By the same author

At-Swim-Two-Birds
The Poor Mouth
The Hard Life
The Dalkey Archive
Stories and Plays
The Various Lives of Keats and Chapman & The Brother
The Hair of the Dogma
The Best of Myles
Further Cuttings from Cruiskeen Lawn
Myles Away from Dublin
Myles Before Myles

FLANN O'BRIEN was one of the many pseudonyms of Brian O'Nolan, born in Strabane, County Tyrone in 1911, the fifth of twelve children. He attended University College, Dublin, where he soon established himself as a brilliantly funny speaker at student debates. In 1935, he joined the Irish Civil Service and until his retirement in 1953 was Private Secretary to successive Ministers for Local Government.

His first novel, *At-Swim-Two-Birds*, was published in 1939. The book had been recommended by Graham Greene, then a reader at Longman Publishers. On publication it was praised highly by many, including Samuel Beckett and the near-blind James Joyce, who read the novel with the aid of a magnifying glass. O'Brien's second novel, *The Third Policeman*, was, however, turned down. Disappointed, O'Brien told everyone that he had lost the manuscript. He was not to write another novel in English for almost twenty years. His third novel, *The Poor Mouth*, was published in 1941 in Gaelic as *An Beal Bocht*. *The Third Policeman* was published posthumously in 1967.

In 1940, under the pseudonym Myles na Gopaleen (civil servants were not permitted to publish under their real names), O'Brien began his celebrated satirical column in the *Irish Times*. Unfailingly witty, feared, respected and loved throughout Ireland, 'Cruiskeen Lawn' (meaning 'Little Brimming Jug') appeared almost daily for nearly thirty years. O'Brien's journalism is published in several collections, including *The Best of Myles* and *The Hair of the Dogma*.

In the 1960s, O'Brien began writing novels again – *The Hard Life* appeared in 1962, *The Dalkey Archive* in 1964. By now he had retired from the Civil Service and was in poor health. He died, not inappropriately, on April Fools' Day, 1966.

FLANN O'BRIEN

The Third Policeman

HARPER PERENNIAL
London, New York, Toronto and Sydney

Harper Perennial
An imprint of HarperCollins*Publishers*
1 London Bridge Street
London SE1 9GF

www.harperperennial.co.uk

This Harper Perennial Modern Classics edition published 2007

15

Previously published in paperback by Flamingo 1960s Series in 2001
Previously published in paperback as a Flamingo Modern Classic in 1993
Previously published in paperback by Paladin in 1988
First published in Great Britain by MacGibbon & Kee Ltd 1967

PS™ is a trademark of HarperCollins*Publishers* Ltd

A catalogue record for this book is available from the British Library

ISBN-13 978-0-00-724717-2
ISBN-10 0-00-724717-6

Set in Melior

Printed and bound by CPI Group (UK) Ltd, Croydon, CR0 4YY

Human existence being an hallucination containing in itself the secondary hallucinations of day and night (the latter an insanitary condition of the atmosphere due to accretions of black air) it ill becomes any man of sense to be concerned at the illusory approach of the supreme hallucination known as death.

DE SELBY

Since the affairs of men rest still uncertain,
Let's reason with the worst that may befall.

SHAKESPEARE

Chapter 1

Not everybody knows how I killed old Phillip Mathers, smashing his jaw in with my spade; but first it is better to speak of my friendship with John Divney because it was he who first knocked old Mathers down by giving him a great blow in the neck with a special bicycle-pump which he manufactured himself out of a hollow iron bar. Divney was a strong civil man but he was lazy and idle-minded. He was personally responsible for the whole idea in the first place. It was he who told me to bring my spade. He was the one who gave the orders on the occasion and also the explanations when they were called for.

I was born a long time ago. My father was a strong farmer and my mother owned a public house. We all lived in the public house but it was not a strong house at all and was closed most of the day because my father was out at work on the farm and my mother was always in the kitchen and for some reason the customers never came until it was nearly bed-time; and well after it at Christmas-time and on other unusual days like that. I never saw my mother outside the kitchen in my life and never saw a customer during the day and even at night I never saw more than two or three together. But then I was in bed part of the time and it is possible that things happened differently with my mother and with the customers late at night. My father I do not remember well but he was a strong man and did not talk much except on Saturdays when he would mention Parnell with the customers and say that Ireland was a queer country. My mother I can recall perfectly. Her face was always red and sore-looking from bending at the fire; she spent her life making tea to pass the time and singing snatches of old songs to pass the meantime. I knew her well but my father and I were strangers and did not converse much; often indeed when I would be studying in the kitchen at night I could hear him through the thin door to the shop talking there from his seat under the oil-lamp for hours on end to Mick the sheepdog. Always it was only the drone of his voice I heard, never the separate bits of words. He was a man who understood all dogs thoroughly and treated them like human beings. My mother owned a cat but it was a foreign outdoor animal and was rarely seen and my mother never took any notice of it. We were all happy enough in a queer separate way.

Then a certain year came about the Christmas-time and when the year was gone my father and mother were gone also. Mick the sheepdog was very tired and sad after my father went and would not do his work with the sheep at all; he too went the next year. I was young and foolish at the time and did not know properly why these people had all left me, where they had gone and why they did not give explanations beforehand. My mother was the first to go and I can remember a fat man with a red face and a black suit telling my father that there was no doubt where she was, that he could be as sure of that as he could of anything else in this vale of tears. But he did not mention where and as I thought the whole thing was very private and that she might be back on Wednesday, I did not ask him where. Later, when my father went, I thought he had gone to fetch her with an outside car but when neither of them came back on the next Wednesday, I felt sorry and disappointed. The man in the black suit was back again. He stayed in the house for two nights and was continually washing his hands in the bed-room and reading books. There were two other men, one a small pale man and one a tall black man in leggings. They had pockets full of pennies and they gave me one every time I asked them questions. I can remember the tall man in the leggings saying to the other man:

'The poor misfortunate little bastard.'

I did not understand this at the time and thought that they were talking about the other man in the black clothes who was always working at the wash-stand in the bedroom. But I understood it all clearly afterwards.

After a few days I was brought away myself on an outside car and sent to a strange school. It was a boarding school filled with people I did not know, some young and some older. I soon got to know that it was a good school and a very expensive one but I did not pay over any money to the people who were in charge of it because I had not any. All this and a lot more I understood clearly later.

My life at this school does not matter except for one thing. It was here that I first came to know something of de Selby. One day I picked up idly an old tattered book in the science master's study and put it in my pocket to read in bed the next morning as I had just earned the privilege of lying late. I was about sixteen then and the date was the seventh of March. I still think that day is the most important in my life and can remember it more readily than I do my birthday. The book was a first edition of *Golden Hours* with the two last pages missing. By the time I was nineteen and had reached the end of my education I knew that the book was valuable and that in keeping it I was stealing it. Nevertheless I packed it in my bag without a qualm and would probably do the same if I had my time again. Perhaps it is important in the story I am going to tell to remember that it was for de Selby I committed my first serious sin. It was for him that I committed my greatest sin.

I had long-since got to know how I was situated in the world. All my people were dead and there was a man called Divney working the farm and living on it until I should return. He did not own any of it and was given weekly cheques of pay by an office full of solicitors in a town far away. I had never met these solicitors and never met Divney but they were really all working for me and my father had paid in cash for these arrangements before he died. When I was younger I thought he was a generous man to do that for a boy he did not know well.

I did not go home direct from school. I spent some months in other places broadening my mind and finding out what a complete edition of de Selby's works would cost me and whether some of the less important of his commentators' books could be got on loan. In one of the places where I was broadening my mind I met one night with a bad accident. I broke my left leg (or, if you like, it was broken for me) in six places and when I was well enough again to go my way I had one leg made of wood, the left one. I knew that I had only a little money, that I was going home to a rocky farm and that my life would not be easy. But I was certain by this time that farming, even if I had to do it, would not be my life work. I knew that if my name was to be remembered, it would be remembered with de Selby's.

I can recall in every detail the evening I walked back into my own house with a travelling-bag in each hand. I was twenty years of age; it was an evening in a happy yellow summer and the door of the public house was open. Behind the counter was John Divney, leaning forward on the low-down porter dash-board with his fork, his arms neatly folded and his face looking down on a newspaper which was spread upon the counter. He had brown hair and was made handsomely enough in a small butty way; his shoulders were broadened out with work and his arms were thick like little tree-trunks. He had a quiet civil face with eyes like cow's eyes, brooding, brown, and patient. When he knew that somebody had come in he did not stop his reading but his left hand strayed out and found a rag and began to give the counter slow damp swipes. Then, still reading, he moved his hands one above the other as if he was drawing out a concertina to full length and said:

'A schooner?'

A schooner was what the customers called a pint of Coleraine blackjack. It was the cheapest porter in the world. I said that I wanted my dinner and mentioned my name and station. Then we closed the shop and went into the kitchen and we were there nearly all night, eating and talking and drinking whiskey.

The next day was Thursday. John Divney said that his work was now done and that he would be ready to go home to where his people were on Saturday. It was not true to say that his work was done because the farm was in a poor way and most of the year's work had not even been started. But on Saturday he said there were a few things to finish and that he could not work on Sunday but that he would be in a position to hand over the place in perfect order on Tuesday evening. On Monday he had a sick pig to mind and that delayed him. At the end of the week he was busier than ever and the passing of another two months did not seem to lighten or reduce his urgent tasks. I did not mind much because if he was idle-minded and a sparing worker, he was satisfactory so far as company was concerned and he never asked for pay. I did little work about the place myself, spending all my time arranging my papers and re-reading still more closely the pages of de Selby.

A full year had not passed when I noticed that Divney was using the word 'we' in his conversation and worse than that, the word 'our'. He said that the place was not everything that it might be and talked of getting a hired man. I did not agree with this and told him so, saying that there was no necessity for more than two men on a small farm and adding, most unhappily for myself, that we were poor. After that it was useless trying to tell him that it was I who owned everything. I began to tell myself that even if I did own everything, he owned me.

Four years passed away happily enough for each of us. We had a good house and plenty of good country food but little money. Nearly all my own time was spent in study. Out of my savings I had now bought the complete works of the two principal commentators, Hatchjaw and Bassett, and a photostat of the de Selby Codex. I had also embarked upon the task of learning French and German thoroughly in order to read the works of other commentators in those languages. Divney had been working after a fashion on the farm by day and talking loudly in the public house by night and serving drinks there. Once I asked him what about the public house and he said he was losing money on it every day. I did not understand this because the customers, judging by their voices through the thin door, were plentiful enough and Divney was continually buying himself suits of clothes and fancy tiepins. But I did not say much. I was satisfied to be left in peace because I knew that my own work was more important than myself.

One day in early winter Divney said to me:

'I cannot lose very much more of my own money on that bar. The customers are complaining about the porter. It is very bad porter because I have to drink a little now and again myself to keep them company and I do not feel well in my health over the head of it. I will have to go away for two days and do some travelling and see if there is a better brand of porter to be had.'

He disappeared the next morning on his bicycle and when he came back very dusty and travel-worn at the end of three days, he told me that everything was all right and that four barrels of better porter could be expected on Friday. It came punctually on that day and was well bought by the customers in the public house that night. It was manufactured in some town in the south and was known as 'The Wrastler'. If you drank three or four pints of it, it was nearly bound to win. The customers praised it highly and when they had it inside them they sang and shouted and sometimes lay down on the floor or on the roadway outside in a great stupor. Some of them complained afterwards that they had been robbed while in this state and talked angrily in the shop the next night about stolen money and gold watches which had disappeared off their strong chains. John Divney did not say much on this subject to them and did not mention it to me at all. He printed the words – BEWARE OF PICKPOCKETS – in large letters on a card and hung it on the back of shelves beside another notice that death with cheques. Nevertheless a week rarely passed without some customer complaining after an evening with 'The Wrastler'. It was not a satisfactory thing.

As time went on Divney became more and more despondent about what he called 'the bar'. He said that he would be satisfied if it paid its way but he doubted seriously if it ever would. The Government were partly responsible for the situation owing to the high taxes. He did not think that he could continue to bear the burden of the loss without some assistance. I said that my father had some old-fashioned way of management which made possible a profit but that the shop should be closed if now continuing to lose money. Divney only said that it was a very serious thing to surrender a licence.

It was about this time, when I was nearly thirty, that Divney and I began to get the name of being great friends. For years before that I had rarely gone out at all. This was because I was so busy with my work that I hardly ever had the time; also my wooden leg was not very good for walking with. Then something very unusual happened to change all this and after it had happened, Divney and I never parted company for more than one minute either night or day. All day I was out with him on the farm and at night I sat on my father's old seat under the lamp in a corner of the public house doing what work I could with my papers in the middle of the blare and the crush and the hot noises which went always with 'The Wrastler'. If Divney went for a walk on Sunday to a neighbour's house I went with him and came home with him again, never before or after him. If he went away to a town on his bicycle to order porter or seed potatoes or even 'to see a certain party', I went on my own bicycle beside him. I brought my bed into his room and took the trouble to sleep only after he was sleeping and to be wide-awake a good hour before he stirred. Once I nearly failed in my watchfulness. I remember waking up with a start in the small hours of a black night and finding him quietly dressing himself in the dark. I asked him where he was going and he said he could not sleep and that he thought a walk would do him good. I said I was in the same condition myself and the two of us went for a walk together into the coldest and wettest night I ever experienced. When we returned drenched I said it was foolish for us to sleep in different beds in such bitter weather and got into his bed beside him. He did not say much, then or at any other time. I slept with him always after that. We were friendly and smiled at each other but the situation was a queer one and neither of us liked it. The neighbours were not long noticing how insepar-able we were. We had been in that condition of being always together for nearly three years and they said that we were the best two Christians in all Ireland. They said that human friendship was a beautiful thing and that Divney and I were the noblest example of it in the history of the world. If other people fell out or fought or disagreed, they were asked why they could not be like me and Divney. It would have been a great shock for everybody if Divney had appeared in any place at any time without myself beside him. And it is not strange that two people never came to dislike each other as bitterly as did I and Divney. And two people were never so polite to each other, so friendly in the face.

I must go back several years to explain what happened to bring about this peculiar situation. The 'certain party' whom Divney went to visit once a month was a girl called Pegeen Meers. For my part I had completed my definitive 'De Selby Index' wherein the views of all known commentators on every aspect of the savant and his work had been collated. Each of us therefore had a large thing on the mind. One day Divney said to me:

'That is a powerful book you have written I don't doubt.'

'It is useful,' I admitted, 'and badly wanted.' In fact it contained much that was entirely new and proof that many opinions widely held about de Selby and his theories were misconceptions based on misreadings of his works.

'It might make your name in the world and your golden fortune in copyrights?'

'It might.'

'Then why do you not put it out?'

I explained that money is required to 'put out' a book of this kind unless the writer already has a reputation. He gave me a look of sympathy that was not usual with him and sighed.

'Money is hard to come by these days,' he said, 'with the drink trade on its last legs and the land starved away to nothing for the want of artificial manures that can't be got for love or money owing to the trickery of the Jewmen and the Freemasons.'

I knew that it was not true about the manures. He had already pretended to me that they could not be got because he did not want the trouble of them. After a pause he said:

'We will have to see what we can do about getting money for your book and indeed I am in need of some myself because you can't expect a girl to wait until she is too old to wait any longer.'

I did not know whether he meant to bring a wife, if he got one, into the house. If he did and I could not stop him, then I would have to leave. On the other hand if marriage meant that he himself would leave I think I would be very glad of it.

It was some days before he talked on this subject of money again. Then he said:

'What about old Mathers?'

'What about him?'

I had never seen the old man but knew all about him. He had spent a long life of fifty years in the cattle trade and now lived in retirement in a big house three miles away. He still did large business through agents and the people said that he carried no less than three thousand pounds with him every time he hobbled to the village to lodge his money. Little as I knew of social proprieties at the time, I would not dream of asking him for assistance.

'He is worth a packet of potato-meal,' Divney said.

'I do not think we should look for charity,' I answered.

'I do not think so either,' he said. He was a proud man in his own way, I thought, and no more was said just then. But after that he took to the habit of putting occasionally into conversations on other subjects some irrelevant remark about our need for money and the amount of it which Mathers carried in his black cash-box; sometimes he would revile the old man, accusing him of being in 'the artificial manure ring' or of being dishonest in his business dealings. Once he said something about 'social justice' but it was plain to me that he did not properly understand the term.

I do not know exactly how or when it become clear to me that Divney, far from seeking charity, intended to rob Mathers; and I cannot recollect how long it took me to realize that he meant to kill him as well in order to avoid the possibility of being identified as the robber afterwards. I only know that within six months I had come to accept this grim plan as a commonplace of our conversation. Three further months passed before I could bring myself to agree to the proposal and three months more before I openly admitted to Divney that my misgivings were at an end. I cannot recount the tricks and wiles he used to win me to his side. It is sufficient to say that he read portions of my 'De Selby Index' (or pretended to) and discussed with me afterwards the serious responsibility of any person who declined by mere reason of personal whim to give the 'Index' to the world.

Old Mathers lived alone. Divney knew on what evening and at what deserted stretch of road near his house we would meet him with his box of money. The evening when it came was in the depth of winter; the light was already waning as we sat at our dinner discussing the business we had in hand. Divney said that we should bring our spades tied on the crossbars of our bicycles because this would make us look like men out after rabbits; he would bring his own iron pump in case we should get a slow puncture.

There is little to tell about the murder. The lowering skies seemed to conspire with us, coming down in a shroud of dreary mist to within a few yards of the wet road where we were waiting. Everything was very still with no sound in our ears except the dripping of the trees. Our bicycles were hidden. I was leaning miserably on my spade and Divney, his iron pump under his arm, was smoking his pipe contentedly. The old man was upon us almost before we realized there was anybody near. I could not see him well in the dim light but I could glimpse a spent bloodless face peering from the top of the great black coat which covered him from ear to ankle. Divney went forward at once and pointing back along the road said:

'Would that be your parcel on the road?'

The old man turned his head to look and received a blow in the back of the neck from Divney's pump which knocked him clean off his feet and probably smashed his neck-bone. As he collapsed full-length in the mud he did not cry out. Instead I heard him say something softly in a conversational tone – something like 'I do not care for celery' or 'I left my glasses in the scullery'. Then he lay very still. I had been watching the scene rather stupidly, still leaning on my spade. Divney was rummaging savagely at the fallen figure and then stood up. He had a black cash-box in his hand. He waved it in the air and roared at me:

'Here, wake up! Finish him with the spade!'

I went forward mechanically, swung the spade over my shoulder and smashed the blade of it with all my strength against the protruding chin. I felt and almost heard the fabric of his skull crumple up crisply like an empty eggshell. I do not know how often I struck him after that but I did not stop until I was tired.

I threw the spade down and looked around for Divney. He was nowhere to be seen. I called his name softly but he did not answer. I walked a little bit up the road and called again. I jumped on the rising of a ditch and peered around into the gathering dusk. I called his name once more as loudly as I dared but there was no answer in the stillness. He was gone. He had made off with the box of money, leaving me alone with the dead man and with a spade which was now probably tinging the watery mud around it with a weak pink stain.

My heart stumbled painfully in its beating. A chill of fright ran right through me. If anybody should come, nothing in the world would save me from the gallows. If Divney was with me still to share my guilt, even that would not protect me. Numb with fear I stood for a long time looking at the crumpled heap in the black coat.

Before the old man had come Divney and I had dug a deep hole in the field beside the road, taking care to preserve the sods of grass. Now in a panic I dragged the heavy sodden figure from where it lay and got it with a tremendous effort across the ditch into the field and slumped it down into the hole. Then I rushed back for my spade and started to throw and push the earth back into the hole in a mad blind fury.

The hole was nearly full when I heard steps. Looking round in great dismay I saw the unmistakable shape of Divney making his way carefully across the ditch into the field. When he came up I pointed dumbly to the hole with my spade. Without a word he went to where our bicycles were, came back with his own spade and worked steadily with me until the task was finished. We did everything possible to hide any trace of what had happened. Then we cleaned our boots with grass, tied the spades and walked home. A few people who came against us on the road bade us good evening in the dark. I am sure they took us for two tired labourers making for home after a hard day's work. They were not far wrong.

On our way I said to Divney:

'Where were you that time?'

'Attending to important business,' he answered. I thought he was referring to a certain thing and said:

'Surely you could have kept it till after.'

'It is not what you are thinking of,' he answered.

'Have you got the box?'

He turned his face to me this time, screwed it up and put a finger on his lip.

'Not so loud,' he whispered. 'It is in a safe place.'

'But where?'

The only reply he gave me was to put the finger on his lip more firmly and make a long hissing noise. He gave me to understand that mentioning the box, even in a whisper, was the most foolish and reckless thing it was possible for me to do.

When we reached home he went away and washed himself and put on one of the several blue Sunday suits he had. When he came back to where I was sitting, a miserable figure at the kitchen fire, he came across to me with a very serious face, pointed to the window and cried:

'Would that be your parcel on the road?'

Then he let out a bellow of laughter which seemed to loosen up his whole body, turn his eyes to water in his head and shake the whole house. When he had finished he wiped the tears from his face, walked into the shop and made a noise which can only be made by taking the cork quickly out of a whiskey bottle.

In the weeks which followed I asked him where the box was a hundred times in a thousand different ways. He never answered in the same way but the answer was always the same. It was in a very safe place. The least said about it the better until things quietened down. Mum was the word. It would be found all in good time. For the purpose of safekeeping the place it was in was superior to the Bank of England. There was a good time coming. It would be a pity to spoil everything by hastiness or impatience.

And that is why John Divney and I became inseparable friends and why I never allowed him to leave my sight for three years. Having robbed me in my own public house (having even robbed my customers) and having ruined my farm, I knew that he was sufficiently dishonest to steal my share of Mathers' money and make off with the box if given the opportunity. I knew that there was no possible necessity for waiting until 'things quietened down' because very little notice was taken of the old man's disappearance. People said he was a queer mean man and that going away without telling anybody or leaving his address was the sort of thing he would do.

I think I have said before that the peculiar terms of physical intimacy upon which myself and Divney found ourselves had become more and more intolerable. In latter months I had hoped to force him to capitulate by making my company unbearably close and unrelenting but at the same time I took to carrying a small pistol in case of accidents. One Sunday night when both of us were sitting in the kitchen – both, incidentally, on the same side of the fire – he took his pipe from his mouth and turned to me:

'Do you know,' he said, 'I think things have quietened down.'

I only gave a grunt.

'Do you get my meaning?' he asked.

'Things were never any other way,' I answered shortly. He looked at me in a superior way.

'I know a lot about these things,' he said, 'and you would be surprised at the pitfalls a man will make if he is in too big a hurry. You cannot be too careful but all the same I think things have quietened down enough to make it safe.'

'I am glad you think so.'

'There are good times coming. I will get the box tomorrow and then we will divide the money, right here on this table.'

'*We* will get the box,' I answered, saying the first word with great care. He gave me a long hurt look and asked me sadly did I not trust him. I replied that both of us should finish what both had started.

'All right,' he said in a very vexed way. 'I am sorry you don't trust me after all the work I have done to try to put this place right but to show you the sort I am I will let you get the box yourself, I will tell you where it is tomorrow.'

I took care to sleep with him as usual that night. The next morning he was in a better temper and told me with great simplicity that the box was hidden in Mathers' own empty house, under the floorboards of the first room on the right from the hall.

'Are you sure?' I asked.

'I swear it,' he said solemnly, raising his hand to heaven.

I thought the position over for a moment, examining the possibility that it was a ruse to part company with me at last and then make off himself to the real hiding-place. But his face for the first time seemed to wear a look of honesty.

'I am sorry if I injured your feelings last night,' I said, 'but to show that there is no ill-feeling I would be glad if you would come with me at least part of the way. I honestly think that both of us should finish what the two of us started.'

'All right,' he said. 'It is all the same but I would like you to get the box with your own hands because it is only simple justice after not telling you where it was.'

As my own bicycle was punctured we walked the distance. When we were about a hundred yards from Mathers' house, Divney stopped by a low wall and said that he was going to sit on it and smoke his pipe and wait for me.

'Let you go alone and get the box and bring it back here. There are good times coming and we will be rich men tonight. It is sitting under a loose board in the floor of the first room on the right, in the corner forenenst the door.'

Perched as he was on the wall I knew that he need never

leave my sight. In the brief time I would be away I could see him any time I turned my head.

'I will be back in ten minutes,' I said.

'Good man,' he answered. 'But remember this. If you meet anybody, you don't know what you're looking for, you don't know in whose house you are, you don't know anything.'

'I don't even know my own name,' I answered.

This was a very remarkable thing for me to say because the next time I was asked my name I could not answer. I did not know.

Chapter 2

De Selby has some interesting things to say on the subject of houses.[1] A row of houses he regards as a row of necessary evils. The softening and degeneration of the human race he attributes to its progressive predilection for interiors and waning interest in the art of going out and staying there. This in turn he sees as the result of the rise of such pursuits as reading, chess-playing, drinking, marriage and the like, few of which can be satisfactorily conducted in the open. Elsewhere[2] he defines a house as 'a large coffin', 'a warren', and 'a box'. Evidently his main objection was to the confinement of a roof and four walls. He ascribed somewhat far-fetched therapeutic values – chiefly pulmonary – to certain structures of his own design which he called 'habitats', crude drawings of which may still be seen in the pages of the *Country Album*. These structures were of two kinds, roofless 'houses' and 'houses' without walls. The former had wide open doors and windows with an extremely ungainly superstructure of tarpaulins loosely rolled on spars against bad weather – the whole looking like a foundered sailing-ship erected on a platform of masonry and the last place where one would think of keeping even cattle. The other type of 'habitat' had the conventional slated roof but no walls save one, which was to be erected in the quarter of the prevailing wind; around the other sides were the inevitable tarpaulins loosely wound on rollers suspended from the gutters of the roof, the whole structure being surrounded by a diminutive moat or pit bearing some resemblance to

[1] *Golden Hours*, ii, 261.
[2] *Country Album*, p. 1,034.

military latrines. In the light of present-day theories of housing and hygiene, there can be no doubt that de Selby was much mistaken in these ideas but in his own remote day more than one sick person lost his life in an ill-advised quest for health in these fantastic dwellings.[3]

My recollections of de Selby were prompted by my visit to the home of old Mr Mathers. As I approached it along the road the house appeared to be a fine roomy brick building of uncertain age, two storeys high with a plain porch and eight or nine windows to the front of each floor.

I opened the iron gate and walked as softly as I could up the weed-tufted gravel drive. My mind was strangely empty. I did not feel that I was about to end successfully a plan I had worked unrelentingly at night and day for three years. I felt no glow of pleasure and was unexcited at the prospect of becoming rich. I was occupied only with the mechanical task of finding a black box.

The hall-door was closed and although it was set far back in a very deep porch the wind and rain had whipped a coating of gritty dust against the panels and deep into the crack where the door opened, showing that it had been shut for years. Standing on a derelict flower-bed, I tried to push up the sash of the first window on the left. It yielded to my strength, raspingly and stubbornly. I clambered through the opening and found myself, not at once in a room, but crawling along the deepest window-ledge I have ever seen. When I reached the floor and jumped noisily down upon it, the open window seemed very far away and much too small to have admitted me.

The room where I found myself was thick with dust,

[3] Le Fournier, the reliable French commentator (in *De Selby – l'Énigme de l'Occident*) has put forward a curious theory regarding these 'habitats'. He suggests that de Selby, when writing the *Album*, paused to consider some point of difficulty and in the meantime engaged in the absent-minded practice known generally as 'doodling', then putting his manuscript away. The next time he took it up he was confronted with a mass of diagrams and drawings which he took to be the plans of a type of dwelling he always had in mind and immediately wrote many pages explaining the sketches. 'In no other way,' adds the severe Le Fournier, 'can one explain so regrettable a lapse.'

musty and deserted of all furniture. Spiders had erected great stretchings of their web about the fireplace. I made my way quickly to the hall, threw open the door of the room where the box was and paused on the threshold. It was a dark morning and the weather had stained the windows with blears of grey wash which kept the brightest part of the weak light from coming in. The far corner of the room was a blur of shadow. I had a sudden urge to have done with my task and be out of this house forever. I walked across the bare boards, knelt down in the corner and passed my hands about the floor in search of the loose board. To my surprise I found it easily. It was about two feet in length and rocked hollowly under my hand. I lifted it up, laid it aside and struck a match. I saw a black metal cash-box nestling dimly in the hole. I put my hand down and crooked a finger into the loose reclining handle but the match suddenly flickered and went out and the handle of the box, which I had lifted up about an inch slid heavily off my finger. Without stopping to light another match I thrust my hand bodily into the opening and just when it should be closing about the box, something happened.

I cannot hope to describe what it was but it had frightened me very much long before I had understood it even slightly. It was some change which came upon me or upon the room, indescribably subtle, yet momentous, ineffable. It was as if the daylight had changed with unnatural suddenness, as if the temperature of the evening had altered greatly in an instant or as if the air had become twice as rare or twice as dense as it had been in the winking of an eye; perhaps all of these and other things happened together for all my senses were bewildered all at once and could give me no explanation. The fingers of my right hand, thrust into the opening in the floor, had closed mechanically, found nothing at all and came up again empty. The box was gone!

I heard a cough behind me, soft and natural yet more disturbing than any sound that could ever come upon the human ear. That I did not die of fright was due, I think, to two things, the fact that my senses were already disarranged and able to interpret to me only gradually what they had perceived and also the fact that the utterance of the cough seemed to bring with it some more awful alteration in everything, just as if it had held the universe standstill for an instant, suspending the planets in their courses, halting the sun and holding in mid-air any falling thing the earth was pulling towards it. I collapsed weakly from my kneeling backwards into a limp sitting-down upon the floor. Sweat broke upon my brow and my eyes remained open for a long time without a wink, glazed and almost sightless.

In the darkest corner of the room near the window a man was sitting in a chair, eyeing me with a mild but unwavering interest. His hand had crept out across the small table by his side to turn up very slowly an oil-lamp which was standing on it. The oil-lamp had a glass bowl with the wick dimly visible inside it, curling in convolutions like an intestine. There were tea things on the table. The man was old Mathers. He was watching me in silence. He did not move or speak and might have been still dead save for the slight movement of his hand at the lamp, the very gentle screwing of his thumb and forefinger against the wick-wheel. The hand was yellow, the wrinkled skin draped loosely upon the bones. Over the knuckle of his forefinger I could clearly see the loop of a skinny vein.

It is hard to write of such a scene or to convey with known words the feelings which came knocking at my numbed mind. How long we sat there, for instance, looking at one another I do not know. Years or minutes could be swallowed up with equal ease in that indescribable and unaccountable interval. The light of morning vanished from my sight, the dusty floor was like nothingness beneath me and my whole body dissolved away, leaving me existing only in the stupid spellbound gaze that went steadily from where I was to the other corner.

I remember that I noticed several things in a cold mechanical way as if I was sitting there with no worry save to note everything I saw. His face was terrifying but his eyes in the middle of it had a quality of chill and horror which made his other features look to me almost friendly. The skin was like faded parchment with an arrangement of puckers and wrinkles which created between them an expression of fathomless inscrutability. But the eyes were horrible. Looking at them I got the feeling that they were not genuine eyes at all but mechanical dummies animated by electricity or the like, with a tiny pinhole in the centre of the 'pupil' through which the real eye gazed out secretively and with great coldness. Such a conception, possibly with no foundation at all in fact, disturbed me agonisingly and gave rise in my mind to interminable speculations as to the colour and quality of the real eye and as to whether, indeed, it was real at all or merely another dummy with its pinhole on the same plane as the first one so that the real eye, possibly behind thousands of these absurd disguises, gazed out through a barrel of serried peep-holes. Occasionally the heavy cheese-like lids would drop down slowly with great languor and then rise again. Wrapped loosely around the body was an old wine-coloured dressing-gown.

In my distress I thought to myself that perhaps it was his twin brother but at once I heard someone say:

Scarcely. If you look carefully at the left-hand side of his neck you will notice that there is sticking-plaster or a bandage there. His throat and chin are also bandaged.

Forlornly, I looked and saw that this was true. He was the man I had murdered beyond all question. He was sitting on a chair four yards away watching me. He sat stiffly without a move as if afraid to hurt the gaping wounds which covered his body. Across my own shoulders a stiffness had spread from my exertions with the spade.

But who had uttered these words? They had not frightened me. They were clearly audible to me yet I knew they did not ring out across the air like the chilling cough of the old man in the chair. They came from deep inside me, from my soul. Never before had I believed or suspected that I had a soul but just then I knew I had. I knew also that my soul was friendly, was my senior in years and was solely concerned for my own welfare. For convenience I called him Joe. I felt a little reassured to know that I was not altogether alone. Joe was helping me.

I will not try to tell of the space of time which followed.

In the terrible situation I found myself, my reason could give me no assistance. I knew that old Mathers had been felled by an iron bicycle-pump, hacked to death with a heavy spade and then securely buried in a field. I knew also that the same man was now sitting in the same room with me, watching me in silence. His body was bandaged but his eyes were alive and so was his right hand and so was all of him. Perhaps the murder by the roadside was a bad dream.

There is nothing dreamy about your stiff shoulders. No, I replied, but a nightmare can be as strenuous physically as the real thing.

I decided in some crooked way that the best thing to do was to believe what my eyes were looking at rather than to place my trust in a memory. I decided to show unconcern, to talk to the old man and to test his own reality by asking about the black box which was responsible, if anything could be, for each of us being the way we were. I made up my mind to be bold because I knew that I was in great danger. I knew that I would go mad unless I got up from the floor and moved and talked and behaved in as ordinary a way as possible. I looked away from old Mathers, got carefully to my feet and sat down on a chair that was not far away from him. Then I looked back at him, my heart pausing for a time and working on again with slow heavy hammer-blows which seemed to make my whole frame shudder. He had remained perfectly still but the live right hand had gripped the pot of tea, raised it very awkwardly and slapped a filling into the empty cup. His eyes had followed me to my new position and were now regarding me again with the same unwavering languorous interest.

Suddenly I began to talk. Words spilled out of me as if they were produced by machinery. My voice, tremulous at first, grew hard and loud and filled the whole room. I do not remember what I said at the beginning. I am sure that most of it was meaningless but I was too pleased and reassured at the natural healthy noise of my tongue to be concerned about the words.

Old Mathers did not move or say anything at first but I was certain that he was listening to me. After a while he began to shake his head and then I was sure I had heard him say No. I became excited at his responses and began to speak carefully. He negatived my inquiry about his health, refused to say where the black box had gone and even denied that it was a dark morning. His voice had a peculiar jarring weight like the hoarse toll of an ancient rusty bell in an ivy-smothered tower. He had said nothing beyond the one word No. His lips hardly moved; I felt sure he had no teeth behind them.

'Are you dead at present?' I asked.

'I am not.'

'Do you know where the box is?'

'No.'

He made another violent movement with his right arm, slapping hot water into his teapot and pouring forth a little more of the feeble brew into his cup. He then relapsed into his attitude of motionless watching. I pondered for a time.

'Do you like weak tea?' I asked.

'I do not,' he said.

'Do you like tea at all?' I asked, 'strong or weak or halfway tea?'

'No,' he said.

'Then why do you drink it?'

He shook his yellow face from side to side sadly and did not say anything. When he stopped shaking he opened up his mouth and poured the cupful of tea in as one would pour a bucket of milk into a churn at churning-time.

Do you notice anything?

No, I replied, nothing beyond the eeriness of this house and the man who owns it. He is by no means the best conversationalist I have met.

I found I spoke lightly enough. While speaking inwardly or outwardly or thinking of what to say I felt brave and normal enough. But every time a silence came the horror of my situation descended upon me like a heavy blanket flung upon my head, enveloping and smothering me and making me afraid of death.

But do you notice nothing about the way he answers your questions?

No.

Do you not see that every reply is in the negative? No matter what you ask him he says No.

That is true enough, I said, but I do not see where that leads me.

Use your imagination.

When I brought my whole attention back to old Mathers I thought he was asleep. He sat over his teacup in a more stooped attitude as if he were a rock or part of the wooden chair he sat on, a man completely dead and turned to stone. Over his eyes the limp lids had drooped down, almost closing them. His right hand resting on the table lay lifeless and abandoned. I composed my thoughts and addressed to him a sharp noisy interrogation.

'Will you answer a straight question?' I asked. He stirred somewhat, his lids opening slightly.

'I will not,' he replied.

I saw that this answer was in keeping with Joe's shrewd suggestion. I sat thinking for a moment until I had thought the same thought inside out.

'Will you refuse to answer a straight question?' I asked

'I will not,' he replied.

This answer pleased me. It meant that my mind had got to grips with his, that I was now almost arguing with him and that we were behaving like two ordinary human beings. I did not understand all the terrible things which had happened to me but I now began to think that I must be mistaken about them.

'Very well,' I said quietly. 'Why do you always answer No?'

He stirred perceptibly in his chair and filled the teacup up again before he spoke. He seemed to have some difficulty in finding words.

'"No" is, generally speaking, a better answer than "Yes",' he said at last. He seemed to speak eagerly, his words coming out as if they had been imprisoned in his mouth for a thousand years. He seemed relieved that I had found a way to make him speak. I thought he even smiled slightly at me but this was doubtless the trickery of the bad morning light or a mischief worked by the shadows of the lamp. He swallowed a long draught of tea and sat waiting, looking at me with his queer eyes. They were now bright and active and moved about restlessly in their yellow wrinkled sockets.

'Do you refuse to tell me why you say that?' I asked.

'No,' he said. 'When I was a young man I led an unsatisfactory life and devoted most of my time to excesses of one kind or another, my principal weakness being Number One. I was also party to the formation of an artificial manure-ring.'

My mind went back at once to John Divney, to the farm and the public house and on from that to the horrible afternoon we had spent on the wet lonely road. As if to interrupt my unhappy thoughts I heard Joe's voice again, this time severe:

No need to ask him what Number One is, we do not want lurid descriptions of vice or anything at all in that line. Use your imagination. Ask him what all this has to do with Yes and No.

'What has that got to do with Yes and No?'

'After a time,' said old Mathers disregarding me, 'I mercifully perceived the error of my ways and the unhappy destination I would reach unless I mended them. I retired from the world in order to try to comprehend it and to find out why it becomes more unsavoury as the years accumulate on a man's body. What do you think I discovered at the end of my meditations?'

I felt pleased again. He was now questioning me.

'What?'

'That No is a better word than Yes,' he replied.

This seemed to leave us where we were, I thought.

On the contrary, very far from it. I am beginning to agree with him. There is a lot to be said for No as a General Principle. Ask him what he means.

'What do you mean?' I inquired.

'When I was meditating,' said old Mathers, 'I took all my sins out and put them on the table, so to speak. I need not tell you it was a big table.'

He seemed to give a very dry smile at his own joke. I chuckled to encourage him.

'I gave them all a strict examination, weighed them and viewed them from all angles of the compass. I asked myself how I came to commit them, where I was and whom I was with when I came to do them.'

This is very wholesome stuff, every word a sermon in itself. Listen very carefully. Ask him to continue.

'Continue,' I said.

I confess I felt a click inside me very near my stomach as if Joe had put a finger to his lip and pricked up a pair of limp spaniel ears to make sure that no syllable of the wisdom escaped him. Old Mathers continued talking quietly.

'I discovered,' he said, 'that everything you do is in response to a request or a suggestion made to you by some other party either inside you or outside. Some of these suggestions are good and praiseworthy and some of them are undoubtedly delightful. But the majority of them are definitely bad and are pretty considerable sins as sins go. Do you understand me?'

'Perfectly.'

'I would say that the bad ones outnumber the good ones by three to one.'

Six to one if you ask me.

'I therefore decided to say No henceforth to every suggestion, request or inquiry whether inward or outward. It was the only simple formula which was sure and safe. It was difficult to practise at first and often called for heroism but I persevered and hardly ever broke down completely. It is now many years since I said Yes. I have refused more requests and negatived more statements than any man living or dead. I have rejected, reneged, disagreed, refused and denied to an extent that is unbelievable.'

An excellent and original régime. This is all extremely interesting and salutary, every syllable a sermon in itself. Very very wholesome.

'Extremely interesting,' I said to old Mathers.

'The system leads to peace and contentment,' he said. 'People do not trouble to ask you questions if they know the

31

answer is a foregone conclusion. Thoughts which have no chance of succeeding do not take the trouble to come into your head at all.'

'You must find it irksome in some ways,' I suggested. 'If, for instance, I were to offer you a glass of whiskey . . .'

'Such few friends as I have,' he answered, 'are usually good enough to arrange such invitations in a way that will enable me to adhere to my system and also accept the whiskey. More than once I have been asked whether I would refuse such things.'

'And the answer is still NO?'

'Certainly.'

Joe said nothing at this stage but I had the feeling that this confession was not to his liking; he seemed to be uneasy inside me. The old man seemed to get somewhat restive also. He bent over his teacup with abstraction as if he were engaged in accomplishing a sacrament. Then he drank with his hollow throat, making empty noises.

A saintly man.

I turned to him again, fearing that his fit of talkativeness had passed.

'Where is the black box which was under the floor a moment ago?' I asked. I pointed to the opening in the corner. He shook his head and did not say anything.

'Do you refuse to tell me?'

'No.'

'Do you object to my taking it?'

'No.'

'Then where is it?'

'What is your name?' he asked sharply.

I was surprised at this question. It had no bearing on my own conversation but I did not notice its irrelevance because I was shocked to realize that, simple as it was, I could not answer it. I did not know my name, did not remember who I was. I was not certain where I had come from or what my business was in that room. I found I was sure of nothing save my search for the black box. But I knew that the other man's name was Mathers, and that he had been killed with a pump and spade. I had no name.

'I have no name,' I replied.

'Then how could I tell you where the box was if you could not sign a receipt? That would be most irregular. I might as well give it to the west wind or to the smoke from a pipe. How could you execute an important Bank document?'

'I can always get a name,' I replied. 'Doyle or Spaldman is a good name and so is O'Sweeny and Hardiman and O'Gara. I can take my choice. I am not tied down for life to one word like most people.'

'I do not care much for Doyle,' he said absently.

The name is Bari. Signor Bari, the eminent tenor. Five hundred thousand people crowded the great piazza when the great artist appeared on the balcony of St Peter's Rome.

Fortunately these remarks were not audible in the ordinary sense of the word. Old Mathers was eyeing me.

'What is your colour?' he asked.

'My colour?'

'Surely you know you have a colour?'

'People often remark on my red face.'

'I do not mean that at all.'

Follow this closely, this is bound to be extremely interesting. Very edifying also.

I saw it was necessary to question old Mathers carefully.

'Do you refuse to explain this question about the colours?'

'No,' he said. He slapped more tea in his cup.

'No doubt you are aware that the winds have colours,' he said. I thought he settled himself more restfully in his chair and changed his face till it looked a little bit benign.

'I never noticed it.'

'A record of this belief will be found in the literature of all ancient peoples.[4] There are four winds and eight sub-winds,

[4] It is not clear whether de Selby had heard of this but he suggests (*Garcia*, p. 12) that night, far from being caused by the commonly accepted theory of planetary movements, was due to accumulations of 'black air' produced by certain volcanic activities of which he does not treat in detail. See also p. 79 and 945, *Country Album*. Le Fournier's comment (in *Homme ou Dieu*) is interesting. 'On ne saura jamais jusqu'à quel point de Selby fut cause de la Grande Guerre, mais, sans aucun doute, ses théories excentriques – spécialement celle que nuit n'est pas un phénomène de nature, mais dans l'atmosphère un état malsain amené par un industrialisme cupide et sans pitié – auraient l'effet de produire un trouble profond dans les masses.'

each with its own colour. The wind from the east is a deep purple, from the south a fine shining silver. The north wind is a hard black and the west is amber. People in the old days had the power of perceiving these colours and could spend a day sitting quietly on a hillside watching the beauty of the winds, their fall and rise and changing hues, the magic of neighbouring winds when they are inter-weaved like ribbons at a wedding. It was a better occupation than gazing at newspapers. The sub-winds had colours of indescribable delicacy, a reddish-yellow half-way between silver and purple, a greyish-green which was related equally to black and brown. What could be more exquisite than a countryside swept lightly by cool rain reddened by the south-west breeze!'

'Can *you* see these colours?' I asked.

'No.'

'You were asking me what my colour was. How do people get their colours?'

'A person's colour,' he answered slowly, 'is the colour of the wind prevailing at his birth.'

'What is your own colour?'

'Light yellow.'

'And what is the point of knowing your colour or having a colour at all?'

'For one thing you can tell the length of your life from it. Yellow means a long life and the lighter the better.'

This is very edifying, every sentence a sermon in itself. Ask him to explain.

'Please explain.'

'It is a question of making little gowns,' he said informatively.

'Little gowns?'

'Yes. When I was born there was a certain policeman present who had the gift of wind-watching. The gift is getting very rare these days. Just after I was born he went outside and examined the colour of the wind that was blowing across the hill. He had a secret bag with him full of certain materials and bottles and he had tailor's instruments also. He was outside for about ten minutes. When he came in

34

again he had a little gown in his hand and he made my mother put it on me.'

'Where did he get this gown?' I asked in surprise.

'He made it himself secretly in the backyard, very likely in the cowhouse. It was very thin and slight like the very finest of spider's muslin. You would not see it at all if you held it against the sky but at certain angles of the light you might at times accidentally notice the edge of it. It was the purest and most perfect manifestation of the outside skin of light yellow. This yellow was the colour of my birth-wind.'

'I see,' I said.

A very beautiful conception.

'Every time my birthday came,' old Mathers said, 'I was presented with another little gown of the same identical quality except that it was put on over the other one and not in place of it. You may appreciate the extreme delicacy and fineness of the material when I tell you that even at five years old with five of these gowns together on me, I still appeared to be naked. It was, however, an unusual yellowish sort of nakedness. Of course there was no objection to wearing other clothes over the gown. I usually wore an overcoat. But every year I got a new gown.'

'Where did you get them?' I asked.

'From the police. They were brought to my own home until I was big enough to call to the barracks for them.'

'And how does all this enable you to predict your span of life?'

'I will tell you. No matter what your colour is, it will be represented faithfully in your birth-gown. With each year and each gown, the colour will get deeper and more pronounced. In my own case I had attained a bright full-blown yellow at fifteen although the colour was so light at birth as to be imperceptible. I am now nearing seventy and the colour is a light brown. As my gowns come to me through the years ahead, the colour will deepen to dark brown, then a dull mahogany and from that ultimately to that very dark sort of brownness one associates usually with stout.'

'Yes?'

'In a word the colour gradually deepens gown by gown

and year by year until it appears to be black. Finally a day will come when the addition of one further gown will actually achieve real and full blackness. On that day I will die.'

Joe and I were surprised at this. We pondered it in silence, Joe, I thought, seeking to reconcile what he had heard with certain principles he held respecting morality and religion.

'That means,' I said at last, 'that if you get a number of these gowns and put them all on together, reckoning each as a year of life, you can ascertain the year of your death?'

'Theoretically, yes,' he replied, 'but there are two difficulties. First of all the police refuse to let you have the gowns together on the ground that the general ascertainment of death-days would be contrary to the public interest. They talk of breaches of the peace and so forth. Secondly, there is a difficulty about stretching.'

'Stretching?'

'Yes. Since you will be wearing as a grown man the tiny gown that fitted you when you were born, it is clear that the gown has stretched until it is perhaps one hundred times as big as it was originally. Naturally this will affect the colour, making it many times rarer than it was. Similarly there will be a proportionate stretch and a corresponding diminution in colour in all the gowns up to manhood – perhaps twenty or so in all.'

I wonder whether it can be taken that this accretion of gowns will have become opaque at the incidence of puberty.

I reminded him that there was always an overcoat.

'I take it, then,' I said to old Mathers, 'that when you say you can tell the length of life, so to speak, from the colour of your shirt, you mean that you can tell roughly whether you will be long-lived or short-lived?'

'Yes,' he replied. 'But if you use your intelligence you can make a very accurate forecast. Naturally some colours are better than others. Some of them, like purple or maroon, are very bad and always mean an early grave. Pink, however, is excellent, and there is a lot to be said for certain shades of green and blue. The prevalence of such colours at birth, however, usually connote a wind that brings bad weather –

thunder and lightning, perhaps – and there might be difficulties such, for instance, as getting a woman to come in time. As you know, most good things in life are associated with certain disadvantages.'

Really very beautiful, everything considered.

'Who are these policemen?' I asked.

'There is Sergeant Pluck and another man called Mac-Cruiskeen and there is a third man called Fox that disappeared twenty-five years ago and was never heard of after. The first two are down in the barracks and so far as I know they have been there for hundreds of years. They must be operating on a very rare colour, something that ordinary eyes could not see at all. There is no white wind that I know of. They all have the gift of seeing the winds.

A bright thought came to me when I heard of these policemen. If they knew so much they would have no difficulty in telling me where I would find the black box. I began to think I would never be happy until I had that box again in my grip. I looked at old Mathers. He had relapsed again to his former passivity. The light had faded from his eyes and the right hand resting on the table looked quite dead.

'Is the barracks far?' I asked loudly.

'No.'

I made up my mind to go there with no delay. Then I noticed a very remarkable thing. The lamplight, which in the beginning had been shining forlornly in the old man's corner only, had now grown rich and yellow and flooded the entire room. The outside light of morning had faded away almost to nothingness. I glanced out of the window and gave a start. Coming into the room I had noticed that the window was to the east and that the sun was rising in that quarter and firing the heavy clouds with light. Now it was setting with last glimmers of feeble red in exactly the same place. It had risen a bit, stopped, and then gone back. Night had come. The policemen would be in bed. I was sure I had fallen among strange people. I made up my mind to go to the barracks the first thing on the morrow. Then I turned again to old Mathers.

'Would you object,' I said to him, 'if I went upstairs and occupied one of your beds for the night? It is too late to go home and I think it is going to rain in any case.'

'No,' he said.

I left him bent at his teaset and went up the stairs. I had got to like him and thought it was a pity he had been murdered. I felt relieved and simplified and certain that I would soon have the black box. But I would not ask the policemen openly about it at first. I would be crafty. In the morning I would go to the barracks and report the theft of my American gold watch. Perhaps it was this lie which was responsible for the bad things that happened to me afterwards. I had no American gold watch.

Chapter 3

I crept out of old Mathers' house nine hours afterwards, making my way on to the firm high-road under the first skies of morning. The dawn was contagious, spreading rapidly about the heavens. Birds were stirring and the great kingly trees were being pleasingly interfered with by the first breezes. My heart was happy and full of zest for high adventure. I did not know my name or where I had come from but the black box was practically in my grasp. The policemen would direct me to where it was. Ten thousand pounds' worth of negotiable securities would be a conservative estimate of what was in it. As I walked down the road I was pleased enough with everything.

The road was narrow, white, old, hard and scarred with shadow. It ran away westwards in the mist of the early morning, running cunningly through the little hills and going to some trouble to visit tiny towns which were not, strictly speaking, on its way. It was possibly one of the oldest roads in the world. I found it hard to think of a time when there was no road there because the trees and the tall hills and the fine views of bogland had been arranged by wise hands for the pleasing picture they made when looked at from the road. Without a road to have them looked at from they would have a somewhat aimless if not a futile aspect.

De Selby has some interesting things to say on the subject of roads.[1] Roads he regards as the most ancient of human monuments, surpassing by many tens of centuries the oldest thing of stone that man has reared to mark his passing. The

---

[1] *Golden Hours*, vi. 156.

tread of time, he says, levelling all else, has beaten only to a more enduring hardness the pathways that have been made throughout the world. He mentions in passing a trick the Celts had in ancient times – that of 'throwing a calculation' upon a road. In those days wise men could tell to a nicety the dimension of a host which had passed by in the night by looking at their tracks with a certain eye and judging them by their perfection and imperfection, the way each footfall was interfered with by each that came after. In this way they could tell the number of men who had passed, whether they were with horse or heavy with shields and iron weapons, and how many chariots; thus they could say the number of men who should be sent after them to kill them. Elsewhere[2] de Selby makes the point that a good road will have character and a certain air of destiny, an indefinable intimation that it is going somewhere, be it east or west, and not coming back from there. If you go with such a road, he thinks, it will give you pleasant travelling, fine sights at every corner and a gentle ease of peregrination that will persuade you that you are walking forever on falling ground. But if you go east on a road that is on its way west, you will marvel at the unfailing bleakness of every prospect and the great number of sore-footed inclines that confront you to make you tired. If a friendly road should lead you into a complicated city with nets of crooked streets and five hundred other roads leaving it for unknown destinations, your own road will always be discernible for its own self and will lead you safely out of the tangled town.

I walked quietly for a good distance on this road, thinking my own thoughts with the front part of my brain and at the same time taking pleasure with the back part in the great and widespread finery of the morning. The air was keen, clear, abundant and intoxicating. Its powerful presence could be discerned everywhere, shaking up the green things jauntily, conferring greater dignity and definition on the stones and boulders, forever arranging and re-arranging the clouds and breathing life into the world. The sun had

[2] *A Memoir of Garcia*, p. 27.

climbed steeply out of his hiding and was now standing benignly in the lower sky pouring down floods of enchanting light and preliminary tinglings of heat.

I came upon a stone stile beside a gate leading into a field and sat down to rest upon the top of it. I was not sitting there long until I became surprised; surprising ideas were coming into my head from nowhere. First of all I remembered who I was – not my name but where I had come from and who my friends were. I recalled John Divney, my life with him and how we came to wait under the dripping trees on the winter's evening. This led me to reflect in wonder that there was nothing wintry about the morning in which I was now sitting. Furthermore, there was nothing familiar about the good-looking countryside which stretched away from me at every view. I was now but two days from home – not more than three hours' walking – and yet I seemed to have reached regions which I had never seen before and of which I had never even heard. I could not understand this because although my life had been spent mostly among my books and papers, I had thought that there was no road in the district I had not travelled, no road whose destination was not well-known to me. There was another thing. My surroundings had a strangeness of a peculiar kind, entirely separate from the mere strangeness of a country where one has never been before. Everything seemed almost too pleasant, too perfect, too finely made. Each thing the eye could see was unmistakable and unambiguous, incapable of merging with any other thing or of being confused with it. The colour of the bogs was beautiful and the greenness of the green fields supernal. Trees were arranged here and there with far-from-usual consideration for the fastidious eye. The senses took keen pleasure from merely breathing the air and discharged their functions with delight. I was clearly in a strange country but all the doubts and perplexities which strewed my mind could not stop me from feeling happy and heart-light and full of an appetite for going about my business and finding the hiding-place of the black box. The valuable contents of it, I felt, would secure me for life in my own house and afterwards I could revisit this mysterious townland upon my bicycle and probe at my leisure the reasons for all its strangenesses. I got down from the stile and continued my walk along the road. It was pleasant easeful walking. I felt sure I was not going against the road. It was, so to speak, accompanying me.

Before going to sleep the previous night I had spent a long time in puzzled thought and also in carrying on inward conversations with my newly-found soul. Strangely enough, I was not thinking about the baffling fact that I was enjoying the hospitality of the man I had murdered (or whom I was sure I had murdered) with my spade. I was reflecting about my name and how tantalizing it was to have forgotten it. All people have names of one kind or another. Some are arbitrary labels related to the appearance of the person, some represent purely genealogical associations but most of them afford some clue as to the parents of the person named and confer a certain advantage in the execution of legal documents.[3] Even a dog has a name which dissociates him from other dogs and indeed my own soul, whom nobody has ever seen on the road or standing at the counter of a public house, had apparently no difficulty in assuming a name which distinguished him from other people's souls.

A thing not easy to account for is the unconcern with which I turned over my various perplexities in my mind.

[3] De Selby (*Golden Hours*, p. 93, *et seq.*) has put forward an interesting theory on names. Going back to primitive times, he regards the earliest names as crude onomatopaeic associations with the appearance of the person or object named – thus harsh or rough manifestations being represented by far from pleasant gutturalities and vice versa. This idea he pursued to rather fanciful lengths, drawing up elaborate paradigms of vowels and consonants purporting to correspond to certain indices of human race, colour and temperament and claiming ultimately to be in a position to state the physiological 'group' of any person merely from a brief study of the letters of his name after the word had been 'rationalised' to allow for variations of language. Certain 'groups' he showed to be universally 'repugnant' to other 'groups'. An unhappy commentary on the theory was furnished by the activities of his own nephew, whether through ignorance or contempt for the humanistic researches of his uncle. The nephew set about a Swedish servant, from whom he was completely excluded by the paradigms, in the pantry of a Portsmouth hotel to such purpose that de Selby had to open his purse to the tune of five or six hundred pounds to avert an unsavoury law case.

Blank anonymity coming suddenly in the middle of life should be at best alarming, a sharp symptom that the mind is in decay. But the unexplainable exhilaration which I drew from my surroundings seemed to invest this situation merely with the genial interest of a good joke. Even now as I walked along contentedly I sensed a solemn question on this subject from within, one similar to many that had been asked the night before. It was a mocking inquiry. I light-heartedly gave a list of names which, for all I knew, I *might* hear:

Hugh Murray.

Constantin Petrie.

Peter Small.

Signor Beniamino Bari.

The Honourable Alex O'Brannigan, Bart.

Kurt Freund.

Mr John P. de Salis, M.A.

Dr Solway Garr.

Bonaparte Gosworth.

Legs O'Hagan.

Signor Beniamino Bari, Joe said, the eminent tenor. Three baton-charges outside La Scala at great tenor's première. Extraordinary scenes were witnessed outside La Scala Opera House when a crowd of some ten thousand devotées, incensed by the management's statement that no more standing-room was available, attempted to rush the barriers. Thousands were injured, 79 fatally, in the wild mêlée. Constable Peter Coutts sustained injuries to the groin from which he is unlikely to recover. These scenes were comparable only to the delirium of the fashionable audience inside after Signor Bari had concluded his recital. The great tenor was in admirable voice. Starting with a phase in the lower register with a husky richness which seemed to suggest a cold, he delivered the immortal strains of Che Gelida Manina, favourite aria of the beloved Caruso. As he warmed to his God-like task, note after golden note spilled forth to the remotest corner of the vast theatre, thrilling all and sundry to the inner core. When he reached the high C where heaven and earth seem married in one great climax of exaltation, the audience arose in their seats and cheered as one man, showering hats, programmes and chocolate-boxes on the great artist.

Thank you very much, I murmured, smiling in wild amusement.

A bit overdone, perhaps, but it is only a hint of the pretensions and vanity that you inwardly permit yourself.

Indeed?

Or what about Dr Solway Garr. The duchess has fainted. Is there a doctor in the audience? The spare figure, thin nervous fingers and iron-grey hair, making its way quietly through the pale excited onlookers. A few brief commands, quietly spoken but imperious. Inside five minutes the situation is well in hand. Wan but smiling, the duchess murmurs her thanks. Expert diagnosis has averted still another tragedy. A small denture has been extracted from the thorax. All hearts go out to the quiet-spoken servant of humanity. His Grace, summoned too late to see aught but the happy ending, is opening his cheque-book and has already marked a thousand guineas on the counterfoil as a small token of his esteem. His cheque is taken but torn to atoms by the smiling medico. A lady in blue at the back of the hall begins to sing O Peace Be Thine and the anthem, growing in volume and sincerity, peals out into the quiet night, leaving few eyes that are dry and hearts that are not replete with yearning ere the last notes fade. Dr Garr only smiles, shaking his head in deprecation.

I think that is quite enough, I said.

I walked on unperturbed. The sun was maturing rapidly in the east and a great heat had started to spread about the ground like a magic influence, making everything, including my own self, very beautiful and happy in a dreamy drowsy way. The little beds of tender grass here and there by the roadside and the dry sheltery ditches began to look seductive and inviting. The road was being slowly baked to a greater hardness, making my walking more and more laborious. After not long I decided that I must now be near the police barracks and that another rest would fit me better for the task I had on hand. I stopped walking and spread my body out evenly in the shelter of the ditch. The day was brand new and the ditch was feathery. I lay back unstintingly, stunned with the sun. I felt a million little influences in my nostril, hay-smells, grass-smells, odours from distant flowers, the reassuring unmistakability of the abiding earth beneath my head. It was a new and a bright day, the day of the world. Birds piped without limitation and incomparable stripe-coloured bees passed above me on their missions and hardly ever came back the same way home. My eyes were shuttered and my head was buzzing with the spinning of the universe. I was not long lying there until my wits deserted me and I fell far into my sleep. I slept there for a long time, as motionless and as devoid of feeling as the shadow of myself which slept behind me.

When I awoke again it was later in the day and a small man was sitting beside me watching me. He was tricky and smoked a tricky pipe and his hand was quavery. His eyes were tricky also, probably from watching policemen. They were very unusual eyes. There was no palpable divergence in their alignment but they seemed to be incapable of giving a direct glance at anything that was straight, whether or not their curious incompatibility was suitable for looking at crooked things. I knew he was watching me only by the way his head was turned; I could not meet his eyes or challenge them. He was small and poorly dressed and on his head was a cloth cap of pale salmon colour. He kept his head in my direction without speaking and I found his presence disquieting. I wondered how long he had been watching me before I awoke.

Watch your step here. A very slippery-looking customer.

I put my hand into my pocket to see if my wallet was there. It was, smooth and warm like the hand of a good friend. When found that I had not been robbed, I decided to talk to him genially and civilly, see who he was and ask him to direct me to the barracks. I made up my mind not to despise the assistance of anybody who could help me, in however small a way, to find the black box. I gave him the time of day and, so far as I could, a look as intricate as any he could give himself.

'More luck to you,' I said.

'More power to yourself,' he answered dourly.

Ask him his name and occupation and inquire what is his destination.

'I do not desire to be inquisitive, sir,' I said, 'but would it be true to mention that you are a bird-catcher?'

'Not a bird-catcher,' he answered.

'A tinker?'

'Not that.'

'A man on a journey?'

'No, not that.'

'A fiddler?'

'Not that one.'

I smiled at him in good-humoured perplexity and said:

'Tricky-looking man, you are hard to place and it is not easy to guess your station. You seem very contented in one way but then again you do not seem to be satisfied. What is your objection to life?'

He blew little bags of smoke at me and looked at me closely from behind the bushes of hair which were growing about his eyes.

'Is it life?' he answered. 'I would rather be without it,' he said, 'for there is a queer small utility in it. You cannot eat it or drink it or smoke it in your pipe, it does not keep the rain out and it is a poor armful in the dark if you strip it and take it to bed with you after a night of porter when you are shivering with the red passion. It is a great mistake and a thing better done without, like bed-jars and foreign bacon.'

'That is a nice way to be talking on this grand lively day,' I chided, 'when the sun is roaring in the sky and sending great tidings into our weary bones.'

'Or like feather-beds,' he continued, 'or bread manufactured with powerful steam machinery. Is it life you say? Life?'

Explain the difficulty of life yet stressing its essential sweetness and desirability.

What sweetness?

Flowers in the spring, the glory and fulfilment of human life, bird-song at evening – you know very well what I mean.

I am not so sure about the sweetness all the same.

'It is hard to get the right shape of it,' I said to the tricky man, 'or to define life at all but if you identify life with enjoyment I am told that there is a better brand of it in the cities than in the country parts and there is said to be a very superior brand of it to be had in certain parts of France. Did you ever notice that cats have a lot of it in them when they are quite juveniles?'

He was looking in my direction crossly.

'Is it life? Many a man has spent a hundred years trying to get the dimensions of it and when he understands it at last and entertains the certain pattern of it in his head, by the hokey he takes to his bed and dies! He dies like a poisoned sheepdog. There is nothing so dangerous, you can't smoke it, nobody will give you tuppence-halfpenny for the half of it and it kills you in the wind-up. It is a queer contraption, very dangerous, a certain death-trap. Life?'

He sat there looking very vexed with himself and stayed for a while without talking behind a little grey wall he had built for himself by means of his pipe. After an interval I made another attempt to find out what his business was.

'Or a man out after rabbits?' I asked.

'Not that. Not that.'

'A travelling man with a job of journey-work?'

'No.'

'Driving a steam thrashing-mill?'

'Not for certain.'

'Tin-plates?'

'No.'

'A town clerk?'

'No.'

'A water-works inspector?'

'No.'

'With pills for sick horses?'

'Not with pills.'

'Then by Dad,' I remarked perplexedly, 'your calling is very unusual and I cannot think of what it is at all, unless you are a farmer like myself, or a publican's assistant or possibly something in the drapery line. Are you an actor or a mummer?'

'Not them either.'

He sat up suddenly and looked at me in a manner that was almost direct, his pipe sticking out aggressively from his tight jaws. He had the world full of smoke. I was uneasy but not altogether afraid of him. If I had my spade with me I knew I would soon make short work of him. I thought the wisest thing to do was to humour him and to agree with everything he said.

'I am a robber,' he said in a dark voice, 'a robber with a knife and an arm that's as strong as an article of powerful steam machinery.'

'A robber?' I exclaimed. My forebodings had been borne out.

Steady here. Take no chances.

'As strong as the bright moving instruments in a laundry. A black murderer also. Every time I rob a man I knock him dead because I have no respect for life, not a little. If I kill enough men there will be more life to go round and maybe then I will be able to live till I am a thousand and not have the old rattle in my neck when I am quite seventy. Have you a money-bag with you?'

Plead poverty and destitution. Ask for the loan of money.

That will not be difficult, I answered.

'I have no money at all, or coins or sovereigns or bankers' drafts,' I replied, 'no pawn-masters' tickets, nothing that is negotiable or of any value. I am as poor a man as yourself and I was thinking of asking you for two shillings to help me on my way.'

I was now more nervous than I was before as I sat looking at him. He had put his pipe away and had produced a long farmer's knife. He was looking at the blade of it and flashing lights with it.

'Even if you have no money,' he cackled, 'I will take your little life.'

'Now look here till I tell you,' I rejoined in a stern voice, 'robbery and murder are against the law and furthermore my life would add little to your own because I have a disorder in my chest and I am sure to be dead in six months. As well as that, there was a question of a dark funeral in my teacup on Tuesday. Wait till you hear a cough.'

I forced out a great hacking cough. It travelled like a breeze across the grass near at hand. I was now thinking that it might be wise to jump up quickly and run away. It would at least be a simple remedy.

'There is another thing about me,' I added, 'part of me is made of wood and has no life in it at all.'

The tricky man gave out sharp cries of surprise, jumped up and gave me looks that were too tricky for description. I smiled at him and pulled up my left trouser-leg to show him my timber shin. He examined it closely and ran his hard finger along the edge of it. Then he sat down very quickly, put his knife away and took out his pipe again. It had been burning away all the time in his pocket because he started to smoke it without any delay and after a minute he had so much blue smoke made, and grey smoke, that I thought his clothes had gone on fire. Between the smoke I could see that he was giving friendly looks in my direction. After a few moments he spoke cordially and softly to me.

'I would not hurt you, little man,' he said.

'I think I got the disorder in Mullingar,' I explained. I knew that I had gained his confidence and that the danger of violence was now passed. He then did something which took me by surprise. He pulled up his own ragged trouser and showed me his own left leg. It was smooth, shapely and fairly fat but it was made of wood also.

'That is a funny coincidence,' I said. I now perceived the reason for his sudden change of attitude.

'You are a sweet man,' he responded, 'and I would not lay a finger on your personality. I am the captain of all the one-leggèd men in the country. I knew them all up to now except one – your own self – and that one is now also my friend into the same bargain. If any man looks at you sideways, I will rip his belly.'

'That is very friendly talk,' I said.

'Wide open,' he said, making a wide movement with his hands. 'If you are ever troubled, send for me and I will save you from the woman.'

'Women I have no interest in at all,' I said smiling.

'A fiddle is a better thing for diversion.'

'It does not matter. If your perplexity is an army or a dog, I will come with all the one-leggèd men and rip the bellies. My real name is Martin Finnucane.'

'It is a reasonable name,' I assented.

'Martin Finnucane,' he repeated, listening to his own voice as if he were listening to the sweetest music in the world. He lay back and filled himself up to the ears with dark smoke and when he was nearly bursting he let it out again and hid himself in it.

'Tell me this,' he said at last. 'Have you a desideratum?'

This queer question was unexpected but I answered it quickly enough. I said I had.

'What desideratum?'

'To find what I am looking for.'

'That is a handsome desideratum,' said Martin Finnucane. 'What way will you bring it about or mature its mutandum and bring it ultimately to passable factivity?'

'By visiting the police barracks,' I said, 'and asking the policemen to direct me to where it is. Maybe you might instruct me on how to get to the barrack from where we are now?'

'Maybe indeed,' said Mr Finnucane. 'Have you an ultimatum?'

'I have a secret ultimatum,' I replied.

'I am sure it is a fine ultimatum,' he said, 'but I will not ask you to recite it for me if you think it is a secret one.'

He had smoked away all his tobacco and was now smoking the pipe itself, judging by the surly smell of it. He put his hand into a pocket at his crotch and took out a round thing.

'Here is a sovereign for your good luck,' he said, 'the golden token of your golden destiny.'

I gave him, so to speak, my golden thank-you but I noticed that the coin he gave me was a bright penny. I put it carefully into my pocket as if it were highly prized and very valuable. I was pleased at the way I had handled this eccentric queerly-spoken brother of the wooden leg. Near the far side of the road was a small river. I stood up and looked at it and watched the white water. It tumbled in the stony bedstead and jumped in the air and hurried excitedly round a corner.

'The barracks are on this same road,' said Martin Finnucane, 'and I left it behind me a mile away this today morning. You will discover it at the place where the river runs away from the road. If you look now you will see the fat trout in their brown coats coming back from the barracks at this hour because they go there every morning for the fine breakfast that is to be had from the slops and the throwings of the two policemen. But they have their dinners down the other way where a man called MacFeeterson has a bakery shop in a village of houses with their rears to the water. Three bread vans he has and a light dog-cart for the high mountain and he attends at Kilkishkeam on Mondays and Wednesdays.'

'Martin Finnucane,' I said, 'a hundred and two difficult thoughts I have to think between this and my destination and the sooner the better.'

He sent me up friendly glances from the smokey ditch.

'Good-looking man,' he said, 'good luck to your luck and do not entertain danger without sending me cognisance.'

I said 'Good-bye, Good-bye' and left him after a handshake. I looked back from down the road and saw nothing but the lip of the ditch with smoke coming from it as if tinkers were in the bottom of it cooking their what-they-had. Before I was gone I looked back again and saw the shape of his old head regarding me and closely studying my disappearance. He was amusing and interesting and had helped me by directing me to the barracks and telling me how far it was. And as I went upon my way I was slightly glad that I had met him.

A droll customer.

Chapter 4

Of all the many striking statements made by de Selby, I do not think that any of them can rival his assertion that 'a journey is an hallucination'. The phrase may be found in the *Country Album*[1] cheek by jowl with the well-known treatise on 'tent-suits', those egregious canvas garments which he designed as a substitute alike for the hated houses and ordinary clothing. His theory, insofar as I can understand it, seems to discount the testimony of human experience and is at variance with everything I have learnt myself on many a country walk. Human existence de Selby has defined as 'a succession of static experiences each infinitely brief', a conception which he is thought to have arrived at from examining some old cinematograph films which belonged probably to his nephew.[2] From this premise he discounts the reality or truth of any progression or serialism in life, denies that time can pass as such in the accepted sense and attributes to hallucinations the commonly experienced sensation of progression as, for instance, in journeying from one place to another or even 'living'. If one is resting at A, he explains, and desires to rest in a distant place B, one can only do so by resting for infinitely brief intervals in innumerable intermediate places. Thus there is no difference essentially between what happens when one is resting at A before the start of the 'journey' and what happens when one

[1] Page 822.
[2] These are evidently the same films which he mentions in *Golden Hours* (p. 155) as having 'a strong repetitive element' and as being 'tedious'. Apparently he had examined them patiently picture by picture and imagined that they would be screened in the same way, failing at that time to grasp the principle of the cinematograph.

is 'en route', i.e., resting in one or other of the intermediate places. He treats of these 'intermediate places' in a lengthy footnote. They are not, he warns us, to be taken as arbitrarily-determined points on the A-B axis so many inches or feet apart. They are rather to be regarded as points infinitely near each other yet sufficiently far apart to admit of the insertion between them of a series of other 'inter-intermediate' places, between each of which must be imagined a chain of other resting-places – not, of course, strictly adjacent but arranged so as to admit of the application of this principle indefinitely. The illusion of progression he attributes to the inability of the human brain – 'as at present developed' – to appreciate the reality of these separate 'rests', preferring to group many millions of them together and calling the result motion, an entirely indefensible and impossible procedure since even two separate positions cannot obtain simultaneously of the same body. Thus motion is also an illusion. He mentions that almost any photograph is conclusive proof of his teachings.

Whatever about the soundness of de Selby's theories, there is ample evidence that they were honestly held and that several attempts were made to put them into practice. During his stay in England, he happened at one time to be living in Bath and found it necessary to go from there to Folkestone on pressing business.[3] His method of doing so was far from conventional. Instead of going to the railway station and inquiring about trains, he shut himself up in a room in his lodgings with a supply of picture postcards of the areas which would be traversed on such a journey, together with an elaborate arrangement of clocks and barometric instruments and a device for regulating the gaslight in conformity with the changing light of the outside day. What happened in the room or how precisely the clocks and other machines were manipulated will never be known. It seems that he emerged after a lapse of seven hours convinced that he was in Folkestone and possibly that he had evolved a formula for travellers which would be extremely

[3] See Hatchjaw's *De Selby's Life and Times*.

distasteful to railway and shipping companies. There is no record of the extent of his disillusionment when he found himself still in the familiar surroundings of Bath but one authority[4] relates that he claimed without turning a hair to have been to Folkestone and back again. Reference is made to a man (unnamed) declaring to have actually seen the savant coming out of a Folkestone bank on the material date.

Like most of de Selby's theories, the ultimate outcome is inconclusive. It is a curious enigma that so great a mind would question the most obvious realities and object even to things scientifically demonstrated (such as the sequence of day and night) while believing absolutely in his own fantastic explanations of the same phenomena.

Of my own journey to the police-barracks I need only say that it was no hallucination. The heat of the sun played incontrovertibly on every inch of me, the hardness of the road was uncompromising and the country changed slowly but surely as I made my way through it. To the left was brown bogland scarred with dark cuttings and strewn with rugged clumps of bushes, white streaks of boulder and here and there a distant house half-hiding in an assembly of little trees. Far beyond was another region sheltering in the haze, purple and mysterious. The right-hand side was a greener country with the small turbulent river accompanying the road at a respectful distance and on the other side of it hills of rocky pasture stretching away into the distance up and down. Tiny sheep could be discerned near the sky far away and crooked lanes ran hither and thither. There was no sign whatever of human life. It was still early morning, perhaps. If I had not lost my American gold watch it would be possible for me to tell the time.

You have no American gold watch.

Something strange then happened to me suddenly. The road before me was turning gently to the left and as I approached the bend my heart began to behave irregularly and an unaccountable excitement took complete possession of me. There was nothing to see and no change of any kind

---

[4] Bassett: *Lux Mundi: A Memoir of de Selby.*

had come upon the scene to explain what was taking place within me. I continued walking with wild eyes.

As I came round the bend of the road an extraordinary spectacle was presented to me. About a hundred yards away on the left-hand side was a house which astonished me. It looked as if it were painted like an advertisement on a board on the roadside and indeed very poorly painted. It looked completely false and unconvincing. It did not seem to have any depth or breadth and looked as if it would not deceive a child. That was not in itself sufficient to surprise me because I had seen pictures and notices by the roadside before. What bewildered me was the sure knowledge deeply-rooted in my mind, that this was the house I was searching for and that there were people inside it. I had no doubt at all that it was the barracks of the policemen. I had never seen with my eyes ever in my life before anything so unnatural and appalling and my gaze faltered about the thing uncomprehendingly as if at least one of the customary dimensions was missing, leaving no meaning in the remainder. The appearance of the house was the greatest surprise I had encountered since I had seen the old man in the chair and I felt afraid of it.

I kept on walking, but walked more slowly. As I approached, the house seemed to change its appearance. At first, it did nothing to reconcile itself with the shape of an ordinary house but it became uncertain in outline like a thing glimpsed under ruffled water. Then it became clear again and I saw that it began to have some back to it, some small space for rooms behind the frontage. I gathered this from the fact that I seemed to see the front and the back of the 'building' simultaneously from my position approaching what should have been the side. As there was no side that I could see I thought the house must be triangular with its apex pointing towards me but when I was only fifteen yards away I saw a small window apparently facing me and I knew from that that there must be *some* side to it. Then I found myself almost in the shadow of the structure, dry-throated and timorous from wonder and anxiety. It seemed ordinary enough at close quarters except that it was very white and still. It was momentous and frightening; the whole morning and the whole world seemed to have no purpose at all save to frame it and give it some magnitude and position so that I could find it with my simple senses and pretend to myself that I understood it. A constabulary crest above the door told me that it was a police station. I had never seen a police station like it.

I cannot say why I did not stop to think or why my nervousness did not make me halt and sit down weakly by the roadside. Instead I walked straight up to the door and looked in. I saw, standing with his back to me, an enormous policeman. His back appearance was unusual. He was standing behind a little counter in a neat whitewashed day-room; his mouth was open and he was looking into a mirror which hung upon the wall. Again, I find it difficult to convey the precise reason why my eyes found his shape unprecedented and unfamiliar. He was very big and fat and the hair which strayed abundantly about the back of his bulging neck was a pale straw-colour; all that was striking but not unheard of. My glance ran over his great back, the thick arms and legs encased in the rough blue uniform. Ordinary enough as each part of him looked by itself, they all seemed to create together, by some undetectable discrepancy in association or proportion, a very disquieting impression of unnaturalness, amounting almost to what was horrible and monstrous. His hands were red, swollen and enormous and he appeared to have one of them half-way into his mouth as he gazed into the mirror.

'It's my teeth,' I heard him say, abstractedly and half-aloud. His voice was heavy and slightly muffled, reminding me of a thick winter quilt. I must have made some sound at the door or possibly he had seen my reflection in the glass for he turned slowly round, shifting his stance with leisurely and heavy majesty, his fingers still working at his teeth; and as he turned I heard him murmuring to himself:

'Nearly every sickness is from the teeth.'

His face gave me one more surprise. It was enormously fat, red and widespread, sitting squarely on the neck of his tunic with a clumsy weightiness that reminded me of a sack of flour. The lower half of it was hidden by a violent red moustache which shot out from his skin far into the air like the antennae of some unusual animal. His cheeks were red and chubby and his eyes were nearly invisible, hidden from above by the obstruction of his tufted brows and from below by the fat foldings of his skin. He came over ponderously to the inside of the counter and I advanced meekly from the door until we were face to face.

'Is it about a bicycle?' he asked.

His expression when I encountered it was unexpectedly reassuring. His face was gross and far from beautiful but he had modified and assembled his various unpleasant features in some skilful way so that they expressed to me good nature, politeness and infinite patience. In the front of his peaked official cap was an important-looking badge and over it in golden letters was the word SERGEANT. It was Sergeant Pluck himself.

'No,' I answered, stretching forth my hand to lean with it against the counter. The Sergeant looked at me incredulously.

'Are you sure?' he asked.

'Certain.'

'Not about a motor-cycle?'

'No.'

'One with overhead valves and a dynamo for light? Or with racing handle-bars?'

'No.'

'In that circumstantial eventuality there can be no question of a motor-bicycle,' he said. He looked surprised and puzzled and leaned sideways on the counter on the prop of his left elbow, putting the knuckles of his right hand between his yellow teeth and raising three enormous wrinkles of perplexity on his forehead. I decided now that he was a simple man and that I would have no difficulty in dealing with him exactly as I desired and finding out from him what had happened to the black box. I did not understand clearly the reason for his questions about bicycles but I made up my mind to answer everything carefully, to bide my time and to be cunning in all my dealings with him. He moved away abstractedly, came back and handed me a bundle of differently-coloured papers which looked like application forms for bull-licences and dog-licences and the like.

'It would be no harm if you filled up these forms,' he said. 'Tell me,' he continued, 'would it be true that you are an itinerant dentist and that you came on a tricycle?'

'It would not,' I replied.

'On a patent tandem?'

'No.'

'Dentists are an unpredictable coterie of people,' he said. 'Do you tell me it was a velocipede or a penny-farthing?'

'I do not,' I said evenly. He gave me a long searching look as if to see whether I was serious in what I was saying, again wrinkling up his brow.

'Then maybe you are no dentist at all,' he said, 'but only a man after a dog licence or papers for a bull?'

'I did not say I was a dentist,' I said sharply, 'and I did not say anything about a bull.'

The Sergeant looked at me incredulously.

'That is a great curiosity,' he said, 'a very difficult piece of puzzledom, a snorter.'

He sat down by the turf fire and began jawing his knuckles and giving me sharp glances from under his bushy brows. If I had horns upon my head or a tail behind me he could not have looked at me with more interest. I was unwilling to give any lead to the direction of the talk and there was complete silence for five minutes. Then his expression eased a bit and he spoke to me again.

'What is your pronoun?' he inquired.

'I have no pronoun,' I answered, hoping I knew his meaning.

'What is your cog?'

'My cog?'

'Your surnoun?'

'I have not got that either.'

My reply again surprised him and also seemed to please him. He raised his thick eyebrows and changed his face into what could be described as a smile. He came back to the counter, put out his enormous hand, took mine in it and shook it warmly.

'No name or no idea of your originality at all?'

'None.'

'Well, by the holy Hokey!'

Signor Bari, the eminent one-leggèd tenor!

'By the holy Irish-American Powers,' he said again, 'by the Dad! Well carry me back to old Kentucky!'

He then retreated from the counter to his chair by the fire and sat silently bent in thought as if examining one by one the by-gone years stored up in his memory.

'I was once acquainted with a tall man,' he said to me at last, 'that had no name either and you are certain to be his son and the heir to his nullity and all his nothings. What way is your pop today and where is he?'

It was not, I thought, entirely unreasonable that the son of a man who had no name should have no name also but it was clear that the Sergeant was confusing me with some-body else. This was no harm and I decided to encourage him. I considered it desirable that he should know nothing about me but it was even better if he knew several things which were quite wrong. It would help me in using him for my own purposes and ultimately in finding the black box.

'He is gone to America,' I replied.

'Is that where,' said the Sergeant. 'Do you tell me that? He was a true family husband. The last time I interviewed him it was about a missing pump and he had a wife and ten sonnies and at that time he had the wife again in a very advanced state of sexuality.'

'That was me,' I said, smiling.

'That was you,' he agreed. 'What way are the ten strong sons?'

'All gone to America.'

'That is a great conundrum of a country,' said the Sergeant, 'a very wide territory, a place occupied by black men and strangers. I am told they are very fond of shooting-matches in that quarter.'

'It is a queer land,' I said.

At this stage there were footsteps at the door and in

marched a heavy policeman carrying a small constabulary lamp. He had a dark Jewish face and hooky nose and masses of black curly hair. He was blue-jowled and black-jowled and looked as if he shaved twice a day. He had white enamelled teeth which came, I had no doubt, from Manchester, two rows of them arranged in the interior of his mouth and when he smiled it was a fine sight to see, like delph on a neat country dresser. He was heavy-fleshed and gross in body like the Sergeant but his face looked far more intelligent. It was unexpectedly lean and the eyes in it were penetrating and observant. If his face alone were in question he would look more like a poet than a policeman but the rest of his body looked anything but poetical.

'Policeman MacCruiskeen,' said Sergeant Pluck.

Policeman MacCruiskeen put the lamp on the table, shook hands with me and gave me the time of day with great gravity. His voice was high, almost feminine, and he spoke with a delicate careful intonation. Then he put the little lamp on the counter and surveyed the two of us.

'Is it about a bicycle?' he asked.

'Not that,' said the Sergeant. 'This is a private visitor who says he did not arrive in the townland upon a bicycle. He has no personal name at all. His dadda is in far Amurikey.'

'Which of the two Amurikeys?' asked MacCruiskeen.

'The Unified Stations,' said the Sergeant.

'Likely he is rich by now if he is in that quarter,' said MacCruiskeen, 'because there's dollars there, dollars and bucks and nuggets in the ground and any amount of rackets and golf games and musical instruments. It is a free country too by all accounts.'

'Free for all,' said the Sergeant. 'Tell me this,' he said to the policeman, 'Did you take any readings today?'

'I did,' said MacCruiskeen.

'Take out your black book and tell me what it was, like a good man,' said the Sergeant. 'Give me the gist of it till I see what I see,' he added.

MacCruiskeen fished a small black notebook from his breast pocket.

'Ten point six,' he said.

'Ten point six,' said the Sergeant. 'And what reading did you notice on the beam?'

'Seven point four.'

'How much on the lever?'

'One point five.'

There was a pause here. The Sergeant put on an expression of great intricacy as if he were doing far-from-simple sums and calculations in his head. After a time his face cleared and he spoke again to his companion.

'Was there a fall?'

'A heavy fall at half-past three.'

'Very understandable and commendably satisfactory,' said the Sergeant. 'Your supper is on the hob inside and be sure to stir the milk before you take any of it, the way the rest of us after you will have our share of the fats of it, the health and the heart of it.'

Policeman MacCruiskeen smiled at the mention of food and went into the back room loosening his belt as he went; after a moment we heard the sounds of coarse slobbering as if he was eating porridge without the assistance of spoon or hand. The Sergeant invited me to sit at the fire in his company and gave me a wrinkled cigarette from his pocket.

'It is lucky for your pop that he is situated in Amurikey,' he remarked, 'if it is a thing that he is having trouble with the old teeth. It is very few sicknesses that are not from the teeth.'

'Yes,' I said. I was determined to say as little as possible and let these unusual policemen first show their hand. Then I would know how to deal with them.

'Because a man can have more disease and germination in his gob than you'll find in a rat's coat and Amurikey is a country where the population do have grand teeth like shaving-lather or like bits of delph when you break a plate.'

'Quite true,' I said.

'Or like eggs under a black crow.'

'Like eggs,' I said.

'Did you ever happen to visit the cinematograph in your travels?'

'Never,' I answered humbly, 'but I believe it is a dark

quarter and little can be seen at all except the photographs on the wall.'

'Well it is there you see the fine teeth they do have in Amurikey,' said the Sergeant.

He gave the fire a hard look and took to handling absently his yellow stumps of teeth. I had been wondering about his mysterious conversation with MacCruiskeen.

'Tell me this much,' I ventured. 'What sort of readings were those in the policeman's black book?'

The Sergeant gave me a keen look which felt almost hot from being on the fire previously.

'The first beginnings of wisdom,' he said, 'is to ask questions but never to answer any. *You* get wisdom from asking and *I* from not answering. Would you believe that there is a great increase in crime in this locality? Last year we had sixty-nine cases of no lights and four stolen. This year we have eighty-two cases of no lights, thirteen cases of riding on the footpath and four stolen. There was one case of wanton damage to a three-speed gear, there is sure to be a claim at the next Court and the area of charge will be the parish. Before the year is out there is certain to be a pump stolen, a very depraved and despicable manifestation of criminality and a blot on the county.'

'Indeed,' I said.

'Five years ago we had a case of loose handlebars. Now there is a rarity for you. It took the three of us a week to frame the charge.'

'Loose handlebars,' I muttered. I could not clearly see the reason for such talk about bicycles.

'And then there is the question of bad brakes. The country is honeycombed with bad brakes, half of the accidents are due to it, runs in families.'

I thought it would be better to try to change the conversation from bicycles.

'You told me what the first rule of wisdom is,' I said. 'What is the second rule?'

'That can be answered,' he said. 'There are five in all. Always ask any questions that are to be asked and never answer any. Turn everything you hear to your own advantage. Always carry a repair outfit. Take left turns as much as possible. Never apply your front brake first.'

'These are interesting rules,' I said dryly.

'If you follow them,' said the Sergeant, 'you will save your soul and you will never get a fall on a slippy road.'

'I would be obliged to you,' I said, 'if you would explain to me which of these rules covers the difficulty I have come here today to put before you.'

'This is not today, this is yesterday,' he said, 'but which of the difficulties is it? What is the *crux rei*?'

Yesterday? I decided without any hesitation that it was a waste of time trying to understand the half of what he said. I persevered with my inquiry.

'I came here to inform you officially about the theft of my American gold watch.'

He looked at me through an atmosphere of great surprise and incredulity and raised his eyebrows almost to his hair.

'That is an astonishing statement,' he said at last.

'Why?'

'Why should anybody steal a watch when they can steal a bicycle?'

Hark to his cold inexorable logic.

'Search me,' I said.

'Who ever heard of a man riding a watch down the road or bringing a sack of turf up to his house on the crossbar of a watch?'

'I did not say the thief wanted my watch to ride it,' I expostulated. 'Very likely he had a bicycle of his own and that is how he got away quietly in the middle of the night.'

'Never in my puff did I hear of any man stealing anything but a bicycle when he was in his sane senses,' said the Sergeant, ' – except pumps and clips and lamps and the like of that. Surely you are not going to tell me at my time of life that the world is changing?'

'I am only saying that my watch was stolen,' I said crossly.

'Very well,' the Sergeant said with finality, 'we will have to institute a search.'

He smiled brightly at me. It was quite clear that he did not believe any part of my story, and that he thought I was in delicate mental health. He was humouring me as if I were a child.

'Thank you,' I muttered.

'But the trouble will only be beginning when we find it,' he said severely.

'How is that?'

'When we find it we will have to start searching for the owner.'

'But I am the owner.'

Here the Sergeant laughed indulgently and shook his head.

'I know what you mean,' he said. 'But the law is an extremely intricate phenomenon. If you have no name you cannot own a watch and the watch that has been stolen does not exist and when it is found it will have to be restored to its rightful owner. If you have no name you possess nothing and you do not exist and even your trousers are not on you although they look as if they were from where I am sitting. On the other separate hand you can do what you like and the law cannot touch you.'

'It had fifteen jewels,' I said despairingly.

'And on the first hand again you might be charged with theft or common larceny if you were mistaken for somebody else when wearing the watch.'

'I feel extremely puzzled,' I said, speaking nothing less than the truth. The Sergeant gave his laugh of good humour.

'If we ever find the watch,' he smiled, 'I have a feeling that there will be a bell and a pump on it.'

I considered my position with some misgiving. It seemed to be impossible to make the Sergeant take cognisance of anything in the world except bicycles. I thought I would make a last effort.

'You appear to be under the impression,' I said coldly and courteously, 'that I have lost a golden bicycle of American manufacture with fifteen jewels. I have lost a watch and there is no bell on it. Bells are only on alarm clocks and I have never in my life seen a watch with a pump attached to it.'

The Sergeant smiled at me again.

'There was a man in this room a fortnight ago,' he said, 'telling me that he was at the loss of his mother, a lady of eighty-two. When I asked him for a description – just to fill up the blanks in the official form we get for half-nothing from the Stationery Office – he said she had rust on her rims and that her back brakes were subject to the jerks.'

This speech made my position quite clear to me. When I was about to say something else, a man put his face in and looked at us and then came in completely and shut the door carefully and came over to the counter. He was a bluff red man in a burly coat with twine binding his trousers at the knees. I discovered afterwards that his name was Michael Gilhaney. Instead of standing at the counter as he would in a public house, he went to the wall, put his arms akimbo and leaned against it, balancing his weight on the point of one elbow.

'Well, Michael,' said the Sergeant pleasantly.

'That is a cold one,' said Mr Gilhaney.

Sounds of shouting came to the three of us from the inner room where Policeman MacCruiskeen was engaged in the task of his early dinner.

'Hand me in a fag,' he called.

The Sergeant gave me another wrinkled cigarette from his pocket and jerked his thumb in the direction of the back room. As I went in with the cigarette I heard the Sergeant opening an enormous ledger and putting questions to the red-faced visitor.

'What was the make,' he was saying, 'and the number of the frame and was there a lamp and a pump on it into the same bargain?'

Chapter 5

The long and unprecedented conversation I had with Policeman MacCruiskeen after I went in to him on my mission with the cigarette brought to my mind afterwards several of the more delicate speculations of de Selby, notably his investigation of the nature of time and eternity by a system of mirrors.[1] His theory as I understand it is as follows:

If a man stands before a mirror and sees in it his reflection, what he sees is not a true reproduction of himself but a picture of himself when he was a younger man. De Selby's explanation of this phenomenon is quite simple. Light, as he points out truly enough, has an ascertained and finite rate of travel. Hence before the reflection of any object in a mirror can be said to be accomplished, it is necessary that rays of light should first strike the object and subsequently impinge on the glass, to be thrown back again to the object – to the eyes of a man, for instance. There is therefore an appreciable and calculable interval of time between the

---

[1] Hatchjaw remarks (unconfirmed, however, by Bassett) that throughout the whole ten years that went to the writing of *The Country Album* de Selby was obsessed with mirrors and had recourse to them so frequently that he claimed to have two left hands and to be living in a world arbitrarily bounded by a wooden frame. As time went on he refused to countenance a direct view of anything and had a small mirror permanently at a certain angle in front of his eyes by a wired mechanism of his own manufacture. After he had resorted to this fantastic arrangement, he interviewed visitors with his back to them and with his head inclined towards the ceiling; he was even credited with long walks backwards in crowded thoroughfares. Hatchjaw claims that his statement is supported by the MS. of some three hundred pages of the *Album*, written backwards, 'a circumstance that made necessary the extension of the mirror principle to the bench of the wretched printer.' (*De Selby's Life and Times*, p. 221.) This manuscript cannot now be found.

throwing by a man of a glance at his own face in a mirror and the registration of the reflected image in his eye.

So far, one may say, so good. Whether this idea is right or wrong, the amount of time involved is so negligible that few reasonable people would argue the point. But de Selby ever loath to leave well enough alone, insists on reflecting the first reflection in a further mirror and professing to detect minute changes in this second image. Ultimately he constructed the familiar arrangement of parallel mirrors, each reflecting diminishing images of an interposed object indefinitely. The interposed object in this case was de Selby's own face and this he claims to have studied backwards through an infinity of reflections by means of 'a powerful glass'. What he states to have seen through his glass is astonishing. He claims to have noticed a growing youthfulness in the reflections of his face according as they receded, the most distant of them – too tiny to be visible to the naked eye – being the face of a beardless boy of twelve, and, to use his own words, 'a countenance of singular beauty and nobility'. He did not succeed in pursuing the matter back to the cradle 'owing to the curvature of the earth and the limitations of the telescope.'

So much for de Selby. I found MacCruiskeen with a red face at the kitchen table panting quietly from all the food he had hidden in his belly. In exchange for the cigarette he gave me searching looks. 'Well, now,' he said.

He lit the cigarette and sucked at it and smiled covertly at me.

'Well, now,' he said again. He had his little lamp beside him on the table and he played his fingers on it.

'That is a fine day,' I said. 'What are you doing with a lamp in the white morning?'

'I can give you a question as good as that,' he responded. 'Can you notify me of the meaning of a bulbul?'

'A bulbul?'

'What would you say a bulbul is?'

This conundrum did not interest me but I pretended to rack my brains and screwed my face in perplexity until I felt it half the size it should be.

'Not one of those ladies who take money?' I said.

'No.'

'Not the brass knobs on a German steam organ?'

'Not the knobs.'

'Nothing to do with the independence of America or such-like?'

'No.'

'A mechanical engine for winding clocks?'

'No.'

'A tumour, or the lather in a cow's mouth, or those elastic articles that ladies wear?'

'Not them by a long chalk.'

'Not an eastern musical instrument played by Arabs?'

He clapped his hands.

'Not that but very near it,' he smiled, 'something next door to it. You are a cordial intelligible man. A bulbul is a Persian nightingale. What do you think of that now?'

'It is seldom I am far out,' I said dryly.

He looked at me in admiration and the two of us sat in silence for a while as if each was very pleased with himself and with the other and had good reason to be.

'You are a B.A. with little doubt?' he questioned.

I gave no direct answer but tried to look big and learned and far from simple in my little chair.

'I think you are a sempiternal man,' he said slowly.

He sat for a while giving the floor a strict examination and then put his dark jaw over to me and began questioning me about my arrival in the parish.

'I do not want to be insidious,' he said, 'but would you inform me about your arrival in the parish? Surely you had a three-speed gear for the hills?'

'I had no three-speed gear,' I responded rather sharply, 'and no two-speed gear and it is also true that I had no bicycle and little or no pump and if I had a lamp itself it would not be necessary if I had no bicycle and there would be no bracket to hang it on.'

'That may be,' said MacCruiskeen, 'but likely you were laughed at on the tricycle?'

'I had neither bicycle nor tricycle and I am not a dentist,'

I said with severe categorical thoroughness, 'and I do not believe in the penny-farthing or the scooter, the velocipede or the tandem-tourer.'

MacCruiskeen got white and shaky and gripped my arm and looked at me intensely.

'In my natural puff,' he said at last, in a strained voice, 'I have never encountered a more fantastic epilogue or a queerer story. Surely you are a queer far-fetched man. To my dying night I will not forget this today morning. Do not tell me that you are taking a hand at me?'

'No,' I said.

'Well Great Crikes!'

He got up and brushed his hair with a flat hand back along his skull and looked out of the window for a long interval, his eyes popping and dancing and his face like an empty bag with no blood in it.

Then he walked around to put back the circulation and took a little spear from a place he had on the shelf.

'Put your hand out,' he said.

I put it out idly enough and he held the spear at it. He kept putting it near me and nearer and when he had the bright point of it about half a foot away, I felt a prick and gave a short cry. There was a little bead of my red blood in the middle of my palm.

'Thank you very much,' I said. I felt too surprised to be annoyed with him.

'That will make you think,' he remarked in triumph, 'unless I am an old Dutchman by profession and nationality.'

He put his little spear back on the shelf and looked at me crookedly from a sidewise angle with a certain quantity of what may be called *roi-s'amuse*.

'Maybe you can explain that?' he said.

'That is the limit,' I said wonderingly.

'It will take some analysis,' he said, 'intellectually.'

'Why did your spear sting when the point was half a foot away from where it made me bleed?'

'That spear' he answered quietly, 'is one of the first things I ever manufactured in my spare time. I think only a little of it now but the year I made it I was proud enough and would not get up in the morning for any sergeant. There is no other spear like it in the length and breadth of Ireland and there is only one thing like it in Amurikey but I have not heard what it is. But I cannot get over the no-bicycle. Great Crikes!'

'But the spear,' I insisted, 'give me the gist of it like a good man and I will tell no one.'

'I will tell you because you are a confidential man,' he said, 'and a man that said something about bicycles that I never heard before. What you think is the point is not the point at all but only the beginning of the sharpness.'

'Very wonderful,' I said, 'but I do not understand you.'

'The point is seven inches long and it is so sharp and thin that you cannot see it with the old eye. The first half of the sharpness is thick and strong but you cannot see it either because the real sharpness runs into it and if you saw the one you could see the other or maybe you would notice the joint.'

'I suppose it is far thinner than a match?' I asked.

'There *is* a difference,' he said. 'Now the proper sharp part is so thin that nobody could see it no matter what light is on it or what eye is looking. About an inch from the end it is so sharp that sometimes – late at night or on a soft bad day especially – you cannot think of it or try to make it the subject of a little idea because you will hurt your box with the excruciation of it.'

I gave a frown and tried to make myself look like a wise person who was trying to comprehend something that called for all his wisdom.

'You cannot have fire without bricks,' I said, nodding.

'Wisely said,' MacCruiskeen answered.

'It was sharp sure enough,' I conceded, 'it drew a little bulb of the red blood but I did not feel the pricking hardly at all. It must be very sharp to work like that.'

MacCruiskeen gave a laugh and sat down again at the table and started putting on his belt.

'You have not got the whole gist of it at all,' he smiled. 'Because what gave you the prick and brought the blood was not the point at all; it was the place I am talking about that is a good inch from the reputed point of the article under our discussion.'

'And what is this inch that is left?' I asked. 'What in heaven's name would you call that?'

'That is the real point,' said MacCruiskeen, 'but it is so thin that it could go into your hand and out in the other extremity externally and you would not feel a bit of it and you would see nothing and hear nothing. It is so thin that maybe it does not exist at all and you could spend half an hour trying to think about it and you could put no thought around it in the end. The beginning part of the inch is thicker than the last part and is nearly there for a fact but I don't think it is if it is my private opinion that you are anxious to enlist.'

I fastened my fingers around my jaw and started to think with great concentration, calling into play parts of my brain that I rarely used. Nevertheless I made no progress at all as regards the question of the points. MacCruiskeen had been at the dresser a second time and was back at the table with a little black article like a leprechaun's piano with diminutive keys of white and black and brass pipes and circular revolving cogs like parts of a steam engine or the business end of a thrashing-mill. His white hands were moving all over it and feeling it as if they were trying to discover some tiny lump on it, and his face was looking up in the air in a spiritual attitude and he was paying no attention to my personal existence at all. There was an overpowering tremendous silence as if the roof of the room had come down half-way to the floor, he at his queer occupation with the instrument and myself still trying to comprehend the sharpness of the points and to get the accurate understanding of them.

After ten minutes he got up and put the thing away. He wrote for a time in his notebook and then lit his pipe.

'Well now,' he remarked expansively.

'Those points,' I said.

'Did I happen to ask you what a bulbul is?'

'You did,' I responded, 'but the question of those points is what takes me to the fair.'

'It is not today or yesterday I started pointing spears,' he said, 'but maybe you would like to see something else that is a medium fair example of supreme art?'

'I would indeed,' I answered.

'But I cannot get over what you confided in me privately *sub-rosa* about the no-bicycle, that is a story that would make your golden fortune if you wrote down in a book where people could pursue it literally.'

He walked back to the dresser, opened the lower part of it, and took out a little chest till he put it on the table for my inspection. Never in my life did I inspect anything more ornamental and well-made. It was a brown chest like those owned by seafaring men or lascars from Singapore, but it was diminutive in a very perfect way as if you were looking at a full-size one through the wrong end of a spy-glass. It was about a foot in height, perfect in its proportions and without fault in workmanship. There were indents and carving and fanciful excoriations and designs on every side of it and there was a bend on the lid that gave the article great distinction. At every corner there was a shiny brass corner-piece and on the lid there were brass corner-pieces beautifully wrought and curved impeccably against the wood. The whole thing had the dignity and the satisfying quality of true art.

'There now,' said MacCruiskeen.

'It is nearly too nice,' I said at last, 'to talk about it.'

'I spent two years manufacturing it when I was a lad,' said MacCruiskeen, 'and it still takes me to the fair.'

'It is unmentionable,' I said.

'Very nearly,' said MacCruiskeen.

The two of us then started looking at it and we looked at it for five minutes so hard that it seemed to dance on the table and look even smaller than it might be.

'I do not often look at boxes or chests,' I said, simply, 'but this is the most beautiful box I have ever seen and I will always remember it. There might be something inside it?'

'There might be,' said MacCruiskeen.

He went to the table and put his hands around the article in a fawning way as if he were caressing a sheepdog and he opened the lid with a little key but shut it down again before I could inspect the inside of it.

'I will tell you a story and give you a synopsis of the ramification of the little plot,' he said. 'When I had the chest made and finished, I tried to think what I would keep in it and what I would use it for at all. First I thought of them letters from Bridie, the ones on the blue paper with the strong smell but I did not think it would be anything but a sacrilege in the end because there was hot bits in them letters. Do you comprehend the trend of my observations?'

'I do,' I answered.

'Then there was my studs and the enamel badge and my presentation iron-pencil with a screw on the end of it to push the point out, an intricate article full of machinery and a Present from Southport. All these things are what are called Examples of the Machine Age.'

'They would be contrary to the spirit of the chest,' I said.

'They would be indeed. Then there was my razor and the spare plate in case I was presented with an accidental bash on the gob in the execution of me duty . . .'

'But not them.'

'Not them. Then there was my certificates and me cash and the picture of Peter the Hermit and the brass thing with straps that I found on the road one night near Matthew O'Carahan's. But not them either.'

'It is a hard conundrum,' I said.

'In the end I found there was only one thing to do to put myself right with my private conscience.'

'It is a great thing that you found the right answer at all,' I countered.

'I decided to myself,' said MacCruiskeen, 'that the only sole correct thing to contain in the chest was another chest of the same make but littler in cubic dimension.'

'That was very competent masterwork,' I said, endeavouring to speak his own language.

He went to the little chest and opened it up again and put his hands down sideways like flat plates or like the fins on a fish and took out of it a smaller chest but one resembling its mother-chest in every particular of appearance and dimension. It almost interfered with my breathing, it was so delightfully unmistakable. I went over and felt it and covered it with my hand to see how big its smallness was. Its brasswork had a shine like the sun on the sea and the colour of the wood was a rich deep richness like a colour deepened and toned only by the years. I got slightly weak from looking at it and sat down on a chair and for the purpose of pretending that I was not disturbed I whistled *The Old Man Twangs His Braces*.

MacCruiskeen gave me a smooth inhuman smile.

'You may have come on no bicycle,' he said, 'but that does not say that you know everything.'

'Those chests,' I said, 'are so like one another that I do not believe they are there at all because that is a simpler thing to believe than the contrary. Nevertheless the two of them are the most wonderful two things I have ever seen.'

'I was two years manufacturing it,' MacCruiskeen said.

'What is in the little one?' I asked.

'What would you think now?'

'I am completely half afraid to think,' I said, speaking truly enough.

'Wait now till I show you,' said MacCruiskeen, 'and give you an exhibition and a personal inspection individually.'

He got two thin butter-spades from the shelf and put them down into the little chest and pulled out something that seemed to me remarkably like another chest. I went over to it and gave it a close examination with my hand, feeling the same identical wrinkles, the same proportions and the same completely perfect brasswork on a smaller scale. It was so faultless and delightful that it reminded me forcibly, strange and foolish as it may seem, of something I did not understand and had never even heard of.

'Say nothing,' I said quickly to MacCruiskeen, 'but go ahead with what you are doing and I will watch here and I will take care to be sitting down.'

He gave me a nod in exchange for my remark and got two straight-handled teaspoons and put the handles into his last chest. What came out may well be guessed at. He opened this one and took another one out with the assistance of two knives. He worked knives, small knives and smaller knives, till he had twelve little chests on the table, the last of them an article half the size of a matchbox. It was so tiny that you would not quite see the brasswork at all only for the glitter of it in the light. I did not see whether it had the same identical carvings upon it because I was content to take a swift look at it and then turn away. But I knew in my soul that it was exactly the same as the others. I said no word at all because my mind was brimming with wonder at the skill of the policeman.

'That last one,' said MacCruiskeen, putting away the knives, 'took me three years to make and it took me another year to believe that I had made it. Have you got the convenience of a pin?'

I gave him my pin in silence. He opened the smallest of them all with a key like a piece of hair and worked with the pin till he had another little chest on the table, thirteen in all arranged in a row upon the table. Queerly enough they looked to me as if they were all the same size but invested with some crazy perspective. This idea surprised me so much that I got my voice back and said:

'These are the most surprising thirteen things I have ever seen together.'

'Wait now, man,' MacCruiskeen said.

All my senses were now strained so tensely watching the policeman's movements that I could almost hear my brain rattling in my head when I gave a shake as if it was drying up into a wrinkled pea. He was manipulating and prodding with his pin till he had twenty-eight little chests on the table and the last of them so small that it looked like a bug or a tiny piece of dirt except that there was a glitter from it. When I looked at it again I saw another thing beside it like something you would take out of a red eye on a windy dry day and I knew then that the strict computation was then twenty-nine.

'Here is your pin,' said MacCruiskeen.

He put it into my stupid hand and went back to the table thoughtfully. He took a something from his pocket that was too small for me to see and started working with the tiny black thing on the table beside the bigger thing which was itself too small to be described.

At this point I became afraid. What he was doing was no longer wonderful but terrible. I shut my eyes and prayed that he would stop while still doing things that were at least possible for a man to do. When I looked again I was happy that there was nothing to see and that he had put no more of the chests prominently on the table but he was working to the left with the invisible thing in his hand on a bit of the table itself. When he felt my look he came over to me and gave me an enormous magnifying-glass which looked like a basin fixed to a handle. I felt the muscles around my heart tightening painfully as I took the instrument.

'Come over here to the table,' he said, 'and look there till you see what you see infra-ocularly.'

When I saw the table it was bare only for the twenty-nine chest articles but through the agency of the glass I was in a position to report that he had two more out beside the last ones, the smallest of all being nearly half a size smaller than ordinary invisibility. I gave him back the glass instrument and took to the chair without a word. In order to reassure myself and make a loud human noise I whistled *The Corncrake Plays the Bagpipes*.

'There now,' said MacCruiskeen.

He took two wrinkled cigarettes from his fob and lit the two at the same time and handed me one of them.

'Number Twenty-Two,' he said, 'I manufactured fifteen years ago and I have made another different one every year since with any amount of nightwork and overtime and piecework and time-and-a-half incidentally.'

'I understand you clearly,' I said.

'Six years ago they began to get invisible, glass or no glass. Nobody has ever seen the last five I made because no glass is strong enough to make them big enough to be regarded truly as the smallest things ever made. Nobody can see me making them because my little tools are invisible into the same bargain. The one I am making now is nearly as small as nothing. Number One would hold a million of them at the same time and there would be room left for a pair of woman's horse-breeches if they were rolled up. The dear knows where it will stop and terminate.'

'Such work must be very hard on the eyes,' I said, determined to pretend that everybody was an ordinary person like myself.

'Some of these days,' he answered, 'I will have to buy spectacles with gold ear-claws. My eyes are crippled with the small print in the newspapers and in the offeecial forms.'

'Before I go back to the day-room,' I said, 'would it be right to ask you what you were performing with that little small piano-instrument, the article with the knobs, and the brass pins?'

'That is my personal musical instrument,' said Mac-Cruiskeen, 'and I was playing my own tunes on it in order to extract private satisfaction from the sweetness of them.'

'I was listening,' I answered, 'but I did not succeed in hearing you.'

'That does not surprise me intuitively,' said Mac-Cruiskeen, 'because it is an indigenous patent of my own. The vibrations of the true notes are so high in their fine frequencies that they cannot be appreciated by the human earcup. Only myself has the secret of the thing and the intimate way of it, the confidential knack of circumventing it. Now what do you think of that?'

I climbed up to my legs to go back to the day-room, passing a hand weakly about my brow.

'I think it is extremely acatalectic,' I answered.

Chapter 6

When I penetrated back to the day-room I encountered two gentlemen called Sergeant Pluck and Mr Gilhaney and they were holding a meeting about the question of bicycles.

'I do not believe in the three-speed gear at all,' the Sergeant was saying, 'it is a new-fangled instrument, it crucifies the legs, the half of the accidents are due to it.'

'It is a power for the hills,' said Gilhaney, 'as good as a second pair of pins or a diminutive petrol motor.'

'It is a hard thing to tune,' said the Sergeant, 'you can screw the iron lace that hangs out of it till you get no catch at all on the pedals. It never stops the way you want it, it would remind you of bad jaw-plates.'

'That is all lies,' said Gilhaney.

'Or like the pegs of a fairy-day fiddle,' said the Sergeant, 'or a skinny wife in the craw of a cold bed in springtime.'

'Not that,' said Gilhaney.

'Or porter in a sick stomach,' said the Sergeant.

'So help me not,' said Gilhaney.

The Sergeant saw me with the corner of his eye and turned to talk to me, taking away all his attention from Gilhaney.

'MacCruiskeen was giving you his talk I wouldn't doubt,' he said.

'He was being extremely explanatory,' I answered dryly.

'He is a comical man,' said the Sergeant, 'a walking emporium, you'd think he was on wires and worked with steam.'

'He is,' I said.

'He is a melody man,' the Sergeant added, 'and very temporary, a menace to the mind.'

'About the bicycle,' said Gilhaney.

'The bicycle will be found,' said the Sergeant, 'when I retrieve and restore it to its own owner in due law and possessively. Would you desire to be of assistance in the search?' he asked me.

'I would not mind,' I answered.

The Sergeant looked at his teeth in the glass for a brief intermission and then put his leggings on his legs and took a hold of his stick as an indication that he was for the road. Gilhaney was at the door operating it to let us out. The three of us walked out into the middle of the day.

'In case we do not come up with the bicycle before it is high dinner-time,' said the Sergeant, 'I have left an official memorandum for the personal information of Policeman Fox so that he will be acutely conversant with the *res ipsa*,' he said.

'Do you hold with rap-trap pedals?' asked Gilhaney.

'Who is Fox?' I asked.

'Policeman Fox is the third of us,' said the Sergeant, 'but we never see him or hear tell of him at all because he is always on his beat and never off it and he signs the book in the middle of the night when even a badger is asleep. He is as mad as a hare, he never interrogates the public and he is always taking notes. If rat-trap pedals were universal it would be the end of bicycles, the people would die like flies.'

'What put him that way?' I inquired.

'I never comprehended correctly,' replied the Sergeant, 'or got the real informative information but Policeman Fox was alone in a private room with MacCruiskeen for a whole hour on a certain 23rd of June and he has never spoken to anybody since that day and he is as crazy as tuppence-half-penny and as cranky as thruppence. Did I ever tell you how I asked Inspector O'Corky about rat-traps? Why are they not made prohibitive, I said, or made specialities like arsenic when you would have to buy them at a chemist's shop and sign a little book and look like a responsible personality?'

'They are a power for the hills,' said Gilhaney.

The Sergeant spat spits on the dry road.

'You would want a special Act of Parliament,' said the Inspector, 'a special Act of Parliament.'

'What way are we going?' I asked, 'or what direction are we heading for or are we on the way back from somewhere else?'

It was a queer country we were in. There was a number of blue mountains around us at what you might call a respectful distance with a glint of white water coming down the shoulders of one or two of them and they kept hemming us in and meddling oppressively with our minds. Half-way to these mountains the view got clearer and was full of humps and hollows and long parks of fine bogland with civil people here and there in the middle of it working with long instruments, you could hear their voices calling across the wind and the crack of the dull carts on the roadways. White buildings could be seen in several places and cows shambling lazily from here to there in search of pasture. A company of crows came out of a tree when I was watching and flew sadly down to a field where there was a quantity of sheep attired in fine overcoats.

'We are going where we are going,' said the Sergeant, 'and this is the right direction to a place that is next door to it. There is one particular thing more dangerous than the rat-trap pedal.'

He left the road and drew us in after him through a hedge.

'It is dishonourable to talk like that about the rat-traps,' said Gilhaney, 'because my family has had their boots in them for generations of their own posterity backwards and forwards and they all died in their beds except my first cousin that was meddling with the suckers of a steam thrashing-mill.'

'There is only one thing more dangerous,' said the Sergeant, 'and that is a loose plate. A loose plate is a scorcher, nobody lives very long after swallowing one and it leads indirectly to asphyxiation.'

'There is no danger of swallowing a rat-trap?' said Gilhaney.

'You would want to have good strong clips if you have a plate,' said the Sergeant, 'and plenty of red sealing-wax to stick it to the roof of your jaws. Take a look at the roots of that bush, it looks suspicious and there is no necessity for a warrant.'

It was a small modest whin-bush, a lady member of the tribe as you might say, with dry particles of hay and sheep's feathers caught in the branches high and low. Gilhaney was on his knees putting his hands through the grass and rooting like one of the lower animals. After a minute he extracted a black instrument. It was long and thin and looked like a large fountain-pen.

'My pump, so help me!' he shouted.

'I thought as much,' said the Sergeant, 'the finding of the pump is a fortunate clue that may assist us in our mission of private detection and smart policework. Put it in your pocket and hide it because it is possible that we are watched and followed and dogged by a member of the gang.'

'How did you know that it was in that particular corner of the world?' I asked in my extreme simplicity.

'What is your attitude to the high saddle?' inquired Gilhaney.

'Questions are like the knocks of beggarmen, and should not be minded,' replied the Sergeant, 'but I do not mind telling you that the high saddle is all right if you happen to have a brass fork.'

'A high saddle is a power for the hills,' said Gilhaney

We were in an entirely other field by this time and in the company of white-coloured brown-coloured cows. They watched us quietly as we made a path between them and changed their attitudes slowly as if to show us all of the maps on their fat sides. They gave us to understand that they knew us personally and thought a lot of our families and I lifted my hat to the last of them as I passed her as a sign of my appreciation.

'The high saddle!' said the Sergeant, 'was invented by a party called Peters that spent his life in foreign parts riding on camels and other lofty animals – giraffes, elephants and birds that can run like hares and lay eggs the size of the bowl you see in a steam laundry where they keep the chemical water for taking the tar out of men's pants. When he came home from the wars he thought hard of sitting on a low saddle and one night accidentally when he was in bed he invented the high saddle as the outcome of his perpetual cerebration and mental researches. His Christian name I do not remember. The high saddle was the father of the low handlebars. It crucifies the fork and gives you a blood rush in the head, it is very sore on the internal organs.'

'Which of the organs?' I inquired.

'Both of them,' said the Sergeant.

'I think this would be the tree,' said Gilhaney.

'It would not surprise me,' said the Sergeant, 'put your hands in under its underneath and start feeling promiscuously the way you can ascertain factually if there is anything there in addition to its own nothing.'

Gilhaney lay down on his stomach on the grass at the butt of a blackthorn and was inquiring into its private parts with his strong hands and grunting from the stretch of his exertions. After a time he found a bicycle lamp and a bell and stood up and put them secretly in his fob.

'That is very satisfactory and complacently articulated,' said the Sergeant, 'it shows the necessity for perseverance, it is sure to be a clue, we are certain to find the bicycle.'

'I do not like asking questions,' I said politely, 'but the wisdom that directed us to this tree is not taught in the National Schools.'

'It is not the first time my bicycle was stolen,' said Gilhaney.

'In *my* day,' said the Sergeant, 'half the scholars in the National Schools were walking around with enough disease in their gobs to decimate the continent of Russia and wither a field of crops by only looking at them. That is all stopped now, they have compulsory inspections, the middling ones are stuffed with iron and the bad ones are pulled out with a thing like the claw for cutting wires.'

'The half of it is due to cycling with the mouth open,' said Gilhaney.

'Nowadays,' said the Sergeant, 'it is nothing strange to see a class of boys at First Book with wholesome teeth and with junior plates manufactured by the County Council for half-nothing.'

'Grinding the teeth half-way up a hill,' said Gilhaney, 'there is nothing worse, it files away the best part of them and leads to a hob-nailed liver indirectly.'

'In Russia,' said the Sergeant, 'they make teeth out of old piano-keys for elderly cows but it is a rough land without too much civilisation, it would cost you a fortune in tyres.'

We were now going through a country full of fine enduring trees where it was always five o'clock in the afternoon. It was a soft corner of the world, free from inquisitions and disputations and very soothing and sleepening on the mind. There was no animal there that was bigger than a man's thumb and no noise superior to that which the Sergeant was making with his nose, an unusual brand of music like wind in the chimney. To every side of us there was a green growth of soft ferny carpeting with thin green twines coming in and out of it and coarse bushes putting their heads out here and there and interrupting the urbanity of the presentation not unpleasingly. The distance we walked in this country I do not know but we arrived in the end at some place where we stopped without proceeding farther. The Sergeant put his finger at a certain part of the growth.

'It might be there and it might not,' he said, 'we can only try because perseverance is its own reward and necessity is the unmarried mother of invention.'

Gilhaney was not long at work till he took his bicycle out of that particular part of the growth. He pulled the briers from between the spokes and felt his tyres with red knowing fingers and furbished his machine fastidiously. The three of us walked back again without a particle of conversation to where the road was and Gilhaney put his toe on the pedal to show he was for home.

'Before I ride away,' he said to the Sergeant, 'what is your true opinion of the timber rim?'

'It is a very commendable invention,' the Sergeant said. 'It gives you more of a bounce, it is extremely easy on your white pneumatics.'

'The wooden rim,' said Gilhaney slowly, 'is a death-trap

in itself, it swells on a wet day and I know a man that owes his bad wet death to nothing else.'

Before we had time to listen carefully to what he was after saying he was half-way down the road with his forked coat sailing behind him on the sustenance of the wind he was raising by reason of his headlong acceleration.

'A droll man,' I ventured.

'A constituent man,' said the Sergeant, 'largely instrumental but volubly fervous.'

Walking finely from the hips the two of us made our way home through the afternoon, impregnating it with the smoke of our cigarettes. I reflected that we would be sure to have lost our way in the fields and parks of bogland only that the road very conveniently made its way in advance of us back to the barrack. The Sergeant was sucking quietly at his stumps and carried a black shadow on his brow as if it were a hat.

As he walked he turned in my direction after a time.

'The County Council has a lot to answer for,' he said.

I did not understand his meaning, but I said that I agreed with him.

'There is one puzzle,' I remarked, 'that is hurting the back of my head and causing me a lot of curiosity. It is about the bicycle. I have never heard of detective-work as good as that being done before. Not only did you find the lost bicycle but you found all the clues as well. I find it is a great strain for me to believe what I see, and I am becoming afraid occasionally to look at some things in case they would have to be believed. What is the secret of your constabulary virtuosity?'

He laughed at my earnest inquiries and shook his head with great indulgence at my simplicity.

'It was an easy thing,' he said.

'How easy?'

'Even without the clues I could have succeeded in ultimately finding the bicycle.'

'It seems a very difficult sort of easiness,' I answered. 'Did you know where the bicycle was?'

'I did.'

'How?'

'Because I put it there.'

'You stole the bicycle yourself?'

'Certainly.'

'And the pump and the other clues?'

'I put them where they were finally discovered also.'

'And why?'

He did not answer in words for a moment but kept on walking strongly beside me looking as far ahead as possible.

'The County Council is the culprit,' he said at last.

I said nothing, knowing that he would blame the County Council at greater length if I waited till he had the blame thought out properly. It was not long till he turned in my direction to talk to me again. His face was grave.

'Did you ever discover or hear tell of the Atomic Theory?' he inquired.

'No,' I answered.

He leaned his mouth confidentially over to my ear.

'Would it surprise you to be told,' he said darkly, 'that the Atomic Theory is at work in this parish?'

'It would indeed.'

'It is doing untold destruction,' he continued, 'the half of the people are suffering from it, it is worse than the smallpox.'

I thought it better to say *something*.

'Would it be advisable,' I said, 'that it should be taken in hand by the Dispensary Doctor or by the National Teachers or do you think it is a matter for the head of the family?'

'The lock stock and barrel of it all,' said the Sergeant, 'is the County Council.'

He walked on looking worried and preoccupied as if what he was examining in his head was unpleasant in a very intricate way.

'The Atomic Theory,' I sallied, 'is a thing that is not clear to me at all.'

'Michael Gilhaney,' said the Sergeant, 'is an example of a man that is nearly banjaxed from the principle of the Atomic Theory. Would it astonish you to hear that he is nearly half a bicycle?'

'It would surprise me unconditionally,' I said.

'Michael Gilhaney,' said the Sergeant, 'is nearly sixty years of age by plain computation and if he is itself, he has spent no less than thirty-five years riding his bicycle over the rocky roadsteads and up and down the hills and into the deep ditches when the road goes astray in the strain of the winter. He is always going to a particular destination or other on his bicycle at every hour of the day or coming back from there at every other hour. If it wasn't that his bicycle was stolen every Monday he would be sure to be more than half-way now.'

'Half-way to where?'

'Half-way to being a bicycle himself,' said the Sergeant.

'Your talk,' I said, 'is surely the handiwork of wisdom because not one word of it do I understand.'

'Did you never study atomics when you were a lad?' asked the Sergeant, giving me a look of great inquiry and surprise.

'No,' I answered.

'That is a very serious defalcation,' he said, 'but all the same I will tell you the size of it. Everything is composed of small particles of itself and they are flying around in concentric circles and arcs and segments and innumerable other geometrical figures too numerous to mention collectively, never standing still or resting but spinning away and darting hither and thither and back again, all the time on the go. These diminutive gentlemen are called atoms. Do you follow me intelligently?'

'Yes.'

'They are lively as twenty leprechauns doing a jig on top of a tombstone.'

A very pretty figure, Joe murmured.

'Now take a sheep,' the Sergeant said. 'What is a sheep only millions of little bits of sheepness whirling around and doing intricate convolutions inside the sheep? What else is it but that?'

'That would be bound to make the beast dizzy,' I observed, 'especially if the whirling was going on inside the head as well.'

The Sergeant gave me a look which I am sure he himself would describe as one of *non-possum* and *noli-me-tangere*.

'That remark is what may well be called buncombe,' he said sharply, 'because the nerve-strings and the sheep's head itself are whirling into the same bargain and you can cancel out one whirl against the other and there you are – like simplifying a division sum when you have fives above and below the bar.'

'To say the truth I did not think of that,' I said.

'Atomics is a very intricate theorem and can be worked out with algebra but you would want to take it by degrees because you might spend the whole night proving a bit of it with rulers and cosines and similar other instruments and then at the wind-up not believe what you had proved at all. If that happened you would have to go back over it till you got a place where you could believe your own facts and figures as delineated from Hall and Knight's Algebra and then go on again from that particular place till you had the whole thing properly believed and not have bits of it half-believed or a doubt in your head hurting you like when you lose the stud of your shirt in bed.'

'Very true,' I said.

'Consecutively and consequentially,' he continued, 'you can safely infer that you are made of atoms yourself and so is your fob pocket and the tail of your shirt and the instrument you use for taking the leavings out of the crook of your hollow tooth. Do you happen to know what takes place when you strike a bar of iron with a good coal hammer or with a blunt instrument?'

'What?'

'When the wallop falls, the atoms are bashed away down to the bottom of the bar and compressed and crowded there like eggs under a good clucker. After a while in the course of time they swim around and get back at last to where they were. But if you keep hitting the bar long enough and hard enough they do not get a chance to do this and what happens then?'

'That is a hard question.'

'Ask a blacksmith for the true answer and he will tell you that the bar will dissipate itself away by degrees if you persevere with the hard wallops. Some of the atoms of the bar will go into the hammer and the other half into the table or the stone or the particular article that is underneath the bottom of the bar.'

'That is well-known,' I agreed.

'The gross and net result of it is that people who spent most of their natural lives riding iron bicycles over the rocky roadsteads of this parish get their personalities mixed up with the personalities of their bicycle as a result of the interchanging of the atoms of each of them and you would be surprised at the number of people in these parts who nearly are half people and half bicycles.'

I let go a gasp of astonishment that made a sound in the air like a bad puncture.

'And you would be flabbergasted at the number of bicycles that are half-human almost half-man, half-partaking of humanity.'

Apparently there is no limit, Joe remarked. *Anything can be said in this place and it will be true and will have to be believed.*

I would not mind being working this minute on a steamer in the middle of the sea, I said, coiling ropes and doing the hard manual work. I would like to be far away from here.

I looked carefully around me. Brown bogs and black bogs were arranged neatly on each side of the road with rectangular boxes carved out of them here and there, each with a filling of yellow-brown brown-yellow water. Far away near the sky tiny people were stooped at their turfwork, cutting out precisely-shaped sods with their patent spades and building them into a tall memorial twice the height of a horse and cart. Sounds came from them to the Sergeant and myself, delivered to our ears without charge by the west wind, sounds of laughing and whistling and bits of verses from the old bog-songs. Nearer, a house stood attended by three trees and surrounded by the happiness of a coterie of fowls, all of them picking and rooting and disputating loudly in the unrelenting manufacture of their eggs. The house was quiet in itself and silent but a canopy of lazy smoke had been erected over the chimney to indicate that people were within engaged on tasks. Ahead of us went the road, running swiftly across the flat land and pausing slightly to climb slowly up a hill that was waiting for it in a place where there was tall grass, grey boulders and rank stunted trees. The whole overhead was occupied by the sky, serene, impenetrable, ineffable and incomparable, with a fine island of clouds anchored in the calm two yards to the right of Mr Jarvis's outhouse.

The scene was real and incontrovertible and at variance with the talk of the Sergeant, but I knew that the Sergeant was talking the truth and if it was a question of taking my choice, it was possible that I would have to forego the reality of all the simple things my eyes were looking at.

I took a sideways view of him. He was striding on with signs of anger against the County Council on his coloured face.

'Are you certain about the humanity of the bicycle?' I inquired of him. 'Is the Atomic Theory as dangerous as you say?'

'It is between twice and three times as dangerous as it might be,' he replied gloomily. 'Early in the morning I often think it is four times, and what is more, if you lived here for a few days and gave full play to your observation and inspection, you would know how certain the sureness of certainty is.'

'Gilhaney did not look like a bicycle,' I said. 'He had no back wheel on him and I did not think he had a front wheel either, although I did not give much attention to his front.'

The Sergeant looked at me with some commiseration.

'You cannot expect him to grow handlebars out of his neck but I have seen him do more indescribable things than that. Did you ever notice the queer behaviour of bicycles in these parts?'

'I am not long in this district.'

Thanks be, said Joe.

'Then watch the bicycles if you think it is pleasant to be surprised continuously,' he said. 'When a man lets things go so far that he is half or more than half a bicycle, you will not see so much because he spends a lot of his time leaning with one elbow on walls or standing propped by one foot at kerbstones. Of course there are other things connected with ladies and ladies' bicycles that I will mention to you separately some time. But the man-charged bicycle is a phenomenon of great charm and intensity and a very dangerous article.'

At this point a man with long coat-tails spread behind him approached quickly on a bicycle, coasting benignly down the road past us from the hill ahead. I watched him with the eye of six eagles, trying to find out which was carrying the other and whether it was really a man with a bicycle on his shoulders. I did not seem to see anything, however, that was memorable or remarkable.

The Sergeant was looking into his black notebook.

'That was O'Feersa,' he said at last. 'His figure is only twenty-three per cent.'

'He is twenty-three per cent bicycle?'

'Yes.'

'Does that mean that his bicycle is also twenty-three per cent O'Feersa?'

'It does.'

'How much is Gilhaney?'

'Forty-eight.'

'Then O'Feersa is much lower.'

'That is due to the lucky fact that there are three similar brothers in the house and that they are too poor to have a separate bicycle apiece. Some people never know how fortunate they are when they are poorer than each other. Six years ago one of the three O'Feersas won a prize of ten pounds in *John Bull*. When I got the wind of this tiding, I knew I would have to take steps unless there was to be two new bicycles in the family, because you will understand that I can steal only a limited number of bicycles in the one week. I did not want to have three O'Feersas on my hands. Luckily I knew the postman very well. The postman! Great holy suffering indiarubber bowls of brown stirabout!' The recollection of the postman seemed to give the Sergeant a pretext for unlimited amusement and cause for intricate gesturing with his red hands.

'The postman?' I said.

'Seventy-one per cent,' he said quietly.

'Great Scot!'

'A round of thirty-eight miles on the bicycle every single day for forty years, hail, rain or snowballs. There is very little hope of ever getting his number down below fifty again.'

'You bribed him?'

'Certainly. With two of the little straps you put around the hubs of bicycles to keep them spick.'

'And what way do these people's bicycles behave?'

'These people's bicycles?'

'I mean these bicycles' people or whatever is the proper name for them – the ones that have two wheels under them and a handlebars.'

'The behaviour of a bicycle that has a high content of humanity,' he said, 'is very cunning and entirely remarkable. You never see them moving by themselves but you meet them in the least accountable places unexpectedly. Did you never see a bicycle leaning against the dresser of a warm kitchen when it is pouring outside?'

'I did.'

'Not very far away from the fire?'

'Yes.'

'Near enough to the family to hear the conversation?'

'Yes.'

'Not a thousand miles from where they keep the eatables?'

'I did not notice that. You do not mean to say that these bicycles *eat food*?'

'They were never seen doing it, nobody ever caught them with a mouthful of steak. All I know is that the food disappears.'

'What!'

'It is not the first time I have noticed crumbs at the front wheels of some of these gentlemen.'

'All this is a great blow to me,' I said.

'Nobody takes any notice,' replied the Sergeant. 'Mick thinks that Pat brought it in and Pat thinks that Mick was instrumental. Very few of the people guess what is going on in this parish. There are other things I would rather not say too much about. A new lady teacher was here one time with a new bicycle. She was not very long here till Gilhaney went away into the lonely country on her female bicycle. Can you appreciate the immorality of that?'

'I can.'

'But worse happened. Whatever way Gilhaney's bicycle managed it, it left itself leaning at a place where the young teacher would rush out to go away somewhere on her bicycle in a hurry. Her bicycle was gone but here was Gilhaney's leaning there conveniently and trying to look very small and comfortable and attractive. Need I inform you what the result was or what happened?'

Indeed he need not, Joe said urgently. *I have never heard of anything so shameless and abandoned. Of course the teacher was blameless, she did not take pleasure and did not know.*

'You need not,' I said.

'Well, there you are. Gilhaney has a day out with the lady's bicycle and vice versa contrarily and it is quite clear that the lady in the case had a high number – thirty-five or forty, I would say, in spite of the newness of the bicycle. Many a grey hair it has put into my head, trying to regulate the people of this parish. If you let it go too far it would be the end of everything. You would have bicycles wanting votes and they would get seats on the County Council and make the roads far worse than they are for their own ulterior motivation. But against that and on the other hand, a good bicycle is a great companion, there is a great charm about it.'

'How would you know a man has a lot of bicycle in his veins?'

'If his number is over Fifty you can tell it unmistakable from his walk. He will walk smartly always and never sit down and he will lean against the wall with his elbow out and stay like that all night in his kitchen instead of going to bed. If he walks too slowly or stops in the middle of the road he will fall down in a heap and will have to be lifted and set in motion again by some extraneous party. This is the unfortunate state that the postman has cycled himself into, and I do not think he will ever cycle himself out of it.'

'I do not think I will ever ride a bicycle,' I said.

'A little of it is a good thing and makes you hardy and puts iron on to you. But walking too far too often too quickly is not safe at all. The continual cracking of your feet on the road makes a certain quantity of road come up into you. When a man dies they say he returns to clay but too much walking fills you up with clay far sooner (or buries bits of you along the road) and brings your death half-way to meet you. It is not easy to know what is the best way to move yourself from one place to another.'

After he had finished speaking I found myself walking nimbly and lightly on my toes in order to prolong my life. My head was packed tight with fears and miscellaneous apprehensions.

'I never heard of these things before,' I said, 'and never knew these happenings could happen. Is it a new development or was it always an ancient fundamental?'

The Sergeant's face clouded and he spat thoughtfully three yards ahead of him on the road.

'I will tell you a secret,' he said very confidentially in a low voice. 'My great-grandfather was eighty-three when he died. For a year before his death he was a horse!'

'A horse?'

'A horse in everything but extraneous externalities. He would spend the day grazing in a field or eating hay in a stall. Usually he was lazy and quiet but now and again he would go for a smart gallop, clearing the hedges in great style. Did you ever see a man on two legs galloping?'

'I did not.'

'Well, I am given to understand that it is a great sight. He always said he won the Grand National when he was a lot younger and used to annoy his family with stories about the intricate jumps and the great height of them.'

'I suppose your great-grandfather got himself into this condition by too much horse riding?'

'That was the size of it. His old horse Dan was in the contrary way and gave so much trouble, coming into the house at night and interfering with young girls during the day and committing indictable offences, that they had to shoot him. The police were unsympathetic, not comprehending things rightly in these days. They said they would have to arrest the horse and charge him and have him up at the next Petty Sessions unless he was done away with. So my family shot him but if you ask me it was my great-grandfather they shot and it is the horse that is buried up in Cloncoonla Churchyard.'

The Sergeant then became thoughtful at the recollection of his ancestors and had a reminiscent face for the next half-mile till we came to the barracks. Joe and I agreed privately that these revelations were the supreme surprise stored for us and awaiting our arrival in the barracks.

When we reached it and the Sergeant led the way in with a sigh. 'The lock, stock and barrel of it all,' he said, 'is the County Council.'

Chapter 7

The severe shock which I encountered soon after re-entry to the barrack with the Sergeant set me thinking afterwards of the immense consolations which philosophy and religion can offer in adversity. They seem to lighten dark places and give strength to bear the unaccustomed load. Not unnaturally my thoughts were never very far from de Selby. All his works – but particularly *Golden Hours* – have what one may term a therapeutic quality. They have a heart-lifted effect more usually associated with spirituous liquors, reviving and quietly restoring the spiritual tissue. This benign property of his prose is not, one hopes, to be attributed to the reason noticed by the eccentric du Garbandier, who said 'the beauty of reading a page of de Selby is that it leads one inescapably to the happy conviction that one is not, of all nincompoops, the greatest.'[1] This is, I think, an overstatement of one of de Selby's most ingratiating qualities. The humanising urbanity of his work has always seemed to me to be enhanced rather than vitiated by the chance obtrusion here and there of his minor failings, all the more pathetic because he regarded some of them as pinnacles of his intellectual prowess rather than indications of his frailty as a human being.

Holding that the usual processes of living were illusory, it is natural that he did not pay much attention to life's adversities and he does not in fact offer much suggestion as to how they should be met. Bassett's anecdote[2] on this point

---

[1] 'Le Suprème charme qu'on trouve à lire une page de de Selby est qu'elle vous conduit inexorablement a l'heureuse certitude que des sots vous n'êtes pas le plus grand.'

[2] In *Lux Mundi*.

may be worth recounting. During de Selby's Bartown days he had acquired some local reputation as a savant 'due possibly to the fact that he was known never to read newspapers.' A young man in the town was seriously troubled by some question regarding a lady and feeling that this matter was weighing on his mind and threatening to interfere with his reason, he sought de Selby for advice. Instead of exorcising this solitary blot from the young man's mind, as indeed could easily have been done, de Selby drew the young man's attention to some fifty imponderable propositions each of which raised difficulties which spanned many eternities and dwarfed the conundrum of the young lady to nothingness. Thus the young man who had come fearing the possibility of a bad thing left the house completely convinced of the worst and cheerfully contemplating suicide. That he arrived home for his supper at the usual time was a happy intervention on the part of the moon for he had gone home by the harbour only to find that the tide was two miles out. Six months later he earned for himself six calendar months' incarceration with hard labour on foot of eighteen counts comprising larceny and offences bearing on interference with railroads. So much for the savant as a dispenser of advice.

As already said, however, de Selby provides some genuine mental sustenance if read objectively for what there is to read. In the *Layman's Atlas*[3] he deals explicitly with bereavement, old age, love, sin, death and the other saliencies of existence. It is true that he allows them only some six lines but this is due to his devastating assertion that they

[3] Now very rare and a collector's piece. The sardonic du Garbandier makes great play of the fact that the man who first printed the *Atlas* (Watkins) was struck by lightning on the day he completed the task. It is interesting to note that the otherwise reliable Hatchjaw has put forward the suggestion that the entire *Atlas* is spurious and the work of 'another hand', raising issues of no less piquancy that those of the Bacon-Shakespeare controversy. He has many ingenious if not quite convincing arguments, not the least of them being that de Selby was known to have received considerable royalties from this book which he did not write, 'a procedure that would be of a piece with the master's ethics.' The theory is, however, not one which will commend itself to the serious student.

are all 'unnecessary'.[4] Astonishing as it may seem, he makes this statement as a direct corollary to his discovery that the earth, far from being a sphere, is 'sausage-shaped.'

Not a few of the critical commentators confess to a doubt as to whether de Selby was permitting himself a modicum of unwonted levity in connection with this theory but he seems to argue the matter seriously enough and with no want of conviction.

He adopts the customary line of pointing out fallacies involved in existing conceptions and then quietly setting up his own design in place of the one he claims to have demolished.

Standing at a point on the postulated spherical earth, he says, one appears to have four main directions in which to move, viz., north, south, east and west. But it does not take much thought to see that there really appear to be only two since north and south are meaningless terms in relation to a spheroid and can connote motion in only *one* direction; so also with west and east. One can reach any point on the north-south band by travelling in either 'direction', the only apparent difference in the two 'routes' being extraneous considerations of time and distance, both already shown to be illusory. North-south is therefore one direction and east-west apparently another. Instead of four directions there are only two. It can be safely inferred,[5] de Selbys says, that there is a further similar fallacy inherent here and that there is in fact only one possible direction properly so-called, because if one leaves any point on the globe, moving and continuing to move in any 'direction', one ultimately reaches the point of departure again.

The application of this conclusion to his theory that 'the earth is a sausage' is illuminating. He attributes the idea that the earth is spherical to the fact that human beings are continually moving in only one known direction (though convinced that they are free to move in any direction) and

[4] Du Garbandier has inquired with his customary sarcasm why a malignant condition of the gall-bladder, a disease which frequently reduced de Selby to a cripple, was omitted from the list of 'unnecessaries'.

[5] Possibly the one weak spot in the argument.

that this one direction is really around the circular circumference of an earth which is in fact sausage-shaped. It can scarcely be contested that if multi-directionality be admitted to be a fallacy, the sphericity of the earth is another fallacy that would inevitably follow from it. De Selby likens the position of a human on the earth to that of a man on a tight-wire who must continue walking along the wire or perish, being, however, free in all other respects. Movement in this restricted orbit results in the permanent hallucination known conventionally as 'life' with its innumerable concomitant limitations, afflictions and anomalies. If a way can be found, says de Selby, of discovering the 'second direction', i.e., along the 'barrel' of the sausage, a world of entirely new sensation and experience will be open to humanity. New and unimaginable dimensions will supersede the present order and the manifold 'unnecessaries' of 'one-directional' existence will disappear.

It is true that de Selby is rather vague as to how precisely this new direction is to be found. It is not, he warns us, to be ascertained by any microscopic subdivision of the known points of the compass and little can be expected from sudden darts hither and thither in the hope that a happy chance will intervene. He doubts whether human legs would be 'suitable' for traversing the 'longitudinal celestium' and seems to suggest that death is nearly always present when the new direction is discovered. As Bassett points out justly enough, this lends considerable colour to the whole theory but suggests at the same time that de Selby is merely stating in an obscure and recondite way something that is well-known and accepted.

As usual, there is evidence that he carried out some private experimenting. He seems to have thought at one time that gravitation was the 'jailer' of humanity, keeping it on the one-directional line of oblivion, and that ultimate freedom lay in some upward direction. He examined aviation as a remedy without success and subsequently spent some weeks designing certain 'barometric pumps' which were 'worked with mercury and wires' to clear vast areas of the earth of the influence of gravitation. Happily for the people of the place as well for their movable chattels he does not seem to have had much result. Eventually he was distracted from these occupations by the extraordinary affair of the water-box.[6]

As I have already hinted, I would have given much for a glimpse of a signpost showing the way along the 'barrel' of the sausage after I had been some two minutes back in the white day-room with Sergeant Pluck.

We were not more than completely inside the door when we became fully aware that there was a visitor present. He had coloured stripes of high office on his chest but he was dressed in policeman's blue and on his head he carried a policeman's hat with a special badge of superior office glittering very brilliantly in it. He was very fat and circular, with legs and arms of the minimum, and his large bush of moustache was bristling with bad temper and self-indulgence. The Sergeant gave him looks of surprise and then a military salute.

'Inspector O'Corky!' he said.

'What is the meaning of the vacuity of the station in routine hours?' barked the Inspector.

The sound his voice made was rough like coarse cardboard rubbed on sandpaper and it was clear that he was not pleased with himself or with other people.

'I was out myself,' the Sergeant replied respectfully, 'on emergency duty and policework of the highest gravity.'

'Did you know that a man called Mathers was found in the crotch of a ditch up the road two hours ago with his belly opened up with a knife or sharp instrument?'

To say this was a surprise which interfered seriously with my heart-valves would be the same as saying that a red-hot poker would heat your face if somebody decided to let you have it there. I stared from the Sergeant to the Inspector and back again with my whole inside fluttering in consternation.

It seems that our mutual friend Finnucane is in the environs, Joe said.

[6] See Hatchjaw: *The de Selby Water-Boxes Day by Day*. The calculations are given in full and the daily variations are expressed in admirably clear graphs.

'Certainly I did,' said the Sergeant.

Very strange. How could he if he has been out with us after the bicycle for the last four hours?

'And what steps have you taken and how many steps?' barked the Inspector.

'Long steps and steps in the right direction,' replied the Sergeant evenly. 'I know who the murderer is.'

'Then why is he not arrested into custody?'

'He is,' said the Sergeant pleasantly.

'Where?'

'Here.'

This was the second thunderbolt. After I had glanced fearfully to my rear without seeing a murderer it became clear to me that I myself was the subject of the private conversation of the two Policemen. I made no protest because my voice was gone and my mouth was bone-dry.

Inspector O'Corky was too angry to be pleased at anything so surprising as what the Sergeant said.

'Then why is he not confined under a two-way key and padlock in the cell?' he roared.

For the first time the Sergeant looked a bit crestfallen and shame-faced. His face got a little redder than it was and he put his eyes on the stone floor.

'To tell you the truth,' he said at last, 'I keep my bicycle there.'

'I see,' said the Inspector.

He stopped quickly and rammed black clips on the extremities of his trousers and stamped on the floor. For the first time I saw that he had been leaning by one elbow on the counter.

'See that you regularize your irregularity instantaneously,' he called as his good-bye, 'and set right your irrectitude and put the murderer in the cage before he rips the bag out of the whole countryside.'

After that he was gone. Sounds came to us of coarse scraping on the gravel, a sign that the Inspector favoured the old-fashioned method of mounting from the back-step.

'Well, now,' the Sergeant said.

He took off his cap and went over to a chair and sat on it,

easing himself on his broad pneumatic seat. He took a red cloth from his fob and decanted the globes of perspiration from his expansive countenance and opened the buttons of his tunic as if to let out on wing the trouble that was imprisoned there. He then took to carrying out a scientifically precise examination of the soles and the toes of his constabulary boots, a sign that he was wrestling with some great problem.

'What is your worry?' I inquired, very anxious by now that what had happened should be discussed.

'The bicycle,' he said.

'The bicycle?'

'How can I put it out of the cell?' he asked.

'I have always kept it in solitary confinement when I am not riding it to make sure it is not leading a personal life inimical to my own inimitability. I cannot be too careful. I have to ride long rides on my constabulary ridings.'

'Do you mean that I should be locked in the cell and kept there and hidden from the world?'

'You surely heard the instructions of the Inspector?'

Ask is it all a joke? Joe said.

'Is this all a joke for entertainment purposes?'

'If you take it that way I will be indefinitely beholden to you,' said the Sergeant earnestly, 'and I will remember you with real emotion. It would be a noble gesture and an unutterable piece of supreme excellence on the part of the deceased.'

'What!' I cried.

'You must recollect that to turn everything to your own advantage is one of the regulations of true wisdom as I informed you privately. It is the following of this rule on my part that makes you a murderer this today evening.

'The Inspector required a captured prisoner as the least tiniest minimum for his inferior *bonhomie* and *mal d'esprit*. It was your personal misfortune to be present adjacently at the time but it was likewise my personal good fortune and good luck. There is no option but to stretch you for the serious offence.'

'Stretch me?'

'Hang you by the windpipe before high breakfast time.'

'That is most unfair,' I stuttered, 'it is unjust . . . rotten . . . fiendish.' My voice rose to a thin tremolo of fear.

'It is the way we work in this part of the country,' explained the Sergeant.

'I will resist,' I shouted, 'and will resist to the death and fight for my existence even if I lose my life in the attempt.'

The Sergeant made a soothing gesture in deprecation. He took out an enormous pipe and when he stuck it in his face it looked like a great hatchet.

'About the bicycle,' he said when he had it in commission.

'What bicycle?'

'My own one. Would it inconvenience you if I neglected to bar you into the inside of the cell? I do not desire to be selfish but I have to think carefully about my bicycle. The wall of this day-room is no place for it.'

'I do not mind,' I said quietly.

'You can remain in the environs on parole and ticket of leave till we have time to build the high scaffold in the backyard.'

'How do you know I will not make excellent my escape?' I asked, thinking that it would be better to discover all the thoughts and intentions of the Sergeant so that my escape would in fact be certain.

He smiled at me as much as the weight of the pipe would let him.

'You will not do that,' he said. 'It would not be honourable but even if it was we would easily follow the track of your rear tyre and besides the rest of everything Policeman Fox would be sure to apprehend you single-handed on the outskirts. There would be no necessity for a warrant.'

Both of us sat silent for a while occupied with our thoughts, he thinking about his bicycle and I about my death.

By the by, Joe remarked, *I seem to remember our friend saying that the law could not lay a finger on us on account of your congenital anonymity.*

'Quite right,' I said. 'I forgot that.'

As things are I fancy it would not be much more than a debating point.

'It is worth mentioning,' I said.

O Lord, yes.

'By the way,' I said to the Sergeant, 'did you recover my American watch for me?'

'The matter is under consideration and is receiving attention,' he said officially.

'Do you recall that you told me that I was not here at all because I had no name and that my personality was invisible to the law?'

'I said that.'

'Then how can I be hanged for a murder, even if I did commit it and there is no trial or preliminary proceedings, no caution administered and no hearing before a Commissioner of the Public Peace?'

Watching the Sergeant, I saw him take the hatchet from his jaws in surprise and knot his brows into considerable corrugations. I could see that he was severely troubled with my inquiry. He looked darkly at me and then doubled his look, giving me a compressed stare along the line of his first vision.

'Well great cripes!' he said.

For three minutes he sat giving my representations his undivided attention. He was frowning so heavily with wrinkles which were so deep that the blood was driven from his face leaving it black and forbidding.

Then he spoke.

'Are you completely doubtless that you are nameless?' he asked.

'Positively certain.'

'Would it be Mick Barry?'

'No.'

'Charlemagne O'Keeffe?'

'No.'

'Sir Justin Spens?'

'Not that.'

'Kimberley?'

'No.'

'Bernard Fann?'

'No.'

'Joseph Poe or Nolan?'

'No.'

'One of the Garvins or the Moynihans?'

'Not them.'

'Rosencranz O'Dowd?'

'No.'

'Would it be O'Benson?'

'Not O'Benson.'

'The Quigleys, The Mulrooneys or the Hounimen?'

'No.'

'The Hardimen or the Merrimen?'

'Not them.'

'Peter Dundy?'

'No.'

'Scrutch?'

'No.'

'Lord Brad?'

'Not him.'

'The O'Growneys, the O'Roartys or the Finnehys?'

'No.'

'That is an amazing piece of denial and denunciation,' he said.

He passed the red cloth over his face again to reduce the moisture.

'An astonishing parade of nullity,' he added.

'My name is not Jenkins either,' I vouchsafed.

'Roger MacHugh?'

'Not Roger.'

'Sitric Hogan?'

'No.'

'Not Conroy?'

'No.'

'Not O'Conroy?'

'Not O'Conroy.'

'There are very few more names that you could have, then,' he said. 'Because only a black man could have a name different to the ones I have recited. Or a red man. Not Byrne?'

'No.'

'Then it is a nice pancake,' he said gloomily. He bent double to give full scope to the extra brains he had at the rear of his head.

'Holy suffering senators,' he muttered.

I think we have won the day.

We are not home and dried yet, I answered.

Nevertheless I think we can relax. Evidently he has never heard of Signor Bari, the golden-throated budgerigar of Milano.

I don't think this is the time for pleasantries.

Or J. Courtney Wain, private investigator and member of the inner bar. Eighteen thousand guineas marked on the brief. The singular case of the red-headed men.

'By Scot!' said the Sergeant suddenly. He got up to pace the flooring.

'I think the case can be satisfactorily met,' he said pleasantly, 'and ratified unconditionally.'

I did not like his smile and asked him for his explanation.

'It is true,' he said, 'that you cannot commit a crime and that the right arm of the law cannot lay its finger on you irrespective of the degree of your criminality. Anything you do is a lie and nothing that happens to you is true.'

I nodded my agreement comfortably.

'For that reason alone,' said the Sergeant, 'we can take you and hang the life out of you and you are not hanged at all and there is no entry to be made in the death papers. The particular death you die is not even a death (which is an inferior phenomenon at the best) only an insanitary abstraction in the backyard, a piece of negative nullity neutralized and rendered void by asphyxiation and the fracture of the spinal string. If it is not a lie to say that you have been given the final hammer behind the barrack, equally it is true to say that nothing has happened to you.'

'You mean that because I have no name I cannot die and that you cannot be held answerable for death even if you kill me?'

'That is about the size of it,' said the Sergeant.

I felt so sad and so entirely disappointed that tears came into my eyes and a lump of incommunicable poignancy swelled tragically in my throat. I began to feel intensely every fragment of my equal humanity. The life that was bubbling at the end of my fingers was real and nearly painful in intensity and so was the beauty of my warm face and the loose humanity of my limbs and the racy health of my red rich blood. To leave it all without good reason and to smash the little empire into small fragments was a thing too pitiful even to refuse to think about.

The next important thing that happened in the day-room was the entry of Policeman MacCruiskeen. He marched in to a chair and took out his black notebook and began perusing his own autographed memoranda, at the same time twisting his lips into an article like a purse.

'Did you take the readings?' the Sergeant asked.

'I did,' MacCruiskeen said.

'Read them till I hear them,' the Sergeant said, 'and until I make mental comparisons inside the interior of my inner head.'

MacCruiskeen eyed his book keenly.[7]

'Ten point five,' he said.

'Ten point five,' said the Sergeant. 'And what was the reading on the beam?'

'Five point three.'

[7] From a chance and momentary perusual of the Policeman's notebook it is possible for me to give here the relative figures for a week's readings. For obvious reasons the figures themselves are fictitious:

PILOT READING	READING ON BEAM	READING ON LEVER	NATURE OF FALL (if any) with time	
10.2	4.9	1.25	Light	4.15
10.2	4.6	1.25	Light	18.16
9.5	6.2	1.7	Light (with lumps)	7.15
10.5	4.25	1.9	Nil	
12.6	7.0	3.73	Heavy	21.6
12.5	6.5	2.5	Black	9.0
9.25	5.0	6.0	Black (with lumps)	14.45

'And how much on the lever?'

'Two point three.'

'Two point three is high,' said the Sergeant. He put the back of his fist between the saws of his yellow teeth and commenced working at his mental comparisons. After five minutes his face got clearer and he looked again to MacCruiskeen.

'Was there a fall?' he asked.

'A light fall at five-thirty.'

'Five-thirty is rather late if the fall was a light one,' he said. 'Did you put charcoal adroitly in the vent?'

'I did,' said MacCruiskeen.

'How much?'

'Seven pounds.'

'I would say eight,' said the Sergeant.

'Seven was satisfactory enough,' MacCruiskeen said, 'if you recollect that the reading on the beam has been falling for the past four days. I tried the shuttle but there was no trace of play or looseness in it.'

'I would still say eight for safety-first,' said the Sergeant, 'but if the shuttle is tight, there can be no need for timorous anxiety.'

'None at all,' said MacCruiskeen.

The Sergeant cleared his face of all the lines of thought he had on it and stood up and clapped his flat hands on his breast pockets. 'Well now,' he said.

He stooped to put the clips on his ankles.

'I must go now to where I am going,' he said, 'and let you,' he said to MacCruiskeen, 'come with me to the exterior for two moments till I inform you about recent events officially.'

The two of them went out together, leaving me in my sad and cheerless loneliness. MacCruiskeen was not gone for long but I was lonely during that diminutive meantime. When he came in again he gave me a cigarette which was warm and wrinkled from his pocket.

'I believe they are going to stretch you,' he said pleasantly. I replied with nods.

'It is a bad time of the year, it will cost a fortune,' he said. 'You would not believe the price of timber.'

'Would a tree not suffice?' I inquired, giving tongue to a hollow whim of humour.

'I do not think it would be proper,' he said, 'but I will mention it privately to the Sergeant.'

'Thank you.'

'The last hanging we had in this parish,' he said, 'was thirty years ago. It was a very famous man called MacDadd. He held the record for the hundred miles on a solid tyre. I need to tell you what the solid tyre did for him. We had to hang the bicycle.'

'Hang the bicycle?'

'MacDadd had a first-class grudge against another man called Figgerson but he did not go near Figgerson. He knew how things stood and gave Figgerson's bicycle a terrible thrashing with a crowbar. After that MacDadd and Figgerson had a fight and Figgerson – a dark man with glasses – did not live to know who the winner was. There was a great wake and he was buried with his bicycle. Did you ever see a bicycle-shaped coffin?'

'No.'

'It is a very intricate piece of wood-working, you would want to be a first-class carpenter to make a good job of the handlebars to say nothing of the pedals and the back-step. But the murder was a bad piece of criminality and we could not find MacDadd for a long time or make sure where the most of him was. We had to arrest his bicycle as well as himself and we watched the two of them under secret observation for a week to see where the majority of MacDadd was and whether the bicycle was mostly in MacDadd's trousers *pari passu* if you understand my meaning.'

'What happened?'

'The Sergeant gave his ruling at the end of the week. His position was painful in the extremity because he was a very close friend of MacDadd after office hours. He condemned the bicycle and it was the bicycle that was hanged. We entered a *nolle prosequi* in the day-book in respect of the other defendant. I did not see the stretching myself because I am a delicate man and my stomach is extremely reactionary.'

He got up and went to the dresser and took out his patent music-box which made sounds too esoterically rarefied to be audible to anybody but himself. He then sat back again in his chair, put his hands through the handstraps and began to entertain himself with the music. What he was playing could be roughly inferred from his face. It had a happy broad coarse satisfaction on it, a sign that he was occupied with loud obstreperous barn-songs and gusty shanties of the sea and burly roaring marching-songs. The silence in the room was so unusually quiet that the beginning of it seemed rather loud when the utter stillness of the end of it had been encountered.

How long this eeriness lasted or how long we were listening intently to nothing is unknown. My own eyes got tired with inactivity and closed down like a public house at ten o'clock. When they opened again I saw that Mac-Cruiskeen had desisted from the music and was making preparations for mangling his washing and his Sunday shirts. He had pulled a great rusty mangle from the shadow of the wall and had taken a blanket from the top of it and was screwing down the pressure-spring and spinning the hand wheel and furbishing the machine with expert hands.

He went over then to the dresser and took small articles like dry batteries out of a drawer and also an instrument like a prongs and glass barrels with wires inside them and other cruder articles resembling the hurricane lamps utilized by the County Council. He put these things into different parts of the mangle and when he had them all satisfactorily adjusted, the mangle looked more like a rough scientific instrument than a machine for wringing out a day's washing.

The time of the day was now a dark time, the sun being about to vanish completely in the red west and withdraw all the light. MacCruiskeen kept on adding small well-made articles to his mangle and mounting indescribably delicate glass instruments about the metal legs and on the superstructure. When he had nearly finished this work the room was almost black, and sharp blue sparks would fly sometimes from the upside-down of his hand when it was at work.

Underneath the mangle in the middle of the cast-iron

handiwork I noticed a black box with coloured wires coming out of it and there was a small ticking sound to be heard as if there was a clock in it. All in all it was the most complicated mangle I ever saw and to the inside of a steam thrashing-mill it was not inferior in complexity.

Passing near my chair to get an additional accessory, MacCruiskeen saw that I was awake and watching him.

'Do not worry if you think it is dark,' he said to me, 'because I am going to light the light and then mangle it for diversion and also for scientific truth.'

'Did you say you were going to mangle the light?'

'Wait till you see now.'

What he did next or which knobs he turned I did not ascertain on account of the gloom but it happened that a queer light appeared somewhere on the mangle. It was a local light that did not extend very much outside its own brightness but it was not a spot of light and still less a bar-shaped light. It was not steady completely but it did not dance like candlelight. It was light of a kind rarely seen in this country and was possibly manufactured with raw materials from abroad. It was a gloomy light and looked exactly as if there was a small area somewhere on the mangle and was merely devoid of darkness.

What happened next is astonishing. I could see the dim contours of MacCruiskeen in attendance at the mangle. He made adjustments with his cunning fingers, stooping for a minute to work at the lower-down inventions on the iron work. He rose then to full life-size and started to turn the wheel of the mangle, slowly, sending out a clamping creakiness around the barrack. The moment he turned the wheel, the unusual light began to change its appearance and situation in an extremely difficult fashion. With every turn it got brighter and harder and shook with such a fine delicate shaking that it achieved a steadiness unprecedented in the world by defining with its outer shakes the two lateral boundaries of the place where it was incontrovertibly situated. It grew steelier and so intense in its livid pallor that it stained the inner screen of my eyes so that it still confronted me in all quarters when I took my stare far away from the mangle in an effort to preserve my sight. MacCruiskeen kept turning slowly at the handle till suddenly to my sick utter horror, the light seemed to burst and disappear and simultaneously there was a loud shout in the room, a shout which could not have come from a human throat.

I sat on the chair's edge and gave frightened looks at the shadow of MacCruiskeen, who was stooping down again at the diminutive scientific accessories of the mangle, making minor adjustments and carrying out running repairs in the dark.

'What was that shouting?' I stuttered over at him.

'I will tell you that in a tick,' he called, 'if you will inform me what you think the words of the shout were. What would you say was said in the shout now?'

This was a question I was already working with in my own head. The unearthly voice had roared out something very quickly with three or four words compressed into one ragged shout. I could not be sure what it was but several phrases sprang into my head together and each of them could have been the contents of the shout. They bore an eerie resemblance to commonplace shouts I had often heard such as *Change for Tinahely and Shillelagh! Two to one the field! Mind the step! Finish him off!* I knew, however, that the shout could not be so foolish and trivial because it disturbed me in a way that could only be done by something momentous and diabolical.

MacCruiskeen was looking at me with a question in his eye.

'I could not make it out,' I said, vaguely and feebly, 'but I think it was railway-station talk.'

'I have been listening to shouts and screams for years,' he said, 'but I never surely catch the words. Would you say that he said "Don't press so hard"?'

'No.'

'Second favourites always win?'

'Not that.'

'It is a difficult pancake,' MacCruiskeen said, 'a very compound crux. Wait till we try again.'

This time he screwed down the rollers of the mangle till

111

they were whining and till it was nearly out of the question to spin the wheel. The light that appeared was the thinnest and sharpest light that I ever imagined, like the inside of the edge of a sharp razor, and the intensification which came upon it with the turning of the wheel was too delicate a process to be watched even sideways.

What happened eventually was not a shout but a shrill scream, a sound not unlike the call of rats yet far shriller than any sound which could be made by man or animal. Again I thought that words had been used but the exact meaning of them or the language they belonged to was quite uncertain.

'"Two bananas a penny"?'

'Not bananas,' I said.

MacCruiskeen frowned vacantly.

'It is one of the most compressed and intricate pancakes I have ever known,' he said.

He put the blanket back over the mangle and pushed it to one side and then lit a lamp on the wall by pressing some knob in the darkness. The light was bright but wavery and uncertain and would be far from satisfactory for reading with. He sat back in his chair as if waiting to be questioned and complimented on the strange things he had been doing.

'What is your private opinion of all that?' he asked.

'What were you doing?' I inquired.

'Stretching the light.'

'I do not understand your meaning.'

'I will tell you the size of it,' he said, 'and indicate roughly the shape of it. It is no harm if you know unusual things because you will be a dead man in two days and you will be held incognito and incommunicate in the meantime. Did you ever hear tell of omnium?'

'Omnium?'

'Omnium is the right name for it although you will not find it in the books.'

'Are you sure that is the right name?' I had never heard this word before except in Latin.

'Certain.'

'How certain?'

'The Sergeant says so.'

'And what is omnium the right name for?'

MacCruiskeen smiled at me indulgently.

'You are omnium and I am omnium and so is the mangle and my boots here and so is the wind in the chimney.'

'That is enlightening,' I said.

'It comes in waves,' he explained.

'What colour?'

'Every colour.'

'High or low?'

'Both.'

The blade of my inquisitive curiosity was sharpened but I saw that questions were putting the matter further into doubt instead of clearing it. I kept my silence till Mac-Cruiskeen spoke again.

'Some people,' he said, 'call it energy but the right name is omnium because there is far more than energy in the inside of it, whatever it is. Omnium is the essential inherent interior essence which is hidden inside the root of the kernel of everything and it is always the same.'

I nodded wisely.

'It never changes. But it shows itself in a million ways and it always comes in waves. Now take the case of the light on the mangle.'

'Take it,' I said.

'Light is the same omnium on a short wave but if it comes on a longer wave it is in the form of noise, or sound. With my own patents I can stretch a ray out until it becomes sound.'

'I see.'

'And when I have a shout shut in that box with the wires, I can squeeze it till I get heat and you would not believe the convenience of it all in the winter. Do you see that lamp on the wall there?'

'I do.'

'That is operated by a patent compressor and a secret instrument connected with that box with the wires. The box is full of noise. Myself and the Sergeant spend our spare time in the summer collecting noises so that we can have light and heat for our official life in the dark winter. That is why the light is going up and down. Some of the noises are noiser than the others and the pair of us will be blinded if we come to the time when the quarry was working last September. It is in the box somewhere and it is bound to come out of it in the due course inevitably.'

'Blasting operations?'

'Dynamiteering and extravagant combustions of the most far-reaching kind. But omnium is the business-end of every-thing. If you could find the right wave that results in a tree, you could make a small fortune out of timber for export.'

'And policemen and cows, are they all in waves?'

'Everything is on a wave and omnium is at the back of the whole shooting-match unless I am a Dutchman from the distant Netherlands. Some people call it God and there are other names for something that is identically resembling it and that thing is omnium also into the same bargain.'

'Cheese?'

'Yes. Omnium.'

'Even braces?'

'Even braces.'

'Did you ever see a piece of it or what colour it is?'

MacCruiskeen smiled wryly and spread his hands into red fans.

'That is the supreme pancake,' he said. 'If you could say what the shouts mean it might be the makings of the answer.'

'And storm-wind and water and brown bread and the feel of hailstones on the bare head, are those all omnium on a different wave?'

'All omnium.'

'Could you not get a piece and carry it in your waistcoat so that you could change the world to suit you when it suited you?'

'It is the ultimate and the inexorable pancake. If you had a sack of it or even the half-full of a small matchbox of it, you could do anything and even do what could not be described by that name.'

'I understand you.'

MacCruiskeen sighed and went again to the dresser, taking

something from the drawer. When he sat down at the table again, he started to move his hands together, performing intricate loops and convolutions with his fingers as if they were knitting something but there were no needles in them at all, nothing to be seen except his naked hands.

'Are you working again at the little chest?' I asked.

'I am,' he said.

I sat watching him idly, thinking my own thoughts. For the first time I recalled the wherefore of my unhappy visit to the queer situation I was in. Not my watch but the black box. Where was it? If MacCruiskeen knew the answer, would he tell me if I asked him? If by chance I did not escape safely from the hangman's morning, would I ever see it or know what was inside it, know the value of the money I could never spend, know how handsome could have been my volume on de Selby? Would I ever see John Divney again? Where was he now? Where was my watch?

You have no watch.

That was true. I felt my brain cluttered and stuffed with questions and blind perplexity and I also felt the sadness of my position coming back into my throat. I felt completely alone, but with a small hope that I would escape safely at the tail end of everything.

I had made up my mind to ask him if he knew anything about the cashbox when my attention was distracted by another surprising thing.

The door was flung open and in came Gilhaney, his red face puffed from the rough road. He did not quite stop or sit down but kept moving restlessly about the day-room, paying no attention to me at all. MacCruiskeen had reached a meticulous point in his work and had his head nearly on the table to make sure that his fingers were working correctly and making no serious mistakes. When he had passed the difficulty he looked up somewhat at Gilhaney.

'Is it about a bicycle?' he asked casually.

'Only about timber,' said Gilhaney.

'And what is your timber news?'

'The prices have been put up by a Dutch ring, the cost of a good scaffold would cost a fortune.'

'Trust the Dutchmen,' MacCruiskeen said in a tone that meant that he knew the timber trade inside out.

'A three-man scaffold with a good trap and satisfactory steps would set you back ten pounds without rope or labour,' Gilhaney said.

'Ten pounds is a lot of money for a hanger,' said MacCruiskeen.

'But a two-man scaffold with a push-off instead of the mechanical trap and a ladder for the steps would cost the best majority of six pound, rope extra.'

'And dear at the same price,' said MacCruiskeen.

'But the ten-pound scaffold is a better job, there is more class about it,' said Gilhaney. 'There is a charm about a scaffold if it is well-made and satisfactory.'

What occurred next I did not see properly because I was listening to this pitiless talk even with my eyes. But something astonishing happened again. Gilhaney had gone near MacCruiskeen to talk down at him seriously and I think he made the mistake of stopping dead completely instead of keeping on the move to preserve his perpendicular balance. The outcome was that he crashed down, half on bent MacCruiskeen and half on the table, bringing the two of them with him into a heap of shouts and legs and confusion on the floor. The policeman's face when I saw it was a frightening sight. It was the colour of a dark plum with passion, but his eyes burned like bonfires in the forehead and there were frothy discharges at his mouth. He said no words for a while, only sounds of jungle anger, wild grunts and clicks of demoniacal hostility. Gilhaney had cowered to the wall and raised himself with the help of it and then retreated to the door. When MacCruiskeen found his tongue again he used the most unclean language ever spoken and invented dirtier words than the dirtiest ever spoken anywhere. He put names on Gilhaney too impossible and revolting to be written with known letters. He was temporarily insane with anger because he rushed ultimately to the dresser where he kept all his properties and pulled out a patent pistol and swept it round the room to threaten the two of us and every breakable article in the house.

'Get down on your four knees, the two of you, on the floor,' he roared, 'and don't stop searching for that chest you have knocked down till you find it!'

Gilhaney slipped down to his knees at once and I did the same thing without troubling to look at the Policeman's face because I could remember distinctly what it looked like the last time I had eyed it. We crawled feebly about the floor, peering and feeling for something that could not be felt or seen and that was really too small to be lost at all.

This is amusing. You are going to be hung for murdering a man you did not murder and now you will be shot for not finding a tiny thing that probably does not exist at all and which in any event you did not lose.

I deserve it all, I answered, for not being here at all, to quote the words of the Sergeant.

How long we remained at our peculiar task, Gilhaney and I, it is not easy to remember. Ten minutes or ten years, perhaps, with MacCruiskeen seated near us, fingering the iron and glaring savagely at our bent forms. Then I caught Gilhaney showing his face to me sideways and giving me a broad private wink. Soon he closed his fingers, got up erect with the assistance of the door-handle and advanced to where MacCruiskeen was, smiling his gappy smile.

'Here you are and here it is,' he said with his closed hand outstretched.

'Put it on the table,' MacCruiskeen said evenly.

Gilhaney put his hand on the table and opened it.

'You can now go away and take your departure,' Mac-Cruiskeen told him, 'and leave the premises for the purpose of attending to the timber.'

When Gilhaney was gone I saw that most of the passion had ebbed from the Policeman's face. He sat silent for a time, then gave his customary sigh and got up.

'I have more to do tonight,' he said to me civilly, 'so I will show you where you are to sleep for the dark night-time.'

He lit a queer light that had wires to it and a diminutive box full of minor noises, and led me into a room where there were two white beds and nothing else.

'Gilhaney thinks he is a clever one and a master mind,' he said.

'He might be or maybe not,' I muttered.

'He does not take much account of coincidental chances.'

'He does not look like a man that would care much.'

'When he said he had the chest he thought he was making me into a prize pup and blinding me by putting his thumb in my eye.'

'That is what it looked like.'

'But by a rare chance he *did* accidentally close his hand on the chest and it was the chest and nothing else that he replaced in due course on the table.'

There was some silence here.

'Which bed?' I asked.

'This one,' said MacCruiskeen.

Chapter 8

After MacCruiskeen had tiptoed delicately from the room like a trained nurse and shut the door without a sound, I found myself standing by the bed and wondering stupidly what I was going to do with it. I was weary in body and my brain was numb. I had a curious feeling about my left leg. I thought that it was, so to speak, spreading – that its wood-enness was slowly extending throughout my whole body, a dry timber poison killing me inch by inch. Soon my brain would be changed to wood completely and I would then be dead. Even the bed was made of wood, not metal. If I were to lie in it –

Will you sit down for Pity's sake and stop standing there like a gawm, Joe said suddenly.

I am not sure what I do next if I stop standing, I answered. But I sat down on the bed for Pity's sake.

There is nothing difficult about a bed, even a child can learn to use a bed. Take off your clothes and get into bed and lie on it and keep lying on it even if it makes you feel foolish.

I saw the wisdom of this and started to undress. I felt almost too tired to go through that simple task. When all my clothes were laid on the floor they were much more numerous than I had expected and my body was surprisingly white and thin.

I opened the bed fastidiously, lay into the middle of it, closed it up again carefully and let out a sigh of happiness and rest. I felt as if all my weariness and perplexities of the day had descended on me pleasurably like a great heavy quilt which would keep me warm and sleepy. My knees opened up like rosebuds in rich sunlight, pushing my shins two inches further to the bottom of the bed. Every joint became loose and foolish and devoid of true utility. Every inch of my person gained weight with every second until the total burden on the bed was approximately five hundred thousand tons. This was evenly distributed on the four wooden legs of the bed, which had by now become an integral part of the universe. My eyelids, each weighing no less than four tons, slewed ponderously across my eyeballs. My narrow shins, itchier and more remote in their agony of relaxation, moved further away from me till my happy toes pressed closely on the bars. My position was completely horizontal, ponderous, absolute and incontrovertible. United with the bed I became momentous and planetary. Far away from the bed I could see the outside night framed neatly in the window as if it were a picture on the wall. There was a bright star in one corner with other smaller stars elsewhere littered about in sublime profusion. Lying quietly and dead-eyed, I reflected on how new the night[1] was, how

[1] Not excepting even the credulous Kraus (see his *De Selby's Leben*), all the commentators have treated de Selby's disquisitions on night and sleep with considerable reserve. This is hardly to be wondered at since he held (a) that darkness was simply an accretion of 'black air', i.e., a staining of the atmosphere due to volcanic eruptions too fine to be seen with the naked eye and also to certain 'regrettable' industrial activities involving coal-tar by-products and vegetable dyes; and (b) that sleep was simply a succession of fainting-fits brought on by semi-asphyxiation due to (a). Hatchjaw brings forward his rather facile and ever-ready theory of forgery, pointing to certain unfamiliar syntactical constructions in the first part of the third so-called 'prosecanto' in *Golden Hours*. He does not, however, suggest that there is anything spurious in de Selby's equally damaging rhodomontade in the *Layman's Atlas* where he inveighs savagely against 'the insanitary conditions prevailing everywhere after six o'clock' and makes the famous *gaffe* that death is merely 'the collapse of the heart from the strain of a lifetime of fits and fainting'. Bassett (in *Lux Mundi*) has gone to considerable pains to establish the date of these passages and shows that de Selby was *hors de combat* from his long-standing gall-bladder disorders at least immediately before the passages were composed. One cannot lightly set aside Bassett's formidable table of dates and his corroborative extracts from contemporary newspapers which treat of an unnamed 'elderly man' being assisted into private houses after having fits in the street. For those who wish to hold the balance for themselves, Henderson's *Hatchjaw and Bassett* is not unuseful. Kraus, usually unscientific and unreliable, is worth reading on this point. (*Leben*, pp. 17–37.)

As in many other of de Selby's concepts, it is difficult to get to grips with his process of reasoning or to refute his curious conclusions. The 'volcanic

distinctive and unaccustomed its individuality. Robbing me of the reassurance of my eyesight, it was disintegrating my bodily personality into a flux of colour, smell, recollection, desire – all the strange uncounted essences of terrestrial and spiritual existence. I was deprived of definition, position and magnitude and my significance was considerably diminished. Lying there, I felt the weariness ebbing from me slowly, like a tide retiring over limitless sands. The feeling was so pleasurable and profound that I sighed again a long sound of happiness. Almost at once I heard another sigh and heard Joe murmuring some contented incoherency. His voice was near me, yet did not seem to come from the accustomed place within. I thought that he must be lying beside me in the bed and I kept my hands carefully at my sides in case I should accidentally touch him, I felt, for no reason, that his diminutive body would be horrible to the human touch – scaly or slimy like an eel or with a repelling roughness like a cat's tongue.

footnote continued

eruptions', which we may for convenience compare to the infra-visual activity of such substances as radium, take place usually in the 'evening' are stimulated by the smoke and industrial combustions of the 'day' and are intensified in certain places which may, for the want of a better term, be called 'dark places'. One difficulty is precisely this question of terms. A 'dark place' is dark merely because it is a place where darkness 'germinates' and 'evening' is a time of twilight merely because the 'day' deteriorates owing to the stimulating effect of smuts on the volcanic processes. De Selby makes no attempt to explain why a 'dark place' such as a cellar need be dark and does not define the atmospheric, physical or mineral conditions which must prevail uniformly in all such places if the theory is to stand. The 'only straw offered', to use Bassett's wry phrase, is the statement that 'black air' is highly combustible, enormous masses of it being instantly consumed by the smallest flame, even an electrical luminance isolated in a vacuum. 'This,' Bassett observes, 'seems to be an attempt to protect the theory from the shock it can be dealt by simply striking matches and may be taken as the final proof that the great brain was out of gear.'

A significant feature of the matter is the absence of any authoritative record of those experiments with which de Selby always sought to support his ideas. It is true that Kraus (see below) gives a forty-page account of certain experiments, mostly concerned with attempts to bottle quantities of 'night' and endless sessions in locked and shuttered bedrooms from which bursts of loud hammering could be heard. He explains that the bottling operations were carried out with bottles which were, 'for obvious reasons', made of black glass. Opaque porcelain jars are also stated to have been used 'with some success'. To use the frigid words of Bassett, 'such information,

That's not very logical – or complimentary either, he said
suddenly.

What isn't?

That about my body. Why scaly?

That's only my joke, I chuckled drowsily. I know you have
no body. Except my own perhaps.

But why scaly?

I don't know. How can I know why I think my thoughts?

By God I won't be called scaly.

His voice to my surprise had become shrill with petul-
ance. Then he seemed to fill the world with his resentment,
not by speaking but by remaining silent after he had spoken.

Now, now, Joe, I murmured soothingly.

*Because if you are looking for trouble you can have your
bellyful*, he snapped.

You have no body, Joe.

---

footnote continued

it is to be feared, makes little contribution to serious deselbiana (*sic*).'

Very little is known of Kraus or his life. A brief biographical note appears
in the obsolete *Bibliographie de de Selby*. He is stated to have been born in
Ahrensburg, near Hamburg, and to have worked as a young man in the
office of his father, who had extensive jam interests in North Germany. He
is said to have disappeared completely from human ken after Hatchjaw had
been arrested in a Sheephaven hotel following the unmasking of the de
Selby letter scandal by *The Times*, which made scathing references to
Kraus's 'discreditable' machinations in Hamburg and clearly suggested his
complicity. If it is remembered that these events occurred in the fateful
June when the *County Album* was beginning to appear in fortnightly parts,
the significance of the whole affair becomes apparent. The subsequent
exoneration of Hatchjaw served only to throw further suspicion on the
shadowy Kraus.

Recent research has not thrown much light on Kraus's identity or his
ultimate fate. Bassett's posthumous *Recollections* contains the interesting
suggestion that Kraus did not exist at all, the name being one of the
pseudonyms adopted by the egregious du Garbandier to further his 'cam-
paign of calumny'. The *Leben*, however, seems too friendly in tone to
encourage such a speculation.

Du Garbandier himself, possibly pretending to confuse the characteristics
of the English and French languages, persistently uses 'black hair' for 'black
air', and makes extremely elaborate fun of the raven-headed lady of the
skies who deluged the world with her tresses every night when retiring.

The wisest course on this question is probably that taken by the little-
known Swiss writer, Le Clerque. 'This matter,' he says, 'is outside the true
province of the conscientious commentator inasmuch as being unable to
say aught that is charitable or useful, he must preserve silence.'

Then why do you say I have? And why scaly?

Here I had a strange idea not unworthy of de Selby. Why was Joe so disturbed at the suggestion that he had a body? What if he *had* a body? A body with another body inside it in turn, thousands of such bodies within each other like the skins of an onion, receding to some unimaginable ultimum? Was I in turn merely a link in a vast sequence of imponderable beings, the world I knew merely the interior of the being whose inner voice I myself was? Who or what was the core and what monster in what world was the final uncontained colossus? God? Nothing? Was I receiving these wild thoughts from Lower Down or were they brewing newly in me to be transmitted Higher Up?

From Lower Down, Joe barked.

Thank you.

I'm leaving.

What?

Clearing out. We will see who is scaly in two minutes.

These few words sickened me instantly with fear although their meaning was too momentous to be grasped without close reasoning.

The scaly idea – where did I get that from? I cried.

Higher Up, he shouted.

Puzzled and frightened I tried to understand the complexities not only of my intermediate dependence and my catenal unintegrity but also my dangerous adjunctiveness and my embarrassing unisolation. If one assumes –

Listen. Before I go I will tell you this. I am your soul and all your souls. When I am gone you are dead. Past humanity is not only implicit in each new man born but is contained in him. Humanity is an ever-widening spiral and life is the beam that plays briefly on each succeeding ring. All humanity from its beginning to its end is already present but the beam has not yet played beyond you. Your earthly successors await dumbly and trust to your guidance and mine and all my people inside me to preserve them and lead the light further. You are not now the top of your people's line any more than your mother was when she had you inside her. When I leave you I take with me all that has made you what

123

you are – I take all your significance and importance and all the accumulations of human instinct and appetite and wisdom and dignity. You will be left with nothing behind you and nothing to give the waiting ones. Woe to you when they find you out! Good-bye!

Although I thought this speech was rather far-fetched and ridiculous, he was gone and I was dead.

Preparations for the funeral were put in hand at once. Lying in my dark blanket-padded coffin I could hear the sharp blows of a hammer nailing down the lid.

It soon turned out that the hammering was the work of Sergeant Pluck. He was standing smiling at me from the doorway and he looked large and lifelike and surprisingly full of breakfast. Over the tight collar of his tunic he wore a red ring of fat that looked fresh and decorative as if it had come directly from the laundry. His moustache was damp from drinking milk.

Thank goodness to be back to sanity, Joe said.

His voice was friendly and reassuring, like pockets in an old suit.

'Good morning to you in the morning-time,' the Sergeant said pleasantly.

I answered him in a civil way and gave particulars of my dream. He leaned listening on the jamb, taking in the difficult parts with a skilled ear. When I had finished he smiled at me in pity and good humour.

'You have been dreaming, man,' he said.

Wondering at him, I looked away to the window. Night was gone from it without a trace, leaving in substitution a distant hill that lay gently against the sky. Clouds of white and grey pillowed it and on its soft shoulder trees and boulders were put pleasingly to make it true. I could hear a morning wind making its way indomitably throughout the world and all the low unsilence of the daytime was in my ear, bright and restless like a caged bird. I sighed and looked back at the Sergeant, who was still leaning and quietly picking his teeth, absent-faced and still.

'I remember well,' he said, 'a dream that I had six years ago on the twenty-third of November next. A nightmare would be a truer word. I dreamt if you please that I had a slow puncture.'

'That is a surprising thing,' I said idly, 'but not astonishing. Was it the work of a tintack?'

'Not a tintack,' said the Sergeant, 'but too much starch.'

'I did not know,' I said sarcastically, 'that they starched the roads.'

'It was not the road, and for a wonder it was not the fault of the County Council. I dreamt that I was cycling on official business for three days. Suddenly I felt the saddle getting hard and lumpy underneath me. I got down and felt the tyres but they were unexceptionable and fully pumped. Then I thought my head was giving me a nervous outbreak from too much overwork. I went into a private house where there was a qualified doctor and he examined me completely and told me what the trouble was. I had a slow puncture.'

He gave a coarse laugh and half-turned to me his enormous backside.

'Here, look,' he laughed.

'I see,' I murmured.

Chuckling loudly he went away for a minute and came back again.

'I have put the stirabout on the table,' he said, 'and the milk is still hot from being inside the cow's milk-bag.'

I put on my clothes and went to my breakfast in the day-room where the Sergeant and MacCruiskeen were talking about their figures.

'Six point nine six three circulating,' MacCruiskeen was saying.

'High,' said the Sergeant. 'Very high. There must be a ground heat. Tell me about the fall.'

'A medium fall at midnight and no lumps.'

The Sergeant laughed and shook his head.

'No lumps indeed,' he chuckled, 'there will be hell to pay tomorrow on the lever if it is true there is a ground heat.'

MacCruiskeen got up suddenly from his chair.

'I will give her half a hundredweight of charcoal,' he announced. He marched straight out of the house muttering calculations, not looking where he was going but staring straight into the middle of his black notebook.

I had almost finished my crock of porridge and lay back to look fully at the Sergeant.

'When are you going to hang me?' I asked, looking fearlessly into his large face. I felt refreshed and strong again and confident that I would escape without difficulty.

'Tomorrow morning if we have the scaffold up in time and unless it is raining. You would not believe how slippery the rain can make a new scaffold. You could slip and break your neck into fancy fractures and you would never know what happened to your life or how you lost it.'

'Very well,' I said firmly. 'If I am to be a dead man in twenty-four hours will you explain to me what these figures in MacCruiskeen's black book are?'

The Sergeant smiled indulgently.

'The readings?'

'Yes.'

'If you are going to be dead completely there is no insoluble impedimentum to that proposal,' he said, 'but it is easier to show you than to tell you verbally. Follow behind me like a good man.'

He led the way to a door in the back passage and threw it open with an air of momentous revelation, standing aside politely to give me a complete and unobstructed view.

'What do you think of that?' he asked.

I looked into the room and did not think much of it. It was a small bedroom, gloomy and not too clean. It was in great disorder and filled with a heavy smell.

'It is MacCruiskeen's room,' he explained.

'I do not see much,' I said.

The Sergeant smiled patiently.

'You are not looking in the right quarter,' he said.

'I have looked everywhere that can be looked,' I said.

The Sergeant led the way in to the middle of the floor and took possession of a walking-stick that was convenient.

'If I ever want to hide,' he remarked, 'I will always go upstairs in a tree. People have no gift for looking up, they seldom examine the lofty altitudes.'

I looked at the ceiling.

'There is little to be seen there,' I said, 'except a bluebottle that looks dead.'

The Sergeant looked up and pointed with his stick.

'That is not a bluebottle,' he said, 'that is Gogarty's outhouse.'

I looked squarely at him in a mixed way but he was paying me no attention but pointing to other tiny marks upon the ceiling.

'That,' he said, 'is Martin Bundle's house and that is Tiernahins and that one there is where the married sister lives. And here we have the lane from Tiernahins to the main telegraph trunk road.' He drew his stick along a wavering faint crack that ran down to join a deeper crack.

'A map!' I cried excitedly.

'And here we have the barrack,' he added. 'It is all as plain as a pikestick.'

When I looked carefully at the ceiling I saw that Mr Mathers' house and every road and house I knew were marked there, and nets of lanes and neighbourhoods that I did not know also. It was a map of the parish, complete, reliable and astonishing.

The Sergeant looked at me and smiled again.

'You will agree,' he said, 'that it is a fascinating pancake and a conundrum of great incontinence, a phenomenon of the first rarity.'

'Did you make it yourself?'

'I did not and nobody else manufactured it either. It was always there and MacCruiskeen is certain that it was there even before that. The cracks are natural and so are small cracks.'

With my cocked eye I traced the road we came when Gilhaney had found his bicycle at the bush.

'The funny thing is,' the Sergeant said, 'that MacCruiskeen lay for two years staring at that ceiling before he saw it was a map of superb ingenuity.'

'Now that was stupid,' I said thickly.

'And he lay looking at the map for five years more before he saw that it showed the way to eternity.'

'To eternity?'

'Certainly.'

'Will it be possible for us to come back from there?' I whispered.

'Of course. There is a lift. But wait till I show you the secret of the map.'

He took up the stick again and pointed to the mark that meant the barracks.

'Here we are in the barracks on the main telegraph trunk road,' he said. 'Now use your internal imagination and tell me what left-hand road you meet if you go forth from the barrack on the main road.'

I thought this out without difficulty.

'You meet the road that meets the main road at Jarvis's outhouse,' I said, 'where we came from the finding of the bicycle.'

'Then that road is the first turn on the left-hand latitude?'

'Yes.'

'And here it is – here.'

He pointed out the left-hand road with his stick and tapped Mr Jarvis's outhouse at the corner.

'And now,' he said solemnly, 'kindly inform me what this is.'

He drew the stick along a faint crack that joined the crack of the main road about half-way between the barrack and the road at Mr Jarvis's.

'What would you call that?' he repeated.

'There is no road there,' I cried excitedly, 'the left-hand road at Jarvis's is the first road on the left. I am not a fool. There is no road there.'

By God if you're not you will be. You're a goner if you listen to much more of this gentleman's talk.

'But there *is* a road there,' the Sergeant said triumphantly, 'if you know how to look knowledgeably for it. And a very old road. Come with me till we see the size of it.'

'Is this the road to eternity?'

'It is indeed but there is no signpost.'

Although he made no move to release his bicycle from solitary confinement in the cell, he snapped the clips adroitly on his trousers and led the way heavily into the middle of the morning. We marched together down the road. Neither of us spoke and neither listened for what the other might have to say.

When the keen wind struck me in the face it snatched away the murk of doubt and fear and wonder that was anchored on my brain like a raincloud on a hill. All my senses, relieved from the agony of dealing with the existence of the Sergeant, became supernaturally alert at the work of interpreting the genial day for my benefit. The world rang in my ear like a great workshop. Sublime feats of mechanics and chemistry were evident on every side. The earth was agog with invisible industry. Trees were active where they stood and gave uncompromising evidence of their strength. Incomparable grasses were forever at hand, lending their distinction to the universe. Patterns very difficult to imagine were made together by everything the eye could see, merging into a supernal harmony their unexceptionable varieties. Men who were notable for the whiteness of their shirts worked diminutively in the distant bog, toiling in the brown turf and heather. Patient horses stood near with their useful carts and littered among the boulders on a hill beyond were tiny sheep at pasture. Birds were audible in the secrecy of the bigger trees, changing branches and conversing not tumultuously. In a field by the road a donkey stood quietly as if he were examining the morning, bit by bit unhurryingly. He did not move, his head was high and his mouth chewed nothing. He looked as if he understood completely these unexplainable enjoyments of the world.

My eye ranged round unsatisfied. I could not see enough in sufficient fulness before I took the left turn for eternity in company with the Sergeant and my thoughts remained entangled in what my eyes were looking at.

You don't mean to say that you believe in this eternity business?

What choice have I? It would be foolish to doubt anything after yesterday.

That is all very well but I think I can claim to be an

authority on the subject of eternity. There must be a limit to this gentleman's monkey-tricks.

I am certain there isn't.

Nonsense. You are becoming demoralized.

I will be hung tomorrow.

That is doubtful but if it has to be faced we will make a brave show.

We?

Certainly. I will be there to the end. In the meantime let us make up our minds that eternity is not up a lane that is found by looking at cracks in the ceiling of a country policeman's bedroom.

Then what *is* up the lane?

I cannot say. If he said that eternity was up the lane and left it at that, I would not kick so hard. But when we are told that we are coming back from there in a lift – well, I begin to think that he is confusing night-clubs with heaven. A lift!

Surely, I argued, if we concede that eternity is up the lane, the question of the lift is a minor matter. That is a case for swallowing a horse and cart and straining at a flea.

No. I bar the lift. I know enough about the next world to be sure that you don't get there and come back out of it in a lift. Besides, we must be near the place now and I don't see any elevator-shaft running up into the clouds.

Gilhaney had no handlebars on him, I pointed out.

Unless the word 'lift' has a special meaning. Like 'drop' when you are talking about a scaffold. I suppose a smash under the chin with a heavy spade could be called a 'lift'. If that is the case you can be certain about eternity and have the whole of it yourself and welcome.

I still think there is an electric lift.

My attention was drawn away from this conversation to the Sergeant, who had now slackened his pace and was making curious inquiries with his stick. The road had reached a place where there was rising ground on each side, rank grass and brambles near our feet, with a tangle of bigger things behind that, and tall brown thickets beset with green creeper plants beyond.

'It is here somewhere,' the Sergeant said, 'or beside a place somewhere near the next place adjacent.'

He dragged his stick along the green margin, probing at the hidden ground.

'MacCruiskeen rides his bicycle along the grass here,' he said, 'it is an easier pancake, the wheels are surer and the seat is a more sensitive instrument than the horny hand.'

After another walk and more probing he found what he was searching for and suddenly dragged me into the undergrowth, parting the green curtains of the branches with a practised hand.

'This is the hidden road,' he called backwards from ahead.

It is not easy to say whether road is the correct name for a place that must be fought through inch by inch at the cost of minor wounds and the sting of strained branches slapping back against the person. Nevertheless the ground was even against the foot and some dim distance to each side I could see the ground banking up sharply with rocks and gloominess and damp vegetation. There was a sultry smell and many flies of the gnat class were at home here.

A yard in front of me the Sergeant was plunging on wildly with his head down, thrashing the younger shoots severely with his stick and calling muffled warnings to me of the strong distended boughs he was about to release in my direction.

I do not know how long we travelled or what the distance was but the air and the light got scarcer and scarcer until I was sure that we were lost in the bowels of a great forest. The ground was still even enough to walk on but covered with the damp and rotting fall of many autumns. I had followed the noisy Sergeant with blind faith till my strength was nearly gone, so that I reeled forward instead of walking and was defenceless against the brutality of the boughs. I felt very ill and exhausted. I was about to shout to him that I was dying when I noticed the growth was thinning and that the Sergeant was calling to me, from where he was hidden and ahead of me, that we were there. When I reached him he was standing before a small stone building and bending to take the clips from his trousers.

'This is it,' he said, nodding his stooped head at the little house.

'This is what?' I muttered.

'The entrance to it,' he replied.

The structure looked exactly like the porch of a small country church. The darkness and the confusion of the branches made it hard for me to see whether there was a larger building at the rear. The little porch was old, with green stains on the stonework and warts of moss in its many crannies. The door was an old brown door with ecclesiastical hinges and ornamental ironwork; it was set far back and made to measure in its peaked doorway. This was the entrance to eternity. I knocked the streaming sweat from my forehead with my hand.

The Sergeant was feeling himself sensually for his keys.

'It is very close,' he said politely.

'Is this the entrance to the next world?' I murmured. My voice was lower than I thought it would be owing to my exertions and trepidation.

'But it is seasonable weather and we can't complain,' he added loudly, paying no attention to my question. My voice, perhaps, had not been strong enough to travel to his ear.

He found a key which he rasped in the keyhole and threw the door open. He entered the dark inside but sent his hand out again to twitch me in after him by the coat sleeve.

Strike a match there!

Almost at the same time the Sergeant had found a box with knobs and wires in it in the wall and did whatever was necessary to make it give out a startling leaping light from where it was. But during the second I was standing in the dark I had ample time to get the surprise of my life. It was the floor. My feet were astonished when they trod on it. It was made of platefuls of tiny studs like the floor of a steam-engine or like the railed galleries that run around a great printing press. It rang with a ghostly hollow noise beneath the hobnails of the Sergeant, who had now clattered to the other end of the little room to fuss with his chain of keys and to throw open another door that was hidden in the wall.

'Of course a nice shower of rain would clear the air,' he called.

I went carefully over to see what he was doing in the little closet he had entered. Here he had operated successfully another unsteady light-box. He stood with his back to me examining panels in the wall. There were two of them, tiny things like matchboxes, and the figure sixteen could be seen in one panel and ten in the other. He sighed and came out of the closet and looked at me sadly.

'They say that walking takes it down,' he said, 'but it is my own experience that walking puts it up, walking makes it solid and leaves plenty of room for more.'

I thought at this stage that a simple and dignified appeal might have some prospect of succeeding.

'Will you please tell me,' I said, 'since I will be a dead man tomorrow – where are we and what are we doing?'

'Weighing ourselves,' he replied.

'Weighing ourselves?'

'Step into the box there,' he said, 'till we see what your registration is by plain record.'

I stepped warily on to more iron plates in the closet and saw the figures change to nine and six.

'Nine stone six pounds,' said the Sergeant, 'and a most invidious weight. I would give ten years of my life to get the beef down.'

He had his back to me again opening still another closet in another wall and passing trained fingers over another light-box. The unsteady light came and I saw him standing in the closet, looking at his large watch and winding it absently. The light was leaping beside his jaw and throwing unearthly leaps of shadow on his gross countenance.

'Will you step over here,' he called to me at last, 'and come in with me unless you desire to be left behind in your own company.'

When I had walked over and stood silently beside him in the steel closet, he shut the door on us with a precise click and leaned against the wall thoughtfully. I was about to ask for several explanations when a cry of horror came bounding from my throat. With no noise or warning at all, the floor was giving way beneath us.

'It is no wonder that you are yawning,' the Sergeant said conversationally, 'it is very close, the ventilation is far from satisfactory.'

'I was only screaming,' I blurted. 'What is happening to this box we are in? Where – '

My voice trailed away to a dry cluck of fright. The floor was falling so fast beneath us that it seemed once or twice to fall faster than I could fall myself so that it was sure that my feet had left it and that I had taken up a position for brief intervals half-way between the floor and the ceiling. In panic I raised my right foot and smote it down with all my weight and my strength. It struck the floor but only with a puny tinkling noise. I swore and groaned and closed my eyes and wished for a happy death. I felt my stomach bounding sickeningly about inside me as if it were a wet football filled with water.

Lord save us!

'It does a man no harm,' the Sergeant remarked pleasantly, 'to move around a bit and see things. It is a great thing for widening out the mind. A wide mind is a grand thing, it nearly always leads to farseeing inventions. Look at Sir Walter Raleigh that invented the pedal bicycle and Sir George Stephenson with his steam-engine and Napoleon Bonaparte and George Sand and Walter Scott – great men all.'

'Are – are we in eternity yet?' I chattered.

'We are not there yet but nevertheless we are nearly there,' he answered. 'Listen with all your ears for a little click.'

What can I say to tell of my personal position? I was locked in an iron box with a sixteen-stone policeman, falling appallingly for ever, listening to talk about Walter Scott and listening for a click also.

Click!

It came at last, sharp and terrible. Almost at once the falling changed, either stopping altogether or becoming a much slower falling.

'Yes,' said the Sergeant brightly, 'we are there now.'·

I noticed nothing whatever except that the thing we were in gave a jolt and the floor seemed to resist my feet suddenly in a way that might well have been eternal. The Sergeant fingered the arrangement of knob-like instruments on the door, which he opened after a time and stepped out.

'That was the lift,' he remarked.

It is peculiar that when one expects some horrible incalculable and devastating thing which does not materialize, one is more disappointed than relieved. I had expected for one thing a blaze of eye-destroying light. No other expectation was clear enough in my brain to be mentioned. Instead of this radiance, I saw a long passage lit fitfully at intervals by the crude home-made noise-machines, with more darkness to be seen than light. The walls of the passage seemed to be made with bolted sheets of pig-iron in which were set rows of small doors which looked to me like ovens or furnace-doors or safe-deposits such as banks have. The ceiling, where I could see it, was a mass of wires and what appeared to be particularly thick wires or possibly pipes. All the time there was an entirely new noise to be heard, not unmusical, sometimes like water gurgling underground and sometimes like subdued conversation in a foreign tongue.

The Sergeant was already looming ahead on his way up the passage, treading heavily on the plates. He swung his keys jauntily and hummed a song. I followed near him, trying to count the little doors. There were four rows of six in every lineal two yards of wall, or a total of many thousands. Here and there I saw a dial or an intricate nest of clocks and knobs resembling a control board with masses of coarse wires converging from all quarters of it. I did not understand the significance of anything but I thought the scene was so real that much of my fear was groundless. I trod firmly beside the Sergeant, who was still real enough for anybody.

We came to a crossroads in the passage where the light was brighter. A cleaner brighter passage with shiny steel walls ran away to each side, disappearing from view only where the distance brought its walls, floor and roof to the one gloomy point. I thought I could hear a sound like hissing steam and another noise like great cogwheels grinding one way, stopping and grinding back again. The Sergeant paused to take a reading from a clock in the wall, then turned sharply to the left and called for me to follow.

I shall not recount the passages we walked or talk of the one with the round doors like portholes or the other place where the Sergeant got a box of matches for himself by putting his hand somewhere into the wall. It is enough to say that we arrived, after walking at least a mile of plate, into a well-lit airy hall which was completely circular and filled with indescribable articles very like machinery but not quite as intricate as the more difficult machines. Large expensive-looking cabinets of these articles were placed tastefully about the floor while the circular wall was one mass of these inventions with little dials and meters placed plentifully here and there. Hundreds of miles of coarse wire were visible running everywhere except about the floor and there were thousands of doors like the strong-hinged doors of ovens and arrangements of knobs and keys that reminded me of American cash registers.

The Sergeant was reading out figures from one of the many clocks and turning a small wheel with great care. Suddenly the silence was split by the sound of loud frenzied hammering from the far end of the hall where the apparatus seemed thickest and most complex. The blood ran away at once from my startled face. I looked at the Sergeant but he still attended patiently to his clock and wheel, reciting numbers under his breath and taking no notice. The hammering stopped.

I sat down to think and gather my scattered wits on a smooth article like an iron bar. It was pleasantly warm and comforting. Before any thought had time to come to me there was another burst of hammering, then silence, then a low but violent noise like passionately-muttered oaths, then silence again and finally the sound of heavy footsteps approaching from behind the tall cabinets of machinery.

Feeling a weakness in my spine, I went over quickly and stood beside the Sergeant. He had taken a long white instrument like a large thermometer or band conductor's baton out of a hole in the wall and was examining the calibrations on it with a frown of great preoccupation. He paid no attention to me or to the hidden presence that was approaching invisibly. When I heard the clanging steps rounding the last cabinet, against my will I looked up wildly. It was Policeman MacCruiskeen. He was frowning heavily and bearing another large baton or thermometer which was orange-coloured. He made straight for the Sergeant and showed him this instrument, putting a red finger on a marking that was on it. They stood there silently examining each other's instruments. The Sergeant looked somewhat relieved, I thought, when he had the matter thought out and marched away to the hidden place that MacCruiskeen had just come from. Soon we heard the sound of hammering, this time gentle and rhythmical.

MacCruiskeen put his baton away into the wall in the hole where the Sergeant's had been and turned to me, giving me generously the wrinkled cigarette which I had come to regard as the herald of unthinkable conversation.

'Do you like it?' he inquired.

'It is neat,' I replied.

'You would not believe the convenience of it,' he remarked cryptically.

The Sergeant came back to us drying his red hands on a towel and looking very satisfied with himself. I looked at the two of them sharply. They received my glance and exchanged it privately between them before discarding it.

'Is this eternity?' I asked. 'Why do you call it eternity?'

'Feel my chin,' MacCruiskeen said, smiling enigmatically.

'We call it that,' the Sergeant explained, 'because you don't grow old here. When you leave here you will be the same age as you were coming in and the same stature and latitude. There is an eight-day clock here with a patent balanced action but it never goes.'

'How can you be sure you don't grow old here?'

'Feel my chin,' MacCruiskeen said again.

'It is simple,' the Sergeant said. 'The beard does not grow and if you are fed you do not get hungry and if you are hungry you don't get hungrier. Your pipe will smoke all day and will still be full and a glass of whiskey will still be there no matter how much of it you drink and it does not matter in any case because it will not make you drunker than your own sobriety.'

'Indeed,' I muttered.

'I have been here for a long time this today morning,' MacCruiskeen said, 'and my jaw is still as smooth as a woman's back and the convenience of it takes my breath away, it is a great thing to downface the old razor.'

'How big is all this place?'

'It has no size at all,' the Sergeant explained, 'because there is no difference anywhere in it and we have no conception of the extent of its unchanging coequality.'

MacCruiskeen lit a match for our cigarettes and then threw it carelessly on the plate floor where it lay looking very much important and alone.

'Could you not bring your bicycle and ride through all of it and see it all and draw a chart?' I asked.

The Sergeant smiled at me as if I were a baby.

'The bicycle is easy,' he said.

To my astonishment he went over to one of the bigger ovens, manipulated some knobs, pulled open the massive metal door and lifted out a brand-new bicycle. It had a three-speed gear and an oil-bath and I could see the vaseline still glistening on the bright parts. He put the front wheel down and spun the back wheel expertly in the air.

'The bicycle is an easy pancake,' he said, 'but it is no use and does not matter. Come and I will demonstrate the *res ipsa.*'

Leaving the bicycle, he led the way through the intricate cabinets and round behind other cabinets and in through a doorway. What I saw made my brain shrink painfully in my head and put a paralysing chill across my heart. It was not so much that this other hall was in every respect an exact replica of the one we had just left. It was more that my burdened eye saw that one of the cabinet doors in the wall was standing open and a brand-new bicycle was leaning against the wall, identically like the other one and leaning even at the same angle.

'If you want to take another walk ahead to reach the same place here without coming back you can walk on till you reach the next doorway and you are welcome. But it will do you no good and even if we stay here behind you it is probable that you will find us there to meet you.'

Here I gave a cry as my eye caught a spent match lying clearly on the floor.

'What do you think of the no-shaving?' MacCruiskeen asked boastfully. 'Surely that is an uninterruptible experiment?'

'It is inescapable and highly intractable,' the Sergeant said.

MacCruiskeen was examining some knobs in a central cabinet. He turned his head and called to me.

'Come over here,' he called, 'till I show you something to tell your friends about.'

Afterwards I saw that this was one of his rare jokes because what he showed me was something that I could tell nobody about, there are no suitable words in the world to tell my meaning. This cabinet had an opening resembling a chute and another large opening resembling a black hole about a yard below the chute. He pressed two red articles like typewriter keys and turned a large knob away from him. At once there was a rumbling noise as if thousands of full biscuit-boxes were falling down a stairs. I felt that these falling things would come out of the chute at any moment. And so they did, appearing for a few seconds in the air and then disappearing down the black hole below. But what can I say about them? In colour they were not white or black and certainly bore no intermediate colour; they were far from dark and anything but bright. But strange to say it was not their unprecedented hue that took most of my attention. They had another quality that made me watch them wild-eyed, dry-throated and with no breathing. I can make no attempt to describe this quality. It took me hours of thought long afterwards to realize why these articles were astonishing. *They lacked an essential property of all known objects.* I cannot call it shape or configuration since shapelessness is not what I refer to at all. I can only say that these objects, not one of which resembled the other, were of no known dimensions. They were not square or rectangular or circular or simply irregularly shaped nor could it be said that their endless variety was due to dimensional dissimilarities. Simply their appearance, if even that word is not inadmissible, was not understood by the eye and was in any event indescribable. That is enough to say.

When MacCruiskeen had unpressed the buttons the Sergeant asked me politely what else I would like to see.

'What else is there?'

'Anything.'

'Anything I mention will be shown to me?'

'Of course.'

The ease with which the Sergeant had produced a bicycle that would cost at least eight pounds ten to buy had set in motion in my head certain trains of thought. My nervousness had been largely reduced to absurdity and nothingness by what I had seen and I now found myself taking an interest in the commercial possibilities of eternity.

'What I would like,' I said slowly, 'is to see you open a door and lift out a solid block of gold weighing half a ton.'

The Sergeant smiled and shrugged his shoulders.

'But that is impossible, it is a very unreasonable requisition,' he said. 'It is vexatious and unconscionable,' he added legally.

My heart sank down at this.

'But you said *anything*.'

'I know, man. But there is a limit and a boundary to everything within the scope of reason's garden.'

'That is disappointing,' I muttered.

MacCruiskeen stirred diffidently.

'Of course,' he said, 'if there would be no objection to me assisting the Sergeant in lifting out the block . . .'

'What! Is that a difficulty?'

'I am not a cart-horse,' the Sergeant said with simple dignity.

'Yet, anyhow,' he added, reminding all of us of his great-grandfather.

'Then we'll all lift it out,' I cried.

And so we did. The knobs were manipulated, the door opened and the block of gold, which was encased in a well-made timber box, was lifted down with all our strength and placed on the floor.

'Gold is a common article and there is not much to see when you look at it,' the Sergeant observed. 'Ask him for something confidential and superior to ordinary pre-eminence. Now a magnifying glass is a better thing because you can look at it and what you see when you look is a third thing altogether.'

Another door was opened by MacCruiskeen and I was handed a magnifying glass, a very ordinary-looking instrument with a bone handle. I looked at my hand through it and saw nothing that was recognizable. Then I looked at several other things but saw nothing that I could clearly see. MacCruiskeen took it back with a smile at my puzzled eye.

'It magnifies to invisibility,' he explained. 'It makes everything so big that there is room in the glass for only the smallest particle of it – not enough of it to make it different from any other thing that is dissimilar.'

My eye moved from his explaining face to the block of gold which my attention had never really left.

'What I would like to see now,' I said carefully, 'is fifty cubes of solid gold each weighing one pound.'

MacCruiskeen went away obsequiously like a trained waiter and got these articles out of the wall without a word, arranging them in a neat structure on the floor. The Sergeant had strolled away idly to examine some clocks and take readings. In the meantime my brain was working coldly and quickly. I ordered a bottle of whiskey, precious stones to the value of £200,000, some bananas, a fountain-pen and writing materials, and finally a serge suit of blue with silk linings. When all these things were on the floor, I remembered other things I had overlooked and ordered underwear, shoes and banknotes, and a box of matches. MacCruiskeen, sweating from his labour with the heavy doors, was complaining of the heat and paused to drink some amber ale. The Sergeant was quietly clicking a little wheel with a tiny ratchet.

'I think that is all,' I said at last.

The Sergeant came forward and gazed at the pile of merchandise.

'Lord, save us,' he said.

'I am going to take these things with me,' I announced.

The Sergeant and MacCruiskeen exchanged their private glance. Then they smiled.

'In that case you will need a big strong bag,' the Sergeant said. He went to another door and got me a hogskin bag worth at least fifty guineas in the open market. I carefully packed away my belongings.

I saw MacCruiskeen crushing out his cigarette on the wall and noticed that it was still the same length as it had been when lit half an hour ago. My own was burning quietly also but was completely unconsumed. I crushed it out also and put it in my pocket.

When about to close the bag I had a thought. I unstooped and turned to the policemen.

'I require just one thing more,' I said. 'I want a small weapon suitable for the pocket which will exterminate any man or any million men who try at any time to take my life.'

Without a word the Sergeant brought me a small black article like a torch.

'There is an influence in that,' he said, 'that will change any man or men into grey powder at once if you point it and press the knob and if you don't like grey powder you can have purple powder or yellow powder or any other shade of powder if you tell me now and confide your favourite colour. Would a velvet-coloured colour please you?'

'Grey will do,' I said briefly.

I put this murderous weapon into the bag, closed it and stood up again.

'I think we might go home now.' I said the words casually and took care not to look at the faces of the policemen. To my surprise they agreed readily and we started off with our resounding steps till we found ourselves again in the endless corridors, I carrying the heavy bag and the policemen conversing quietly about the readings they had seen. I felt happy and satisfied with my day. I felt changed and regenerated and full of fresh courage.

'How does this thing work?' I inquired pleasantly, seeking to make friendly conversation. The Sergeant looked at me.

'It has helical gears,' he said informatively.

'Did you not see the wires?' MacCruiskeen asked, turning to me in some surprise.

'You would be astonished at the importance of the charcoal,' the Sergeant said. 'The great thing is to keep the beam reading down as low as possible and you are doing very well if the pilot-mark is steady. But if you let the beam rise, where are you with your lever? If you neglect the charcoal feedings you will send the beam rocketing up and there is bound to be a serious explosion.'

'Low pilot, small fall,' MacCruiskeen said. He spoke neatly and wisely as if his remark was a proverb.

'But the secret of it all-in-all,' continued the Sergeant, 'is the daily readings. Attend to your daily readings and your conscience will be as clear as a clean shirt on Sunday morning. I am a great believer in the daily readings.'

'Did I see everything of importance?'

At this the policemen looked at each other in amazement and laughed outright. Their raucous roars careered away from us up and down the corridor and came back again in pale echoes from the distance.

'I suppose you think a smell is a simple thing?' the Sergeant said smiling.

'A smell?'

'A smell is the most complicated phenomenon in the world,' he said, 'and it cannot be unravelled by the human snout or understood properly although dogs have a better way with smells than we have.'

'But dogs are very poor riders on bicycles,' MacCruiskeen said, presenting the other side of the comparison.

'We have a machine down there,' the Sergeant continued, 'that splits up any smell into its sub- and inter-smells the way you can split up a beam of light with a glass instrument. It is very interesting and edifying, you would not believe the dirty smells that are inside the perfume of a lovely lily-of-the mountain.'

'And there is a machine for tastes,' MacCruiskeen put in,

'the taste of a fried chop, although you might not think it, is forty per cent the taste of . . .'

He grimaced and spat and looked delicately reticent.

'And feels,' the Sergeant said. 'Now there is nothing so smooth as a woman's back or so you might imagine. But if that feel is broken up for you, you would not be pleased with women's backs, I'll promise you that on my solemn oath and parsley. Half of the inside of the smoothness is as rough as a bullock's hips.'

'The next time you come here,' MacCruiskeen promised, 'you will see surprising things.'

This in itself, I thought, was a surprising thing for anyone to say after what I had just seen and after what I was carrying in the bag. He groped in his pocket, found his cigarette, re-lit it and proffered me the match. Hampered with the heavy bag, I was some minutes finding mine but the match still burnt evenly and brightly at its end.

We smoked in silence and went on through the dim passage till we reached the lift again. There were clock-faces or dials beside the open lift which I had not seen before and another pair of doors beside it. I was very tired with my bag of gold and clothes and whiskey and made for the lift to stand on it and put the bag down at last. When nearly on the threshold I was arrested in my step by a call from the Sergeant which rose nearly to the pitch of a woman's scream.

'Don't go in there!'

The colour fled from my face at the urgency of his tone. I turned my head round and stood rooted there with one foot before the other like a man photographed unknowingly in the middle of a walk.

'Why?'

'Because the floor will collapse underneath the bottom of your feet and send you down where nobody went before you.'

'And why?'

'The bag, man.'

'The simple thing is,' MacCruiskeen said calmly, 'that you cannot enter the lift unless you weigh the same weight as you weighed when you weighed into it.'

'If you do,' said the Sergeant, 'it will extirpate you uncon- ditionally and kill the life out of you.'

I put the bag, clinking with its bottle and gold cubes, rather roughly on the floor. It was worth several million pounds. Standing there on the plate floor, I leaned on the plate wall and searched my wits for some reason and understanding and consolation-in-adversity. I understood little except that my plans were vanquished and my visit to eternity unavailing and calamitous. I wiped a hand on my damp brow and stared blankly at the two policemen, who were now smiling and looking knowledgeable and compla- cent. A large emotion came swelling against my throat and filling my mind with great sorrow and a sadness more remote and desolate than a great strand at evening with the sea far away at its distant turn. Looking down with a bent head at my broken shoes, I saw them swim and dissolve in big tears that came bursting on my eyes. I turned to the wall and gave loud choking sobs and broke down completely and cried loudly like a baby. I do not know how long I was crying. I think I heard the two policemen discussing me in sympathetic undertones as if they were trained doctors in a hospital. Without lifting my head I looked across the floor and saw MacCruiskeen's legs walking away with my bag. Then I heard an oven door being opened and the bag fired roughly in. Here I cried loudly again, turning to the wall of the lift and giving complete rein to my great misery.

At last I was taken gently by the shoulders, weighed and guided into the lift. Then I felt the two large policemen crowding in beside me and got the heavy smell of blue official broadcloth impregnated through and through with their humanity. As the floor of the lift began to resist my feet, I felt a piece of crisp paper rustling against my averted face. Looking up in the poor light I saw that MacCruiskeen was stretching his hand in my direction dumbly and meekly across the chest of the Sergeant who was standing tall and still beside me. In the hand was a small white paper bag. I glanced into it and saw round coloured things the size of florins.

'Creams,' MacCruiskeen said kindly.

He shook the bag encouragingly and started to chew and suck loudly as if there was almost supernatural pleasure to be had from these sweetmeats. Beginning for some reason to sob again, I put my hand into the bag but when I took a sweet, three or four others which had merged with it in the heat of the policeman's pocket came out with it in one sticky mass of plaster. Awkwardly and foolishly I tried to disentangle them but failed completely and then rammed the lot into my mouth and stood there sobbing and sucking and snuffling. I heard the Sergeant sighing heavily and could feel his broad flank receding as he sighed.

'Lord, I love sweets,' he murmured.

'Have one,' MacCruiskeen smiled, rattling his bag.

'What are you saying, man,' the Sergeant cried, turning to view MacCruiskeen's face, 'are you out of your mind, man alive? If I took one of these – not one but half of a corner of the quarter of one of them – I declare to the Hokey that my stomach would blow up like a live landmine and I would be galvanized in my bed for a full fortnight roaring out profanity from terrible stoons of indigestion and heartscalds. Do you want to kill me, man?'

'Sugar barley is a very smooth sweet,' MacCruiskeen said, speaking awkwardly with his bulging mouth. 'They give it to babies and it is a winner for the bowels.'

'If I ate sweets at all,' the Sergeant said, 'I would live on the "Carnival Assorted". Now *there* is a sweet for you. There is great sucking in them, the flavour is very spiritual and one of them is good for half an hour.'

'Did you ever try Liquorice Pennies?' asked MacCruiskeen.

'Not them but the "Fourpenny Coffee-Cream Mixture" have a great charm.'

'Or the Dolly Mixture?'

'No.'

'They say,' MacCruiskeen said, 'that the Dolly Mixture is the best that was ever made and that it will never be surpassed and indeed I could eat them and keep eating till I got sick.'

'That may be,' the Sergeant said, 'but if I had my health I would give you a good run for it with the Carnival Mixture.'

As they wrangled on about sweets and passed to chocolate bars and sticks of rock, the floor was pressing strongly from underneath. Then there was a change in the pressing, two clicks were heard and the Sergeant started to undo the doors, explaining to MacCruiskeen his outlook on Ju-jubes and jelly-sweets and Turkish Delights.

With sloped shoulders and a face that was stiff from my dried tears, I stepped wearily out of the lift into the little stone room and waited till they had checked the clocks. Then I followed them into the thick bushes and kept behind them as they met the attacks of the branches and fought back. I did not care much.

It was not until we emerged, breathless and with bleeding hands, on the green margin of the main road that I realized that a strange thing had happened. It was two or three hours since the Sergeant and I had started on our journey yet the country and the trees and all the voices of every thing around still wore an air of early morning. There was incommunicable earliness in everything, a sense of waking and beginning. Nothing had yet grown or matured and nothing begun had yet finished. A bird singing had not yet turned finally the last twist of tunefulness. A rabbit emerging still had a hidden tail.

The Sergeant stood monumentally in the middle of the hard grey road and picked some small green things delicately from his person. MacCruiskeen stood stooped in knee-high grass looking over his person and shaking himself sharply like a hen. I stood myself looking wearily into the bright sky and wondering over the wonders of the high morning.

When the Sergeant was ready he made a polite sign with his thumb and the two of us set off together in the direction of the barrack. MacCruiskeen was behind but he soon appeared silently in front of us, sitting without a move on the top of his quiet bicycle. He said nothing as he passed us and stirred no breath or limb and he rolled away from us down the gentle hill till a bend received him silently.

As I walked with the Sergeant I did not notice where we were or what we passed by on the road, men, beasts or houses. My brain was like an ivy near where swallows fly. Thoughts were darting around me like a sky that was loud and dark with birds but none came into me or near enough. Forever in my ear was the click of heavy shutting doors, the whine of boughs trailing their loose leaves in a swift springing and the clang of hobnails on metal plates.

When I reached the barrack I paid no attention to anything or anybody but went straight to a bed and lay on it and fell into a full and simple sleep. Compared with this sleep, death is a restive thing, peace is a clamour and darkness a burst of light.

Chapter 9

I was awakened the following morning by sounds of loud hammering[1] outside the window and found myself immediately recalling – the recollection was an absurd paradox – that I had been in the next world yesterday. Lying there half awake, it is not unnatural that my thoughts should turn to de Selby. Like all the greater thinkers, he has been looked to for guidance on many of the major perplexities of existence. The commentators, it is to be feared, have not succeeded in extracting from the vast store-house of his writings any consistent, cohesive or comprehensive corpus of spiritual belief and praxis. Nevertheless, his ideas of paradise are not

[1] Le Clerque (in his almost forgotten *Extensions and Analyses*) has drawn attention to the importance of percussion in the de Selby dialectic and shown that most of the physicist's experiments were extremely noisy. Unfortunately the hammering was always done behind locked doors and no commentator has hazarded even a guess as to what was being hammered and for what purpose. Even when constructing the famous water-box, probably the most delicate and fragile instrument ever made by human hands, de Selby is known to have smashed three heavy coal-hammers and was involved in undignified legal proceedings with his landlord (the notorious Porter) arising from an allegation of strained floor-joists and damage to a ceiling. It is clear that he attached considerable importance to 'hammerwork'. (v. *Golden Hours*, p. 48–9). In *The Layman's Atlas* he publishes a rather obscure account of his inquiries into the nature of hammering and boldly attributes the sharp sound of percussion to the bursting of 'atmosphere balls' evidently envisaging the air as being composed of minute balloons, a view scarcely confirmed by later scientific research. In his disquisitions elsewhere on the nature of night and darkness, he refers in passing to the straining of 'air-skins', *al.* 'air-balls' and 'bladders'. His conclusion was that 'hammering is anything but what it appears to be'; such a statement, if not open to explicit refutation, seems unnecessary and unenlightening.

Hatchjaw has put forward the suggestion that loud hammering was a device resorted to by the savant to drown other noises which might give some indication of the real trend of the experiments. Bassett has concurred in this view, with, however, two reservations.

149

without interest. Apart from the contents of the famous de Selby 'Codex',[2] the main references are to be found in the *Rural Atlas* and in the so-called 'substantive' appendices to

[2] The reader will be familiar with the storms which have raged over this most tantalizing of holograph survivals. The 'Codex' (first so-called by Bassett in his monumental *De Selby Compendium*) is a collection of some two thousand sheets of foolscap closely hand-written on both sides. The signal distinction of the manuscript is that not one word of the writing is legible. Attempts made by different commentators to decipher certain passages which look less formidable than others have been characterized by fantastic divergencies, not in the meaning of the passages (of which there is no question) but in the brand of nonsense which is evolved. One passage, described by Bassett as being 'a penetrating treatise on old age' is referred to by Henderson (biographer of Bassett) as 'a not unbeautiful description of lambing operations on an unspecified farm'. Such disagreement, it must be confessed, does little to enhance the reputation of either writer.

Hatchjaw, probably displaying more astuteness than scholastic acumen, again advances his forgery theory and professes amazement that any person of intelligence could be deluded by 'so crude an imposition'. A curious contretemps arose when, challenged by Bassett to substantiate this cavalier pronouncement, Hatchjaw casually mentioned that eleven pages of the 'Codex' were all numbered '88'. Bassett, evidently taken by surprise, performed an independent check and could discover no page at all bearing this number. Subsequent wrangling disclosed the startling fact that both commentators claimed to have in their personal possession the 'only genuine Codex'. Before this dispute could be cleared up, there was a further bombshell, this time from far-off Hamburg. The Norddeutsche Verlag published a book by the shadowy Kraus purporting to be an elaborate exegesis based on an authentic copy of the 'Codex' with a transliteration of what was described as the obscure code in which the document was written. If Kraus can be believed, the portentously-named 'Codex' is simply a collection of extremely puerile maxims on love, life, mathematics and the like, couched in poor ungrammatical English and entirely lacking de Selby's characteristic reconditeness and obscurity. Bassett and many of the other commentators, regarding this extraordinary book as merely another manifestation of the mordant du Garbandier's spleen, pretended never to have heard of it notwithstanding the fact that Bassett is known to have obtained, presumably by questionable means, a proof of the work many months before it appeared. Hatchjaw alone did not ignore the book. Remarking dryly in a newspaper article that Kraus's 'aberration' was due to a foreigner's confusion of the two English words code and codex, declared his intention of publishing 'a brief brochure' which would effectively discredit the German's work and all similar 'trumpery frauds'. The failure of this work to appear is popularly attributed to Kraus's machinations in Hamburg and lengthy sessions on the transcontinental wire. In any event, the wretched Hatchjaw was again arrested, this time at the suit of his own publishers who accused him of the larceny of some of the firm's desk fittings. The case was adjourned and subsequently struck out owing to the failure to appear of certain unnamed witnesses from abroad. Clear as it is

the *Country Album*. Briefly he indicates that the happy state is 'not unassociated with water' and that 'water is rarely absent from any wholly satisfactory situation'. He does not give any closer definition of this hydraulic elysium but mentions that he has written more fully on the subject elsewhere.[3] It is not clear, unfortunately, whether the reader is expected to infer that a wet day is more enjoyable than a dry one or that a lengthy course of baths is a reliable method of achieving peace of mind. He praises the equilibrium of water, its circumambiency, equiponderance and equitableness, and declares that water, 'if not abused'[4] can achieve 'absolute superiority.' For the rest, little remains save the record of his obscure and unwitnessed experiments. The story is one of a long succession of prosecutions for water

footnote continued

that this fantastic charge was without a vestige of foundation, Hatchjaw failed to obtain any redress from the authorities.

It cannot be pretended that the position regarding this 'Codex' is at all satisfactory and it is not likely that time or research will throw any fresh light on a document which cannot be read and of which four copies at least, all equally meaningless, exist in the name of being the genuine original.

An amusing diversion in this affair was unwittingly caused by the mild Le Clerque. Hearing of the 'Codex' some months before Bassett's authoritative 'Compendium' was published, he pretended to have read the 'Codex' and in an article in the *Zuercher Tageblatt* made many vague comments on it, referring to its 'shrewdness', 'compelling if novel arguments', 'fresh viewpoint', etc. Subsequently he repudiated the article and asked Hatchjaw in a private letter to denounce it as a forgery. Hatchjaw's reply is not extant but it is thought that he refused with some warmth to be party to any further hanky-panky in connection with the ill-starred 'Codex'. It is perhaps unnecessary to refer to du Garbandier's contribution to this question. He contented himself with an article in *l'Avenir* in which he professed to have decyphered the 'Codex' and found it to be a repository of obscene conundrums, accounts of amorous adventures and erotic speculation, 'all too lamentable to be repeated even in broad outline.'

[3] Thought to be a reference to the 'Codex'.

[4] Naturally, no explanation is given of what is meant by 'abusing' water but it is noteworthy that the savant spent several months trying to discover a satisfactory method of 'diluting' water, holding that it was 'too strong' for many of the novel uses to which he desired to put it. Bassett suggests that the de Selby Water Box was invented for this purpose although he cannot explain how the delicate machinery is set in motion. So many fantastic duties have assigned to this inscrutable mechanism (witness Kraus's absurd sausage theory) that Bassett's speculation must not be allowed the undue weight which his authoritative standing would tend to lend it.

wastage at the suit of the local authority. At one hearing it was shown that he had used 9,000 gallons in one day and on another occasion almost 80,000 gallons in the course of a week. The word 'used' in this context is the important one. The local officials, having checked the volume of water entering the house daily from the street connection, had sufficient curiosity to watch the outlet sewer and made the astonishing discovery that *none of the vast quantity of water drawn in ever left the house.* The commentators have seized avidly on this statistic but are, as usual, divided in their interpretations. In Bassett's view the water was treated in the patent water-box and diluted to a degree that made it invisible – in the guise of water, at all events – to the untutored watchers at the sewer. Hatchjaw's theory in this regard is more acceptable. He tends to the view that the water was boiled and converted, probably through the water-box, into tiny jets of steam which were projected through an upper window into the night in an endeavour to wash the black 'volcanic' stains from the 'skins' or 'air-bladders' of the atmosphere and thus dissipate the hated and 'insanitary' night. However far-fetched this theory may appear, unexpected colour is lent to it by a previous court case when the physicist was fined forty shillings. On this occasion, some two years before the construction of the water-box, de Selby was charged with playing a fire hose out of one of the upper windows of his house at night, an operation which resulted in several passers-by being drenched to the skin. On another occasion[5] he had to face the curious charge of hoarding

[5] Almost all of the numerous petty litigations in which de Selby was involved afford a salutary example of the humiliations which great minds may suffer when forced to have contact with the pedestrian intellects of the unperceiving laity. On one of the water-wastage hearings the Bench permitted itself a fatuous inquiry as to why the defendant did not avail himself of the metered industrial rate 'if bathing is to be persisted in so immoderately'. It was on this occasion that de Selby made the famous retort that 'one does not readily accept the view that paradise is limited by the capacity of a municipal waterworks or human happiness by water-meters manufactured by unemancipated labour in Holland.' It is some consolation to recall that the forcible medical examination which followed was characterized by an enlightenment which redounds to this day to the credit of the medical profession. De Selby's discharge was unconditional and absolute.

water, the police testifying that every vessel in his house, from the bath down to a set of three ornamental egg-cups, was brimming with the liquid. Again a trumped-up charge of attempted suicide was preferred merely because the savant had accidentally half-drowned himself in a quest for some vital statistic of celestial aquatics.

It is clear from contemporary newspapers that his inquiries into water were accompanied by persecutions and legal pin-prickings unparalleled since the days of Galileo. It may be some consolation to the minions responsible to know that their brutish and barbaric machinations succeeded in denying posterity a clear record of the import of these experiments and perhaps a primer of esoteric water science that would banish much of our worldly pain and unhappiness. Virtually all that remains of de Selby's work in this regard is his house where his countless taps[6] are still as he left them, though a newer generation of more delicate mind has had the water turned off at the main.

Water? The word was in my ear as well as in my brain. Rain was beginning to beat on the windows, not a soft or friendly rain but large angry drops which came spluttering with great force upon the glass. The sky was grey and stormy and out of it I heard the harsh shouts of wild geese and ducks labouring across the wind on their coarse pinions. Black quails called sharply from their hidings and a swollen stream was babbling dementedly. Trees, I knew, would be angular and ill-tempered in the rain and boulders would gleam coldly at the eye.

I would have sought sleep again without delay were it not

---

[6] Hatchjaw (in his invaluable *Conspectus of the de Selby Dialectic*) has described the house as 'the most water-piped edifice in the world.' Even in the living-rooms there were upwards of ten rough farmyard taps, some with zinc troughs and some (as those projecting from the ceiling and from converted gas-brackets near the fireplace) directed at the unprotected floor. Even on the stairs a three-inch main may still be seen nailed along the rail of the balustrade with a tap at intervals of one foot, while under the stairs and in every conceivable hiding-place there were elaborate arrangements of cisterns and storage-tanks. Even the gas pipes were connected up with this water system and would gush strongly at any attempt to provide the light.

Du Garbandier in this connection has permitted himself some coarse and cynical observations bearing upon cattle lairages.

for the loud hammering outside. I arose and went on the cold floor to the window. Outside there was a man with sacks on his shoulders hammering at a wooden framework he was erecting in the barrack yard. He was red-faced and strong-armed and limped around his work with enormous stiff strides. His mouth was full of nails which bristled like steel fangs in the shadow of his moustache. He extracted them one by one as I watched and hammered them perfectly into the wet wood. He paused to test a beam with his great strength and accidentally let the hammer fall. He stooped awkwardly and picked it up.

Did you notice anything?

No.

The Hammer, man.

It looks an ordinary hammer. What about it?

You must be blind. It fell on his foot.

Yes?

And he didn't bat an eyelid. It might have been a feather for all the sign he gave.

Here I gave a sharp cry of perception and immediately threw up the sash of the window and leaned out into the inhospitable day, hailing the workman excitedly. He looked at me curiously and came over with a friendly frown of interrogation on his face.

'What is your name?' I asked him.

'O'Feersa, the middle brother,' he answered. 'Will you come out here,' he continued, 'and give me a hand with the wet carpentry?'

'Have you a wooden leg?'

For answer he dealt his left thigh a mighty blow with the hammer. It echoed hollowly in the rain. He cupped his hand clownishly at his ear as if listening intently to the noise he had made. Then he smiled.

'I am building a high scaffold here,' he said, 'and it is lame work where the ground is bumpy. I could find use for the assistance of a competent assistant.'

'Do you know Martin Finnucane?'

He raised his hand in a military salute and nodded.

'He is almost a relation,' he said, 'but not completely. He

is closely related to my cousin but they never married, never had the time.'

Here I knocked my own leg sharply on the wall.

'Did you hear that?' I asked him.

He gave a start and then shook my hand and looked brotherly and loyal, asking me was it the left or the right?

Scribble a note and send him for assistance. There is no time to lose.

I did so at once, asking Martin Finnucane to come and save me in the nick of time from being strangled to death on the scaffold and telling him he would have to hurry. I did not know whether he could come as he had promised he would but in my present danger anything was worth trying.

I saw Mr O'Feersa going quickly away through the mists and threading his path carefully through the sharp winds which were racing through the fields, his head down, sacks on his shoulders and resolution in his heart.

Then I went back to bed to try to forget my anxiety. I said a prayer that neither of the other brothers was out on the family bicycle because it would be wanted to bring my message quickly to the captain of the one-leggèd men. Then I felt a hope kindling fitfully within me and I fell asleep again.

Chapter 10

When I awoke again two thoughts came into my head so closely together that they seemed to be stuck to one another; I could not be sure which came first and it was hard to separate them and examine them singly. One was a happy thought about the weather, the sudden brightness of the day that had been vexed earlier. The other was suggesting to me that it was not the same day at all but a different one and maybe not even the next day after the angry one. I could not decide that question and did not try to. I lay back and took to my habit of gazing out of the window. Whichever day it was, it was a gentle day – mild, magical and innocent with great sailings of white cloud serene and impregnable in the high sky, moving along like kingly swans on quiet water. The sun was in the neighbourhood also, distributing his enchantment unobtrusively, colouring the sides of things that were unalive and livening the hearts of living things. The sky was a light blue without distance, neither near nor far. I could gaze at it, through it and beyond it and see still illimitably clearer and nearer the delicate lie of its nothingness. A bird sang a solo from nearby, a cunning blackbird in a dark hedge giving thanks in his native language. I listened and agreed with him completely.

Then other sounds came to me from the nearby kitchen. The policemen were up and about their incomprehensible tasks. A pair of their great boots would clump across the flags, pause and then clump back. The other pair would clump to another place, stay longer and clump back again with heavier falls as if a great weight were being carried. Then the four boots would clump together solidly far away to the front door and immediately would come the long slash of thrown-water on the road, a great bath of it flung in a lump to fall flat on the dry ground.

I arose and started to put on my clothes. Through the window I could see the scaffold of raw timber rearing itself high into the heavens, not as O'Feersa had left it to make his way methodically through the rain, but perfect and ready for its dark destiny. The sight did not make me cry or even sigh. I thought it was sad, too sad. Through the struts of the structure I could see the good country. There would be a fine view from the top of the scaffold on any day but on this day it would be lengthened out by five miles owing to the clearness of the air. To prevent my tears I began to give special attention to my dressing.

When I was nearly finished the Sergeant knocked very delicately at the door, came in with great courtesy and bade me good morning.

'I notice the other bed has been slept in,' I said for conversation. 'Was it yourself or MacCruiskeen?'

'That would likely be Policeman Fox. MacCruiskeen and I do not do our sleeping here at all, it is too expensive, we would be dead in a week if we played that game.'

'And where do you sleep then?'

'Down below – over there – beyant.'

He gave my eyes the right direction with his brown thumb. It was down the road to where the hidden left turn led to the heaven full of doors and ovens.

'And why?'

'To save our lifetimes, man. Down there you are as young coming out of a sleep as you are going into it and you don't fade when you are inside your sleep, you would not credit the time a suit or a boots will last you and you don't have to take your clothes off either. That's what charms Mac-Cruiskeen – that and the no shaving.' He laughed kindly at the thought of his comrade. 'A comical artist of a man,' he added.

'And Fox? Where does he live?'

'Beyant, I think.' He jerked again to the place that was to the left. 'He is down there beyant somewhere during the daytime but we have never seen him there, he might be in a distinctive portion of it that he found from a separate ceiling in a different house and indeed the unreasonable jumps of the lever-reading would put you in mind that there is unauthorized interference with the works. He is as crazy as bedamned, an incontestable character and a man of ungovernable inexactitudes.'

'Then why does he sleep here?' I was not at all pleased that this ghostly man had been in the same room with me during the night.

'To spend it and spin it out and not have all of it forever unused inside him.'

'All what?'

'His lifetime. He wants to get rid of as much as possible, undertime and overtime, as quickly as he can so that he can die as soon as possible. MacCruiskeen and I are wiser and we are not yet tired of being ourselves, we save it up. I think he has an opinion that there is a turn to the right down the road and likely that is what he is after, he thinks the best way to find it is to die and get all the leftness out of his blood. I do not believe there is a right-hand road and if there is it would surely take a dozen active men to look after the readings alone, night and morning. As you are perfectly aware the right is much more tricky than the left, you would be surprised at all the right pitfalls there are. We are only at the beginning of our knowledge of the right, there is nothing more deceptive to the unwary.'

'I did not know that.'

The Sergeant opened his eyes wide in surprise.

'Did you ever in your life,' he asked, 'mount a bicycle from the right?'

'I did not.'

'And why?'

'I do not know. I never thought about it.'

He laughed at me indulgently.

'It is nearly an insoluble pancake,' he smiled, 'a conundrum of inscrutable potentialities, a snorter.'

He led the way out of the bedroom to the kitchen where he had already arranged my steaming meal of stirabout and milk on the table. He pointed to it pleasantly, made a motion as if lifting a heavily-laden spoon to his mouth and then made succulent spitty sounds with his lips as if they were dealing with the tastiest of all known delicacies. Then he swallowed loudly and put his red hands in ecstasy to his stomach. I sat down and took up the spoon at this encouragement.

'And why is Fox crazy?' I inquired.

'I will tell you that much. In MacCruiskeen's room there is a little box on the mantelpiece. The story is that when MacCruiskeen was away one day that happened to fall on the 23rd of June inquiring about a bicycle, Fox went in and opened the box and looked into it from the strain of his unbearable curiosity. From that day to this . . .'

The Sergeant shook his head and tapped his forehead three times with his finger. Soft as porridge is I nearly choked at the sound his finger made. It was a booming hollow sound, slightly tinny, as if he had tapped an empty watering-can with his nail.

'And what was in the box?'

'That is easily told. A card made of cardboard about the size of a cigarette-card, no better and no thicker.'

'I see,' I said.

I did not see but I was sure that my easy unconcern would sting the Sergeant into an explanation. It came after a time when he had looked at me silently and strangely as I fed solidly at the table.

'It was the colour,' he said.

'The colour?'

'But then maybe it was not that at all,' he mused perplexedly.

I looked at him with a mild inquiry. He frowned thoughtfully and looked up at a corner of the ceiling as if he expected certain words he was searching for to be hanging there in coloured lights. No sooner had I thought of that than I glanced up myself, half expecting to see them there. But they were not.

'The card was not red,' he said at last doubtfully.

'Green?'

'Not green. No.'

'Then what colour?'

'It was not one of the colours a man carries inside his head like nothing he ever looked at with his eyes. It was . . . different. MacCruiskeen says it is not blue either and I believe him, a blue card would never make a man batty because what is blue is natural.'

'I saw colours often on eggs,' I observed, 'colours which have no names. Some birds lay eggs that are shaded in a way too delicate to be noticeable to any instrument but the eye, the tongue could not be troubled to find a noise for anything so nearly not-there. What I would call a green sort of complete white. Now would that be the colour?'

'I am certain it would not,' the Sergeant replied immediately, 'because if birds could lay eggs that would put men out of their wits, you would have no crops at all, nothing but scarecrows crowded in every field like a public meeting and thousands of them in their top hats standing together in knots on the hillsides. It would be a mad world completely, the people would be putting their bicycles upside down on the roads and pedalling them to make enough mechanical movement to frighten the birds out of the whole parish.' He passed a hand in consternation across his brow. 'It would be a very unnatural pancake,' he added.

I thought it was a poor subject for conversation, this new colour. Apparently its newness was new enough to blast a man's brain to imbecility by the surprise of it. That was enough to know and quite sufficient to be required to believe. I thought it was an unlikely story but not for gold or diamonds would I open that box in the bedroom and look into it.

The Sergeant had wrinkles of pleasant recollection at his eyes and mouth.

'Did you ever in your travels meet with Mr Andy Gara?' he asked me.

'No.'

'He is always laughing to himself, even in bed at night he laughs quietly and if he meets you on the road he will go into roars, it is a most enervating spectacle and very bad for nervous people. It all goes back to a certain day when

MacCruiskeen and I were making inquiries about a missing bicycle.'

'Yes?'

'It was a bicycle with a criss-cross frame,' the Sergeant explained, 'and I can tell you that it is not every day in the week that one like that is reported, it is a great rarity and indeed it is a privilege to be looking for a bicycle like that.'

'Andy Gara's bicycle?'

'Not Andy's. Andy was a sensible man at the time but a very curious man and when he had us gone he thought he would do a clever thing. He broke his way into the barrack here in open defiance of the law. He spent valuable hours boarding up the windows and making MacCruiskeen's room as dark as night time. Then he got busy with the box. He wanted to know what the inside of it felt like, even if it could not be looked at. When he put his hand in he let out a great laugh, you could swear he was very amused at something.'

'And what did it feel like?'

The Sergeant shrugged himself massively.

'MacCruiskeen says it is not smooth and not rough, not gritty and not velvety. It would be a mistake to think it is a cold feel like steel and another mistake to think it blankety. I thought it might be like the damp bread of an old poultice but no, MacCruiskeen says that would be a third mistake. And not like a bowl-full of dry withered peas, either. A contrary pancake surely, a fingerish atrocity but not without a queer charm all its own.'

'Not hens' piniony under-wing feeling?' I questioned keenly. The Sergeant shook his head abstractedly.

'But the criss-cross bicycle,' he said, 'it is no wonder it went astray. It was a very confused bicycle and was shared by a man called Barbery with his wife and if you ever laid your eye on big Mrs Barbery I would not require to explain this thing privately to you at all.'

He broke off his utterance in the middle of the last short word of it and stood peering with a wild eye at the table. I had finished eating and had pushed away my empty bowl.

Following quickly along the line of his stare, I saw a small piece of folded paper lying on the table where the bowl had been before I moved it. Giving a cry the Sergeant sprang forward with surpassing lightness and snatched the paper up. He took it to the window, opened it out and held it far away from him to allow for some disorder in his eye. His face was puzzled and pale and stared at the paper for many minutes. Then he looked out of the window fixedly, tossing the paper over at me. I picked it up and read the roughly printed message:

'ONE-LEGGED MEN ON THEIR WAY TO RESCUE PRISONER. MADE A CALCULATION ON TRACKS AND ESTIMATE NUMBER IS SEVEN. SUBMITTED PLEASE. — FOX.'

My heart began to pound madly inside me. Looking at the Sergeant I saw that he was still gazing wild-eyed into the middle of the day, which was situated at least five miles away, like a man trying to memorize forever the perfection of the lightly clouded sky and the brown and green and boulder-white of the peerless country. Down some lane of it that ran crookedly through the fields I could see inwardly my seven true brothers hurrying to save me in their lame walk, their stout sticks on the move together.

The Sergeant still kept his eye on the end of five miles away but moved slightly in his monumental standing. Then he spoke to me.

'I think,' he said, 'we will go out and have a look at it, it is a great thing to do what is necessary before it becomes essential and unavoidable.'

The sounds he put on these words were startling and too strange. Each word seemed to rest on a tiny cushion and was soft and far away from every other word. When he had stopped speaking there was a warm enchanted silence as if the last note of some music too fascinating almost for comprehension had receded and disappeared long before its absence was truly noticed. He then moved out of the house before me to the yard, I behind him spellbound with no thought of any kind in my head. Soon the two of us had mounted a ladder with staid unhurrying steps and found ourselves high beside the sailing gable of the barrack, the two of us on the lofty scaffold, I the victim and he my hangman. I looked blankly and carefully everywhere, seeing for a time no difference between any different things, inspecting methodically every corner of the same unchanging sameness. Nearby I could hear his voice murmuring again:

'It is a fine day in any case,' he was saying.

His words, now in the air and out of doors, had another warm breathless roundness in them as if his tongue was lined with furry burrs and they came lightly from him like a string of bubbles or like tiny things borne to me on thistledown in very gentle air. I went forward to a wooden railing and rested my weighty hands on it, feeling perfectly the breeze coming chillingly at their fine hairs. An idea came to me that the breezes high above the ground are separate from those which play on the same level as men's faces: here the air was newer and more unnatural, nearer the heavens and less laden with the influences of the earth. Up here I felt that every day would be the same always, serene and chilly, a band of wind isolating the earth of men from the far-from-understandable enormities of the girdling universe. Here on the stormiest autumn Monday there would be no wild leaves to brush on any face, no bees in the gusty wind. I sighed sadly.

'Strange enlightenments are vouchsafed,' I murmured, 'to those who seek the higher places.'

I do not know why I said this strange thing. My own words were also soft and light as if they had no breath to liven them. I heard the Sergeant working behind me with coarse ropes as if he were at the far end of a great hall instead of at my back and then I heard his voice coming back to me softly called across a fathomless valley:

'I heard of a man once,' he said, 'that had himself let up into the sky in a balloon to make observations, a man of great personal charm but a divil for reading books. They played out the rope till he was disappeared completely from all appearances, telescopes or no telescopes, and then they played out another ten miles of rope to make sure of first-class observations. When the time-limit for the observations was over they pulled down the balloon again but lo and behold there was no man in the basket and his dead body was never found afterwards lying dead or alive in any parish ever afterwards.'

Here I heard myself give a hollow laugh, standing there with a high head and my two hands still on the wooden rail.

'But they were clever enough to think of sending up the balloon again a fortnight later and when they brought it down the second time lo and behold the man was sitting in the basket without a feather out of him if any of my information can be believed at all.'

Here I gave some sound again, hearing my own voice as if I was a bystander at a public meeting where I was myself the main speaker. I had heard the Sergeant's words and understood them thoroughly but they were no more significant than the clear sounds that infest the air at all times – the far cry of gulls, the disturbance a breeze will make in its blowing and water falling headlong down a hill. Down into the earth where dead men go I would go soon and maybe come out of it again in some healthy way, free and innocent of all human perplexity. I would perhaps be the chill of an April wind, an essential part of some indomitable river or be personally concerned in the ageless perfection of some rank mountain bearing down upon the mind by occupying forever a position in the blue easy distance. Or perhaps a smaller thing like movement in the grass on an unbearable breathless yellow day, some hidden creature going about its business – I might well be responsible for that or for some important part of it. Or even those unaccountable distinctions that make an evening recognizable from its own morning, the smells and sounds and sights of the perfected and matured essences of the day, these might not be innocent of my meddling and my abiding presence.

'So they asked where he was and what had kept him but he gave them no satisfaction, he only let out a laugh like one that Andy Gara would give and went home and shut himself up in his house and told his mother to say he was not at home and not receiving visitors or doing any entertaining. That made the people very angry and inflamed their passions to a degree that is not recognized by the law. So they held a private meeting that was attended by every member of the general public except the man in question and they decided to get out their shotguns the next day and break into the man's house and give him a severe threatening and tie him up and heat pokers in the fire to make him tell what happened in the sky the time he was up inside it. That is a nice piece of law and order for you, a terrific indictment of democratic self-government, a beautiful commentary on Home Rule.'

Or perhaps I would be an influence that prevails in water, something sea-borne and far away, some certain arrangement of sun, light and water unknown and unbeheld, something far-from-usual. There are in the great world whirls of fluid and vaporous existences obtaining in their own unpassing time, unwatched and uninterpreted, valid only in their essential un-understandable mystery, justified only in their eyeless and mindless immeasurability, unassailable in their actual abstraction; of the inner quality of such a thing I might well in my own time be the true quintessential pith. I might belong to a lonely shore or be the agony of the sea when it bursts upon it in despair.

'But between that and the next morning there was a stormy night in between, a loud windy night that strained the trees in their deep roots and made the roads streaky with broken branches, a night that played a bad game with root-crops. When the boys reached the home of the balloon-man the next morning, lo and behold the bed was empty and no trace of him was ever found afterwards dead or alive, naked or with an overcoat. And when they got back to where the balloon was, they found the wind had torn it up out of the ground with the rope spinning loosely in the windlass and it invisible to the naked eye in the middle of the clouds. They pulled in eight miles of rope before they got it down but lo and behold the basket was empty again. They all said that the man had gone up in it and stayed up but it is an insoluble conundrum, his name was Quigley and he was by all accounts a Fermanagh man.'

Parts of this conversation came to me from different parts of the compass as the Sergeant moved about at his tasks, now right, now left and now aloft on a ladder to fix the hang-rope on the summit of the scaffold. He seemed to dominate the half of the world that was behind my back with his presence – his movements and his noises – filling it up with himself to the last farthest corner. The other half of the world which lay in front of me was beautifully given a shape of sharpness or roundness that was faultlessly suitable to its nature. But the half behind me was black and evil and composed of nothing at all except the menacing policeman who was patiently and politely arranging the mechanics of my death. His work was now nearly finished and my eyes were faltering as they gazed ahead, making little sense of the distance and taking a smaller pleasure in what was near.

There is not much that I can say.

No.

Except to advise a brave front and a spirit of heroic resignation.

That will not be difficult. I feel too weak to stand up without support.

In a way that is fortunate. One hates a scene. It makes things more difficult for all concerned. A man who takes into consideration the feelings of others even when arranging the manner of his own death shows a nobility of character which compels the admiration of all classes. To quote a well-known poet, 'even the ranks of Tuscany could scarce forbear to cheer'. Besides, unconcern in the face of death is in itself the most impressive gesture of defiance.

I told you I haven't got the strength to make a scene.

Very good. We will say no more about it.

A creaking sound came behind me as if the Sergeant was swinging red-faced in mid-air to test the rope he had just fixed. Then came the clatter of his great hobs as they came again upon the boards of the platform. A rope which would stand his enormous weight would never miraculously give way with mine.

You know, of course, that I will be leaving you soon?

That is the usual arrangement.

I would not like to go without placing on record my pleasure in having been associated with you. It is no lie to say that I have always received the greatest courtesy and consideration at your hands. I can only regret that it is not practicable to offer you some small token of my appreciation.

Thank you. I am very sorry also that we must part after having been so long together. If that watch of mine were found you would be welcome to it if you could find some means of taking it.

But you have no watch.

I forgot that.

Thank you all the same. You have no idea where you are going . . . when all this is over?

No, none.

Nor have I. I do not know, or do not remember, what happens to the like of me in these circumstances. Sometimes I think that perhaps I might become part of . . . the world, if you understand me?

I know.

I mean – the wind, you know. Part of that. Or the spirit of the scenery in some beautiful place like the Lakes of Killarney, the inside meaning of it if you understand me.

I do.

Or perhaps something to do with the sea. 'The light that never was on sea or land, the peasant's hope and the poet's dream.' A big wave in mid-ocean, for instance, it is a very lonely and spiritual thing. Part of that.

I understand you.

Or the smell of a flower, even.

Here from my throat bounded a sharp cry rising to a scream. The Sergeant had come behind me with no noise and fastened his big hand into a hard ring on my arm, started to drag me gently but relentlessly away from where I was to the middle of the platform where I knew there was a trapdoor which could be collapsed with machinery.

Steady now!

My two eyes, dancing madly in my head, raced up and down the country like two hares in a last wild experience of the world I was about to leave for ever. But in their hurry and trepidation they did not fail to notice a movement that was drawing attention to itself in the stillness of everything far far down the road.

'The one-leggèd men!' I shouted.

I know that the Sergeant behind me had also seen that the far part of the road was occupied for his grip, though still unbroken, had stopped pulling at me and I could almost sense his keen stare running out into the day parallel with my own but gradually nearing it till the two converged a quarter of a mile away. We did not seem to breathe or be alive at all as we watched the movement approaching and becoming clearer.

'MacCruiskeen, by the Powers!' the Sergeant said softly.

My lifted heart subsided painfully. Every hangman has an assistant. MacCruiskeen's arrival would make the certainty of my destruction only twice surer.

When he came nearer we could see that he was in a great hurry and that he was travelling on his bicycle. He was lying almost prostrate on top of it with his rear slightly higher than his head to cut a passage through the wind and no eye could travel quickly enough to understand the speed of his flying legs as they thrashed the bicycle onwards in a savage fury. Twenty yards away from the barrack he threw up his head, showing his face for the first time, and saw us standing on the top of the scaffold engaged in watching him with all our attention. He leaped from the bicycle in some complicated leap which was concluded only when the bicycle had been spun round adroitly to form a seat for him with its bar while he stood there, wide-legged and diminutive, looking up at us and cupping his hands at his mouth to shout his breathless message upwards:

'The lever – nine point six nine!' he called.

For the first time I had the courage to turn my head to the Sergeant. His face had gone instantly to the colour of ash as if every drop of blood had left it, leaving it with empty pouches and ugly loosenesses and laxities all about it. His lower jaw hung loosely also as if it were a mechanical jaw on a toy man. I could feel the purpose and the life running out of his gripping hand like air out of a burst bladder. He spoke without looking at me.

'Let you stay here till I come back reciprocally,' he said.

For a man of his weight he left me standing there alone with a speed that was astonishing. With one jump he was at the ladder. Coiling his arms and legs around it, he slid to the ground out of view with a hurry that was not different in any way from an ordinary fall. In the next second he was seated on the bar of MacCruiskeen's bicycle and the two of them were disappearing into the end of a quarter of a mile away.

When they had gone an unearthly weariness came down upon me so suddenly that I almost fell in a heap on the platform. I called together all my strength and made my way inch by inch down the ladder and back into the kitchen of the barrack and collapsed helplessly into a chair that was near the fire. I wondered at the strength of the chair for my body seemed now to be made of lead. My arms and legs were too heavy to move from where they had fallen and my eyelids could not be lifted higher than would admit through them a small glint from the red fire.

For a time I did not sleep, yet I was far from being awake. I did not mark the time that passed or think about any question in my head. I did not feel the ageing of the day or the declining of the fire or even the slow return of my strength. Devils or fairies or even bicycles could have danced before me on the stone floor without perplexing me or altering by one whit my fallen attitude in the chair. I am sure I was nearly dead.

But when I did come to think again I knew that a long time had passed, that the fire was nearly out and that MacCruiskeen had just come into the kitchen with his bicycle and wheeled it hastily into his bedroom, coming out again without it and looking down at me.

'What has happened?' I whispered listlessly.

'We were just in time with the lever,' he replied, 'it took our combined strengths and three pages of calculations and rough-work but we got the reading down in the nick of zero-hour, you would be surprised at the coarseness of the lumps and the weight of the great fall.'

'Where is the Sergeant?'

'He instructed me to ask your kind pardon for his delays. He is lying in ambush with eight deputies that were sworn in as constables on the spot to defend law and order in the public interest. But they cannot do much, they are outnumbered and they are bound to be outflanked into the same bargain.'

'Is it for the one-leggèd men he is waiting?'

'Surely yes. But they took a great rise out of Fox. He is certain to get a severe reprimand from headquarters over the head of it. There is not seven of them but fourteen. They took off their wooden legs before they marched and tied themselves together in pairs so that there were two men for every two legs, it would remind you of Napoleon on the retreat from Russia, it is a masterpiece of military technocratics.'

This news did more to revive me than would a burning drink of finest brandy. I sat up. The light appeared once more in my eyes.

'Then they will win against the Sergeant and his policemen?' I asked eagerly.

MacCruiskeen gave a smile of mystery, took large keys from his pocket and left the kitchen. I could hear him opening the cell where the Sergeant kept his bicycle. He reappeared almost at once carrying a large can with a bung in it such as painters use when they are distempering a house. He had not removed his sly smile in his absence but now wore it more deeply in his face. He took the can into his bedroom and came out again with a large handkerchief in his hand and his smile still in use. Without a word he came behind my chair and bound the handkerchief tightly across my eyes, paying no attention to my movements and my surprise. Out of my darkness I heard his voice:

'I do not think the hoppy men will best the Sergeant,' he said, 'because if they come to where the Sergeant lies in secret ambush with his men before I have time to get back

there, the Sergeant will delay them with military man-
oeuvres and false alarms until I arrive down the road on my
bicycle. Even now the Sergeant and his men are all blindfolded like yourself, it is a very queer way for people to be
when they are lying in an ambush but it is the only way to
be when I am expected at any moment on my bicycle.'

I muttered that I did not understand what he had said.

'I have a private patent in that box in my bedroom,' he
explained, 'and I have more of it in that can. I am going to
paint my bicycle and ride it down the road in full view of
the hoppy lads.'

He had been going away from me in my darkness while
saying this and now he was in his bedroom and had shut
the door. Soft sounds of work came to me from where he
was.

I sat there for half an hour, still weak, bereft of light and
feebly wondering for the first time about making my escape.
I must have come back sufficiently from death to enter a
healthy tiredness again for I did not hear the policeman
coming out of the bedroom again and crossing the kitchen
with his unbeholdable and brain-destroying bicycle. I must
have slept there fitfully in my chair, my own private darkness reigning restfully behind the darkness of the
handkerchief.

Chapter 11

It is an unusual experience to waken restfully and slowly, to let the brain climb lazily out of a deep sleep and shake itself and yet have no encounter with the light to guarantee that the sleep is really over. When I awoke I first thought of that, then the scare of blindness came upon me and finally my hand joyously found MacCruiskeen's handkerchief. I tore it off and gazed around. I was still splayed stiffly in my chair. The barrack seemed silent and deserted, the fire was out and the evening sky had the tones of five o'clock. Nests of shadow had already gathered in the corners of the kitchen and in under the table.

Feeling stronger and fresher, I stretched forth my legs and braced my arms with exertions of deep chesty strength. I reflected briefly on the immeasurable boon of sleep, more particularly on my own gift of sleeping opportunely. Several times I had gone asleep when my brain could no longer bear the situations it was faced with. This was the opposite of a weakness which haunted no less a man than de Selby. He, for all his greatness, frequently fell asleep for no apparent reason in the middle of everyday life, often even in the middle of a sentence.[1]

---

[1] Le Fournier, the conservative French commentator (in his *De Selby – Dieu ou Homme?*) has written exhaustively on the non-scientific aspects of de Selby's personality and has noticed several failings and weaknesses difficult to reconcile with his dignity and eminence as a physicist, ballistician, philosopher and psychologist. Though he did not recognize sleep as such, preferring to regard the phenomenon as a series of 'fits' and heart-attacks, his habit of falling asleep in public earned for him the enmity of several scientific brains of the inferior calibre. These sleeps took place when walking in crowded thoroughfares, at meals and on at least one occasion in a public lavatory. (Du Garbandier has given this latter incident malignant publicity in his pseudo-scientific 'redaction' of the police court

I arose and stretched my legs up and down the floor. From my chair by the fire I had noticed idly that the front wheel of a bicycle was protruding into view in the passage leading to the rear of the barrack. It was not until I sat down again on the chair after exercising for a quarter of an hour that I found myself staring at this wheel in some surprise. I could have sworn it had moved out farther in the interval because three-quarters of it was now visible whereas I could not see the hub the last time. Possibly it was an illusion due to an altered position between my two sittings but this was quite unlikely because the chair was small and would not permit of much variation of seat if there was any question of studying comfort. My surprise began to mount to astonishment.

I was on my feet again at once and had reached the passage in four long steps. A cry of amazement – now almost a habit with me – escaped from my lips as I looked around. MacCruiskeen in his haste had left the door of the cell wide open with the ring of keys hanging idly in the lock. In the back of the small cell was a collection of paint-cans, old ledgers, punctured bicycle tubes, tyre repair outfits and a mass of peculiar brass and leather articles not unlike ornamental horse harness but clearly intended for some wholly different office. The front of the cell was where my attention was. Leaning half-way across the lintel was the Sergeant's bicycle. Clearly it could not have been put there by Mac-Cruiskeen because he had returned instantly from the cell with his can of paint and his forgotten keys were proof that he had not gone back there before he rode away. During my

footnote continued

proceedings to which he added a virulent preface assailing the savant's moral character in terms which, however intemperate, admit of no ambiguity.) It is true that some of these sleeps occurred without warning at meetings of learned societies when the physicist had been asked to state his views on some abstruse problem but there is no inference, *pace* du Garbandier, that they were 'extremely opportune'.

Another of de Selby's weaknesses was his inability to distinguish between men and women. After the famous occasion when the Countess Schnapper had been presented to him (her *Glauben ueber Ueberalls* is still read) he made flattering references to 'that man', 'that cultured old gentleman', 'crafty old

absence in my sleep it is unlikely that any intruder would have come in merely to move the bicycle half-way out of where it was. On the other hand I could not help recalling what the Sergeant had told me about his fears for his bicycle and his decision to keep it in solitary confinement. If there

footnote continued

boy' and so on. The age, intellectual attainments and style of dress of the Countess would make this a pardonable error for anybody afflicted with poor sight but it is feared that the same cannot be said of other instances when young shop-girls, waitresses and the like were publicly addressed as 'boys'. In the few references which he ever made to his own mysterious family he called his mother 'a very distinguished gentleman' (*Lux Mundi* p. 307), 'a man of stern habits' (ibid, p. 308) and 'a man's man' (Kraus: *Briefe*, xvii). Du Garbandier (in his extraordinary *Histoire de Notre Temps*) has seized on this pathetic shortcoming to outstep, not the prudent limits of scientific commentary but all known horizons of human decency. Taking advantage of the laxity of French law in dealing with doubtful or obscene matter, he produced a pamphlet masquerading as a scientific treatise on sexual idiosyncracy in which de Selby is arraigned by name as the most abandoned of all human monsters.

Henderson and several lesser authorities on the Hatchjaw-Bassett school have taken the appearance of this regrettable document as the proximate cause of Hatchjaw's precipitate departure for Germany. It is now commonly accepted that Hatchjaw was convinced that the name 'du Garbandier' was merely a pseudonym adopted for his own ends by the shadowy Kraus. It will be recalled that Bassett took the opposite view, holding that Kraus was a name used by the mordant Frenchman for spreading his slanders in Germany. It may be observed that neither of these theories is directly supported by the writings of either commentator: du Garbandier is consistently virulent and defamatory while much of Kraus's work, blemished as it is by his inaccurate attainments in scholarship, is not at all unflattering to de Selby. Hatchjaw seems to take account of this discrepancy in his farewell letter to his friend Harold Barge (the last he is known to have written) when he states his conviction that Kraus was making a considerable fortune by publishing tepid refutations of du Garbandier's broadsides. This suggestion is not without colour because, as he points out, Kraus had extremely elaborate books on the market – some containing expensive plates – within an incredibly short time of the appearance of a poisonous volume under the name of du Garbandier. In such circumstances it is not easy to avoid the conclusion that both books were produced in collaboration if not written by the one hand. Certainly it is significant that the balance of the engagements between Kraus and du Garbandier was unfailingly to the disadvantage of de Selby.

Too much credit cannot be given to Hatchjaw for his immediate and heroic decision to go abroad 'to end once and for all a cancerous corruption which has become an intolerable affront to the decent instincts of humanity.' Bassett, in a note delivered at the quay-side at the moment of departure, wished Hatchjaw every success in his undertaking but deplored the fact

is good reason for locking a bicycle in a cell like a dangerous criminal, I reflected, it is fair enough to think that it will try to escape if given the opportunity. I did not quite believe this and I thought it was better to stop thinking about the mystery before I was compelled to believe it because if a

footnote continued

that he was in the wrong ship, a sly hint that he should direct his steps to Paris rather than to Hamburg. Hatchjaw's friend Harold Barge has left an interesting record of the last interview in the commentator's cabin. 'He seemed nervous and out of sorts, striding up and down the tiny floor of his apartment like a caged animal and consulting his watch at least once every five minutes. His conversation was erratic, fragmentary and unrelated to the subjects I was mentioning myself. His lean sunken face, imbued with unnatural pallor, was livened almost to the point of illumination by eyes which burned in his head with a sickly intensity. The rather old-fashioned clothes he wore were creased and dusty and bore every sign of having been worn and slept in for weeks. Any recent attempts which he had made at shaving or washing were clearly of the most perfunctory character; indeed, I recall looking with mixed feelings at the sealed port-hole. His disreputable appearance, however, did not detract from the nobility of his personality or the peculiar spiritual exaltation conferred on his features by his selfless determination to bring to a successful end the desperate task to which he had set his hand. After we had traversed certain light mathematical topics (not, alas, with any degree of dialectical elegance), a silence fell between us. Both of us, I am sure, had heard the last boat-train (run, as it happened, in two sections on this occasion) draw alongside and felt that the hour of separation could not be long delayed. I was searching in my mind for some inanity of a non-mathematical kind which I could utter to break the tension when he turned to me with a spontaneous and touching gesture of affection, putting a hand which quivered with emotion upon my shoulder. Speaking in a low unsteady voice, he said: "You realize, no doubt, that I am unlikely to return. In destroying the evil things which prevail abroad, I do not exclude my own person from the ambit of the cataclysm which will come and of which I have the components at this moment in my trunk. If I should leave the world the cleaner for my passing and do even a small service to that man whom I love, then I shall measure my joy by the extent to which no trace of either of us will be found after I have faced my adversary. I look to you to take charge of my papers and books and instruments, seeing that they are preserved for those who may come after us." I stammered some reply, taking his proffered hand warmly in my own. Soon I found myself stumbling on the quay again with eyes not innocent of emotion. Ever since that evening I have felt that there is something sacred and precious in my memory of that lone figure in the small shabby cabin, setting out alone and almost unarmed to pit his slender frame against the snake-like denizen of far-off Hamburg. It is a memory I will always carry with me proudly so long as one breath animates this humble temple.'

Barge, it is feared, was actuated more by kindly affection for Hatchjaw than for any concern for historical accuracy when he says that the latter

man is alone in a house with a bicycle which he thinks is edging its way along a wall he will run away from it in fright; and I was by now so occupied with the thought of my escape that I could not afford to be frightened of anything which could assist me.

footnote continued

was 'almost unarmed'. Probably no private traveller has ever gone abroad accompanied by a more formidable armoury and nowhere outside a museum has there been assembled a more varied or deadly collection of lethal engines. Apart from explosive chemicals and the unassembled components of several bombs, grenades and landmines, he had four army-pattern revolvers, two rook-rifles, angler's landing gear (!), a small machine-gun, several minor firing-irons and an unusual instrument resembling at once a pistol and a shotgun, evidently made to order by a skilled gunsmith and designed to take elephant ball. Wherever he hoped to corner the shadowy Kraus, it is clear that he intended that the 'cataclysm' should be widespread.

The reader who would seek a full account of the undignified fate which awaited the courageous crusader must have recourse to the page of history. Newspaper readers of the older generation will recall the sensational reports of his arrest for *impersonating himself*, being arraigned at the suit of a man called Olaf (var. Olafsohn) for obtaining credit in the name of a world-famous literary 'Gelehrter'. As was widely remarked at the time, nobody but either Kraus or du Garbandier could have engineered so malignant a destiny. (It is noteworthy that du Garbandier, in a reply to a suggestion of this kind made by the usually inoffensive Le Clerque, savagely denied all knowledge of Hatchjaw's whereabouts on the continent but made the peculiar statement that he had thought for many years that 'a similar impersonation' had been imposed on the gullible public at home many years before there was any question of 'a ridiculous adventure' abroad, implying apparently that Hatchjaw was not Hatchjaw at all but either another person of the same name or an impostor who had successfully maintained the pretence, in writing and otherwise, for forty years. Small profit can accrue from pursuing so peculiar a suggestion.) The facts of Hatchjaw's original incarceration are not now questioned by any variety of fates after being released. None of these can be regarded as verified fact and many are too absurd to be other than morbid conjecture. Mainly they are: (1) that he became a convert to the Jewish faith and entered the ministry of that persuasion; (2) that he had resort to petty crime and drug-peddling and spent much of his time in jail; (3) that he was responsible for the notorious 'Munich Letter' incident involving an attempt to use de Selby as the tool of international financial interests; (4) that he returned home in disguise with his reason shattered; and (5) that he was last heard of as a Hamburg brothel-keeper's nark or agent in the lawless dockland fastnesses of that maritime cosmopolis. The definitive work on this strange man's life is, of course, that of Henderson but the following will also repay study: Bassett's *Recollections*, Part vii; *The Man Who Sailed Away: A Memoir* by H. Barge; Le Clerque's Collected Works, Vol. III, pp. 118–287; Peachcroft's *Thoughts in a Library* and the Hamburg chapter in Goddard's *Great Towns*.

The bicycle itself seemed to have some peculiar quality of shape or personality which gave it distinction and importance far beyond that usually possessed by such machines. It was extremely well-kept with a pleasing lustre on its dark-green bars and oil-bath and a clean sparkle on the rustless spokes and rims. Resting before me like a tame domestic pony, it seemed unduly small and low in relation to the Sergeant yet when I measured its height against myself I found it was bigger than any other bicycle that I knew. This was possibly due to the perfect proportion of its parts which combined merely to create a thing of surpassing grace and elegance, transcending all standards of size and reality and existing only in the absolute validity of its own unexceptionable dimensions. Notwithstanding the sturdy cross-bar it seemed ineffably female and fastidious, posing there like a mannequin rather than leaning idly like a loafer against the wall, and resting on its prim flawless tyres with irreproachable precision, two tiny points of clean contact with the level floor. I passed my hand with unintended tenderness – sensuously, indeed – across the saddle. Inexplicably it reminded me of a human face, not by any simple resemblance of shape or feature but by some association of textures, some incomprehensible familiarity at the finger-tips. The leather was dark with maturity, hard with a noble hardness and scored with all the sharp lines and finer wrinkles which the years with their tribulations had carved into my own countenance. It was a gentle saddle yet calm and courageous, unembittered by its confinement and bearing no mark upon it save that of honourable suffering and honest duty. I knew that I liked this bicycle more than I had ever liked any other bicycle, better even than I had liked some people with two legs. I liked her unassuming competence, her docility, the simple dignity of her quiet way. She now seemed to rest beneath my friendly eyes like a tame fowl which will crouch submissively, awaiting with out-hunched wings the caressing hand. Her saddle seemed to spread invitingly into the most enchanting of all seats while her two handlebars, floating finely with the wild grace of alighting wings, beckoned to me to lend my mastery for free and joyful journeyings, the lightest of light running in the company of the swift groundwinds to safe havens far away, the whir of the true front wheel in my ear as it spun perfectly beneath my clear eye and the strong fine back wheel with unadmired industry raising gentle dust on the dry roads. How desirable her seat was, how charming the invitation of her slim encircling handle-arms, how unaccountably competent and reassuring her pump resting warmly against her rear thigh!

With a start I realized that I had been communing with this strange companion and – not only that – conspiring with her. Both of us were afraid of the same Sergeant, both were awaiting the punishments he would bring with him on his return, both were thinking that this was the last chance to escape beyond his reach; and both knew that the hope of each lay in the other, that we would not succeed unless we went together, assisting each other with sympathy and quiet love.

The long evening had made its way into the barrack through the windows, creating mysteries everywhere, erasing the seam between one thing and another, lengthening out the floors and either thinning the air or putting some refinement on my ear enabling me to hear for the first time the clicking of a cheap clock from the kitchen.

By now the battle would be over, Martin Finnucane and his one-leggèd men would be stumbling away into the hills with blinded eyes and crazy heads, chattering to each other poor broken words which nobody understood. The Sergeant would now be making his way inexorably through the twilight homewards, arranging in his head the true story of his day for my amusement before he hanged me. Perhaps MacCruiskeen would remain behind for the present, waiting for the blackest of the night's darkness by some old wall, a wrinkled cigarette in his mouth and his bicycle now draped with six or seven greatcoats. The deputies would also be going back to where they came from, still wondering why they had been blindfolded to prevent them seeing something wonderful – a miraculous victory with no fighting, nothing but a bicycle bell ringing madly and the screams of demented men mixing madly in their darkness.

In the next moment I was fumbling for the barrack latch with the Sergeant's willing bicycle in my care. We had travelled the passage and crossed the kitchen with the grace of ballet dancers, silent, swift and faultless in our movements, united in the acuteness of our conspiracy. In the country which awaited us outside we stood for a moment undecided, looking into the lowering night and inspecting the dull sameness of the gloom. It was to the left the Sergeant had gone with MacCruiskeen, to that quarter the next world lay and it was leftwards that all my troubles were. I led the bicycle to the middle of the road, turned her wheel resolutely to the right and swung myself into the centre of her saddle as she moved away eagerly under me in her own time.

How can I convey the perfection of my comfort on the bicycle, the completeness of my union with her, the sweet responses she gave me at every particle of her frame? I felt that I had known her for many years and that she had known me and that we understood each other utterly. She moved beneath me with agile sympathy in a swift, airy stride, finding smooth ways among the stony tracks, swaying and bending skilfully to match my changing attitudes, even accommodating her left pedal patiently to the awkward working of my wooden leg. I sighed and settled forward on her handlebars, counting with a happy heart the trees which stood remotely on the dark roadside, each telling me that I was further and further from the Sergeant.

I seemed to cut an unerring course between two sharp shafts of wind which whistled coldly past each ear, fanning my short side hairs. Other winds were moving about in the stillness of the evening, loitering in the trees and moving leaves and grasses to show that the green world was still present in the dark. Water by the roadside, always overshouted in the roistering day, now performed audibly in its hidings. Flying beetles came against me in their broad loops and circles, whirling blindly against my chest; overhead geese and heavy birds were calling in the middle of a journey. Aloft in the sky I could see the dim tracery of the stars struggling out here and there between the clouds. And all the time she was under me in a flawless racing onwards, touching the road with the lightest touches, surefooted, straight and faultless, each of her metal bars like spear-shafts superbly cast by angels.

A thickening of the right-hand night told me that we were approaching the mass of a large house by the road. When we were abreast of it and nearly past it, I recognized it. It was the house of old Mathers, not more than three miles from where my own house was. My heart bounded joyfully. Soon I would see my old friend Divney. We would stand in the bar drinking yellow whiskey, he smoking and listening and I telling him my strange story. If he found any part of it difficult to believe completely I would show him the Sergeant's bicycle. Then the next day we could both begin again to look for the black cashbox.

Some curiosity (or perhaps it was the sense of safety which comes to a man on his own hillside) made me stop pedalling and pull gently at the queenly brake. I had intended only to look back at the big house but by accident I had slowed the bicycle so much that she shuddered beneath me awkwardly, making a gallant effort to remain in motion. Feeling that I had been inconsiderate I jumped quickly from the saddle to relieve her. Then I took a few paces back along the road, eyeing the outline of the house and the shadows of its trees. The gate was open. It seemed a lonely place with no life or breath in it, a dead man's empty house spreading its desolation far into the surrounding night. Its trees swayed mournfully, gently. I could see the faint glinting of the glass in the big sightless windows and fainter, the sprawl of ivy at the room where the dead man used to sit. I eyed the house up and down, happy that I was near my own people. Suddenly my mind became clouded and confused. I had some memory of seeing the dead man's ghost while in the house searching for the box. It seemed a long time ago now and doubtless was the memory of a bad dream. I had killed Mathers with my spade. He was dead for a long time. My adventures had put a strain upon my mind.

I could not now remember clearly what had happened to me during the last few days. I recalled only that I was fleeing from two monstrous policemen and that I was now near my home. I did not just then try to remember anything else.

I had turned away to go when a feeling came upon me that the house had changed the instant my back was turned. This feeling was so strange and chilling that I stood rooted to the road for several seconds with my hands gripping the bars of the bicycle, wondering painfully whether I should turn my head and look or go resolutely forward on my way. I think I had made up my mind to go and had taken a few faltering steps forward when some influence came upon my eyes and dragged them round till they were again resting upon the house. They opened widely in surprise and once more my startled cry jumped out from me. A bright light was burning in a small window in the upper storey.

I stood watching it for a time, fascinated. There was no reason why the house should not be occupied or why a light should not be showing, no reason why the light should frighten me. It seemed to be the ordinary yellow light of an oil lamp and I had seen many stranger things than that – many stranger lights, also – in recent days. Nevertheless I could not persuade myself that there was anything the least usual in what my eyes were looking at. The light had some quality which was wrong, mysterious, alarming.

I must have stood there for a long time, watching the light and fingering the reassuring bars of the bicycle which would take me away swiftly at any time I chose to go. Gradually I took strength and courage from her and from other things which were lurking in my mind – the nearness of my own house, the nearer nearness of Courahans, Gillespies, Cavanaghs, and the two Murrays, and not further than a shout away the cottage of big Joe Siddery, the giant blacksmith. Perhaps whoever had the light may have found the black box and would yield it willingly to anyone who had suffered so much in search of it as I had. Perhaps it would be wise to knock and see.

I laid the bicycle gently against the gate-pier, took some string from my pocket and tied her loosely to the bars of the ironwork; then I walked nervously along the crunching gravel towards the gloom of the porch. I recalled the great thickness of the walls as my hand searched for the door in the pitch darkness at the rear of it. I found myself well into the hall before I realized that the door was swinging half-open, idly at the mercy of the wind. I felt a chill come upon me in this bleak open house and thought for a moment of returning to the bicycle. But I did not do so. I found the door and grasped the stiff metal knocker, sending three dull rumbling thuds through the house and out around the dark empty garden. No sound or movement answered me as I stood there in the middle of the silence listening to my heart. No feet came hurrying down the stairs, no door above opening with a flood of lamplight. Again I knocked on the hollow door, got no response and again thought of returning to the companionship of my friend who was at the gate. But again I did not do so. I moved farther into the hallway, searched for matches and struck one. The hall was empty with all doors leading from it closed; in a corner of it the wind had huddled a blowing of dead leaves and along the walls was the stain of bitter inblown rain. At the far end I could glimpse the white winding stairway. The match spluttered in my fingers and went out, leaving me again standing in the dark in indecision, again alone with my heart.

At last I summoned all my courage and made up my mind to search the upper storey and finish my business and get back to the bicycle as quickly as possible. I struck another match, held it high above my head and marched noisily to the stairs, mounting them with slow heavy footfalls. I remembered the house well from the night I had spent in it after spending hours searching it for the black box. On the top landing I paused to light another match and gave a loud call to give warning of my approach and awaken anybody who was asleep. The call, when it died away without reply, left me still more desolate and alone. I moved forward quickly and opened the door of the room nearest me, the room where I thought I once slept. The flickering match showed me that it was empty and had been long unoccupied. The bed was stripped of all its clothes, four chairs were locked together, two up-ended, in a corner and a white sheet was draped over a dressing-table. I slammed the door shut and paused to light another match, listening intently for any sign that I was watched. I heard nothing at all. Then I went along the passage throwing open the door of every room to the front of the house. They were all empty, deserted, with no light or sign of light in any of them. Afraid to stand still, I went quickly to all the other rooms, but found them all in the same way and ended by running down the stairs in growing fright and out of the front door. Here I stopped dead in my tracks. The light from the upper window was still streaming out and lying against the dark. The window seemed to be in the centre of the house. Feeling frightened, deluded, cold and bad-tempered I strode back into the hall, up the stairs and looked down the corridor where the doors of all the rooms to the front of the house were. I had left them all wide open on my first visit yet no light now came from any one of them. I walked the passage quickly to make sure that they had not been closed. They were all still open. I stood in the silence for three or four minutes barely breathing and making no sound, thinking that perhaps whatever was at work would make some move and show itself. But nothing happened, nothing at all.

I then walked into the room which seemed most in the centre of the house and made my way over to the window in the dark, guiding myself with my hands outstretched before me. What I saw from the window startled me painfully. The light was streaming from the window of the room next door on my right-hand side, lying thickly on the misty night air and playing on the dark-green leaves of a tree that stood nearby. I remained watching for a time, leaning weakly on the wall; then I moved backwards, keeping my eyes on the faintly-lighted tree-leaves, walking on my toes and making no sound. Soon I had my back to the rear wall, standing within a yard of the open door and the dim light on the tree still plainly visible to me. Then almost in one bound I was out into the passage and into the next room. I could not have spent more than one quarter of a second in that jump and yet I found the next room dusty and deserted with no life or light in it. Sweat was gathering on my brow, my heart was thumping loudly and the bare wooden floors seemed to tingle still with the echoing noises my feet had made. I moved to the window and looked out. The yellow light was still lying on the air and shining on the same tree-leaves but now it was streaming from the window of the room I had just left. I felt I was standing within three yards of something unspeakably inhuman and diabolical which was using its trick of light to lure me on to something still more horrible.

I stopped thinking, closing up my mind with a snap as if it were a box or a book. I had a plan in my head which seemed almost hopelessly difficult, very nearly beyond the extremity of human effort, desperate. It was simply to walk out of the room, down the stairs and out of the house on to the rough solid gravel, down the short drive and back to the company of my bicycle. Tied down there at the gate she seemed infinitely far away as if now in another world.

Certain that I would be assailed by some influence and prevented from reaching the hall door alive, I put my hands down with fists doubled at my sides, cast my eyes straight at my feet so that they should not look upon any terrible thing appearing in the dark, and walked steadily out of the room and down the black passage. I reached the stairs without mishap, reached the hall and then the door and soon found myself on the gravel feeling very much relieved and surprised. I walked down to the gate and out through it. She was resting where I had left her, leaning demurely against the stone pier; my hand told me that the string was unstrained, just as I had tied it. I passed my hands about her hungrily, knowing that she was still my accomplice in the plot of reaching home unharmed. Something made me turn my head again to the house behind me. The light was still burning peacefully in the same window, for all the world as if there was somebody in the room lying contentedly in bed reading a book. If I had given (or had been able to give) unrestricted rein to either fear or reason I should have turned my back forever on this evil house and rode away there and then upon the bicycle to the friendly home which was waiting for me beyond four bends of the passing road. But there was some other thing interfering with my mind. I could not take my eye from the lighted window and perhaps it was that I could resign myself to going home with no news about the black box so long as something was happening in the house where it was supposed to be. I stood there in the gloom, my hands gripping the handlebars of the bicycle and my great perplexity worrying me. I could not decide what was the best thing for me to do.

It was by accident that an idea came to me. I was shifting my feet as I often did to ease my bad left leg when I noticed that there was a large loose stone on the ground at my feet. I stooped and picked it up. It was about the size of a bicycle-lamp, smooth and round and easily fired. My heart had again become almost audible at the thought of hurling it through the lighted window and thus provoking to open action whoever was hiding in the house. If I stood by with the bicycle I could get away quickly. Having had the idea, I knew that I should have no contentment until the stone was fired; no rest would come to me until the unexplainable light had been explained.

I left the bicycle and went back up the drive with the stone swinging ponderously in my right hand. I paused under the window, looking up at the shaft of light. I could see some large insect flitting in and out of it. I felt my limbs weakening under me and my whole body becoming ill and faint with apprehension. I glanced at the nearby porch half expecting to glimpse some dreadful apparition watching me covertly from the shadows. I saw nothing but the impenetrable patch of deeper gloom. I then swung the stone a few times to and fro at the end of my straight arm and lobbed it strongly high into the air. There was a loud smash of glass, the dull thuds of the stone landing and rolling along the wooden floor and at the same time the tinkle of broken glass falling down upon the gravel at my feet. Without waiting at all I turned and fled at top speed down the drive until I had again reached and made contact with the bicycle.

Nothing happened for a time. Probably it was four or five seconds but it seemed an interminable delay of years. The whole upper half of the glass had been carried away, leaving jagged edges protruding about the sash; the light seemed to stream more clearly through the gaping hole. Suddenly a shadow appeared, blotting out the light on the whole left-hand side. The shadow was so incomplete that I could not recognize any part of it but I felt certain it was the shadow of a large being or presence who was standing quite still at the side of the window and gazing out into the night to see who had thrown the stone. Then it disappeared, making me realize for the first time what had happened and sending a new and deeper horror down upon me. The certain feeling that something else was going to happen made me afraid to make the smallest move lest I should reveal where I was standing with the bicycle.

The developments I expected were not long in coming. I was still gazing at the window when I heard soft sounds behind me. I did not look round. Soon I knew they were the footsteps of a very heavy person who was walking along the grass margin of the road to deaden his approach. Thinking he would pass without seeing me in the dark recess of the gateway, I tried to remain even more still than my original utter immobility. The steps suddenly clattered out on the roadway not six yards away, came up behind me and then stopped. It is no joke to say that my heart nearly stopped also. Every part of me that was behind me – neck, ears, back and head – shrank and quailed painfully before the presence confronting them, each expecting an onslaught of indescrib-able ferocity. Then I heard words.

'This is a brave night!'

I swung round in amazement. Before me, almost blocking out the night, was an enormous policeman. He looked a policeman from his great size but I could see the dim sign of his buttons suspended straight before my face, tracing out the curvature of his great chest. His face was completely hidden in the dark and nothing was clear to me except his overbearing policemanship, his massive rearing of wide strengthy flesh, his domination and his unimpeachable reality. He dwelt upon my mind so strongly that I felt many times more submissive than afraid. I eyed him weakly, my hand faltering about the bars of the bicycle. I was going to try to make my tongue give some hollow answer to his salutation when he spoke again, his words coming in thick friendly lumps from his hidden face.

'Will you follow after me till I have a conversation with you privately,' he said, 'if it was nothing else you have no light on your bicycle and I could take your name and address for the half of that.'

Before he had finished speaking he had eased off in the dark like a battleship, swinging his bulk ponderously away the same way as he had come. I found my feet obeying him without question, giving their six steps for every two of his, back along the road past the house. When we were about to pass it he turned sharply into a gap in the hedge and led the way into shrubberies and past the boles of dark forbidding trees, leading me to a mysterious fastness by the gable of the house where branches and tall growings filled the darkness and flanked us closely on both sides, reminding me of my journey to the underground heaven of Sergeant Pluck. In the presence of this man I had stopped wondering or even thinking. I watched the swaying outline of his back in the murk ahead of me and hurried after it as best I could. He said nothing and made no sound save that of the air labouring in his nostrils and the brushing strides of his boots on the grass-tangled ground, soft and rhythmical like a well-wielded scythe laying down a meadow in swaths.

He then turned sharply in towards the house and made for a small window which looked to me unusually low and near the ground. He flashed a torch on it, showing me as I peered from behind his black obstruction four panes of dirty glass set in two sashes. As he put his hand out to it I thought he was going to lift the lower sash up but instead of that he swung the whole window outwards on hidden hinges as if it were a door. Then he stooped his head, put out the light and began putting his immense body in through the tiny opening. I do not know how he accomplished what did not look possible at all. But he accomplished it quickly, giving no sound except a louder blowing from his nose and the groaning for a moment of a boot which had become wedged in some angle. Then he sent the torchlight back at me to show the way, revealing nothing of himself except his feet and the knees of his blue official trousers. When I was in, he leaned back an arm and pulled the window shut and then led the way ahead with his torch.

The dimensions of the place in which I found myself were most unusual. The ceiling seemed extraordinarily high while the floor was so narrow that it would not have been possible for me to pass the policeman ahead if I had desired to do so. He opened a tall door and, walking most awkwardly half-sideways, led the way along a passage still narrower. After passing through another tall door we began to mount an unbelievable square stairs. Each step seemed about a foot in depth, a foot in height and a foot wide. The policeman was walking up them fully sideways like a crab with his face turned still ahead towards the guidance of his torch. We went through another door at the top of the stairs and I found myself in a very surprising apartment. It was slightly wider than the other places and down the middle of it was a table about a foot in width, two yards in length and attached permanently to the floor by two metal legs. There was an oil-lamp on it, an assortment of pens and inks, a number of small boxes and file-covers and a tall jar of official gum. There were no chairs to be seen but all around the walls were niches where a man could sit. On the walls themselves were pinned many posters and notices dealing with bulls and dogs and regulations about sheep-dipping and school-going and breaches of the Firearms Act. With the figure of the policeman, who still had his back to me making an entry on some schedule on the far wall, I had no trouble in know-that I was standing in a tiny police station. I looked around again, taking everything in with astonishment. Then I saw that there was a small window set deeply in the left wall and that a cold breeze was blowing in through a gaping hole in the lower pane. I walked over and looked out. The lamplight was shining dimly on the foliage of the same tree and I knew that I was standing, not in Mathers' house, *but inside the walls of it*. I gave again my surprised cry, supported myself at the table and looked weakly at the back of the policeman. He was carefully blotting the figures he had entered on the paper on the wall. Then he turned round and replaced his pen on the table. I staggered quickly to one of the niches and sat down in a state of complete collapse, my eyes glued on his face and my mouth drying up like a raindrop on a hot pavement. I tried to say something several times but at first my tongue would not respond. At last I stammered out the thought that was blazing in my mind:

'I thought you were dead!'

The great fat body in the uniform did not remind me of anybody that I knew *but the face at the top of it belonged to old Mathers*. It was not as I had recalled seeing it last whether in my sleep or otherwise, deathly and unchanging; it was now red and gross as if gallons of hot thick blood had been pumped into it. The cheeks were bulging out like two ruddy globes marked here and there with straggles of purple discolouration. The eyes had been charged with unnatural life and glistened like beads in the lamplight. When he answered me it was the voice of Mathers.

'That is a nice thing to say,' he said, 'but it is no matter because I thought the same thing about yourself. I do not understand your unexpected corporality after the morning on the scaffold.'

'I escaped,' I stammered.

He gave me long searching glances.

'Are you sure?' he asked.

Was I sure? Suddenly I felt horribly ill as if the spinning of the world in the firmament had come against my stomach for the first time, turning it all to bitter curd. My limbs weakened and hung about me helplessly. Each eye fluttered like a bird's wing in its socket and my head throbbed, swelling out like a bladder at every surge of blood. I heard the policeman speaking at me again from a great distance.

'I am Policeman Fox,' he said, 'and this is my own private police station and I would be glad to have your opinion on it because I have gone to great pains to make it spick and span.'

I felt my brain struggling on bravely, tottering, so to speak, to its knees but unwilling to fall completely. I knew that I would be dead if I lost consciousness for one second. I knew that I could never awaken again or hope to understand afresh the terrible way in which I was if I lost the chain of the bitter day I had had. I knew that he was not Fox but Mathers. I knew Mathers was dead. I knew that I would have to talk to him and pretend that everything was natural and try perhaps to escape for the last time with my life to the bicycle. I would have given everything I had in the world and every cashbox in it to get at that moment one look at the strong face of John Divney.

'It is a nice station,' I muttered, 'but why is it inside the walls of another house?'

'That is a very simple conundrum, I am sure you know the answer of it.'

'I don't.'

'It is a very rudimentary conundrum in any case. It is fixed this way to save the rates because if it was constructed the same as any other barracks it would be rated as a separate hereditament and your astonishment would be flabbergasted if I told you what the rates are in the present year.'

'What?'

'Sixteen and eightpence in the pound with thruppence in the pound for bad yellow water that I would not use and fourpence by your kind leave for technical education. Is it any wonder the country is on its final legs with the farmers crippled and not one in ten with a proper bull-paper? I have eighteen summonses drawn up for nothing else and there will be hell to pay at the next Court. Why had you no light at all, big or small, on your bicycle?'

'My lamp was stolen.'

'Stolen? I thought so. It is the third theft today and four pumps disappeared on Saturday last. Some people would steal the saddle from underneath you if they thought you would not notice it, it is a lucky thing the tyre cannot be taken off without undoing the wheel. Wait till I take a deposition from you. Give me a description of the article and tell me all and do not omit anything because what may seem unimportant to yourself might well give a wonderful clue to the trained investigator.'

I felt sick at heart but the brief conversation had steadied me and I felt sufficiently recovered to take some small interest in the question of getting out of this hideous house. The policeman had opened a thick ledger which looked like the half of a longer book which had been sawn in two to fit the narrow table. He put several questions to me about the lamp and wrote down my replies very laboriously in the book, scratching his pen noisily and breathing heavily through his nose, pausing occasionally in his blowing when some letter of the alphabet gave him special difficulty. I surveyed him carefully as he sat absorbed in his task of writing. It was beyond all doubt the face of old Mathers but now it seemed to have a simple childlike quality as if the wrinkles of a long lifetime, evident enough the first time I looked at him, had been suddenly softened by some benign influence and practically erased. He now looked so innocent and good-natured and so troubled by the writing down of simple words that hope began to flicker once again within me. Surveyed coolly, he did not look a very formidable enemy. Perhaps I was dreaming or in the grip of some horrible hallucination. There was much that I did not understand and possibly could never understand to my dying day – the face of old Mathers whom I thought I had buried in a field on so great and fat a body, the ridiculous police station within the walls of another house, the other two monstrous policemen I had escaped from. But at least I was near my own house and the bicycle was waiting at the gate to take me there. Would this man try to stop me if I said I was going home? Did he know anything about the black box?

He had now carefully blotted his work and passed the book to me for my signature, proffering the pen by the handle with great politeness. He had covered two pages in a large childish hand. I thought it better not to enter into any discussion on the question of my name and hastily made an intricate scrawl at the bottom of the statement, closed the book and handed it back. Then I said as casually as I could:

'I think I will be going now.'

He nodded regretfully.

'I am sorry I cannot offer you anything,' he said, 'because it is a cold night and it would not do you a bit of harm.'

My strength and courage had been flowing back into my body and when I heard these words I felt almost completely strong again. There were many things to be thought about but I would not think of them at all until I was secure in my own house. I would go home as soon as possible and on the way I would not put my eye to right or left. I stood up steadily.

'Before I go,' I said, 'there is one thing I would like to ask you. There was a black cashbox stolen from me and I have been searching for it for several days. Would you by any chance have any information about it?'

The instant I had this said I was sorry I had said it because if it actually was Mathers brought miraculously back to life he might connect me with the robbery and the murder of himself and wreak some terrible vengeance. But the policeman only smiled and put a very knowing expression on his face. He sat down on the edge of the very narrow table and drummed upon it with his nails. Then he looked me in the eye. It was the first time he had done so and I was dazzled as if I had accidentally glanced at the sun.

'Do you like strawberry jam?' he asked.

His stupid question came so unexpectedly that I nodded and gazed at him uncomprehendingly. His smile broadened.

'Well if you had that box here,' he said, 'you could have a bucket of strawberry jam for your tea and if that was not enough you could have a bathful of it to lie in it full-length and if that much did not satisfy you, you could have ten acres of land with strawberry jam spread on it to the height of your two oxters. What do you think of that?'

'I do not know what to think of it,' I muttered. 'I do not understand it.'

'I will put it another way,' he said good-humouredly. 'You could have a house packed full of strawberry jam, every room so full that you could not open the door.'

I could only shake my head. I was becoming uneasy again.

'I would not require all that jam,' I said stupidly.

The policeman sighed as if despairing to convey to me his

that I had not known what was in the box. If I could believe him he had been sitting in this room presiding at four ounces of this inutterable substance, calmly making ribbons of the natural order, inventing intricate and unheard of machinery to delude the other policemen, interfering drastically with time to make them think they had been leading their magical lives for years, bewildering, horrifying and enchanting the whole countryside. I was stupefied and appalled by the modest claim he had made so cheerfully, I could not quite believe it, yet it was the only way the terrible recollections which filled my brain could be explained. I felt again afraid of the policeman but at the same time a wild excitement gripped me to think that this box and what was in it was at this moment resting on the table of my own kitchen. What would Divney do? Would he be angry at finding no money, take this awful omnium for a piece of dirt and throw it out on the manure heap? Formless speculations crowded in upon me, fantastic fears and hopes, inexpressible fancies, intoxicating foreshadowing of creations, changes, annihilations and god-like interferences. Sitting at home with my box of omnium I could do anything, see anything and know anything with no limit to my powers save that of my own imagination. Perhaps I could use it even to extend my imagination. I could destroy, alter and improve the universe at will. I could get rid of John Divney, not brutally, but by giving him ten million pounds to go away. I could write the most unbelievable commentaries on de Selby ever written and publish them in bindings unheard of for their luxury and durability. Fruits and crops surpassing anything ever known would flower on my farm, in earth made inconceivably fertile by unparalleled artificial manures. A leg of flesh and bone yet stronger than iron would appear magically upon my left thigh. I would improve the weather to a standard day of sunny peace with gentle rain at night washing the world to make it fresher and more enchanting to the eye. I would present every poor labourer in the world with a bicycle made of gold, each machine with a saddle made of something as yet uninvented but softer than the softest softness, and I would arrange that a warm gale would blow behind every man on every journey, even when two were going in opposite directions on the same road. My sow would farrow twice daily and a man would call immediately offering ten million pounds for each of the piglings, only to be outbid by a second man arriving and offering twenty million. The barrels and bottles in my public house would still be full and inexhaustible no matter how much was drawn out of them. I would bring de Selby himself back to life to converse with me at night and advise me in my sublime undertakings. Every Tuesday I would make myself invisible –

'You would not believe the convenience of it,' said the policeman bursting in upon my thoughts, 'it is very handy for taking the muck off your leggings in the winter.'

'Why not use it for preventing the muck getting on your leggings at all?' I asked excitedly. The policeman looked at me in wide-eyed admiration.

'By the Hokey I never thought of that,' he said. 'You are very intellectual and I am certain that I am nothing but a gawm.'

'Why not use it,' I almost shouted, 'to have no muck anywhere at any time?'

He dropped his eyes and looked very disconsolate.

'I am the world's champion gawm,' he murmured.

I could not help smiling at him, not, indeed, without some pity. It was clear that he was not the sort of person to be entrusted with the contents of the black box. His oafish underground invention was the product of a mind which fed upon adventure books of small boys, books in which every extravagance was mechanical and lethal and solely concerned with bringing about somebody's death in the most elaborate way imaginable. I was lucky to have escaped from his preposterous cellars with my life. At the same time I recalled that I had a small account to settle with Policeman MacCruiskeen and Sergeant Pluck. It was not the fault of these gentlemen that I had not been hanged on the scaffold and prevented from ever recovering the black box. My life had been saved by the policeman in front of me, probably by accident, when he decided to rush up an alarming reading on the lever. He deserved some consideration for that. I would probably settle ten million pounds upon him when I had time to consider the matter fully. He looked more a fool than a knave. But MacCruiskeen and Pluck were in a different class. It would probably be possible for me to save time and trouble by adapting the underground machinery to give both of them enough trouble, danger, trepidation, work and inconvenience to make them rue the day they first threatened me. Each of the cabinets could be altered to contain, not bicycles and whiskey and matches, but putrescent offals, insupportable smells, unbeholdable corruptions containing tangles of gleaming slimy vipers each of them deadly and foul of breath, millions of diseased and decayed monsters clawing the inside latches of the ovens to open them and escape, rats with horns walking upside down along the ceiling pipes trailing their leprous tails on the policemen's heads, readings of incalculable perilousness mounting hourly upon the –

'But it is a great convenience for boiling eggs,' the policeman put in again, 'if you like them soft you get them soft and the hard ones are as hard as iron.'

'I think I will go home,' I said steadily, looking at him almost fiercely. I stood up. He only nodded, took out his torch and swung his leg off the table.

'I do not think an egg is nice at all if it is underdone,' he remarked, 'and there is nothing so bad for heartburn and indigestion, yesterday was the first time in my life I got my egg right.'

He led the way to the tall narrow door, opened it and passed out before me down the dark stairs, flashing the torch ahead and swinging it politely back to me to show the steps. We made slow progress and remained silent, he sometimes walking sideways and rubbing the more bulging parts of his uniform on the wall. When we reached the window, he opened it and got out into the shrubberies first, holding it up until I had scrambled out beside him. Then he went ahead of me again with his light in long swishing steps through the long grass and undergrowth, saying nothing until we had reached the gap in the hedge and were again standing on the hard roadside. Then he spoke. His voice was strangely diffident, almost apologetic.

'There was something I would like to tell you,' he said, 'and I am half-ashamed to tell you because it is a question of principle and I do not like taking personal liberties because where would the world be if we all did that?'

I felt him looking at me in the dark with his mild inquiry. I was puzzled and a little disquieted. I felt he was going to make some further devastating revelation.

'What is it?' I asked.

'It is about my little barrack . . .' he mumbled.

'Yes?'

'I was ashamed of my life of the shabbiness of it and I took the liberty of having it papered the same time as I was doing the hard-boiled egg. It is now very neat and I hope you are not vexed or at any loss over the head of it.'

I smiled to myself, feeling relieved, and told him that he was very welcome.

'It was a sore temptation,' he continued eagerly to reinforce his case, 'it was not necessary to go to the trouble of taking down the notices off the wall because the wallpaper put itself up behind them while you would be saying nothing.'

'That is all right,' I said. 'Good night and thank you.'

'Goodbye to you,' he said, saluting me with his hand, 'and you can be certain I will find the stolen lamp because they cost one and sixpence and you would want to be made of money to keep buying them.'

I watched him withdrawing through the hedge and going back into the tangle of trees and bushes. Soon his torch was only an intermittent flicker between the trunks and at last he disappeared completely. I was again alone upon the roadway. There was no sound to be heard save the languorous stirring of the trees in the gentle night air. I gave a sigh of relief and began to walk back towards the gate to get my bicycle.

Chapter 12

The night seemed to have reached its middle point of intensity and the darkness was now much darker than before. My brain was brimming with half-formed ideas of the most far-reaching character but I repressed them firmly and determined to confine myself wholly to finding the bicycle and going home at once.

I reached the embrasure of the gateway and moved about it gingerly, stretching forth my hands into the blackness in search of the reassuring bars of my accomplice. At every move and reach I either found nothing or my hand came upon the granite roughness of the wall. An unpleasant suspicion was dawning on me that the bicycle was gone. I started searching with more speed and agitation and investigated with my hands what I am sure was the whole semicircle of the gateway. She was not there. I stood for a moment in dismay, trying to remember whether I had untied her the last time I had raced down from the house to find her. It was inconceivable that she had been stolen because even if anybody had passed at that unearthly hour, it would not be possible to see her in the pitch darkness. Then as I stood, something quite astonishing happened to me again. Something slipped gently into my right hand. It was the grip of a handlebar – *her* handlebar. It seemed to come to me out of the dark like a child stretching out its hand for guidance. I was astonished yet could not be certain afterwards whether the thing actually had entered my hand or whether the hand had been searching about mechanically while I was deep in thought and found the handlebar without the help or interference of anything unusual. At any other time I would have meditated in wonder on this curious incident but I now repressed all thought of it, passed my hands about the rest of the bicycle and found her leaning awkwardly against the wall with the string hanging loosely from her crossbar. She was not leaning against the gate where I had tied her.

My eyes had become adjusted to the gloom and I could now see clearly the lightish road bounded by the formless obscurities of the ditch on either side. I led the bicycle to the centre, started upon her gently, threw my leg across and settled gently into her saddle. She seemed at once to communicate to me some balm, some very soothing and pleasurable relaxation after the excitements of the tiny police station. I felt once more comfortable in mind and body, happy in the growing lightness of my heart. I knew that nothing in the whole world could tempt me from the saddle on this occasion until I reached my home. Already I had left the big house a far way behind me. A breeze had sprung up from nowhere and pushed tirelessly at my back, making me flit effortlessly through the darkness like a thing on wings. The bicycle ran truly and faultlessly beneath me, every part of her functioning with precision, her gentle saddle-springs giving unexceptionable consideration to my weight on the undulations of the road. I tried as firmly as ever to keep myself free of the wild thought of my four ounces of omnium but nothing I could do could restrain the profusion of half-thought extravagances which came spilling forth across my mind like a horde of swallows – extravagances of eating, drinking, inventing, destroying, changing, improving, awarding, punishing and even loving. I knew only that some of these undefined wisps of thought were celestial, some horrible, some pleasant and benign; all of them were momentous. My feet pressed down with ecstasy on the willing female pedals.

Courahan's house, a dull silent murk of gloom, passed away behind me on the right-hand side and my eyes narrowed excitedly to try to penetrate to my own house two hundred yards further on. It formed itself gradually exactly in the point I knew it stood and I nearly roared and cheered and yelled out wild greetings at the first glimpse of these four simple walls. Even at Courahan's – I admitted it to myself now – I could not quite convince myself beyond all doubt that I would ever again see the house where I was born, but now I was dismounting from the bicycle outside it. The perils and wonders of the last few days seemed magnificent and epic now that I had survived them. I felt enormous, important and full of power. I felt happy and fulfilled.

The shop and the whole front of the house was in darkness. I wheeled the bicycle smartly up to it, laid it against the door and walked round to the side. A light was shining from the kitchen window. Smiling to myself at the thought of John Divney, I tiptoed up and looked in.

There was nothing altogether unnatural in what I saw but I encountered another of those chilling shocks which I thought I had left behind me forever. A woman was standing at the table with some article of clothing neglected in her hands. She was facing up the kitchen towards the fireplace where the lamp was and she was talking quickly to some-body at the fire. The fireplace could not be seen from where I stood. The woman was Pegeen Meers whom Divney had once talked of marrying. Her appearance amazed me far more than her presence in my own kitchen. She seemed to have grown old, very fat and very grey. Looking at her sideways I could see that she was with child. She was talking rapidly, even angrily, I thought. I was certain she was talking to John Divney and that he was seated with his back to her at the fire. I did not stop to think on this queer situation but walked past the window, lifted the latch of the door, opened the door quickly and stood there looking in. In the one glance I saw two people at the fire, a young lad I had never seen before and my old friend John Divney. He was sitting with his back half-towards me and I was greatly startled by his appearance. He had grown enormously fat and his brown hair was gone, leaving him quite bald. His strong face had collapsed to jowls of hanging fat. I could discern a happy glimmer from the side of his fire-lit eye; an open bottle of whiskey was standing on the floor beside his chair. He turned lazily towards the open door, half-rose and gave a scream which pierced me and pierced the house and careered up to reverberate appallingly in the vault of the heavens. His eyes were transfixed and motionless as they stared at me, his loose face shrunk and seemed to crumble to a limp pallid rag of flesh. His jaws clicked a few times like a machine and then he fell forward on his face with another horrible shriek which subsided to heartrending moans.

I was very frightened and stood pale and helpless in the doorway. The boy had jumped forward and tried to lift Divney up; Pegeen Meers had given a frightened cry and rushed forward also. They pulled Divney round upon his back. His face was twisted in a revolting grimace of fear. His eyes again looked in my direction upside down and backwards and he gave another piercing scream and frothed foully at the mouth. I took a few steps forward to assist in getting him up from the floor but he made a demented convulsive movement and choked out the four words 'Keep away, keep away,' in such a tone of fright and horror that I halted in my tracks, appalled at his appearance. The woman pushed the pale-faced boy distractedly and said:

'Run and get the doctor for your father, Tommy! Hurry, hurry!'

The boy mumbled something and ran out of the open door without giving me a glance. Divney was still lying there, his face hidden in his hands, moaning and gibbering in broken undertones; the woman was on her knees trying to lift his head and comfort him. She was now crying and muttered that she knew something would happen if he did not stop his drinking. I went a little bit forward and said:

'Could I be of any help?'

She took no notice of me at all, did not even glance at me. But my words had a stange effect on Divney. He gave a whining scream which was muffled by his hands; then it died down to choking sobs and he locked his face in his hands so firmly that I could see the nails biting into the loose white flesh beside his ears. I was becoming more and more alarmed. The scene was eerie and disturbing. I took another step forward.

'If you will allow me,' I said loudly to the woman Meers,

'I will lift him and get him into bed. There is nothing wrong with him except that he has taken too much whiskey.'

Again the woman took no notice whatever but Divney was siezed by a convulsion terrible to behold. He half-crawled and rolled himself with grotesque movements of his limbs until he was a crumpled heap on the far side of the fireplace, spilling the bottle of whiskey on his way and sending it clattering noisily across the floor. He moaned and made cries of agony which chilled me to the bone. The woman followed him on her knees, crying pitifully and trying to mumble soothing words to him. He sobbed convulsively where he lay and began to cry and mutter things disjointedly like a man raving at the door of death. It was about me. He told me to keep away. He said I was not there. He said I was dead. He said that what he had put under the boards in the big house was not the black box but a mine, a bomb. It had gone up when I touched it. He had watched the bursting of it from where I had left him. The house was blown to bits. I was dead. He screamed to me to keep away. I was dead for sixteen years.

'He is dying,' the woman cried.

I do not know whether I was surprised at what he said, or even whether I believed him. My mind became quite empty, light, and felt as if it were very white in colour. I stood exactly where I was for a long time without moving or thinking. I thought after a time that the house was strange and I became uncertain about the two figures on the floor. Both were moaning and wailing and crying.

'He is dying, he is dying,' the woman cried again.

A cold biting wind was sweeping in through the open door behind me and staggering the light of the oil-lamp fitfully. I thought it was time to go away. I turned with stiffer steps and walked out through the door and round to the front of the house to get my bicycle. It was gone. I walked out upon the road again, turning leftwards. The night had passed away and the dawn had come with a bitter searing wind. The sky was livid and burdened with ill omen. Black angry clouds were piling in the west, bulging and glutted, ready to vomit down their corruption and drown the dreary world in it. I felt sad, empty, and without a thought. The trees by the road were rank and stunted and moved their stark leafless branches very dismally in the wind. The grasses at hand were coarse and foul. Waterlogged bog and healthless marsh stretched endlessly to left and right. The pallor of the sky was terrible to look upon.

My feet carried my nerveless body unbidden onwards for mile upon mile of rough cheerless road. My mind was completely void. I did not recall who I was, where I was or what my business was upon earth. I was alone and desolate yet not concerned about myself at all. The eyes in my head were open but they saw nothing because my brain was void.

Suddenly I found myself noticing my own existence and taking account of my surroundings. There was a bend in the road and when I came round it an extraordinary spectacle was presented to me. About a hundred yards away was a house which astonished me. It looked as if it were painted like an advertisement on a board on the roadside and, indeed, very poorly painted. It looked completely false and unconvincing. It did not seem to have any depth or breadth and looked as if it would not deceive a child. That was not in itself sufficient to surprise me because I had seen pictures and notices by the roadside before. What bewildered me was the sure knowledge, deeply rooted in my mind, that this was the house I was searching for and that there were people inside it. I had never seen with my eyes ever in my life before anything so unnatural and appalling and my gaze faltered about the thing uncomprehendingly as if at least one of the customary dimensions were missing, leaving no meaning in the remainder. The appearance of the house was the greatest surprise I had encountered ever, and I felt afraid of it.

I kept on walking but walked more slowly. As I approached, the house seemed to change its appearance. At first, it did nothing to reconcile itself with the shape of an ordinary house but it became uncertain in outline like a thing glimpsed under ruffled water. Then it became clear again and I saw that it began to have some back to it, some small space for rooms behind the frontage. I gathered this from the fact that I seemed to see the front and the back simultaneously from my position approaching what should have been the side. As there was no side that I could see I thought that the house must be triangular with its apex pointing towards me but when I was only fifteen yards away I saw a small window facing me and I knew from that that there must be *some* side to it. Then I found myself almost in the shadow of the structure, dry-throated and timorous from wonder and anxiety. It seemed ordinary enough at close quarters except that it was very white and still. It was momentous and frightening; the whole morning and the whole world seemed to have no purpose at all save to frame it and give it some magnitude and position so that I could find it with my simple senses and pretend to myself that I understood it. A constabulary crest above the door told me that it was a police station. I had never seen a police station like it.

I stopped in my tracks, I heard distant footsteps on the road behind me, heavy footsteps hurrying after me. I did not look round but remained standing motionless ten yards from the police station, waiting for the hurrying steps. They grew louder and louder and heavier and heavier. At last he came abreast of me. It was John Divney. We did not look at each other or say a single word. I fell into step beside him and both of us marched into the police station. We saw, standing with his back to us, an enormous policeman. His back appearance was unusual. He was standing behind a little counter in a neat whitewashed day-room; his mouth was open and he was looking into a mirror which hung upon the wall.

'It's my teeth,' we heard him say abstractedly and half-aloud. 'Nearly every sickness is from the teeth.'

His face, when he turned, surprised us. It was enormously fat, red and widespread, sitting squarely on the neck of his tunic with a clumsy weightiness that reminded me of a sack of flour. The lower half of it was hidden by a violent red moustache which shot out from his skin far into the air like the antennae of some unusual animal. His cheeks were red and chubby and his eyes were nearly invisible, hidden from above by the obstruction of his tufted brows and from below by the fat foldings of his skin. He came over ponderously to the inside of the counter and Divney and I advanced meekly from the door until we were face to face.

'Is it about a bicycle?' he asked.

Publisher's Note

On St Valentine's Day, 1940, the author wrote to William Saroyan about this novel, as follows:

I've just finished another book. The only thing good about it is the plot and I've been wondering whether I could make a crazy . . . play out of it. When you get to the end of this book you realize that my hero or main character (he's a heel and a killer) has been dead throughout the book and that all the queer ghastly things which have been happening to him are happening in a sort of hell which he earned for the killing. Towards the end of the book (before you know he's dead) he manages to get back to his own house where he used to live with another man who helped in the original murder. Although he's been away three days, this other fellow is twenty years older and dies of fright when he sees the other lad standing in the door. Then the two of them walk back along the road to the hell place and start thro' all the same terrible adventures again, the first fellow being surprised and frightened at everything just as he was the first time and as if he'd never been through it before. It is made clear that this sort of thing goes on for ever – and there you are. It is supposed to be very funny but I don't know about that either . . . I think the idea of a man being dead all the time is pretty new. When you are writing about the world of the dead – and the damned – where none of the rules and laws (not even the law of gravity) holds good, there is any amount of scope for back-chat and funny cracks.'

14 February, 1940.
B. O'N.

Elsewhere, the author wrote:

'Joe had been explaining things in the meantime. He said it was again the beginning of the unfinished, the re-discovery of the familiar, the re-experience of the already suffered, the fresh-forgetting of the unremembered. Hell goes round and round. In shape it is circular and by nature it is interminable, repetitive and very nearly unbearable.'

P.S.

Ideas,
interviews
& features...

About the Author(s)

FLANN O'BRIEN WAS born Brian O'Nolan in 1911 in Strabane, County Tyrone, Northern Ireland, the fifth of twelve children. Following several uprootings, his family moved to Dublin in 1925, and in 1929 he enrolled in University College, Dublin, ostensibly to study German, Irish and English, but where he devoted much of his time to developing his skills at debating, billiards and raising glasses of stout. He also began writing while at college, contributing to a magazine, *Fair Play*, then editing a short-lived publication called *Blather*. He wrote the majority of *Blather*'s content for its five or six issues, which consisted of fictitious news items, highly elaborate puns and vicious parodies. For this he adopted the *nom de plume* Brother Barnabas, and dealt in anecdotes about one 'The O'Blather' and his half-wit son, 'Blazes O'Blather'.

In 1935, he joined the Irish Civil Service, remaining there until ill health forced him to retire in 1953, by which time he had been appointed secretary to a number of ministers.

Since it was forbidden for civil servants to publish under their own name, O'Nolan adopted a slew of pseudonyms including Flann O'Brien for his (English) books, and Lir O'Connor, the quaintly sounding George Knowall and Myles na Gopaleen for his journalism.

From 1940 until 1966, under the last of these names, he began writing a highly satirical column in the *Irish Times* called *Cruiskeen Lawn*, or *Little Brimming Jug*. Appearing almost daily, the column ranged from mordantly comic anecdotes and examinations of Dublin life to lively if vitriolic attacks on his readers, as well as increasingly bitter political harangues in which he employed his fierce intellect to decimate Irish officialdom, assorted bores and timewasters (including a number of his fellow civil servants). One column found him delivering the following broadside to his faithful, if masochistic, readers: 'you smug, self-righteous swine...self-opinionated, sod-minded, suet-brained, ham-faced, mealy-mouthed, streptococcus-ridden gang of natural gobdaws!' Small wonder that he was obliged to conceal himself behind pseudonyms.

Despite rumours and untruths offered by the man himself, O'Brien only left Ireland once, taking a very brief trip to Germany in 1934, about which there has been much speculation. According to a feature in *Time* magazine in 1943, he went there to study German, and also met and married an eighteen-year-old girl named Clara Ungerland, the daughter of a basket-weaver from Cologne. She was blonde, played the violin and died of tuberculosis a month later. Coupled with a further account he gave of an extended trip to Cologne, enjoying, as he put it, 'many months on the Rhineland and at Bonn, drifting away from the strict pursuit of study', and an admission that he had got involved in some kind of altercation with the Nazis in a beer hall, much of the German episode sounds like *Erfindung* – fiction.

In 1948, to the surprise of many of his ▶

❝ One column found him delivering the following broadside to his faithful, if masochistic, readers: 'you smug, self-righteous swine ... self-opinionated, sod-minded, suet-brained, ham-faced, mealy-mouthed, streptococcus-ridden gang of natural gobdaws! ❞

About the Author(s) *(continued)*

◄ friends, O'Brien did actually marry. Her name was Evelyn McDonnell and she too was a civil servant, a typist in the same department as O'Brien. They had no children but the marriage seemed happy enough, helped by Evelyn's enormous respect for her husband's talents and his undoubted individuality.

O'Brien published his first novel, *At-Swim-Two-Birds*, in 1939, at the behest of Graham Greene, who was then a reader for Longman. His second novel, *The Third Policeman*, was rejected by the same publisher but a third book, *The Poor Mouth*, was published in Gaelic in 1941 and was followed, twenty years later, by *The Hard Life* (1961) and *The Dalkey Archive* (1964). O'Brien also wrote plays, including a sketch called *Thirst* which was shown at Dublin's Gate Theatre as part of a Christmas show entitled *Jack-in-the-Box*. Recently restaged in New York, it was praised by critic Richard Watts, who claimed that O'Brien 'made drink more attractive than Wilde made lust'.

O'Brien died of cancer in 1966, on April Fools' Day. Numerous plays and collections of journalism were published posthumously over the following two decades. ■

A Curious Tale

A PUBLISHER'S NOTE at the end of *The Third Policeman* displays a letter, written in 1940 by O'Brien to the American author William Saroyan, in which he explains some of its eccentricities.

By the time they reach this letter, readers will already have marvelled at the book's many themes: man's search for God, for eternal youth, for unimaginable power and treasures, and his relationship with nature, with the soul, with the myriad mysteries of the universe and, crucially, with the bicycle.

A beguiling and curious combination of many books and styles – part *Alice's Adventures in Wonderland*, part *Gulliver's Travels*, part *Seventh Voyage of Sinbad* – *The Third Policeman* drifts from bizarre fantasy to sheer nonsense and back again, propelled by frequent draughts of dry wit. It is, in the immortal words of one of the policemen, 'nearly an insoluble pancake'.

Almost as strange as the novel's plot is its history. It was written after the publication of O'Brien's first novel, *At-Swim-Two-Birds*, but was rejected by his publishers who wrote: 'We realize the author's ability but think that he should become less fantastic and in this new novel he is more so.' He had been thinking about adapting it for the stage, probably influenced by Saroyan's success as a playwright, but abandoned the idea after this blow.

Nonetheless, he did try his luck abroad, sending the manuscript to literary agents in America through a contact of Saroyan's, with the perhaps more apposite title of ▶

5

A Curious Tale *(continued)*

◀ *Hell Goes Round and Round*. However, further enquiries revealed that they had mislaid it. Perhaps enraged, or inspired, by this carelessness, he abandoned all attempts to place it with anyone and began telling friends that *he* had mislaid the manuscript, even inventing different fates for it. These ranged from the simple mistake of leaving it on a tramcar or showing it to someone at the Dolphin Hotel and then leaving without it, to the inspired notion that he had taken it on a trip to Donegal by car only for the pages to have somehow been blown out of the boot. To an actor friend who knew a film director and who felt that it might be adapted into a script he offered the rather undramatic yarn of having left it on a train. Only his friend Donagh McDonagh knew the truth and, after O'Brien had asked him to look at the novel again to see what was wrong with it, McDonagh replied 'nothing'. Despite this reassurance, it lay unread for twenty-six years.

Yet various chunks of *The Third Policeman* did appear in O'Brien's final novel, *The Dalkey Archive*. Largely concerned with bicycles and policemen, some of the material has been lifted, word for word, from the original source. And a short story published under the pseudonym Myles na Gopaleen, called 'Two in One', also borrowed from the unpublished novel. But when O'Brien's friend and biographer Anthony Cronin suggested that the story should be published under the byline Flann O'Brien, the latter replied ominously, 'I don't know that fellow any more.' ■

Hats Off

PUBLISHED POSTHUMOUSLY IN 1967 to
critical acclaim, *The Third Policeman* was
reviewed in the *New Yorker* by Howard Moss,
who noted that it was 'a comic but sinister
invention: on the one hand a regional farce
in which a criminal struggles with a regional
bureaucracy, and, on the other, a mysterious
allegory with universal pitfalls'. Though he
compared it to the work of James Joyce and
Alice's Adventures in Wonderland, Moss
acknowledged nonetheless that it was
'completely original'. And in closing, he put
his finger on one of the novel's most
interesting, if elusive, qualities: 'for no reason
one can definitely point to, it is as strangely
affecting as it is funny'.

Jonathan Lethem paid tribute to the novel
by including an extract in his anthology, *The
Vintage Book of Amnesia*, an appropriate
volume to feature a segment from a book
that lay forgotten until its author's death. It
finds the narrator waking up in the police
station and having a customary elliptical
conversation both with his soul and with
Sergeant Pluck. O'Brien appears alongside
such august contributors as Jorge Luis
Borges, Oliver Sacks, Dennis Potter, Philip K.
Dick and Vladimir Nabokov – not a bad
crowd in which to find yourself. ■

De Selby: Idiot/Savant

SIGNIFICANT PORTIONS OF *The Third Policeman* are taken up with the findings and otherwise of de Selby, 'a physicist, ballistician, philosopher and psychologist'. Referred to throughout the copious and frequent footnotes as a 'savant', de Selby may well have been based partly on Des Esseintes, the reclusive savant and protagonist of Huysmans's *A Rebours*, which O'Brien read during that time. But there have been other ideas as to the origin of the character's name, notably the De Selby Quarries situated on Mount Seskin Road on the number 65 bus route, and the De Selby company. This company may have piqued O'Brien's interest as it had a connection with Walter Conan, maker of academic gowns and some kind of inventor, among whose successes was an index card system, heated gas lamps and a method of preserving meat.

In O'Brien's subsequent novel, *The Dalkey Archive*, De Selby (as well as having acquired a capital 'D') emerges from the chrysalis of sundry footnotes and appears as a fully formed character who talks, drinks, eats and grandly displays his matchless intellectual prowess, arrogance and extreme misanthropy.

De Selby isn't unique to O'Brien's novels however: the character also appears in the work of Robert Anton Wilson (aka RAW), co-author with Robert Shea of the cult classic, *The Illuminatus Trilogy*, where de Selby appears in a great many footnotes. And just as O'Brien employs James Joyce as a character in *The Dalkey Archive*, so Wilson features him in his novel, *Masks of the Illuminati*. ∎

Lost? Call a Policeman

SALES OF O'BRIEN'S novel escalated when it was announced that the Emmy award-winning television show *Lost* would prominently feature *The Third Policeman* and that the book would go some way to explaining the warp and weave of the show's labyrinthine plot. Scriptwriter and producer Craig Wright's promise that *The Third Policeman* 'was chosen very specifically for a reason' and his tantalising offering that 'whoever goes out and buys the book will have a lot more ammunition in their back pocket as they theorize about the show' must have seemed like a tangible lifeline to all those befuddled viewers.

In the three weeks after being shown on *Lost*, the novel sold 15,000 copies, apparently the same number sold in the last six years by its American publisher, Dalkey Archive (itself named after O'Brien's final novel). Although not the first literary reference to have been featured in the programme – in other episodes the character Sawyer was seen reading *Watership Down* and *A Wrinkle in Time*, a novel about time travel – media interest was piqued and stories about the relationship between book and television show appeared in the *Guardian*, *Independent*, *Daily Telegraph*, *New York Times*, *USA Today* and *LA Weekly*. Nonetheless, last word on the subject must belong to Craig Wright, who points out that those *Lost* fans who bravely decide to delve into O'Brien's world 'will have a lot more to speculate about – and, no small thing, they will have read a really great book'. ■

Have You Read?

Best of Myles
Under the pseudonym Myles na Gopaleen,
Flann O' Brien wrote a daily column in the
Irish Times called *Cruiskeen Lawn*. For over
twenty years it hilariously satirised the
absurdities and solemnities of Dublin life
and, with its shameless irony and relentless
high spirits, became the most feared,
respected and uproarious newspaper
column in the whole of Ireland.

'Brilliant, morosely inventive comic turns
devoted to O'Brien's favourite topics: the
literary life, the Gaelic Revival, civil service
bureaucracy, booze and its discontent'
Observer

....

The Dalkey Archive
An ingenious and riotous depiction of the
extraordinary events surrounding theologian
and mad scientist De Selby's attempt to
destroy the world by removing all the
oxygen from the atmosphere. Only Michael
Shaughnessy, 'a lowly civil servant', and
James Joyce, alive and well and working as
a barman in the nearby seaside resort of
Skerries, can stop the inimitable De Selby
in his tracks.

'Flann O'Brien is inventive, his storytelling is
swift and sure, making the eccentric seem
natural and the commonplace hilarious'
The Times

Points on a Similar Map

The following is a short list of publications that, partially or otherwise, contain much of the same spirit as O'Brien's novel.

Complete Prose
Woody Allen
Published originally in three separate volumes and written between the 1960s and 1970s, these short pieces are classics of comic prose and represent some of Allen's finest work. The resemblance in style and humour between the de Selby footnotes and many of the pieces here, such as *The Metterling Lists*, *The Gossage-Vardebeian Papers*, *Conversations with Helmholtz* and the sublime *Yes, But Can the Steam Engine Do This?* is quite substantial. Possibly Allen was aware of O'Brien because one of his biggest influences – S.J. Perelman – was such a fan.

Pale Fire
Vladimir Nabokov
One of Nabokov's finest works, this is part epic poem, part series of complicated annotations on that poem. The story of the possibly fictitious kingdom of Zembla and the assassination of this country's King Charles is interwoven with the dazzling mystery of who wrote the poem, who annotated it, who got shot and much more.

If on a Winter's Night a Traveller
Italo Calvino
Calvino's ingenious series of tales within a ▶

Points on a Similar Map (continued)

◄ tale concerns two people, the Reader and the Other Reader, who both end up finding each other as they search for the book that they thought was by the writer Italo Calvino! Each book they get turns out to be by someone else, with its story told in a different genre. By the time they've uncovered ten of them they have fallen in love and have their own tale to tell.

The Living End
Stanley Elkin
This short, very funny, novel deals with the afterlife, as a perfectly normal man, who dies in an armed raid, goes to Heaven, which resembles a theme park, before being sent down to Hell for committing what seem to be the most inconsequential of sins.

Puckoon
Spike Milligan
Set in 1920s Ireland, when the Boundary Commission is deciding where to divide Northern Ireland from the Republic and they put the border through the middle of the village of Puckoon, this is quite probably the funniest novel ever written.

The New Policeman
Kate Thompson
A book for children, this is an inventive and stylishly written novel about magic and myth and which, title and all, owes something to Flann O'Brien's work.

Vicious Circles & Infinities: a Panoply of Paradoxes by Patrick Hughes/George Brecht, *Flatland* by Edwin Abbott and the *Graphic Works of M.C. Escher*
These three books explore semantically, mathematically and visually some terrain similar to that charted by O'Brien.

BIOGRAPHIES

For more information about the author's life and times, check out:

No Laughing Matter: The Life and Times of Flann O'Brien
by Anthony Cronin

Flann O'Brien: A Portrait of the Artist as a Young Post-Modernist
by Keith Hopper

A Colder Eye: The Modern Irish Writers
by Hugh Kenner

The Web Detective

There's scads of material on the Internet concerning O'Brien, his life and books but here are a few fine examples.

http://www.themodernword.com/scriptorium/obrien.html
An excellent site, full of fascinating material on the man and his works.

http://www.hellshaw.com/flann/
and
http://www.blather.net/blather/2003/11/flann_obrien_comic_genius.html
These two pages are part of sites that are both fantastic and full of wonderful stuff on O'Brien. The latter is named after O'Brien's magazine, *Blather*, of course.

http://www.centerforbookculture.org/dalkey/backlist/obrien.html
This is the webpage for the Dalkey Archive Press, O'Brien's American publishers, which contains a list of all of his books, plus lots of other interesting stuff.

http://www.necessaryprose.com/obrien.html
A useful biographical introduction to the man whom they refer to as 'sodden with whisky'.

LEGENDS

OF

ICELAND

ICELANDIC LEGENDS

COLLECTED BY

JÓN ARNASON

TRANSLATED BY

GEORGE E. J. POWELL

AND

EIRÍKUR MAGNÚSSON

WITH TWENTY-EIGHT ILLUSTRATIONS

Facsimile reprint, 1995,
Llanerch Publishers,
Felinfach.
ISBN 1 897853 71 8

First published by Richard Bentley,
London, 1864.

George E.J. Powell and Eiríkur Magnússon, *Icelandic
Legends*. London, 1864.

Foreward to the 1994 reprint.

With the publication in 1864 and 1866 of two volumes
of *Icelandic Legends*, translated by George Powell and
Eiríkur Magnússon, Icelandic folk-tales took their
proper place on the shelves of those many Victorian
philologists and antiquaries who were drawn to the
misty world of Northern folklore and antiquity.
Victorian readers, long familiar with tales collected or
created by the Brothers Grimm and Hans Christian
Anderson, could now engage with the Norwegian folk
narratives collected by Peter Christian Asbjørnsen and
Jørgen Moe (and translated in Sir George Dasent's
much reprinted *Popular Tales from the Norse*, 1859,
and *Tales from the Fjeld*, 1874), and also with Jón
Árnason's Icelandic corpus, as represented in the two
Powell-Eiríkur Magnússon volumes.

It was the eccentric, Copenhagen-based, Scandophile
scholar George Stephens who in 1845 had first
proposed the systematic collection and publication of
Icelandic folktales.   Jón Árnason (1819-88), scholar,
schoolmaster, and librarian, promoted the idea in
Iceland.   He published selections of folktales in
Reykjavík in 1852 and 1855-6, but the enterprise
ultimately required the energising presence in Iceland
in 1858 of Konrad Maurer, a visiting German scholar
of formidable learning and enthusiasm. It was Maurer
who published his own German translations of some of
the tales (1860); he also arranged for the Icelandic
texts to be published in Leipzig in two hefty volumes,
Islenzkar þjóðsögur og ævintýri (1862-4); he
supervised the printing and (more daunting) the proof
reading of the Leipzig books; and, with Jón inaccessibly

distant in Iceland, Maurer arranged for Guðbrandur Vigfússon to write a necessarily hasty but learned introduction. Appropriately, the first volume was dedicated to Jakob Grimm, whose brother had died in 1859.

By 1864 Guðbrandur Vigfússon and his (then) friend Eiríkur Magnússon had both made their way to Britain, where they were to remain until their respective deaths in 1889 and 1913. Guðbrandur, as a protégé of George Dasent, had come to work on the long-delayed *Icelandic-English Dictionary* (1874). Eiríkur's early patrons included the prosperous young Welsh Icelandophile George Powell. The two men had first met either during Powell's Icelandic travels in the summer of 1862 or as fellow passengers on the homeward passage to Britain. They subsequently read Icelandic texts together, in both London and Aberystwyth, translating folktales and sagas for pleasure and, they hoped, publication. The 1864 *Icelandic Legends* selection from the Jón Árnason corpus was the first fruit of their labours. They had worked quickly---the manuscript was with the publisher as early as January 1863.

The volume enjoyed much critical approval but little commercial success. Reviewers and readers engaged eagerly with the trolls, elves, sprites, nixies and other hidden people; they relished the images of stoicism and canniness played out amidst the lava and lyme grass, the fire and ice of 66 degrees North; and they could now add eery legends of Icelandic outlaws to the more familiar 'rymes' of Robin Hood and Hereward the Wake. To the student of comparative religion, the tales represented the rich, but fragmented residuum of Northern mythology; to the politicised philologist, the stories reflected the imaginative energy of a 'freeborn people'; and to the white-knuckled Protestant, the narratives revealed an Icelandic spirit immune to the 'prosy-nonsense' of medieval Saints lives, works 'born in the bigoted brains of monks, and committed by them to countless reams of dingy vellum'. The selection of material and the style of the translations were shrewdly judged by Powell and his Icelandic colleague. Recognising that 'so sensitive is the English moral nature, and so prone to blush the English cheek', the translators had sought deftly to navigate the dangerous seaway between the 'rude but ingenious simplicity' of the texts, and the 'refined delicacy' of their Victorian target audience.

A critical success, for sure, and yet the 1864 *Icelandic Legends* was something of a financial flop. When Bentley the publisher went bankrupt in 1867, 475 of the 1000 copies printed remained unsold, and in a letter to George Powell the publisher's son comments sourly that the book 'entirely ceased to be in demand two months after publication'. It was, accordingly, Longmans who published the 1866 second volume. George Powell's own financial commitment to the 1864 enterprise cannot be doubted. For the design and preparation of the icicle-festooned frontispiece, with each inset picture relating to one of the translated tales, Powell paid £400. This represents twice the annual salary which his young collaborator Eiríkur Magnússon was eventually to achieve as a librarian in the University Library in Cambridge.

Andrew Wawn,
Leeds, 1994.

PREFACE.

THOSE who are thoroughly acquainted with the literature
of Iceland are agreed that, so far as the historical part of
it is concerned, it holds a distinguished place among the
literatures of the world, next indeed to the classics of
ancient Greece and Rome. And though its historians,
the authors of its noble sagas, have been men of high
learning and cultivated minds, its peasants, uncultivated
and unlearned, have been those who have handed down
to us the traditional lore of the country, the poetical and
imaginative tales of elves, trolls, ghosts, goblins, and
monsters; some contenting themselves with telling them
often by the winter fire; others adding stories from their
own mental testimonies. And thus, in the course of
many years, the mass of such stories has accumulated,
until at length, becoming perhaps too unwieldy for oral
tradition, it has been committed to paper by the peasants
and others, who were its guardians and possessors, at
the earnest and constant request of Mr. Jón Arnason,

who, with a diligence and perseverance which have rightly earned for him the name of "The Grimm of Iceland," has gathered into one great mass the mighty body of Icelandic folk-lore.

From this immense collection Mr. Arnason published, in 1862, a volume called "Íslenzkar Þjóðsögur og Æfintýri" (Icelandic National Stories and Tales), at Leipzig, of which the first part has appeared this year. It is from these volumes that the present selection has been made. As we have intended this volume more for amusement than instruction, we have wilfully omitted the able introduction written by Mr. Guðbrandr Vigfússon (a learned Icelander, at Copenhagen), which treats of the Icelandic superstition in all its branches. For the same reason we have also left out many topographical names and allusions, which, to be of any use to the general public, would require an elaborately finished map and long explanatory notes.

And here, perhaps, a few extracts from Mr. Vigfússon's preface might not be out of place.

"Iceland, from the times of its earliest settlement, has abounded with tales of elves, goblins, trolls, and super-natural beings of every description, as will be at once acknowledged by anyone who is conversant with the sagas. These tales are closely coherent with, and have risen and grown in the company of, the historical sagas, as, in those long gone-by days, history and tradition lived in the greatest union. Both, as twin sisters, are begotten

in the same bosom, and both can therefore be called
national; and to this name the superstitional tales have
perhaps the highest claims, since they are the offspring
of fancy and popular poetry, never dying out so long as
the flame of imagination is not extinct in the minds of
the people, and assuming a new form with every age,
according to the way in which the spirit of that age
regards the world of wonders. When times are dark,
and superstition gloomy, we find tales of goblins and
witchcraft to be most prevalent. But on the dawning
of brighter days, the quaint and elegant stories of elves
become the objects of popular poetry."

We still quote from Mr. Vigfússon.

"At first it was intended to apply to this collection of
stories some name that savoured strongly of the past, but
it soon appeared that such a denomination would not
be applicable to all the stories. The author, therefore,
changed his intention, and has called the work 'Icelandic
National Stories and Tales.' Because the olden time is the
mother of the present, people are too often inclined to
make it the standard of everything good, and to institute
invidious comparisons, declaring that all that we have
and know has been handed down from those bygone
days, from man to man and from mouth to mouth; we,
of the modern days, doing nothing but picking up and
piecing together the fragments we find. And applying
this theory to literature, they disparage all folk-lore which

is not avowedly ancient. But they do not consider that as long as nation is nation, and life is life, old things either die out and become extinct, or else change their colours; are either replaced by, or closely mingled with, the new. That nation, therefore, which does nothing but remember, must be looked upon as dead, as petrified, as no longer to be numbered among the living and acting. These stories will show clearly that the Icelanders are not so utterly deprived of mental life as to be unable to replace old with new, and to add to their literary treasure-heap. Many of them are of quite modern origin, and will not suffer from a comparison with those of older date."

Mr. Jón Arnason, the talented collector of these tales (the two volumes hitherto published being but a tithe of the entire mass which lies in his hand), is the librarian of the only public library in Iceland, that of Reykjavík Cathedral, and secretary to the bishop. We seize with high pleasure this opportunity of paying our tribute of praise to his energy and zeal as a collector, for he has spent thirty years, and large sums of money, in searching for, and obtaining from all quarters of the island these "records of the lower classes;" to his conscientiousness as an editor, for he has published the stories intact as he received them; to his great talents as a scholar; and last, though by no means least, to his uprightness and modesty as a gentleman, and his kindness as a friend.

From Mr. Arnason's Selection we have selected still further, reducing the work to about a third of its original dimensions. Many of the stories given in the Icelandic edition we have omitted on account of their want of interest and climax. Others, because they were but repetitions, with slight and unimportant variations, of stories taken. Others, of high beauty and originality, we have most reluctantly left out, from the fact of their being founded on incidents which would shock the sensibility of many readers; and it is our earnest hope, that among our reading public will be numbered many children. Of these last-named stories we may particularly mention " Skapti Sœmundsson the Surgeon," and " The Sorb-trees ;" the former remarkable for its singular mixture of fact and fiction, the latter for its extreme beauty and poetical fancy.

An apologetic Preface is never worth much ; if a book is bad, it does not improve it, and if a book is good it is superfluous : it is either a sop for Cerberus, or a line cast out for compliments. But, in conclusion, we will say a few words, not apologetically, concerning our manner of treating the stories herein contained. We have not translated closely; we have amplified, we have expunged, we have inverted. Where stories were told barely and nakedly, we have coloured and clothed them ; where irrelevancies occurred, we have either got rid of them or harmonized them with the text ; where incidents or descriptions have

been given out of their proper places, we have changed
their position. In Icelandic, tautology, if well managed,
is looked upon as a merit; in English, on the contrary, it
is regarded as a sign of clumsiness: we have therefore
expunged all repetitions. We have confined ourselves
throughout to straightforward language, adopting sometimes words and forms of speech which may, perhaps, be
looked upon as stiff and obsolete, but which, in such a
work as the present, replace well the rounded periods and
ingenious Latinisms of the most modern English. And
as our great example in this, we have Dr. Dasent, who
alone of men has hitherto made the noblest Icelandic
language breathe freely in an English dress, and who, by
the purity of his writings, and the consummate skill with
which he has introduced true and expressive old English
words and phrases, has gained the admiration of all the
philological world.

In the case of one story, however, that of "Grímur who
killed Skeljungur," we have adhered pretty closely to the
text, as we wished our readers to see how an Icelandic
peasant (who is still living) could tell a classical tale.

Subsequent to the conclusion of Part IV., there fell
into our hands a little work, entitled "Icelandic Stories and
Fairy Tales, translated into English by the Rev. Olaf
Pálsson, Dean and Rector of Reykjavík Cathedral, revised
and edited by David Mackinlay and Andrew James
Symington," which contained several stories which we had

already translated from the original text; namely, that about Una, that about Hildur, and "The Father of Eighteen Elves," called by Mr. Pálsson "The Changeling." Besides these, there were the stories of Sœmundur the Learned, upon which we were engaged, and several others we do not include in our work. We refrained from *reading* the book until our own was concluded. We therefore absolve ourselves from any charge of plagiarism.

We are indebted for the illustrations to Messrs. Worms, Zwecker, Powell, &c.

GEORGE E. J. POWELL.
EIRÍKUR MAGNÚSSON.

LONDON,
January, 1864.

CONTENTS.

STORIES OF ELVES.

STORIES OF WATER-MONSTERS.

STORIES OF TROLLS.

STORIES OF GHOSTS AND GOBLINS.

STORIES OF ELVES.

" And purchased another in a dark and dismal valley, over which the sun seldom shone in summer and never in winter, and in the darkest and gloomiest recess intended to take up her abode." —p. 116.

[*To face page* 19.

LEGENDS OF ICELAND.

THE GENESIS OF THE HID-FOLK.

ONCE upon a time, God Almighty came to visit Adam and
Eve. They received him with joy, and showed him everything they had in the house. They also brought their
children to him, to show him, and these He found promising
and full of hope. Then He asked Eve whether she had no
other children than these whom she now showed him.
She said " None."

But it so happened that she had not finished washing

them all, and, being ashamed to let God see them dirty, had hidden the unwashed ones. This God knew well, and said therefore to her, " What man hides from God, God will hide from man." These unwashed children became forthwith invisible, and took up their abode in mounds, and hills, and rocks. From these are the elves descended, but we men from those of Eve's children whom she had openly and frankly shown to God. And it is only by the will and desire of the elves themselves that men can ever see them.

A traveller once lost his way, and knew not whither to turn or what to do. At last, after wandering about for some time, he came to a hut, which he had never seen before; and on his knocking at the door, an old woman opened it, and invited him to come in, which he gladly did. Inside, the house seemed to be a clean and good one. The old woman led him to the warmest room, where were sitting two young and beautiful girls. Besides these there were none else in the house. He was well received and kindly treated, and having eaten a good supper was shown to bed.

He asked whether one of the girls might stay with him, as his companion for the night, and his request was granted.

And now wishing to kiss her, the traveller turned towards her, and placed his hand upon her; but his hand sank through her, as if she had been of mist, and though he could well see her lying beside him, he could grasp nothing but the air. So he asked what this all meant, and she said, " Be not astonished, for I am a spirit. When the devil, in times gone by, made war in heaven, he, with all his armies, was driven into outer darkness. Those who turned their eyes to look after him as he fell, were also driven out of heaven; but those who were neither for nor against him, were sent to the earth and commanded to dwell there in the rocks and mountains. These are called Elves and Hid-folk. They can live in company with none but their own race. They do either good or evil, which they will, but what they do they do thoroughly. They have no bodies as you other mortals, but can take a human form and be seen of men when they wish. I am one of these fallen spirits, and so you can never hope to embrace me."

To this fate the traveller yielded himself, and has handed down to us this story.

THE FISHERMAN OF GÖTUR.

It is told, that long ago, a peasant living at Götur in Mýrdalur, went out fishing round the island of Dyrhólar. In returning from the sea, he had to cross a morass. It happened once, that, on his way home, after nightfall, he came to a place where a man had lost his horse in the bog, and was unable to recover it without help. The fisherman,

to whom this man was a stranger, aided him in freeing his
horse from the peat.

When the animal stood again safe and sound upon the
dry earth, the stranger said to the fisherman, " I am your
neighbour, for I live in Hvammsgil, and am, as you,
returning from the sea. But I am so poor, that I cannot
pay you for this service, as you ought to be paid. I will
promise you, however, this much—that you shall never go
to sea without catching fish, nor ever, if you will take my
advice, return with empty hands. But you must never
put to sea without having first seen me pass your house
as if going towards the shore. Obey me in this matter
and I promise you that you shall launch, at no time, your
boat in vain."

The fisherman thanked him for this advice, and sure
enough it was, that, for three years afterwards, never
putting to sea till he had first seen his neighbour pass his
door, he always launched his boat safely, and always came
home full-handed.

But at the end of the three years, it fell out that one
day, in the early morning, the fisherman looking out from
his house, saw the wind and weather favourable and all
other fishers hurrying down to the sea, to make the best
of so good a time. But though he waited hour after hour,
in the hope of seeing his neighbour pass, the man of
Hvammsgil never came. At last losing his patience, he
started out without having seen him go by. When he

came down to the shore, he found that all the boats were launched and far away.

Before night the wind rose and became a storm, and every boat that had that day put to sea was wrecked, and every fisher drowned, the peasant of Götur alone escaping, for he had been unable to go out fishing. The next night he had a strange dream, in which his neighbour from Hvammsgil came to him and said, " Although you did not yesterday follow my advice, I yet so far felt kindly towards you, that I hindered you from going out to sea, and saved you thus from drowning ; but look no more forth to see me pass, for we have met for the last time." And never again did the peasant see his neighbour pass his door.

THE GRATEFUL ELFWOMAN.

A peasant's wife once dreamed that a woman came to her bedside, whom she knew to be a Huldukona, and who begged her to give her milk for her child, two quarts a day, for the space of a month, placing it always in a part of the house which she pointed out. The goodwife promised to do so, and remembered her promise when she awoke. So she put a milkbowl every morning in the place which the other had chosen, and left it there, always on her return finding it empty. This went on for a month ; and at the end of the month she dreamed that the same woman came to her, thanked her for her kindness, and begged her to accept the belt which she should find in the bed when she awoke, and then vanished. In the morning the goodwife found beneath her pillow, a silver belt, beautifully and rarely wrought, the promised gift of the grateful elf-woman.

THÓRDUR OF THRASTASTADIR.

A certain man named Thórdur lived at Thrastastadir, in Skagafiördur.

One day, in the winter, he started from home, intending to go to the trading-town of Hofsós, but the snow had drifted so deeply that the way was thought unsafe. Not caring for this, he carried his merchandise in a bag and walked off across a bog, which he knew to be his shortest path to Hofsós. When he had gone a little way, he quite lost the track, but still walked straight on till nightfall, when he saw before him some warehouses, so lofty and so beautiful that they filled him with surprise. Going up to them he discovered a light in one of the windows, and at the same time heard some delightful music. So he looked in at the window and saw a number of people dancing. He then went to the door and knocked, and immediately it was opened by a well-dressed man, who asked him what he would? Thórdur told him how he had lost his way, and begged, if it were possible, for a night's shelter.

"Come in and be welcome," said the man, "you shall have shelter here. Bring in your bag too, and to-morrow I will trade with you, and I promise you that you shall not find the bargains of Hofsós better than mine."

Thórdur could scarcely believe his ears, but thought he must be dreaming. So the man let him into the chief room, spite of Thórdur's plain and muddy dress. There were many assembled there; the lady of the house, her children, and her servants, all gaily and brightly drest, making merry.

The man who had opened the door to Thórdur, and who was no other than the master of the house, said to the lady, "Wife, here is a man who has lost his way and who needs both rest and food: treat him well."

"I grieve to hear of his distress," replied she, and rising, brought in a good and plentiful supper, which she set before Thórdur, while the master of the house fetched wine and glasses, and begged Thórdur to drink with him. Thórdur did so, and thought he had never tasted such wine in all his life, nor ever met such goodly company, though he could not, for all that, help wondering at the strangeness of the adventure. Glass after glass of wine he drank, and by-and-by, becoming tipsy, went to bed and fell into a deep sleep.

Next morning, at breakfast, he was offered wine even better than that of the night before, and having drunk it, was conducted by the master to the trading-room, which was well filled with every kind of merchandise. Then and there Thórdur showed the man his wares, and received from him in exchange more than half again what he would have got for them at Hofsós. With the money he bought corn and linen, and many other small things, at a much lower price than he was wont to pay elsewhere for the like, and filled with them his sack.

When the trading was finished the master offered him as a gift, a cloak for his wife and cakes for his children, saying to him, " These and many other good turns shall you have at my hands, as tokens of my gratitude to you for having saved my son from death." Thórdur wondered what the man could mean, but the other said, " Once, you were standing under the rock called Thórdarhöfdi, in company with other young men, waiting for a good wind to take your boat to Drángey. Your companions amused themselves by throwing stones against the rock, under which, as the sun was very hot, my son had laid himself down to sleep; for he was tired, having been up all the night. You bade them cease their sport, for it was a foolish one, you said, and a useless. They laughed at you for this notion of yours, and called you strange and fanciful for your pains. But had you not prevented them from throwing stones, they would have killed my son."

After this Thórdur took leave of all in the house, for the sky was now clear and the path good, and started on his homeward way, the master walking some steps with him,

to wish him "God-speed." Thórdur marched on steadily
for a while; but chancing to look back for the house
wherein he had passed the night, he saw nothing of it,
but, in its place, the rocks of the Thórdarhöfdi. Then he
understood that the kind merchant was an elf, and hastening
home, told his wife all that had befallen him, and gave her
the cloak. As for the wares he had got instead of his own,
he showed them to all his neighbours, and never were the
like of them, for goodness, seen in all that country, nor in
any other country under the sun.

THE MAGIC SCYTHE.

A certain day-labourer once started from his home in
the south, to earn wages for hay-cutting, in the north
country. In the mountains, he was suddenly overtaken
by a thick mist and sleet-storm, and lost his way. Fearing
to go on further, he pitched his tent in a convenient spot,
and taking out his provisions, began to eat.

While he was engaged upon his meal, a brown dog came
into the tent, so ill-favoured, dirty, wet, and fierce-eyed,
that the poor man felt quite afraid of it, and gave it as
much bread and meat as it could devour. This the dog
swallowed greedily, and ran off again into the mist. At
first the man wondered much to see a dog in such a wild
place, where he never expected to meet with a living

creature, but after a while he thought no more about the matter, and having finished his supper, fell asleep, with his saddle for a pillow.

At midnight he dreamed that he saw a tall and aged woman enter his tent, who spoke thus to him, "I am beholden to you, good man, for your kindness to my daughter, but am unable to reward you as you deserve. Here is a scythe which I place beneath your pillow: it is the only gift I can make you, but despise it not. It will surely prove useful to you, as it can cut down all that lies before it. Only beware of putting it into the fire to temper it. Sharpen it, however, you will, but in that way never." So saying she was seen no more.

When the man awoke and looked forth, he found the mist all gone and the sun high in heaven; so getting all his things together and striking his tent, he laid them upon the pack-horses, saddling, last of all, his own horse. But on lifting his saddle from the ground, he found beneath it a small scythe-blade, which seemed well worn and was rusty. On seeing this he, at once, recalled to mind his dream, and taking the scythe with him, set out once more on his way. He soon found again the road which he had lost, and made all speed to reach the well-peopled district to which he was bound.

When he arrived at the north country, he went from house to house, but did not find any employment, for every farmer had labourers enough, and one week of hay-harvest was already past. He heard it said, however, that one old woman in the district, generally thought by her neighbours to be skilled in magic and very rich, always began her hay-cutting a week later than anybody else, and though she seldom employed a labourer, always contrived to finish it by the end of the season. When, by any chance—and it was a rare one—she did engage a workman, she was never known to pay him for his work.

Now the peasant from the south was advised to ask this old woman for employment, having been warned of her strange habits.

He accordingly went to her house, and offered himself to her as a day-labourer. She accepted his offer, and told him that he might, if he chose, work a week for her, but must expect no payment.

"Except," she said, "you can cut more grass in the whole week than I can rake in on the last day of it."

To these terms he gladly agreed, and began mowing. And a very good scythe he found that to be which the woman had given him in his dream; for it cut well, and never wanted sharpening, though he worked with it for five days unceasingly. He was well content, too, with his place, for the old woman was kind enough to him.

One day, entering the forge next to her house, he saw a vast number of scythe-handles and rakes, and a big heap of blades, and wondered beyond measure what the old lady could want with all these. It was the fifth day—the

Friday—and when he was asleep that night, the same elf-woman whom he had seen upon the mountains, came again to him, and said:

"Large as are the meadows you have mown, your employer will easily be able to rake in all that hay to-morrow, and if she does so, will—as you know—drive you away without paying you. When, therefore, you see yourself worsted, go into the forge, take as many scythe-handles as you think proper, fit their blades to them and carry them out into that part of the land where the hay is yet uncut. There you must lay them on the ground, and you shall see how things go."

This said, she disappeared, and in the morning the labourer getting up, set to work, as usual, at his mowing.

At six o'clock the old witch came out, bringing five rakes with her, and said to the man:

"A goodly piece of ground you have mowed, indeed!"

And so saying she spread the rakes upon the hay. Then the man saw, to his astonishment, that though the one she held in her hand raked in great quantities of hay, the other four raked in no less, each, all of their own accord and with no hand to wield them.

At noon, seeing that the old woman would soon get the best of him, he went into the forge and took out several scythe-handles, to which he fixed their blades, and bringing them out into the field laid them down upon the grass which was yet standing. Then all the scythes set to work of their own accord, and cut down the grass so quickly that the rakes could not keep pace with them. And so they went on all the rest of the day, and the old woman was unable to rake in all the hay which lay in the fields. After dark, she told him to gather up his scythes and take them into the house again, while she collected her rakes, saying to him :

" You are wiser than I took you to be, and you know more than myself: so much the better for you, for you may stay as long with me as you like."

He spent the whole summer in her employment, and they agreed very well together, mowing with mighty little trouble a vast amount of hay. In the autumn she sent him away, well laden with money, to his own home in the south. Next summer, and more than one summer following he spent in her employ, always being paid as his heart could desire, at the end of the season.

After some years, he took a farm of his own in the south country, and was always looked upon by all his neighbours as an honest man, a good fisherman, and an able workman in whatever work he might put his hand to. He always cut his own hay, never using any scythe but that which the elf-woman had given him upon the mountains; nor did any of his neighbours ever finish their mowing before him.

One summer it chanced that, while he was out fishing, one of his neighbours came to his house and asked his wife to lend him her husband's scythe, as he had lost his own. The farmer's wife looked for one, but could only find the one upon which her husband set such store. This, however, a little loth, she lent to the man, begging him at the same time never to temper it in the fire, for that, she said, her good man never did. So the neighbour promised, and taking it with him, bound it to a handle and began to work with it. But, sweep as he would, and strain as he would (and sweep and strain he did right lustily), not a single blade of grass fell. Wroth at this, the man tried to sharpen it, but with no avail. Then he took it into his forge, intending to temper it, for, thought he, what harm could that possibly do; but as soon as the flames touched it, the steel melted like wax, and nothing of it was left but a little heap of ashes. Seeing this, he went in haste to the farmer's house, where he had borrowed it, and told the woman what had happened: she was at her wits' end with fright and shame when she heard it, for she knew well enough how her husband set store by this scythe, and how angry he would be at its loss.

And angry indeed he was, when he came home, and he beat his wife well for her folly in lending what was not hers to lend. But his wrath was soon over, and he never again, as he never had before, laid the stick about his wife's shoulders.

GRÍMSBORG.

In the north country, near a farm called Keta, stands a high and steep rock, named Grímsborg. It is said that, in this wild castle, elves have dwelt for many ages, and that their chief has always been called Grímur. Certain old folk, not long dead, used to declare that in their time, four elves dwelt in the Grímsborg, two men and two women, and that of these each pair went in turn to church at Keta, when there was worship, leaving the others at home.

It happened that a bad season, for a long time prevailing, cut off from the inhabitants of that district their supply of food, and drove them into the very jaws of death. Once, during the famine, the farmer of Keta, chancing to pass the Elf-castle, bethought him of what hope might lie in an appeal to the good-will of the chief elf, and going close to the foot of the borg, said in a loud voice :—

> " Rich Grímur of the castle, hear our sorrow!
> And, of thy pity, ere shall dawn to-morrow,
> Cast up beneath the rocks, upon the shore,
> A mighty whale, that we may starve no more."

Then he waited to hear if there should be any answer to these words. In a few minutes a voice came from the Elf-castle, saying :—

> " Whale, come to land!
> Lie stretched upon the sand
> In death, that those who fear to die
> From famine, find salvation nigh."

C

As soon as he heard these words, the farmer returned
home joyfully, knowing that the days of the famine were
ended, since the elves vouchsafed their help. And next
morning, going with a large band of men down to the
beach, what should he see lying dead upon the rocks, but
a fine whale, which had been driven up by the surf in the
night!

So ended the famine of Keta, for before the people had
finished the flesh of the whale, the season changed and
good days came back again.

"OLD BEGGAR."

Near a certain farm, long ago, three children were playing on a grass-mound, a little girl and two boys. After
they had played for some time, the girl, who was the youngest of them, found a deep hole in the ground, so deep that
she could not see the bottom of it. Stooping down she
thrust her hand into it, and shutting her eyes, cried out
in fun, "Put something into the palm of an old beggar,
and old beggar shall not see." No sooner had she said
the words, than a large silver button was placed in her
hand.

When the other children saw her good luck they were
fit to burst with envy, and the eldest of them stooping
down stuck his hand into the hole too, and said, "Put

something into the hand of an old beggar, and old beggar shall not see," for he hoped to get something at least as good as the little girl had got, if not better indeed.

But no! Far from it. When he drew his hand out again, he only found that he had lost the use of it, and what is more, never recovered it again. For the elf, who hated envy more than anything in the world, had given it a squeeze.

TÚNGUSTAPI.

In the olden times, many years ago, a rich farmer lived at Sœlíngsdalstúnga. Of his children, two were sons, by name Arnór and Sveinn. These brothers were both full of promise, though as different in character from one another as day and night. Arnór was a brave, stirring, and active youth; Sveinn, a quiet, gentle, and timid one.

Arnór, who was full of life and spirits, spent all his time in out-door sports and games, in company with the other young men who lived in that valley, and who used to meet together at a rocky hill standing near the farm Túnga, which was called Túngustapi. Their favourite amusement in the winter was to slide in sleighs down the snowy sides of the hill, and in the evenings, the rocks used to echo again with their shouts and merriment, Arnór being always ringleader.

Sveinn scarcely ever took part in their sports, but was wont generally to pass his time in the church, and to wander alone about the foot of the hill, when the rest were not playing there. People used to point at him, and to say that he had to do with the elves who dwelt in the mountain.

Certain it was that, without fail, every new year's night, he used to disappear, and nobody knew where he went to. He often warned his brother not to make such riot on the hill, but Arnór always laughed at him for his pains, and said that " no doubt the elves were none the worse for it. As for stopping their sports on the hill, he saw no fun in that, and go on he would." And go on he did, just the same as ever, though Sveinn assured him, over and over again, that harm would come of his folly.

One new year's night Sveinn had disappeared as usual, but stayed much longer away from home than was his custom. Arnór offered to go and look for him, saying in joke, " He is certainly enjoying the company of his friends the elves." So starting out, he took his way to the mountain.

The night was dark and stormy. When he had arrived at that side of the hill which faced the farm, the rock opened suddenly before him of its own accord, and he saw, within, endless rows of the brightest lamps. At the same time he heard the sound of music, and bethought himself that this must surely be the time for the elves' public worship. And drawing nearer he came to an open door, through which he looked, and saw vast crowds of people assembled within. One, who seemed to be a priest, stood, dressed in splendid robes, by an altar, round which were placed numberless burning candles. Arnór then went further in still, and saw his brother Sveinn kneeling before the altar, while the priest, laying his hands on his head, was speaking some words over him. Round about him stood many others, all in sacred robes, so that Arnór guessed at once that they were making his brother an elfin-priest.

Then he cried aloud, " Sveinn! Come! Come with me! You are running the risk of death!"

Whereupon Sveinn started up, and, turning towards the door near which his brother stood, made as if he would hurry to him. But the priest, who stood before the altar, said :

" Shut instantly the door! and let us wreak vengeance upon the man who has dared to place his feet within our holy place. But thou, Sveinn, must go from among us for thy brother's fault; and, inasmuch as thou wert willing to go to him, and loved more his shameless call than these our sacred rites, thou shalt fall down dead whenever thine eyes again see me standing in my robes before this altar."

Arnór now saw those who had been standing round the altar, lift his brother in their arms and vanish with him

through a distant arch of rock. At the same moment the
sound of a bell rang out above him, and all the assembled
crowd rushed with one accord to the doorway. He himself ran through it first, back into the outer night, and
sped towards his home. But soon he heard behind him
the sound of following feet, and the weird tramp of fleet
elfin horses. And one of the foremost riders cried with a
loud voice—

> "Ride! Ride! Ride on!
> For the slopes are dark and the path is dim;
> He flees before, ride after him!
> Let us, with fell enchantment, spread
> Confusion o'er his feet and head,
> In order that he
> May never see
> To-morrow's sun! Ride! Ride! Ride on!"

Then the whole troop rode between Arnór and the farm
and drove him back. On they went over hill and rock
and morass, Arnór, whose dread clogged his feet, knowing
not whither he fled. At last he came to some slopes far
east of his home, and there, his strength forsaking him,
he fell down fainting, and the whole elfin-troop rode over
him, bruising him with the hoofs of their goblin-horses,
till he was more dead than alive.

As to Sveinn, he came home just when the household,
tired of waiting, were going to bed. He did not utter a
word about himself or his own long absence, but bade them
at once make search for his brother Arnór. All the

" *Then the whole troop rode between Arnór and the farm, and drove him back.*"

[*To face page* 38.

servants, therefore, went out and spent the rest of the
night in vainly trying to find him. But he was found at
last by a farmer who lived to the eastward, and who, as he
rode to early worship, at Túnga, next morning, stumbled
across him lying at the foot of the slopes. Arnór was
sensible, but dying, and so weak that he only found
strength and words to tell the farmer what had happened,
and to beg him not to take him home again, but leave
him, before he fell back dead.

Ever since that those mounds have been called " the
slopes of death !"

Sveinn was never himself again, but became more sullen,
silent, and strange than he had been before. And it was
noticed from that time forth he neither went near nor
looked towards the rocky mountain, Túngustapi. He
seemed to care no more for worldly things, and at last
gave them up with their interests for ever, by becoming a
monk, and shutting himself up in the monastery of Helga-
fell. He was so learned that none of the brethren were
by any means a match for him, and he sang the mass so
sweetly that the like of it—they said—had never been
heard before. So they looked on him with awe, and as
on one who is not of this world, and he was, as it were,
head over them all.

Now, after a while, his father, at Túnga, being far on
in years, fell sick for the last time, and yearning to see
his son before he died, sent for Sveinn to come to him.

Sveinn at once obeyed the bidding, but, as he departed, said sadly to the monks who had assembled to wish him God-speed:

" May it fare well with you all for ever, for perchance I may never come back with life again."

He arrived at Túnga the Saturday before Easter, and found his father so void of strength as to be scarcely able to speak. But the old man made it understood that he wished his son to sing the mass on Easter day in the church, whither he himself would be carried to die. Sveinn, strangely loth, consented, but only on condition that the church door should be kept firmly shut during the whole service, for upon the fulfilment of this something told him that his life depended.

Easter morning has arrived, and the dying man is borne by his servants into the church. Then Sveinn, attired in his priestly robes, stands upon the steps of the altar and sweetly sings the mass. So sweetly, that all there present think that never before have they heard a voice like this, and they kneel with the very breath hushed upon their lips to listen to him the better.

But when, at the close of the service, the priest turns from the altar, and with outstretched hands pronounces solemnly the blessing, suddenly a strong wind from the west strikes the church, and the door, bursting from its fastenings, falls heavily inwards. All turn to look, and they see through the empty frame that the rocky hill

near at hand yawns open, and that within it gleam
countless rows of burning lamps. And when they turn
again towards the altar, Sveinn has fallen down and lies
dead where he has just pronounced the blessing. And
his father has fallen also from his couch, his face likewise
white with death.

Then the people knew whence the west wind came, and
how Sveinn has been slain by the revengeful elves.

For the farmer, who had found Arnór at the foot of
the slopes, has long ago told them the story; and they
whisper to one another that Sveinn has seen the elfin-
priest standing robed at his altar.

So the father and son were buried on the same day.

But the church at Túnga now stands elsewhere, that it
may be out of sight of the elfin temple, whose altar is
to the west and whose door to the east.

The Father of Eighteen Elves.

At a certain farm, long ago, it happened that all the
household were out one day, making hay, except the
goodwoman and her only child, a boy of four years old.
He was a strong, handsome, lusty little fellow, who could
already speak almost as well as his elders, and was looked
upon by his parents with great pride and hope. But
as his mother had plenty of other work to do besides

watching him, she was obliged to leave him alone for a short time, while she went down to the brook to wash the milk-pails. So she left him playing in the door of the cottage, and came back again as soon as she had placed the milk-pails to dry.

Directly she spoke to the child, it began to cry in a strange and unnatural way, which amazed her not a little, as it had always been so quiet and sweet-tempered. When she tried to make the child speak to her, as it was wont to do, it only yelled the more, and so it went on for a long time, always crying and never would be soothed, till the mother was in despair at so wonderful a change in her boy, who now seemed to have lost his senses.

Filled with grief, she went to ask the advice of a learned and skilful woman in the neighbourhood, and confided to her all her trouble.

Her neighbour asked her all sorts of questions—How long ago this change in the child's manner had happened? What his mother thought to be the cause of it? and so forth. To all of which the wretched woman gave the best answers she could. At last the wise woman said:

"Do you not think, my friend, that the child you now have is a changeling? Without doubt it was put at your cottage door in the place of your son, while you were washing the milk-pails."

"I know not," replied the other, "but advise me how to find it out."

So the wise woman said, " I will tell you. Place the child where he may see something he has never seen before, and let him fancy himself alone. As soon as he believes no one to be near him, he will speak. But you must listen attentively, and if the child says something that declares him to be a changeling, then beat him without mercy."

That was the wise woman's advice, and her neighbour, with many thanks for it, went home.

When she got to her house, she set a cauldron in the middle of the hearth, and taking a number of rods, bound them end to end, and at the bottom of them fastened a porridge-spoon. This she stuck into the cauldron in such a way that the new handle she had made for it reached right up the chimney: as soon as she had prepared everything, she fetched the child, and placing him on the floor of the kitchen left him and went out, taking care, however, to leave the door ajar, so that she could hear and see all that went·on.

When she had left the room, the child began to walk round and round the cauldron, and eye it carefully, and after a while he said :

" Well ! I am old enough, as anybody may guess from my beard, and the father of eighteen elves, but never, in all my life, have I seen so long a spoon to so small a pot."

On hearing this the goodwoman waited not a moment,

but rushed into the room and snatching up a bundle of fire-wood flogged the changeling with it, till he kicked and screamed again. In the midst of all this, the door opened, and a strange woman, bearing in her arms a beautiful boy, entered and said, "See how we differ! I cherish and love your son, while you beat and illuse my husband;" with these words, she gave back to the farmer's wife her own son, and taking the changeling by the hand, disappeared with him.

But the little boy grew up to manhood, and fulfilled all the hope and promise of his youth.

BLUE FACE.

It happened once that a farmer's daughter in the east country was lost, and, though great search was made for her, was never found again. Her parents were over-whelmed with grief, and the farmer went to the house of a priest who was deemed wiser than his neighbours, and who received him kindly, listening attentively to the man's account of his misfortune, and to his request for help to find out whether his daughter were living or dead. The priest told him that the girl had been stolen by elves, adding, "Nor would seeing her again be any pleasure to you."

But the father could not think this, so fond had he been of his daughter, but urged the priest over and over again to aid him in getting her back. At length, the latter, worn out by continual entreaties, agreed to do so, and appointed an evening on which the farmer should come to his house.

At the appointed time the farmer repaired to the priest's dwelling, who, as soon as the rest of his household had retired to bed, led him out of the house to where a horse was standing ready saddled. The priest mounted the horse, and making the farmer mount behind him, put spurs to his steed, and they rode away. After they had ridden for a time, the peasant knew not how long, they came to the sea, over which the horse galloped as if it had been dry land. At last they came to some high rocks, which rose sheer from the sea, and upon which the waves dashed. Under these the priest guided the horse, until they saw before them an opening like the door of a house, into which the peasant looked and could perceive a bright light, and many people hurrying to and fro. Among them was a woman whose face was pale-blue and who had upon her forehead a white cross. Then the priest asked the peasant how he admired this woman. "Not at all," said he. The priest answered, "That is your daughter, and I can, if you will it, get her back again for you; but I warn you that on account of her having lived with the elves, and through the force of their strange arts, her nature has been changed into a wild one like theirs." The peasant said, "Nay! let us return at once; my heart does not yearn towards her."

So they returned over the sea and over the land, and their fleet horse took them home again ere any knew of their departure.

THE BISHOP AND THE ELVES.

A bishop, travelling to visit the various parts of his diocese, took with him, among other servants, as was the custom in those times (for this was long ago), a maid-servant to cook his meals for him. One evening he rested and caused the tents to be pitched, and the camp for the night to be made upon a certain mountain.

Next morning the maid was missing. Search was made, high and low, far and wide, for her, but all in vain, and the bishop shrewdly suspected that she had been stolen by the elves.

Now he had in his retinue of servants a certain man, who, from his great stature and strength, went by the name of "John the Giant." Accordingly he called John the Giant to him, and said to him:

"Sit you here, upon my bed, while I go out, and do not stir for an instant from the tent. If it should happen that the maid come in, seize her and hold her fast; and, above all things, do not let her go till I return, however much she may struggle, and however much she may beg. Take care, too, how you believe what she says, for to deceive you into leaving her free, she will not stick at a lie."

With these words, the bishop took his staff, and going out drew with it three circles, one within the other, on the ground outside the tent, and went away without anybody seeing in what direction.

Meanwhile John the Giant sat upon the bed and waited, listening and looking intently, but moving neither hand nor foot. After a little while the maid, who had been lost, appeared near the tent, without any shoes upon her feet, and running into it, went up to the pillow of the bishop's bed as if to get something from underneath it. But John the Giant was too quick for her, and starting up flung his arms round her and held her tight. At first she begged him to let her go, saying that the bishop had sent her, and that she must make haste back to him again. Then, as soon as she saw that John the Giant turned a deaf ear to all her entreaties, and did not believe or care for a word she said, she began to struggle, and fought so sturdily, that it was almost more than he could do to hold her.

Just at this time the other servants outside saw twelve mounted men, dressed in blue, ride towards the tent, stopping, however, suddenly, as if they had been shot, when they came to the circles which were drawn round it, and immediately vanishing away.

For these were magic circles which the bishop had made with his holy staff, and nothing evil or ungodly could pass beyond them.

Soon afterwards the bishop himself returned and told his serving men to bind the maid until such time as her temper should be less perverse. Then he again went away, and before long the girl came to her own good senses again. When the others saw this they asked her to tell them what had befallen her, and how she had left the camp without awakening anybody. She declared that in the night a man had come to her bedside, taken her hand and led her out, she not knowing why or whither they were going till they came to a certain mound, into which they entered. That here she found a great many people assembled in a large hall, at the end of which was a raised daïs, with many women collected together upon it. That these women had made her go to bed, and placed beside her couch a spinning-wheel and bundle of hemp, bidding her spin it when she awoke. "But," she said, "in the morning the bishop, with his staff in his hand, came to my bedside and bade me run back here and fetch his keys from under his pillow. I rose and ran in such haste that I had not even time to put on my shoes."

And this was the end of the matter. The bishop came

back soon afterwards, not ill-pleased with his morning's work; for being pretty well skilled in magic and the like, and being, moreover, a very holy man, and a right-determined one to boot, he had played the elves a pretty trick that day, in getting his maid-servant out of their hands almost as soon as they had got her into theirs. And, as far as that went, he could have done it a hundred times just as easily as once; and in a different way each time.

Who built Reynir Church?

A certain farmer once lived at Reynir, in the district of Mýrdal. He was ordered by the bishop to build a good church hard by his farm-house, but had so much difficulty in getting enough timber before the hay-making season, and then so much trouble in finding proper builders, that he feared he should be unable to finish the work before the winter.

One day as he was walking in his field, thinking sadly over the matter, and how he should excuse himself to the bishop for failing to obey his bidding, a strange man, whom he had never seen before, met him, and stopping him, offered him his services in building the church, declaring that he should require the services of no other workman. Then the farmer asked him what payment he would think the due meed of such labour, and the man made the following condition—that the farmer should either find out his name before he had finished the church, or else give him his son, who was then a little boy six years old. The farmer thought these easy terms enough, forsooth, and laughing in his sleeve, gladly consented to them.

So the strange builder set to work, and worked with a will, by day and by night, speaking but little to anybody, until the church rose beneath his hands as quickly as if by magic, and the farmer plainly foresaw that it would be finished even before the hay-making was over.

. But by this time he had rather changed his mind about the payment he had before thought so easy, and was very far from feeling glad that the end of the church-building was so near ; for do what he would, ask whom he would, and search the country round as he would, and had done, he could not, for the life of him, find out the name of his quick-handed mason. Still the church went on not a whit slower for his anxiety, and autumn came, and a very little more labour would finish the building.

One day, the last day of the work, he happened to be wandering outside his field, brooding, in deep grief, over what now seemed to be the heavy price he would have to pay to his master-builder, and threw himself down upon a grass-mound which he came to ; he had scarcely lain there a minute, when he heard some one singing, and listening, he found that the voice was that of a mother lulling her child, and came from inside the mound upon which he had flung himself down. This is what it said :

> " Soon will thy father Finnur come from Reynir,
> Bringing a little playmate for thee, here."

And these words were repeated over and over again ; but the farmer, who pretty soon guessed what they meant, did not wait to hear how many times the mother thought fit to sing them, or what the child seemed to think of them, but started up and ran with all speed, his heart filled with joy, to the church, in which he found the builder just nailing the last plank over the altar.

" Well done, friend Finnur !" said he, " how soon you have finished your work !"

No sooner had these words passed his lips than friend Finnur, letting the plank fall from his hand, vanished, and was never seen again.

KATLA'S DREAM.

A certain chief, named Már, lived, long ago, at Reyk-hólar. His wife, who was of noble family, was called Katla. Once, as was his custom, Már had ridden to the Diet, leaving his wife at home.

One morning, during his absence, Katla, feeling tired and heavy, went to bed, not very long after she had risen from it, and fell into a deep sleep. At noon her attendants went to her to call her, but, try as they would, could not wake her; so, fearing that she was dead, they called her foster-father, who lived in the house, and told him of her state. He went to the side of her bed, and himself endeavoured to rouse her, but quite in vain. Then, looking attentively at her, he said, "She is not dead: the flame of life is still flickering in her bosom, but I am no more able to wake her than you were." And, with these words, he sat down beside her couch, and kept close watch over her for four whole days and nights.

On the fifth day Katla awoke, and seemed to be overcome with sorrow; but no one dared to ask her what was the cause of it.

Soon after this her husband came back home from the Diet; but his wife was no longer the same that he had left behind him. She was changed. She neither went to

meet him, as she was wont to do, nor when he came did
she say " Welcome " to him, nor salute him with her usual
love, nor show joy to see him safe.

Wondering and grieved at her strange manner, he asked
her attendants apart what had befallen her, and why she
behaved thus; but they could only tell him that she had
slept unceasingly for four days and four nights, and on
awaking had shown this sorrow, without ever telling anybody the reason of it, or what ailed her. On hearing this,
Már took Katla herself apart, and urged her to tell him
what ailed her,—whether aught had befallen her in her
long sleep, assuring her that she would lighten her load
of sorrow in thus giving him the half of it. At last,
yielding to her husband's prayers, she spoke as follows :—

" As you know, my husband, I fell into a deep sleep
early one morning while you were away. I had not slept
long, when there came to my bedside a beautiful lady, richly
dressed, who spoke sweetly to me, and telling me that she
lived at the farm Thverá, not far hence, begged me to go
back with her some part of the way thither. As soon as
I rose to comply with her wish, she placed her gloves in
my bed, saying, ' These shall take your place while you
are away.' Then we went out, and came soon to a large
lake, as clear and as smooth as glass, upon which, nea
the shore, a gaily-painted boat was moored. Here I would
part from the lady, and wished her God-speed; but she,
thanking me for having come so far with her, held out her

hand, as if to bid me farewell, crying, 'Will you not say farewell to Alvör ? '

"No sooner had I stretched forth mine in return, than she grasped it tightly, and leaping from the shore into the skiff with me, rowed it swiftly to a small island which stood in the midst of the lake. Now, indeed, I felt only too well that she had all power over me, and that I was unable to resist her. She saw that I was filled with dread, and tried to calm my fears, showing me every kindness and courtesy, and assuring me that it was Fate alone which had compelled her to treat me thus. 'I will,' she said, 'soon take you safely home again.'

"When we had come to the island, I saw that there stood upon it a castle, more beautiful than anything I had ever seen or heard of before. 'This is mine,' said Alvör; and leading me into it by the hand, she took me to her own room, where many ladies were sitting. There she made me enter a bath of sweet water, and when I had bathed, she took me to a beautiful bed which stood in the room, covered with curtains of the richest stuff, and filled with soft down. In this I fell asleep after I had drunk a cup of some rare wine which was handed me. When I awoke, I found on a couch near me a mantle worked richly in gold, which the lady who sat by my side bade me put on, together with an embroidered dress which she gave me. When I was dressed, she threw also over me her own mantle, which was daintily wrought in gold and

" No sooner had I stretched forth mine in return, than she grasped it tightly, and leaping from the shore into the skiff with me, rowed it swiftly to a small island.'

[To face page 54.

lined with fur. Besides all this, she gave me five rings of
red gold, a golden band for my hair, and a costly belt,
begging me to keep them all as gifts. After I had thus
attired myself, she bade me follow her to the dining-hall,
and we went there with her, eight ladies in all.

"All the walls of the room were hung with cloth of
woven gold, and the tables were crowded with silver vessels
and flagons, and with gold inlaid horns; and round the
table sat many handsome men, splendidly attired. At
the high table stood a throne, and near this I saw a man,
dressed in rich silk, lying asleep on a couch. Alvör went up
to him and woke him, and I heard that she called him Kári.

"He started up from his slumber, and said to her,
'Why have you broken my rest? Have you aught of
good tidings to tell me? or, perchance, have you brought
Katla hither?'

"As soon as he saw that I was in the hall, he came to
me, and taking me by the hand, led me to the throne,
where he made me sit, and sat beside me. Then the Lady
Alvör pointed to us, and cried out to the guests, 'See!
the bride and bridegroom!' Whereupon they shouted, as
with one voice, and drank and made merry till nightfall.
And through all this din of revel, Alvör told me that for
that night I was to share the couch of Kári; but I, full
wroth, withdrawing myself from her side, said:

"'Never will I do this thing! Far too dearly do I
love my husband to share the love of any other.'

"The lady answered, 'If you say nay, bale and bann will cling to you for ever: be wise, therefore, and consent.'

"Wretched that I was, I knew not what to do, or whither to turn myself, for neither comfort nor aid was near, and I was as a lamb in the midst of a herd of wolves. They led me to the couch in which I had slept before, and then Kári came to me, and offered me all he had, if I would only love him. I told him that his love was hopeless, but he would not hear me. Then he brought me a horn of wine; and after he had tasted it himself first, made me drink of it, saying:

"'Rather would I struggle with Helja than see sorrow in your eyes. Be comforted; you shall soon return to your home.'

"With these words he lay beside me; and whether it were the force of his entreaties, or the beauty of his presence, or the weight of the wine upon my soul, I cannot tell, but I no longer opposed his love, though the while my heart was filled with grief.

"And so in sorrow passed two days and nights; nor could all the kindness of the attendants, and of all around me, comfort me. At last Kári said to me, 'Call the son whom you shall bear to me by my name, and give him from his father, whom he shall never see, this belt of wrought gold, and this knife with the haft of cunning workmanship, and let them be heirlooms in his family.' And he bade me place the belt and knife, together with the embroidered garments and costly ornaments which I had worn while with him, in a sack, and take them home with me.

"'Show them,' he said, 'to your husband Már, and tell him the whole truth, though it be a grief and woe to your heart to do so; for it is but just, and your duty. Let him aid you in building a farm at Thverá, where you shall see two small hillocks, which shall be your money-mounds. In that place you shall found a great and noble family. Now I must leave you, and you will never see me again, for,' said he sadly, 'the hours of my life are numbered.'

" When he had finished speaking, Alvör the lady took my hand and led me out; and as I left the hall I heard a loud and echoing sound, and turning my head to see whence it came, behold Kári lay dead, for his heartstrings had broken with exceeding love and sorrow. So the lady rowed me again in the boat across the lake and brought me home, and took the gloves out of my bed.

" As she left me she said, ' May it fare well with you, though you have caused but sorrow to me in breaking my son's heart for love and anguish. Enjoy all the wealth you have, and be happy.' So saying, she was no more with me.

" This is the end of my dream. Therefore, my husband, as you are a just and true man, weigh my fault against its causes, and forgive me. Truly my love for you has not one whit departed."

So she showed Már all the beautiful and costly things
that she had brought with her from Alvör's castle.

In the summer she gave birth to a son, a lovely child,
and exceeding all other children in mind and form, whom
she called, as she had promised his father—Kári. But
she never loved the boy with a true mother's love ; though
on the other hand Már doted upon him as if he had been
his own son. Soon after, they built a new farm at Thverá,
where they found the two money-mounds, as Kári had
promised, and, unestranged by Katla's dream, dwelt there
happy and prosperous to a ripe old age.

The Elfin Lover.

A certain rich farmer and his wife had two daughters,
who were named Margrèt and Olöf.

Margrèt was the darling of her parents' hearts, and used
in the summer to take care of a dairy and pasture in the
mountains, for her father and mother always put more trust
in her than in anybody else.

One summer it happened, that, while she was sitting
milking the ewes, a little boy came to her several evenings
in succession, and brought with him a small wooden jug,
which he asked her to fill for him with milk. This Margrèt always refused to do, and as he still came day after
day with the same request, she at last became angry, and

one evening threatened him with a good whipping if he
troubled her again.

"For," she said, "I should think I had plenty to do
without giving milk to all the little boys who choose to
come with jugs for it. Begone!"

At this the child ran back crying to his mother, who
was an elfwoman, and who lived near the mountain-farm,
and told her how harshly Margrèt had spoken to him.
The elfwoman was mighty wroth at this, and said:

"Harsh words shall meet with a harsh lot. This shall
be Margrèt's fate. She shall spend and fritter away everything that comes into her hands just as lavishly as she has
stingily refused to give you milk. She shall try how she
likes poverty and loss of trust." And true enough she
certainly did become such a spendthrift, that her father and
mother soon noticed it, and not caring that she should
waste all they had, withdrew her from the mountain pasture and sent Olöf there in her stead.

When the latter had been there some little time, the
same child came to her as she sat out in the evening milking the ewes, and, holding out his little porringer, said:

"Olöf, my mother sends her love to you, and begs you
to give her a little milk for her child. When your sister
Margrèt was here I often asked her for some, but she was
harsh and said nay, and drove me out of her sight."

Olöf was tender-hearted, and willingly gave the boy some
milk to drink himself and filled his jug for him, at the same

time telling him to come whenever he liked. The boy ran off to his mother and told her how different things were now, and how kindly the girl had spoken to him and treated him. Whereupon the elfwoman said:

" Good words shall have a good reward. ᵥ This shall be Olöf's fate. All that comes into her hands shall turn to fair luck, and all she has shall increase as many-fold as her kindness to you has been greater than her sister's cruelty."

So for some summers the boy came often to Olöf for milk. Now one autumn her companions in the mountain-farm noticed that she was soon to give birth to a child, but being discreet, and moreover loving her well, they kept their discovery from all else, though they could not help whispering among themselves that the boy who used to beg for milk was just as fond of Olöf herself as of her milk-pails, if not more so.

One night Olöf was delivered of a child. As soon as it was born, an old man and old woman, together with the boy who had so often visited Olöf on the mountains, came into the cottage, and taking the child in their arms went out with it, after bidding her an affectionate farewell. All this her companions saw, and that the youth often came and spoke with her, though Olöf fully believed that not only the birth of her child, but also the visits of the elves, were unknown to all but herself.

Time passed without any new occurrence, until Olöf's mother fell into a sickness which was her last. After her mother's death, Olöf took her place in keeping the house, but never seemed quite happy after what had happened at the mountain-hut. Many fine young fellows wooed and wished to win her, but she said nay to them all, and sent them all off without so much as turning her head to look after them.

At last one came, to whom Olöf's father, wearied with her eternal refusals, bade her give herself. For some while she would not listen to him, but at length consented to marry him only on the condition that he would never allow anyone to pass the winter with them, until he had first spoken to her and asked her leave to do so. He made her this promise, and they were speedily married and went to live at the husband's farm (for he was a farmer, well to do), which was in the mountains, far from her old home.

She had not been there long, when her mother-in-law saw that some weight lay upon Olöf's heart, and that her eyes were often filled with tears, and begged her to tell her the cause of her grief. But Olöf would not be persuaded, for a long time, and always put the other off with shirking answers. At last, however, her mother-in-law promised never, as long as she lived, to repeat to anyone the truth, if Olöf would only tell it her. So Olöf told it her, and when she found how the good woman pitied her, and how kind and leal was that heart into which she poured her sorrow, she wondered why she had not trusted her at first.

For there is no balm like pity to a wounded soul, how-

ever deep the wound and however long it may have ached
in secret.

In the third year after Olöf's marriage, but the twelfth
from the birth of her child in the mountain-hut, it happened
at autumntide, towards the end of the hay harvest, that a
man and a young boy came to the farmer's house and gave
him greeting. He had never seen them before, but he
noticed that they kept their hats slouched down over their
brows, as if they were unwilling to be known. When the
farmer had returned kindly their salutation, they begged
him to allow them to pass the winter in his house. The
farmer answered:

"It is not my custom to receive strangers thus. It is
long since I have done so."

But on their becoming more urgent, he said:

"I cannot bid you welcome, nor will I send you away,
until I have first seen my wife, and spoken to her about
it."

The man answered, "Truly you do well, and it becomes
you to let your wife have the upper hand of you. If you
send us away, be sure that all your neighbours shall know
which of you two is master."

This taunt was more than the farmer could bear, so he
promised to let them stay with him. Then going into
the house he met Olöf, who said to him:

"What men are these?"

"I know not," he replied: "they have come to me to

ask lodging for the winter, and they urged me so, that I promised it them, and bade them welcome to stay with us."

Then Olöf said, "In so doing you have broken your promise to me, but some voice in this matter I will have. These men shall not sleep in the house with the rest of the servants, but shall spend the winter in one of the outbuildings."

And she left him, and went to her own room weeping.

So the farmer made ready one of the outlying buildings, furnishing it with every necessary from the farm, and gave it up as a winter dwelling for the two strangers; but his wife never set foot inside its door, nor went near it. The man and boy took up their abode there, joining the farmer's family every evening in the family room, as was the custom, but always sitting apart in a dark corner, and never speaking unless the farmer first addressed them. Olöf always seemed as if she did not see them, never even once looking at or speaking to them. Thus the winter passed away and spring came.

Now it happened one Sunday, that the farmer and his wife were going to church in order to take the Holy Communion, having bidden farewell to all their household. When they were a little way from home, the farmer asked Olöf:

"Have you bidden farewell to all at home?"

She said, "To all."

Then he asked again, " Have you bidden farewell to the strangers also ? "

" No," she said, " I have not, nor need I, for the whole winter through I have neither spoken to nor looked at them. How then can I have trespassed against them ? "

But the farmer was not well-pleased at this, and urged her to return and bid the strangers farewell, and the more she refused, the more he waxed wroth, till at length she seeing that he would be obeyed, said :

" Well ! I will return, as you have bidden, but for what comes of it, blame yourself, not me."

She went, and the farmer waited for her, but she stayed so long away that he turned back after her, to see what had delayed her. When he came to the outhouse in which the two strangers lived, he found the door unlatched, and stopping by it to listen if his wife were there, he heard her say these words:

" This is the sweetest draught that ever passed my lips from thine."

He waited yet a while to hear if more would be said, but no other sound came from the house. So he went in, and there on the couch lay his wife and the stranger dead (for their hearts had broken from love and sorrow) ; and over them the young boy stood weeping. When he asked the lad what this meant, and how death had befallen them, he only said, " These are my parents."

But his mother told him Olöf's story, for she held

herself free from her promise now that Olöf was dead.
And the farmer, full of grief, bade the lad welcome to stay
with him, and as he had been Olöf's child, so to be his.
But from the moment when Olöf and her elfin lover were
hidden by the earth, the boy was no more seen.

The Man-Whale.

In ancient times, in the south part of the country, it
was the custom to go in a boat, at a certain season of the
year, from the mainland to the cliffs, Geirfuglasker, to
procure sea-birds and the eggs which they were in the
habit of laying there. The passage to these rocks was
always looked upon as an unsafe one, as they stood some
way out at sea, and a constant and heavy surf beat upon
them.

It happened once that some men went thither in a boat
at the proper season for the purpose, as the weather seemed
to promise a long calm. When they arrived at the rocks,
some of them landed, the rest being left to take care of
the boat. Suddenly a heavy wind came on, and the latter
were forced to leave the island in haste, as the sea became
dangerous and the surf beat furiously upon the cliffs. All
those who had landed were enabled to reach the boat in time,
at the signal from their companions, except one, a young
and active man, who, having gone in his zeal higher and

E

farther than the others, was longer in getting down to the beach again. By the time he did get down, the waves were so high, that though those in the boat wrought their best to save him, they could not get near enough to him, and so were compelled for their own lives' sake to row to shore. They determined, however, when the storm should abate its fury, to return to the rocks and rescue him, knowing that unless they did so and the wind were soon spent, the youth could not but perish from cold and hunger. Often they tried to row to the Geirfuglasker, but, the whole season through, they were unable to approach them, as the wind and surf always drove them back. At last, deeming the young man dead, they gave up the attempt and ceased to risk their lives in seas so wrathful.

So time passed away, until the next season for seeking sea-birds came round, and the weather being now calm, the peasants embarked in their boat for the Geirfuglasker. When they landed upon the cliffs, great was their astonishment at seeing come towards them a man, for they thought that no one could live in so wild and waste a spot. When the man drew near them, and they recognized him as the youth who had been left there the year before, and whom they had long ago given up as lost, their wonder knew no bounds, and they guessed that he had the elves to thank for his safety. They asked him all sorts of questions. What had he lived upon? Where had he slept at night?

What had he done for fire in the winter? and so forth,
but he would give them none but vague replies, which left
them just as wise as they were before. He said, however,
he had never once left the cliff, and that he had been very
comfortable there, wanting for nothing. They then rowed
him to land, where all his friends and kin received him
with unbounded amazement and joy, but, question him as
they would, could get but mighty little out of him concerning his life on the cliffs the whole year through. With
time, the strangeness of this event and the wonder it had
awakened passed away from men's minds, and it was little
if at all more spoken of.

One Sunday in the summer, certain things that took
place in the church at Hvalsnes filled people with astonishment. There were large numbers there, and among them
the young man who had passed a year on the cliffs of the
Geirfuglasker. When the service was over and the folk
began to leave the church, what should they find standing
in the porch but a beautiful cradle with a baby in it.
The coverlet was richly embroidered, and wrought of a
stuff that nobody had ever seen before. But the strangest
part of the business was, that though everybody looked at
the cradle and child, nobody claimed either one or the other,
or seemed to know anything whatever about them. Last of
all came the priest out of church, who, after he had admired
and wondered at the cradle and child as much as the others,
asked whether there was no one present to whom they

belonged. No one answered. Then he asked whether there was no one present who had enough interest in the child to desire him to baptize it. No one either answered or came forward.

At this moment the priest happened to cast his eyes on the young peasant, concerning whose sojourn on the Geirfuglasker rocks he had always felt particularly suspicious, and calling him aside, asked him whether he had any idea who its father was, and whether he would like the child baptized. But the youth turning angrily from him declared that he knew nothing whatever about the child or its father.

" What care I," he said, " whether you baptize the child or no ? Christen it or drown it, just which you think fit ; neither it, nor its father, nor its mother, are aught to me."

As these words left his lips, there suddenly appeared in the porch a woman, handsomely apparelled, of great beauty and noble stature, whom no one had ever seen before. She snatched the coverlet from the cradle, and flinging it in through the door of the church, said :

" Be witnesses all, that I wish not the church to lose its dues for this child's baptism."

Then turning to the young peasant, and stretching out her hands towards him, she cried, " But thou, O faithless coward, disowner of thy child, shalt become a whale, the fiercest and most dreaded in the whole wide sea ! "

With these words, she seized the cradle and disappeared.

The priest, however, took the coverlet which she had flung into the church, and made of it an altar-cloth, the handsomest that had ever been seen. As for the young peasant, he went mad on the spot; and, rushing down to the Holmur Cliffs, which rise sheer from the deep water, made as if he would throw himself from them. But while he hesitated for a moment on the brink, lo! a fearful change came over him, and he began to swell to a vast size, till, at last, he became so large, that the rock could no longer bear him, but crumbling beneath him hurled him into the sea. There he was changed into a great whale, and the red cap which he had been wearing, became a red head.

After this, his mother confessed that her son had spent the year with the elves upon the Geirfuglasher. On his being left on the rocks by his companions (so he had declared to her), he had at first wandered about in despair, filled only with the thought of throwing himself into the waves to die a speedy death rather than suffer all the pangs of hunger and cold; but a lovely girl had come to him, and telling him she was an elf, had asked him to spend the winter with her. She had borne him a child before the end of the year, and only allowed him to go to shore when his companions came again to the cliffs, on condition that he would have this child baptized when he should find it in the church-porch, threatening him, if he failed in the fulfilment of this, with the severest punishment and most hapless fate.

Now Redhead, the whale, took up his abode in the Faxafjörd, and wrought mischief there without end, destroying boats innumerable, and drowning all their crews, so that at last it became unsafe to cross any part of the bay, and nothing could either prevent his ravages or drive him away. After matters had gone on like this for some time, the whale began to haunt a 'narrow gulf between Akranes and Kjarlarnes, which is now called after him, Hvalfjördur.

At that time there lived at Saurbœr, in Hvalfjardar-strönd, an aged priest, who, though hale and hearty, was blind. He had two sons and a daughter, who were all in the flower of their youth, and who were their father's hope and stay, and, as it were, the very apple of his eye. His sons were in the habit of fishing in Hvalfjördur, and one day when they were out they encountered the whale, Redhead, who overthrew their boat and drowned them both. When their father heard of their death, and how it had been brought about, he was filled with grief, but uttered not a word at the time.

Now it must be known that this old priest was well skilled in all magical arts.

Not long after this, one fine morning in the summer, he bade his daughter take his hand and guide him down to the sea-shore. When he arrived there, he planted the end of the staff which he had brought with him, in the waves, and leaning on the handle fell into deep thought.

After a few minutes he asked his daughter, "How looks the sea?"

She answered, "My father, it is as bright and smooth as a mirror."

Again, a few minutes, and he repeated, "How looks the sea?"

She replied, "I see on the horizon a black line, which draws nearer and nearer, as it were a shoal of whales, swimming quickly into the bay."

When the old man heard that the black line was approaching them, he bade the girl lead him along the shore towards the inland end of the bay. She did so, and the black surging sea followed them constantly. But as the water became shallower, the girl saw that the foam arose, not from a shoal of whales, as she had thought at first, but from the swimming of a single huge whale with a red head, who came rapidly towards them along the middle of the bay, as if drawn to them by some unseen power. A river ran into the extreme end of the gulf, and the old priest begged his daughter to lead him still on along its banks. As they went slowly up the stream, the old man feeling every footstep before him, the whale followed them, though with a heavy struggle, as the river contained but little water for so vast a monster to swim in. Yet forward they went, and the whale still after them, till the river became so narrow between its high walls of rock, that the ground beneath their feet quaked as the whale followed

them. After a while they came to a waterfall, up which
the monster leaped with a spring that made the land
tremble far and wide, and the very rocks totter. But they
came at last to a lake, from which the river rose, whose
course they had followed from the sea; the lake Hvalvatn.
Here the heart of the monster broke from very toil and
anguish, and he disappeared from their eyes.

When the old priest returned home, after having charmed
the whale thus to his death, all the people from far and
near thanked him for having rid their coasts of so dread a
plague.

And in case anybody should doubt the truth of this
story of Redhead, the man-whale, we may as well say that
on the shores of the lake Hvalvatn, mighty whale-bones
were found lying long after the date of this tale.

Valbjörg the Unelfed.

In the east country, not far from the Lakes of Wool,
as they are called, lived a certain farmer, who had a son
named Sigurdur.

It happened one year, that this peasant had lost all his
sheep upon the mountains, and, as his flocks were nearly
all that he had to depend upon for his livelihood, had taken
the loss very much to heart, and sent four or five men in
succession to search far and near, through hill and valley,

" *After a while they came to a waterfall, up which the monster leaped with a spring that made the land tremble far and wide.*"

[*To face page* 72.

for the missing sheep, which could not, in the short time
that had passed since they were lost sight of, have strayed
very far.

But to the farmer's great distress neither sheep nor
shepherds ever came to light again.

One fine day Sigurdur, who was a sturdy fellow and
brave to boot, said to his father, " My father, I will go and
try my luck in searching for your lost servants and flocks ;
give me God speed."

His parents were mightily against this, " for," said they,
" we would rather lose a thousand servants and a thousand
flocks than our son."

But Sigurdur laughed at their fears, and said " go he
would, and go he must." Accordingly, go he did, having
asked the blessing of his parents. Over hill and through
valley he went, just as he had heard his father bid the
shepherds go ; but though he looked far and near, and
though he toiled himself well weary, nothing did he see of
either men or sheep. At last he came to some large lakes,
round the shores of which lay vast masses of wool spread
out for drying. On the other side of these, lay some
pasture lands of the richest grass, upon which he saw
flocks grazing and shepherds watching them. Thinking,
at once, that they must be the sheep that had been lost
and of which he was in search, he made his way, with all
speed, towards them. But he had scarcely gone near
enough to count them, when a woman of handsome

presence walked up to him and saluted him kindly. When he had returned her greeting, he asked her what she was called.

"I am called," she said, "Vandrád or Valbjörg, which you please, and am glad to see you here and welcome you, friend Sigurdur."

"Surely I have never seen you before," replied he; "how then do you know my name?"

The woman answered, "I know well both you and your father Andres, and what is more, I know that you are now in search of his missing flocks and herdsmen. To tell you the truth, it was I that both lost your father his sheep and killed his shepherds. And you, since you have been fool-hardy enough to wander about on the same errand, shall lose your life in the same way as the others have done, if you will not agree, better than they, to what I ask you."

"What is your will?" said Sigurdur. "Tell me what you wish me to do."

Then she said, "My will is that you stay here and live with me and never try to escape."

"But," replied Sigurdur again, "I must know first to what manner of woman I pledge myself; and if you refuse to tell me I will rather die, for I know not fear, than say you yea."

Upon this she answered, "I am one of the race of elves, and I dwell in yonder hillock."

Then Sigurdur consented to live with her, on condition

that she would, firstly, let him build a house for himself
after his own manner; secondly, that she would let his
father know that he still lived and did well; and lastly,
that she would restore safe and sound his father's flocks.
All these things she promised to do, and bade Sigurdur
follow her. Pretty well content with the bargain he had
made, and not altogether cold to Valbjörg's charms, he
followed her till they came to the hillock, into which they
entered through a door of carved wood. As Sigurdur was
looking round him and admiring the beauty of the rooms
and the traces of wealth which they contained, Valbjörg
said to him:

"Two years have I lived here quite alone, since I lost
my parents, and weary and lonely have I been. And I
have been unwilling to dwell with one of my own race, as
my father prophesied that I should have children by a
human being. Therefore, when the herdsmen came here
to look after the lost flocks, I asked them to stay with me
and comfort me, and when each refused, I slew him by
magic art. But I am well pleased, Sigurdur, that your
heart has inclined towards me, as now my father's words
will be accomplished."

So Sigurdur built himself a hut close to the hillock, and
lived with Valbjörg; and though, at first, he found his
new life irksome to him, and his soul yearned for home,
yet after a short time he became accustomed to everything
about him, and his love for Valbjörg increased.

One morning, when Andres, Sigurdur's father, rose from
sleep and looked forth from the farm, he saw the flock of
sheep which he had lost grazing in the home-field, and
on going to count them, he found that not one was missing.
Much rejoiced at this, he thought that Sigurdur, and
perhaps the missing shepherds, had come back during the
night, and were now in the family room. But no! nothing
had either been seen or heard of them, and Andres was
constrained to send out twenty of his neighbours to search
for them. All in vain, however; for search as they would,
far and near, high and low, over hill and through valley,
not a trace was to be found of the lost men. When they
all came back to the farm with this bad news, the farmer
took it so much to heart, that he fell ill and kept to his
bed.

It happened one night, some little time after this, that
Andres had a dream, in which he saw a woman of handsome presence come to him, who said—

" Fear not, my friend, for your son's life. He is well,
and lives happily with me, who am an elfwoman. It was
I who stole your sheep, but your son made me restore
them."

Upon this she left him, and he woke, full of joy that
his son was still alive; and in the morning he rose again,
restored to health by these happy tidings, and went about
among his servants, attending to the management of the
farm, as he had done before the illness smote him.

Three years went by, and still nothing was heard of Sigurdur. In the autumn of the third year, however, the farmer Andres had a dream, in which his son came to him, and after he had saluted him, said:

" Come, my father, I entreat you, on Christmas-eve, to the Lakes of Wool, and bring with you the priest Eiríkur. By the shores of the lakes you will see my house standing, and will find the door thrown open. Come into the house yourself, but bid Eiríkur stand in the entrance and grasp tightly the woman who shall run out from the family-room as if to leave the house. On no account must he let her go, do or say what she will, as on his holding her fast depend my safety and happiness. If she escape him that Christmas-eve, you will never see me more."

With these words he vanished, and Andres woke. After pondering a while over this dream, which he felt to be no idle fancy, but well fraught with meaning, he determined to do as Sigurdur had bidden him, and rising went forthwith to Eiríkur's house to take counsel with him thereupon. When the priest had heard the dream, he said to the farmer:

" My friend, this but confirms what I have always thought, namely, that the elves withhold your son from you, and right willingly will I aid you in this matter, whatever turn it may take."

Accordingly in due time Andres and Eiríkur addressed themselves to their journey, and on Christmas-eve arrived at the shores of the Lakes of Wool. They at once saw

Sigurdur's house, and going up to it found the door thrown open. · Then Andres went in, leaving the priest in the doorway, as his son had told him in the dream to do. When he entered the family-room he saw, by the light of a candle that was burning there, his son Sigurdur carding wool upon a wooden chest. Near him was a bed, on which sat a woman with a child in her arms, and another child lying in a cradle before her feet.

So the farmer saluted them, saying, "God be here."

No sooner were the words out of his mouth than the woman, flinging down the child she held in her arms, and leaping over the cradle which lay at her feet, ran hastily from the family-room, and made as if she would leave the house. But Eiríkur, the priest, who stood in the doorway, was too quick for her, and seizing her in his arms, held her fast. And that was no easy matter, for she struggled so that the priest, who had the strength of two men, and who was moreover skilled in wrestling and manly arts, had much ado to resist her. When they heard the noise, Sigurdur and his father went out from the family-room, taking the light with them, and helped the priest to bring her back into the house and lay her down on the bed. After Eiríkur had laid his hand gently upon her she became quieter, and he watched over her all that night. From time to time she fainted, and when she came again to her senses, wept till it made the blood of all who heard her run cold. And she entreated the priest to let her go

free, by all he loved best; but he was not to be moved
from his firm though gentle watch and ward. At last,
after day had broken, Sigurdur and his father collected all
the house-wealth together, packed it on horses, and set
forth, taking the priest and Valbjörg and the children with
them, and driving the flocks before them. When they
had left the hut and the mound a little way behind them,
Sigurdur turned round and cast a spell over the place,
which is the reason why nobody can find it.

Now the weather being fine and the nights bright and
calm, the whole company travelled without resting till they
came to Andres' farm, where the priest Eiríkur dwelt with
them a week, trying, through much watching and prayer,
to tame the savage temper of Valbjörg.

But at the end of that time Sigurdur and his father
thought best that he should take the woman to his own
house for the remainder of the winter, which he did; and
before the spring time, he had quite subdued her elfin
nature.

In the meantime Sigurdur took care of his two children
at the farm, and his flocks wandered about the hills, taking
care of themselves and trusting to kind neighbours.

In the spring Eiríkur joined Sigurdur and Valbjörg in
marriage, and a very loving and happy couple they were,
now that all Valbjörg's elfin nature had left her. So they
dwelt to a good age in the parish of which the worthy
Eiríkur was priest, and Valbjörg was much loved and

looked up to, as a Christian woman and a good housewife.
Four children they had, whose descendants may no doubt
be found in the East of Iceland, by anybody who cares to
look for them.

UNA THE ELFWOMAN.

A certain man named Geir lived at a farm called Randa-
fell, and was rich, young, and active, and a widower at
the time to which this story refers. Once, in the hay-
making season, a large quantity of hay being left for the
women to rake up—almost more than they could do, for
he kept but few maid-servants—Geir saw a young and
fair woman enter the field, and begin raking up the hay
with the others. She uttered not a word to anybody, but
worked quietly, and so quickly, that, very soon after she
arrived, the hay was all got in, till the farmer fancied there
must be some magic power in the rake she used. Every
evening, when the work was over, she went away, but
came on the morrow, and every day through the season,
always doing more work than all the rest, and always
departing at nightfall without exchanging a syllable with
anybody. On the last night of the hay-cutting, however,
the farmer went up to her, and thanked her for having
worked so diligently all the summer. She received his
thanks kindly, and they talked a long time together, the
farmer concluding by asking her to come to his house and

act thenceforth as his housekeeper. She consented, and went away.

Next morning she came to Raudafell, bringing with her a large chest, and at once entered upon her duties in the house. The chest was put into one of the outhouses, as she was unwilling, for some reasons of her own, to keep it in the farm itself. She stayed there through the winter, and Geir had every cause to be pleased with her management of the house, for she was clean and thrifty, and an active manager. She never would tell the farmer whence she came, but went so far as to allow that her name was Una: nor would she ever enter the church, though urged to do so over and over again by the farmer; and this was the only cause of offence which he could find in her.

It was the custom on Christmas-eve for every inmate of the farm to go to church except one, who was left behind to take care of the house. On this occasion Una always refused to go with the rest, which much displeased the farmer; she remained at home, and when the family returned from church, had finished all the household work.

Three years passed, during which time Una remained with the farmer, who became so fond of her, that were it not for her one fault—her dislike of going to church—he would have married her.

On Christmas-eve in the third winter Una was, as usual, while the others went to service, left alone in the house. When the family had gone some little distance

F

from home on their way to church, one of the men-servants
declared himself unwell, and, sitting on a stone, said that
he would remain there till the illness passed over, and that
he did not wish anyone to remain behind with him. The
farmer, therefore, and the rest of the family left him there,
and went on to the church.

When they were out of sight, the man got up and
went back to the farm—for his illness was only feigned in
order to enable him to play the spy upon Una. On arriving
there he saw that Una was sweeping and washing the
whole house, and seemed in great haste to finish her work.
He hid himself so that Una should not know of his return,
and, when she had finished her work, saw her leave the
house. He followed her, and saw her go to the outhouse
and unlock her chest, from which she took out handsome
and cunningly-embroidered clothes, and, having dressed
herself in them, she looked so lovely, that the man-servant
thought he had never seen anybody so beautiful before.
Then she took out of the chest a red cloth, which she put
under her arm, and, locking the box, left the outhouse,
and closed the door behind her. She ran across the meadow near the farm till she came to a soft slough, upon the
surface of which she spread the scarlet cloth, and stepped
into the centre of it, just leaving room by chance at
one of the corners for the man-servant, who (having by
magical arts, in which he was well skilled, made himself
quite invisible) stepped on to the cloth after her.

No sooner was he there than the cloth sank with them through the earth, which seemed like smoke round them, until they came to some wide and fair green fields, where Una stepped off the cloth and put it again under her arm. Some little way off stood a vast and stately palace, into which Una went, and the man after her. Here he found a great number of people assembled, who rose at her entrance, and received her with every show of love and respect. The whole hall in which they stood was adorned as if for a feast. When they had greeted Una they all sat down again, Una amongst them, and the most costly dainties, and rarest wines in gold and silver vessels, were set before them.

But as for our invisible friend, the man-servant, all he could get hold of was a rib-bone of smoked mutton, wonderfully fat and good, which he, without tasting, thrust into his pocket.

When the supper was over, the guests amused themselves with drinking and various games, and kept up the revel all night with a great show of joy. About daybreak Una rose and declared that she must now depart, as the farmer, her master, and his family would by this time be leaving church. Then bidding a courteous farewell to all, she went out again into the fair green fields, where she spread the cloth out once more, and stepped upon it, and the man-servant on to the corner, as before. The cloth rose with them through the earth, till they arrived at the slough, whence they had started. And now, gathering up the cloth under her arm, Una ran into the outhouse, where she locked it, together with her handsome clothes in the chest, and again donning her every-day apparel, went back to the farmer's house. Pretty well content with having seen all this, the man-servant took his visible form, and hastened back to the stone, where he had feigned illness the evening before. On their way homewards from church, the farmer and his family found him; and inquiring how he was, received for answer that he had passed a wretched night, but was much better, and was now able to return home with them, which he did.

When they were all assembled at breakfast, and were eating, the farmer (suspecting nothing) took up a rib-bone of mutton from his plate, and holding it up, said:

" Did any of you ever see so fat a rib-bone as this?"

" Possibly, my master," replied the man-servant; and taking from his pocket the rib-bone of mutton he had stolen from the elfin-feast, held it up.

Directly she saw it, Una changed colour, and without a word vanished from their sight: nor was she ever seen afterwards. So the man told the farmer all that he had seen in the night, and Geir no longer wondered why Una should avoid going to church.

Hildur, the Queen of the Elves.

Once, in a mountainous district, there lived a certain farmer, whose name and that of his farm have not been handed down to us; so we cannot tell them. He was unmarried, and had a housekeeper named Hildur, concerning whose family and descent he knew nothing whatever. She had all the indoor affairs of the farm under her charge, and managed them wondrous well. All the inmates of the house, the farmer himself to boot, were fond of her, as she was clean and thrifty in her habits, and kind and gentle in speech.

Everything about the place flourished exceedingly, but the farmer always found the greatest difficulty in hiring a herdsman; a very important matter, as the well-being of the farm depended not a little on the care taken of the sheep. This difficulty did not arise from any fault of the farmer's own, or from neglect on the part of the housekeeper to the comforts of the servants, but from the fact, that no herdsman who entered his service lived more than a year, each one being without fail found dead in his bed, on the morning of Christmas-day. No wonder, therefore, the farmer found herdsmen scarce.

In those times it was the custom of the country to spend the night of Christmas-eve at church, and this occasion for service was looked upon as a very solemn one.

But so far was this farm from the church, that the herds-men, who did not return from their flocks till late in the evening, were unable to go to it on that night until long after the usual time; and as for Hildur, she always remained behind to take care of the house, and always had so much to do in the way of cleaning the rooms and dealing out the rations for the servants, that the family used to come home from church and go to bed long before she had finished her work, and was able to go to bed herself.

The more the reports of the death of herdsman after herdsman, on the night of Christmas-eve, were spread abroad, the greater became the difficulty the farmer found in hiring one, although it was never supposed for an instant that violence was used towards the men, as no mark had ever been found on their bodies; and as, more-over, there was no one to suspect. At length the farmer declared that his conscience would no longer let him thus hire men only in order that they might die, so he deter-mined in future to let luck take care of his sheep, or the sheep take care of themselves.

Not long after he had made this determination, a bold and hardy-looking man came to him and made him a proffer of his services. The farmer said:

"My good friend, I am not in so great need of your services as to hire you."

Then the man asked him, "Have you, then, taken a herdsman for this winter?"

The farmer said, "No; for I suppose you know what a terrible fate has hitherto befallen every one I have hired."

"I have heard of it," said the other, "but the fear of it shall neither trouble me nor prevent my keeping your sheep this winter for you, if you will but make up your mind to take me."

But the farmer would not hear of it at first; "For," said he, "it is a pity, indeed, that so fine a fellow as you should lose your chance of life. Begone, if you are wise, and get work elsewhere."

Yet still the man declared, again and again, that he cared not a whit for the terrors of Christmas-eve, and still urged the farmer to hire him.

At length the farmer consented, in answer to the man's urgent prayer, to take him as herdsman; and very well they agreed together. For everyone, both high and low, liked the man, as he was honest and open, zealous in everything he laid his hands to, and willing to do anyone a good turn, if need were.

On Christmas-eve, towards nightfall, the farmer and all his family went (as has been before declared to be the custom) to church, except Hildur, who remained behind to look after household matters, and the herdsman, who could not leave his sheep in time. Late in the evening, the latter as usual returned home, and after having eaten his supper, went to bed. As soon as he was well between the sheets, the remembrance struck him of what had befallen all the former herdsmen in his position on the same evening, and he thought it would be the best plan for him to lie awake and thus to be ready for any accident, though he was mighty little troubled with fear. Quite late at night, he heard the farmer and his family return from church, enter the house, and having taken supper, go to bed. Still, nothing happened, except that whenever he closed his eyes for a moment, a strange and deadly faintness stole over him, which only acted as one reason the more for his doing his best to keep awake.

Shortly after he had become aware of these feelings, he heard some one creep stealthily up to the side of his bed, and looking through the gloom at the figure, fancied he recognized Hildur the housekeeper. So he feigned to be fast asleep, and felt her place something in his mouth, which he knew instantly to be the bit of a magic bridle, but yet allowed her to fix it on him, without moving. When she had fastened the bridle, she dragged him from his bed with it, and out of the farmhouse, without his being either able or willing to make the least resistance. Then mounting on his back, she made him rise from the ground as if on wings, and rode him through the air, till they arrived at a huge and awful precipice, which yawned, like a great well, down into the earth.

She dismounted at a large stone, and fastening the reins to it, leaped into the precipice. But the herdsman, objecting strongly to being tied to this stone all night, and

" So he managed to get the bridle of his head, and leapt into the precipice."

[*To face page* 88.

thinking to himself that it would be no bad thing to know what became of the woman, tried to escape, bridle and all, from the stone. This he found, however, to be impossible, for as long as the bit was in his mouth, he was quite powerless to get away. So he managed, after a short struggle, to get the bridle off his head, and having so done, leapt into the precipice, down which he had seen Hildur disappear. After sinking for a long, long time, he caught a glimpse of Hildur beneath him, and at last they came to some beautiful green meadows.

From all this, the man guessed that Hildur was by no means a common mortal, as she had before made believe to be, and feared if he were to follow her along these green fields, and she turn round and catch sight of him, he might, not unlikely, pay for his curiosity with his life. So he took a magic stone which he always carried about him, the nature of which was to make him invisible when he held it in his palm, and placing it in the hollow of his hand, ran after her with all his strength.

When they had gone some way along the meadows, a splendid palace rose before them, with the way to which Hildur seemed perfectly well acquainted. At her approach a great crowd of people came forth from the doors, and saluted Hildur with respect and joy. Foremost of these walked a man of kingly and noble aspect, whose salutation seemed to be that of a lover or a husband: all the rest bowed to her as if she were their queen. This man was accompanied by two children, who ran up to Hildur, calling her mother, and embraced her. After the people had welcomed their queen, they all returned to the palace, where they dressed her in royal robes, and loaded her hands with costly rings and bracelets.

The herdsman followed the crowd, and posted himself where he would be least in the way of the company, but where he could catch sight easily of all that passed, and lose nothing. So gorgeous and dazzling were the hangings of the hall, and the silver and golden vessels on the table, that he thought he had never, in all his life before, seen the like; not to mention the wonderful dishes and wines which seemed plentiful there, and which, only by the look of them, filled his mouth with water, while he would much rather have filled it with something else.

After he had waited a little time, Hildur appeared in the hall, and all the assembled guests were begged to take their seats, while Hildur sat on her throne beside the king; after which all the people of the court ranged themselves on each side of the royal couple, and the feast commenced.

When it was concluded, the various guests amused themselves, some by dancing, some by singing, others by drinking and revel; but the king and queen talked together, and seemed to the herdsman to be very sad.

While they were thus conversing, three children, younger than those the man had seen before, ran in, and

clung round the neck of their mother. Hildur received
them with all a mother's love, and, as the youngest was
restless, put it on the ground and gave it one of her rings
to play with.

After the little one had played a while with the ring he
lost it, and it rolled along the floor towards the herdsman,
who, being invisible, picked it up without being perceived,
and put it carefully into hisc poket. Of course all search
for it by the guests was in vain.

When the night was far advanced, Hildur made preparations for departure, at which all the people assembled
showed great sorrow, and begged her to remain longer.

The herdsman had observed, that in one corner of the
hall sat an old and ugly woman, who had neither received
the queen with joy nor pressed her to stay longer.

As soon as the king perceived that Hildur addressed
herself to her journey, and that neither his entreaties nor
those of the assembly could induce her to stay, he went
up to the old woman, and said to her :

" Mother, rid us now of thy curse ; cause no longer my
queen to live apart and afar from me. Surely her short
and rare visits are more pain to me than joy."

The old woman answered him with a wrathful face.

" Never will I depart from what I have said. My words
shall hold true in all their force, and on no condition will
I abolish my curse."

On this the king turned from her, and going up to his

wife, entreated her in the fondest and most loving terms
not to depart from him.

The queen answered, "The infernal power of thy
mother's curse forces me to go, and perchance this may be
the last time that I shall see thee. For lying, as I do,
under this horrible ban, it is not possible that my constant murders can remain much longer secret, and then I
must suffer the full penalty of crimes which I have committed against my will."

While she was thus speaking the herdsman sped from
the palace and across the fields to the precipice, up which
he mounted as rapidly as he had come down, thanks to
the magic stone.

When he arrived at the rock he put the stone into his
pocket, and the bridle over his head again, and awaited the
coming of the elf-queen. He had not long to wait, for
very soon afterwards Hildur came up through the abyss,
and mounted on his back, and off they flew again to the
farmhouse, where Hildur, taking the bridle from his
head, placed him again in his bed, and retired to her
own. The herdsman, who by this time was well tired
out, now considered it safe to go to sleep, which he did, so
soundly as not to wake till quite late on Christmas-
morning.

Early that same day the farmer rose, agitated and filled
with the fear that, instead of passing Christmas in joy, he
should assuredly, as he so often had before, find his herds-

man dead, and pass it in sorrow and mourning. So he
and all the rest of the family went to the bedside of the
herdsman.

When the farmer had looked at him and found him
breathing, he praised God aloud for his mercy in preserving
the man from death.

Not long afterwards the man himself awoke and got up.

Wondering at his strange preservation the farmer asked
him how he had passed the night, and whether he had
seen or heard anything.

The man replied, " No; but I have had a very curious
dream."

" What was it ? " asked the farmer.

Upon which the man related everything that had passed
in the night, circumstance for circumstance, and word for
word, as well as he could remember. When he had finished
his story every one was silent for wonder, except Hildur,
who went up to him and said :

" I declare you to be a liar in all that you have said,
unless you can prove it by sure evidence."

Not in the least abashed, the herdsman took from his
pocket the ring which he had picked up on the floor of the
hall in Elf-land, and showing it to her said :

" Though my dream needs no proof, yet here is one
you will not doubtless deem other than a sure one ; for is
not this your gold ring, Queen Hildur ? "

Hildur answered, " It is, no doubt, my ring. Happy

man! may you prosper in all you undertake, for you have released me from the awful yoke which my mother-in-law laid, in her wrath, upon me, and from the curse of a yearly murder."

And then Hildur told them the story of her life as follows :—

" I was born of an obscure family among the elves. Our king fell in love with me and married me, in spite of the strong disapproval of his mother. She swore eternal hatred to me in her anger against her son, and said to him, 'Short shall be your joy with this fair wife of yours, for you shall see her but once a year, and that only at the expense of a murder. This is my curse upon her, and it shall be carried out to the letter. She shall go and serve in the upper world, this queen, and every Christmas-eve shall ride a man, one of her fellow-servants, with this magic bridle, to the confines of Elf-land, where she shall pass a few hours with you, and then ride him back again till his very heart breaks with toil, and his very life leaves him. Let her thus enjoy her queenship.'

" And this horrible fate was to cling to me until I should either have these murders brought home to me, and be condemned to death, or should meet with a gallant man, like this herdsman, who should have nerve and courage to follow me down into Elf-land, and be able to prove afterwards that he had been there with me, and seen the customs of my people. And now I must confess that all the former herdsmen were slain by me, but no penalty shall touch me for their murders, as I committed them against my will. And as for you, O courageous man, who have dared, the first of human beings, to explore the realms of Elf-land, and have freed me from the yoke of this awful curse, I will reward you in times to come, but not now.

"A deep longing for my home and my loved ones impels me hence. Farewell!"

With these words Hildur vanished from the sight of the astonished people, and was never seen again.

But our friend the herdsman, leaving the service of the farmer, built a farm for himself, and prospered, and became one of the chief men in the country, and always ascribed, with grateful thanks, his prosperity to Hildur, Queen of the Elves.

The Man-servant and the Water-elves.

In a large house, where all the chief rooms were panelled, there lived, once upon a time, a farmer, whose ill fate it was that every servant of his that was left alone to guard the house on the night of Christmas-eve, while the rest of the family went to church, was found dead when the family returned home. As soon as the report of this was spread abroad, the farmer had the greatest difficulty in procuring servants who would consent to watch alone in the house on that night; until at last one day a man, a strong fellow, offered him his services to sit up alone and guard the house. The farmer told him what fate awaited him for his rashness, but the man despised such a fear, and persisted in his determination.

On Christmas-eve, when the farmer and all his family, except the new man-servant, were preparing for church, the farmer said to him:

" Come with us to church; I cannot leave you here to die."

But the other replied, "I intend to stay here, for it would be unwise in you to leave your house unprotected; and, besides, the cattle and sheep must have their food at the proper time."

"Never mind the beasts," answered the farmer. "Do not be so rash as to remain in the house this night, for whenever we have returned from church on this night, we have always found every living thing in the house dead, with all its bones broken."

But the man was not to be persuaded, as he considered all these fears beneath his notice; so the farmer and the rest of the servants went away and left him behind, alone in the house.

As soon as he was by himself, he began to consider how to guard against anything that might occur, for a dread had stolen over him, in spite of his courage, that something strange was about to take place. At last he thought that the best thing to do was, first of all to light up the family room, and then to find some place in which to hide himself. As soon as he had lighted all the candles, he moved two planks out of the wainscot at the end of the room, and, creeping into the space between it and the wall, restored the planks to their places, so that he could see plainly into the room, and yet avoid being himself discovered.

He had scarcely finished concealing himself, when two fierce and strange-looking men entered the room and began looking about.

One of them said, " I smell a human being."

" No," replied the other, " there is no human being here."

Then they took a candle and continued their search, until they found the man's dog asleep under one of the beds. They took it up, and, having dashed it on the ground till every bone in its body was broken, hurled it from them. When the man-servant saw this, he congratulated himself on not having fallen into their hands.

Suddenly the room was filled with people, who were laden with tables and all kinds of table furniture, silver, cloths, and all, which they spread out, and having done so, sat down to a rich supper, which they had also brought with them. They feasted noisily, and spent the remainder of the night in drinking and dancing. Two of them were appointed to keep guard, in order to give the company due warning of the approach either of anybody, or of the day. Three times they went out, always returning with the news that they saw neither the approach of any human being, nor yet the break of day.

But when the man-servant suspected the night to be pretty far spent, he jumped from his place of concealment into the room, and clashing the two planks together with as much noise as he could make, shouted like a madman :

" The day ! the day ! the day ! "

On these words the whole company rose scared from their seats, and rushed headlong out, leaving behind them not only their tables and all the silver dishes, but even the very clothes they had taken off for ease in dancing. In the hurry of flight many were wounded and trodden under foot, while the rest ran into the darkness, the man-servant after them, clapping the planks together, and shrieking, " The day ! the day ! the day ! " until they came to a large lake, into which the whole party plunged headlong and disappeared.

From this, the man knew them to be water-elves.

Then he returned home, gathered the corpses of the elves who had been killed in the flight, killed the wounded ones, and making a great heap of them all, burned them. When he had finished this task, he cleaned up the house and took possession of all the treasures the elves had left behind them.

On the farmer's return, his servant told him all that had occurred, and showed him the spoils. The farmer praised him for a brave fellow, and congratulated him on having escaped with his life. The man gave him half the treasures of the elves, and ever afterwards prospered exceedingly.

This was the last visit the water-elves ever paid to *that* house.

THE CROSSWAYS.

It is supposed that among the hills there are certain cross-roads from the centre of which you can see four churches, one at the end of each road.

If you sit at the crossing of these roads, on Christmaseve (or as others say, on New Year's-eve), elves come from every direction and cluster round you, and ask you, with all sorts of blandishments and fair promises, to go with them; but you must continue silent. Then they bring to you rarities and delicacies of every description, gold, silver, and precious stones, meats and wines, of which they beg you to accept; but you must neither move a limb nor accept a single thing they offer you. If you get so far as this without speaking, elfwomen come to you in the likeness of your mother, your sister, or any other relation, and beg you to come with them, using every art and entreaty; but beware you neither move nor speak. And if you can continue to keep silent and motionless all the night, until you see the first streak of dawn, then start up, and cry aloud :

" Praise be to God !   His daylight filleth the heavens !"

As soon as you have said this, the elves will leave you, and with you, all the wealth they have used to entice you, which will now be yours.

But should you either answer, or accept of their offers, you will from that moment become mad.

On the night of one Christmas-eve, a man named Fusi was out on the cross-roads, and managed to resist all the entreaties and proffers of the elves, until one of them offered him a large lump of mutton-suet, and begged him to take a bite of it. Fusi, who had up to this time gallantly resisted all such offers as gold and silver and diamonds, and such filthy lucre, could hold out no longer, and crying, " Seldom have I refused a bite of mutton-suet," he went mad.

STORIES OF WATER-MONSTERS.

The Merman.

Long ago a farmer lived at Vogar, who was a mighty
fisherman, and, of all the farms round about, not one was
so well situated with regard to the fisheries as his.

One day, according to custom, he had gone out fishing,
and having cast down his line from the boat, and waited
awhile, found it very hard to pull up again, as if there were
something very heavy at the end of it. Imagine his astonishment when he found that what he had caught was a
great fish, with a man's head and body! When he saw
that this creature was alive, he addressed it and said,
"Who and whence are you?"

"A merman from the bottom of the sea," was the reply.

The farmer then asked him what he had been doing when the hook caught his flesh.

The other replied, "I was turning the cowl of my mother's chimney-pot, to suit it to the wind. So let me go again, will you?"

"Not for the present," said the fisherman. "You shall serve me awhile first."

So without more words he dragged him into the boat and rowed to shore with him.

When they got to the boat-house, the fisherman's dog came to him and greeted him joyfully, barking and fawning on him, and wagging his tail. But his master's temper being none of the best, he struck the poor animal; whereupon the merman laughed for the first time.

Having fastened the boat, he went towards his house, dragging his prize with him, over the fields, and stumbling over a hillock, which lay in his way, cursed it heartily; whereupon the merman laughed for the second time.

When the fisherman arrived at the farm, his wife came out to receive him, and embraced him affectionately, and he received her salutations with pleasure; whereupon the merman laughed for the third time.

Then said the farmer to the merman, "You have laughed three times, and I am curious to know why you have laughed. Tell me, therefore."

"Never will I tell you," replied the merman, "unless you promise to take me to the same place in the sea wherefrom you caught me, and there to let me go free again." So the farmer made him the promise.

"Well," said the merman, "I laughed the first time because you struck your dog, whose joy at meeting you was real and sincere. The second time, because you cursed the mound over which you stumbled, which is full of golden ducats. And the third time, because you received with pleasure your wife's empty and flattering embrace, who is faithless to you, and a hypocrite. And now be an honest man and take me out to the sea whence you have brought me."

The farmer replied : "Two things that you have told me I have no means of proving, namely, the faithfulness of my dog and the faithlessness of my wife. But the third I will try the truth of, and if the hillock contain gold, then I will believe the rest."

Accordingly he went to the hillock, and having dug it up, found therein a great treasure of golden ducats, as the merman had told him. After this the farmer took the merman down to the boat, and to that place in the sea whence he had caught him. Before he put him in, the latter said to him :

"Farmer, you have been an honest man, and I will reward you for restoring me to my mother, if only you have skill enough to take possession of property that I shall throw in your way. Be happy and prosper."

Then the farmer put the merman into the sea, and he sank out of sight.

It happened that not long after, seven sea-grey cows were seen on the beach, close to the farmer's land. These cows appeared to be very unruly, and ran away directly the farmer approached them. So he took a stick and ran after them, possessed with the fancy that if he could burst the bladder which he saw on the nose of each of them, they would belong to him. He contrived to hit out the bladder on the nose of one cow, which then became so tame that he could easily catch it, while the others leaped into the sea and disappeared. The farmer was convinced that this was the gift of the merman. And a very useful gift it was, for better cow was never seen nor milked in all the land, and she was the mother of the race of grey cows so much esteemed now.

And the farmer prospered exceedingly, but never caught any more mermen. As for his wife, nothing further is told about her, so we can repeat nothing.

NENNIR, OR THE ONE WHO FEELS INCLINED.

There was once a girl who had been charged by her master to look after some ewes which were lost. She had gone a long way after them, until she was quite tired, when suddenly she saw before her a grey horse. Much delighted at this, she went up to it and bound her garter into its mouth for a bridle, but just as she was going to mount she said, "I feel afraid, I am half-inclined not to mount this horse." As soon as the animal heard these words it leaped into some water that stood near, and disappeared.

Then the girl saw that this was a river-horse.

Now the nature of this animal is that it cannot bear to hear its own name "Nennir, or the one who feels inclined," which is the reason why it jumped into the water when the girl said, "I feel afraid, I am half-inclined not to mount this horse."

The same is the effect on the river-horse if it hears the name of the devil.

Listen to another story.

Three children were playing together on the shingly bank of a river, when they saw a grey horse standing near them and went up to it to look at it. One of the children mounted on its back and after him another, to have a ride for pleasure, and only the eldest one was left. They asked him to follow, "for," they said, "the horse's back is surely long enough for all three of us."

But the child refused, and said, "I do not feel inclined." No sooner were the words out of his mouth, than the horse leaped into the river with the two other children, who

were both drowned, while only the eldest survived to tell
us this story of Nennir the grey river-horse.

THE LAKE-MONSTER.

In the last century a man lived in the north country,
called Kolbeinn, who was very poor. But everybody liked
him for his good heart, and treated him with kindness.

Once, on the day before Christmas-eve, late at night, he
went over the lake of Vesturhóp, which was frozen, to beg
some food for the next day, from one of the farmers on the
other side. The farmer gave him a smoked carcase of
mutton, with which Kolbeinn returned joyfully homewards.

When he was about the middle of the lake, he heard a
noise behind him, and turning round saw the ice crack
and a monster rise from it, having eight feet, and looking
like two horses joined by their tails, with their heads facing
opposite ways. This monster ran after Kolbeinn, who saw
no chance of escape, so he dropped the carcase of mutton
and took to his heels with all the speed he could muster.

Next morning he went out again on to the ice to see
how much might be left of his mutton, but only found a
few chewed bones. He took some of his neighbours to
look at these bones, and they pitied him so much that
they soon made up his loss to him.

" Turning round, he saw the ice crack and a monster rise from it, having eight feet, and looking like two horses."

[To face page 108.

NADDI.

In ancient times there was a main road from Njardvík, to Borgar-fjördur, which passed over a very steep mountain, sloping down to the sea. But this road became unfrequented because a monster, half-man, half-beast, took up his abode upon it, and after nightfall used to destroy so many travellers that the way was at length considered impassable. This creature hid itself in a rocky gulf on the sea-side of the mountains, which has since been called the gulf of Naddi. This name arose from the fact that as people passed, a strange rattling was heard among the stones at the bottom.

It happened once, in autumn, that a certain man stopped at a farm in the neighbourhood, who intended late in the evening to cross this part of the mountain, and was not to be dissuaded from his determination by the entreaties of the farmer and his family. So he started off with the words "as long as I fear nothing, nothing can harm me."

When he came to the gulf he met with the monster, and at once attacked it, and they had a long and fearful struggle together. In their fight they came together to the verge of a precipice which has been since called Krossjadar. Over this the man hurled the monster. Afterwards upon this very spot was raised a cross, with this inscription :—

"Effigiem Christi, qui prodis, pronus honora."

The man came to Njarðvík, black and blue with his struggle, and, after having kept his bed for a month, recovered.

Never was this fearful sea-monster seen after it had been vanquished by a human being. The man soon forgot his bruises in the glory of having rid his country of such a plague.

STORIES OF TROLLS.

GOLD-BROW.

LONG ago, a certain woman named Audur the wealthy lived at a farm called Hvammur, in the west country. The farm stood on the bank of a river, on the opposite side of which were rich corn-fields. But Audur had forbidden any seed to be sown on a particular spot where the land happened to be best, nor did she allow her servants to graze any cattle there, and if by chance any cows had been there, she forbade them to be milked the next day.

Once it happened that when Audur was very old, a young and handsome woman came to Hvammur, who declared her name to be Gold-brow, but nobody knew either whence she came or who she was. The only person she could find to speak to was the superintendent, but Audur herself she did not see. The woman asked him why a particular spot in the field was not sown with corn, nor grazed, and the superintendent answered that Audur had forbidden it to be so. At this Gold-brow laughed heartily, and asked him to sell her the ground.

"For," she said, " I will give more for a single hillock of that land than for all the great farm of Hvammur. I have a certain foreboding that on that ground a custom will be introduced, and that sort of house built, of which I have the greatest dread and dislike. Sell me, therefore, the spot of ground without asking Audur about it."

With these words she took out a large purse filled with coin.

When the manager saw the glitter of her gold he said to himself, " Audur is old and has but little to do with the management;" and forthwith sold the land to Gold-brow.

But when Audur came to know what had been done, she was exceedingly wroth, and sent her manager away, saying to him, " You will never fatten on this gold. I suspect the woman who paid it to you to be the most evil of witches, and knew long ago what would happen to that ground. No harm, however, can come home to Hvammur, for a good spirit watches over it." Then the steward thought that he would pacify the old lady by giving her some of the contents of the purse he had just received. So he undid the strings, and lo! instead of gold out poured from it a heap of worms which smelt so horrible that the man forthwith went mad and died. After this the man and his purse were buried in a little hollow of that spot of ground which Gold-brow had purchased, which is called to this day " worm-hollow."

Audur did not endeavour to reclaim from Gold-brow the ground which she had bought, but destroyed all the corn-fields round it from the sea to a rocky river-gulf in one direction, and from the mountain to the river in the other. She also set up three crosses where the gulf joined the mountain (whence its name Cross-gulf), and said, " During my life Gold-brow shall never cross this boundary." And this came true, for during the life of Audur, Gold-brow neither brought her sheep and cattle to graze anywhere near the crops nor approached them herself. Now Gold-brow built on her piece of ground a farm and a large temple, where she made great offerings, and performed all sorts of witchcraft. It is told as a curious thing, that whenever she was using her incantations, and happened to look either towards Hvammur, or the crosses by the mountains, all her spells went wrong, which she declared was because at each of these points she always saw a light, whose rays were so dazzling as to make her forget at once all her magic words and signs.

Audur, who was a Christian, died shortly after all this

H 2

and was buried in some ground which she had caused, in
her lifetime, to be consecrated, by the sea, not far from
the land belonging to Gold-brow, who found herself now·
in a sort of prison, what with the sacred remains of
Audur on one side and the crosses on the other. So she
sold her piece of ground to the heathen successor of'
Audur, at Hvammur, and purchased another in a dark
and dismal valley, over which the sun seldom shone in
summer and never in winter, and in the darkest and
gloomiest recess intended to take up her abode. But when
it came to passing out of her old property to go to her·
new one, by the road which led near the crosses, she found
herself nearly powerless, and going into her temple was
compelled to use the strongest charms to strengthen her-·
self; and then ordering her servants to bind her eyes so
that she should not see, she took from the temple a large
chest of gold, on to which she had fastened a ring from
the temple-door, mounted her horse, holding the chest in
front of her, and caused the horse to be led quickly along
the path. She particularly commanded her servants to
avoid looking toward the crosses. But when they came
to the Cross-gulf, one of them looked in the forbidden
direction, and, being frightened, caused the horse to stumble, so that the chest of gold burst away from its ring and
fell to the ground. Gold-brow being· astonished at this,
tore the bandage from her eyes, and looked to see what
had become of it, but in so doing happened to see the

"In the gulf she pointed out, there was a vast waterfall, and under the waterfall a cave, and the water at the foot of the fall was very deep and its eddying awful."

[*To face page* 116.

crosses not far off. At this she shrieked aloud, and declaring that their brightness was greater than she could bear, bade her servants hurry on as quickly as possible, and bring the chest after her. Then looking at her hand she saw the ring from which the box had fallen, and flung it away in a rage, saying, " All my life will I repent of having brought you with me. Different, indeed, to the purpose for which I intended you, and most hateful to me will be the use to which you will be put."

As soon as she had passed the gulf, a fierce and burning pain seized her eyes, so that before she had reached her new abode she was perfectly blind. In this gloomy valley she lived no long time, suffering perpetual tortures till she died.

On her death-bed, she told her servants to bury her in a deep and precipitous gulf, where neither was the sun ever seen, nor church-bells ever heard. In the gulf she pointed out, there was a vast waterfall, and under the waterfall a cave, and the water at the foot of the fall was very deep and its eddying awful. To this cave Gold-brow was carried, and in it buried, with her head upon the chest of gold. Long afterwards her ghost haunted all the mountains round, so that neither man nor beast was safe after twilight, and much mischief was done.

At this time a farmer lived at Hvammur, named Skeggi, who was a heathen, and addicted to witchcraft. This man suffered much from the persecutions of the goblin

Gold-brow, who killed his herdsmen and his sheep for him one after the other. Skeggi became more wroth with her every day, and in proportion to his anger increased his desire to become possessed of her golden treasures under the waterfall, for he considered that her gold would be of infinitely more use to a living man than to a dead witch. With this idea in his head, he one day started off for the waterfall; but so long was the way that it was evening before he arrived there. He commanded his two servants whom he had brought with him, to let him down into the gulf with a rope. They did so, and he disappeared into the cave under the waterfall. The two men who held the end of the rope, heard, after a little while, the sound of heavy blows and loud shrieks beneath the water, and it was plain that some fearful struggle was going on there. At last they became so horrified as to be on the point of taking flight, when Skeggi gave them the sign to pull up the rope. When they did so they found the chest full of gold fastened to the end of it. They had scarcely pulled it up to the edge of the gulf before they saw the whole valley filled with a strange and spectral fire, whose flames flared higher than the very mountains, and letting go of the rope in their fright, took to their heels, while the chest fell down again into the abyss.

Skeggi came home some time afterwards very weary, and covered with bruises and blood, but bringing on one of his arms, a kettle full of gold which he had managed to take out of the chest of Gold-brow, and climb with up the rope. But though he had fought hard with the ghost of the troll, he had been unable to subdue her, and she became now more dangerous than ever, killing his sheep and his herdsmen, till at last he could get no servants at all. Skeggi from this time became a changed man, and was so affected by the constant loss of his servants, that he fell ill and took, for a long while, to his bed.

At last one day, after his recovery, being without any herdsman, he went out himself as if to watch the flocks. But he did not return either that night or the next. On the third day, however, he came back, more dead than alive, bearing on his back Gold-brow's treasure-chest.

He said, "You will not see much more either of the troll or of me."

And after these words took to his bed, whence he never rose again.

Before he died, he ordered that the gold contained in the kettle should be expended in timber for building a church at Hvammur.

"For," he continued, "the first time I went to the waterfall and struggled with the ghost of Gold-brow, I called upon Thor to aid me, but he deceived me and played me false. The last time I fought with her, in my despair and anguish I called upon Christ the God of the Christians to aid me, promising to build a church to him. Suddenly a bright gleam of light struck full into the eyes of the phantom-troll, and she became a stone in the midst of the gulf."

But in spite of all this, Skeggi died a heathen, and refused to be buried in the consecrated ground of the church which he had commanded to be built. So they buried him in the open country, and under his head placed the chest of Gold-brow.

Whether he slept more calmly upon this pillow than the troll had done, this tale saith not.

The Troll of Mjóifjördur.

In the east of Iceland, a bay runs into the land between two steep mountains, which is called Mjóifjördur. In one of the mountains is a deep rocky gulf called Mjóafjardargil. This gulf was inhabited by a troll, who used to draw into her power by magic spells the priests living at the farm Fjördur. She was wont, while the priest was preaching, to lay one of her hands upon the window over the pulpit in church. As soon as the strange hand prevented the light from falling on the paper on which the sermon was written, the priests became mad, and used to cry out to their congregation :

" Take my bowels out, for I must be off to the gulf, to the gulf of Mjóifjördur."

With these words the priests disappeared from the church in the direction of the gulf, and were never heard of again.

A traveller, happening to pass the gulf, once saw the troll sitting on a ledge of rock, kicking her heels and holding something in her hand.

He said to her, "Well, old hag, what have you got there?"

"Oh," replied the other, "I am gnawing the last piece of the skull of Snjóki, your late priest."

After this, no priest would take the charge of the church, until one intrepid man declared that he would do so in spite of the troll and all her tricks. The first time he had to perform service in his new church, he told the boldest of his parishioners to look out for his changing his demeanour in the pulpit, and then to act as follows :—

"Six of you," said he, "must run and catch hold of me, and not let me go, however much I struggle; other six of you shall ring the bells as loud as you can; and ten more of you shall run to the door and place your backs against it."

Shortly after the priest had mounted the pulpit, the hand of the troll was seen moving backwards and forwards outside the window, and at the same moment the priest went mad and said :

"Out with my bowels, out with my bowels, and I must away to the gulf, to the gulf of Mjóifjördur."

With these words he endeavoured to rush out of the church.

But the six men, whom he had previously selected,

seized him and held him back; six others rang the bells with all their might; and the remaining ten ran to the door and set their backs against it. When the troll heard the bells ring, she took to her heels and jumped from the church on to the wall of the churchyard. When she touched this her foot slipped back, and she cried:

"May you never stand again."

From the churchyard she ran to the gulf, and was never more seen.

But the gap in the churchyard wall which her foot had made, could never be mended perfectly, however well the workmen worked, and however good the materials.

The troll's iron shoe, which had tumbled off, was found there, and used by a farmer for an ash-scuttle.

TROLL'S STONE.

In the neighbourhood of Kirkjubœr, in Hróarstúnga, stand some curious rocks under which is a cave. In this cave, ages ago, dwelt a troll named Thórir, with his wife. Every year, these trolls contrived to entice into their clutches, by magic arts, either the priest or the herdsmen, from Kirkjubœr, and thus matters went on until a priest arrived at the place, named Eiríkur, a spiritual man, who was able by his prayers to protect both himself and his herdsmen from the magic spells of this worthy couple.

One Christmas-eve, the female troll had tried her incantations quite in vain, and went to her husband, saying, " I have tried my utmost to entice the priest or the herdsman, but to no purpose, for, as soon as ever I begin my spells, a hot wind blows upon me which forces me by the scorching heat to desist, as if it would consume all my joints. So you must go and procure something for our Christmas dinner, as we have nothing left to eat in the cave."

The giant expressed great unwillingness to trouble himself, being rather lazy, but was at length compelled to go, by the entreaties of his wife, and accordingly marched off to a lake in the neighbourhood which since was called by his name. There he broke a hole through the ice, and lying down on his face, cast in a line and caught trout. When he thought he had caught enough for the Christmas dinner, he wanted to get up again, in order to take them home ; but the frost had been so hard while he was intent upon his fishing that it had frozen him tight to the ice, so that he could not rise from it. He struggled desperately to escape, but in vain, and the frost seized upon his heart and killed him where he lay.

The female troll finding her husband rather long in returning, and becoming very hungry, sallied out in search of him, and discovered him lying dead upon the ice. She ran to him and tried to tear his body up from the ice, but failing in this, seized the string of trout, and placing it over her shoulder started off.

Before she went, she said, " A curse on thee, thou wicked lake ! Never shall a living fish be caught in thee again."

Which words have indeed proved fatal to the fishery, for the lake since then has never yielded a single fish.

Then she went back homewards with great strides. As she came, however, to the edge of the neighbouring hill, she saw the day-break in the east, and heard from the south the sound of the Kirkjubœr church-bells (two things, which, as everyone knows, are fatal to trolls), upon which she was instantly changed into the rock which now bears the name of Troll's Stone.

GELLIVÖR.

Near the end of the Roman Catholic times, a certain married couple lived at a farm named Hvoll, situated on a firth in the east part of the country. The farmer was well to do, and wealthy in sheep and cattle. It was commonly reported that a female troll lived on the south side of the firth, who was supposed to be mild and not given to mischief.

One Christmas-eve, after dark, the farmer went out and never returned again, and all search for him was in vain. After the man's disappearance one of the servants took the management of the farm, but was lost in the same manner, after dark on the Christmas-eve following. After this the widow of the farmer determined to remove all her goods from the house and live elsewhere for the winter, leaving only the sheep and herds under the charge of shepherds, and returning to pass the summer there. As soon as the winter approached she made preparations for leaving Hvoll, until the next spring, and set the herdsmen to take care of the sheep and cattle, and feed them during the cold season.

For home-use she always kept four cows, one of which had just had a calf.

Two days before her intended departure, a woman came to her in her dreams, who was dressed in an old-fashioned dress of poor appearance. The stranger addressed her with these words: " Your cow has just calved, and I have no hope of getting nourishment for my children, unless you will every day, when you deal out the rations, put a share for me in a jug in the dairy. I know that your intention is to move to another farm in two days, as you dare not live here over Christmas, for you know not what has become of your husband and of the servant, on the last two Christmas-eves. But I must tell you that a female troll lives in the opposite mountains, herself of mild temper, but who, two years ago, had a child of such curious appetite and disposition, that she was forced to provide fresh human flesh for it each Christmas. If, however, you will do willingly for me what I have asked you to do, I will give you good advice as to how you may get rid of the troll from this neighbourhood."

With these words the woman vanished. When the widow awoke she remembered her dream, and getting up, went to the dairy, where she filled a wooden jug with new milk and placed it on the appointed spot. No sooner had she done so than it disappeared. The next evening the jug stood again in the same place, and so matters went on till Christmas.

On Christmas-eve she dreamt again that the woman came to her with a friendly salutation, and said, " Surely you are not inquisitive, for you have not yet asked to whom you give milk every day. I will tell you. I am an elfwoman, and live in the little hill near your house. You have treated me well all through the winter, but henceforth I will ask you no more for milk, as my cow had yesterday a calf. And now you must accept the little gift which you will find on the shelf where you have been accustomed to place the jug for me; and I intend, also, to deliver you from the danger which awaits you to-morrow night. At midnight you will awake and feel yourself irresistibly urged to go out, as if something attracted you; do not struggle against it, but get up and leave the house. Outside the door you will find a giantess standing, who will seize you and carry you in her arms across your grass-field, stride over the river,

and make off with you in the direction of the mountains
in which she lives. When she has carried you a little
way from the river, you must cry, ' What did I hear
then?' and she will immediately ask you, ' What did
you hear?' You must answer, ' I heard some one cry,
" Mamma Gellivör, Mamma Gellivör!"' which she will think
very extraordinary, for she knows that no mortal ever
yet heard her name. She will say, ' Oh, I suppose it is
that naughty child of mine,' and will put you down and
run to the mountains. But in the meantime, while she
is engaged with you, I will be in the mountain and
will thump and pinch her child without mercy. Directly
she has left you, turn your back upon the mountain and
run as fast as you possibly can towards the nearest farm
along the river banks. When the troll comes back and
overtakes you, she will say, ' Why did you not stand
still, you wretch?' and will take you again in her arms
and stride away with you. As soon as you have gone
a little way you must cry again, ' What did I hear then?'
She will ask as at first, ' What did you hear?' Then
you shall reply again, ' I thought I heard some one calling " Mamma Gellivör, Mamma Gellivör!"' on which she
will fling you down as before, and run towards the mountain. And now you must make all speed to reach the
nearest church before she can catch you again, for if she
succeed in doing so she will treat you horribly in her
fury at finding that I have pinched and thumped her

child to death. If, however, you fail in getting to the
church in time, I will help you."

When, after this dream, the widow awoke, the day had
dawned, so she got up and went to the shelf upon which
the jug was wont to stand. Here she found a large bundle,
which contained a handsome dress and girdle, and cap, all
beautifully embroidered.

About midnight on Christmas-day, when all the rest of
the farm people at Hvoll were asleep, the widow felt an
irresistible desire to go out, as the elfwoman had warned
her, and she did so. Directly she had passed the threshold, she felt herself seized and lifted high in the air by
the arms of the gigantic troll, who stalked off with her
over the river and towards the mountain. Everything
turned out exactly as the elf had foretold, until the giantess
flung down her burden for the second time, and the
widow made speed to reach the church. On the way, it
seemed to her as if some one took hold of her arms and
helped her along. Suddenly she heard the sound of a
tremendous land-slip on the troll's mountain, and turning
round saw in the clear moonlight the giantess striding
furiously towards her over the morasses. At this sight she
would have fainted with fear, had not she felt herself lifted
from the ground and hurried through the air into the
church, the door of which closed immediately behind her.
It happened that the priests were about to celebrate early
mass, and all the people were assembled. Directly after

"Suddenly she heard the sound of a tremendous land-slip, and turning round saw in the clear moonlight the giantess striding furiously towards her over the morasses."

she came into the church the bells began to ring, and the congregation heard the sound of some heavy fall outside. Looking from one of the windows they saw the troll hurry away from the noise of the bells, and, in her flight, stumble over the wall of the churchyard, part of which fell. Then the troll said to it, " Never stand again," and hurrying away took up her abode in another mountain beyond the confines of the parish of Hvoll.

Here is something more about Gellivör. A mountain in the south of the country, called Bláskógar, was so haunted by this troll, who had now become mischievous, as to be impassable. For two years things went on thus.

It happened at this time that the inhabitants of Thíngeyarsýsla became confused in their computation of dates, and forgot when Christmas-day fell. In their difficulty they determined that their only chance was to send to the bishop at Skálholt, and ask him to put them right again, and they chose as their messenger a certain bold and active man named Olafur. On his way to Skálholt this Olafur passed, late in the day, over the mountain Bláskógar, and being unwilling to linger there went on his way as quickly as possible. When twilight had fallen, he saw a great giantess standing in the way before him, who addressed him with these words :

I

> " Are you going south,
> Olafur mouth ?
> Wry-mouth, I would fain
> Warn you, go home again.
> Blow your nose, wry-face,
> And return with shame to your own place."

Then he replied :

> " Oh troll, sitting on Bláfell,
> All hail ! may you fare well."

To which she replied :

> " Of old, few greeted me so well ;
> Dearest darling, fare thee well,"—

and let him pass without molesting him.

So Olafur went on to Skálholt, where the bishop solved his difficulty immediately for him.

On his way home, as he passed over Bláskógar he met again with the troll, who did not appear so formidable as she had done the first time. She gave him a book, which he looked at and found to be a troll-almanack. In giving him this calendar she said :

" If Christ, the Son of Mary, had done as much for us trolls as you declare that He has done for you human beings, we should scarcely have been so ungrateful as to forget the date of his birth-day."

Then Olafur (whose powers of gratitude certainly do seem to have been rather limited) said to her, " Look eastward ! Who rides there on a white horse ? "

Whereupon the troll turned round, and as she saw nothing but daybreak, was instantly turned into stone.

So Olafur went home rejoicing.

THE SHEPHERDESS.

Once upon a time, in Dalasyslu, a little shepherdess went to church and took the sacrament. When she left the church, instead of going home to dinner, she went to look after her ewes. As she was passing some rocks, she heard a voice from one of them say :

" Ragnhildur in the Red rock !"

Then a voice from the opposite side answered :

" What is the matter, O giant, in the triple rocks ?"

" There is a tender little steer running along the road ; let us take her ; let us eat her."

" Faugh," replied the other, " leave her alone ; she looks as if she had been chewing coals."

So the little girl ran away as fast as she could, and heard no more about it.

JÓRA THE TROLL.

A farmer's daughter, young and hopeful, but gifted with a fearful temper, acted as housekeeper to her father. Her name was Jóra.

One day it happened that a horse-fight was held near the farm at which she lived, and one of the combatants was a horse of her father's, of which she was very fond. She was present at the fight, together with many other women; but at the commencement she saw that her favourite horse was getting the worst of it. So she jumped furiously down from her seat, and running up to the victor, seized one of its hind-legs and tore it off. Then she ran off with the leg so quickly, that nobody could catch her. When she came to the river Olfusá, where it forms in a deep gulf a waterfall called Laxfoss, she seized a large rock from the wall of the abyss, and hurling it into the middle of the fall, used it as a stepping-stone, and leaped over, with these words—

> " Here is a jump for a maiden like me,
>
> Though soon comes the time when a wife I shall be."

Ever after this, that passage of the river has been called " Troll's-leap."

From this place she ran on for a long way, till she came to a mountain called Heingill, where she took up her abode in a cave (since called "Jóra's Cave"), and became the most malignant troll possible: killing man and beast without mercy. She used to sit on a high peak, which has since been called " Jóra's-seat," and from this eminence looked out for passers-by in all directions; and if she saw one, killed him and ate him up. At last, nearly the whole neighbourhood had fallen victims to her, and the roads became void, except when, from time to time, large troops of people came, with the vain idea of destroying her.

In this state of affairs, when no means could be found of destroying this wicked troll, a young man, who had been a sailor, went to the King of Norway, and told him of this monster who lived in the Mountain Heingill; at the same time asking his advice how to overcome her.

The king answered, " You must attack Jóra at sunrise on Whit-Sunday; for there is no monster, however fearful, and no troll, however strong, that is not fast asleep at that time. You will find her sleeping with her face to the ground. Here is an axe of silver, which I will give you. With this you must make a chop between her shoulder-bones. Then Jóra, feeling the pain, will turn and say to you, ' May your hands grow to the handle.' But you must instantly answer—' Blade, leave the handle.' Then she will roll down into a lake near the foot of the peak, and be drowned."

With these words he dismissed the young man, who returned to the Heingill, and did as the King of Norway had told him, and killed Jóra.

So that was the end of Jóra the Troll.

KATLA.

Once it happened that the Abbot of the Monastery of Thykkvaboe had a housekeeper whose name was Katla, and who was an evil-minded and hot-tempered woman. She possessed a pair of shoes whose peculiarity was, that whoever put them on was never tired of running. Every body was afraid of Katla's bad disposition and fierce temper, even the Abbot himself. The herdsman of the monastery farm, whose name was Bardi, was often dreadfully ill-treated by her, particularly if he had chanced to lose any of the ewes.

One day in the autumn the Abbot and his housekeeper went to a wedding, leaving orders with Bardi to drive in the sheep and milk them before they came home. But unhappily, when the time came, the herdsman could not find all the ewes; so he went into the house, put on Katla's magic shoes, and sallied out in search of the stray sheep. He had a long way to run before he discovered them, but felt no fatigue, so drove all the flock in quite briskly.

When Katla returned, she immediately perceived that the herdsman had been using her shoes, so she took him and drowned him in a large tubful of curds. Nobody knew what had become of the man, and as the winter went on, and the curds in the tub sank lower and lower,

Katla was heard to say these words to herself: "Soon will the waves of milk break upon the foot-soles of Bardi!"

Shortly after this, dreading that the murder should be found out, and that she would be condemned to death, she took her magic shoes, and ran from the monastery to a great ice-mountain, into a rift of which she leaped, and was never seen again.

As soon as she had disappeared, a fearful eruption took place from the mountain, and the lava rolled down and destroyed the monastery at which she had lived. People declared that her witchcraft had been the cause of this, and called the crater of the mountain "The Rift of Katla."

OLAFUR AND THE TROLLS.

Some people who lived in the south part of the country, at Biskupstúngur, once went into the forest to cut wood for charcoal, and took with them a young lad to hold their horses. While he was left to look after the animals he disappeared, and, though they searched in every direction for him, they failed in finding him.

After three years had passed, the same people were cutting wood in exactly the same place, when the lost boy Olafur came running to them. They asked him where he had been all this time, and how he had gone away.

He said, " While I was looking after the horses, and had

strolled a short distance from them, I suddenly met a
gigantic troll-woman, who came rushing towards me and
seized me in her arms, and ran off with me until she came
into the heart of the wilderness to some great rocks. In
these rocks was her cave, into which she carried me. When
I was there I saw another giantess coming towards me, of
younger appearance than the former, but both were immensely tall. They were dressed in tunics of horse-leather,
falling to their feet in front, but very short behind. Here
they kept me, and fed me with trout, which one was always
out catching, while the other watched me. During the
night they forced me to sleep between them on their bed
of horse-skins. Sometimes they used to lull me to sleep
by singing magical songs in my ears, so that I was
enchanted by wonderful dreams. They both were very
kind to me, and watched me carefully lest I should wish to
escape from them. One day when I had been left alone, I
was standing outside the cave, and saw, on the other side
of the wilderness, the smoke of the charcoal-burners; so,
as I knew that neither of the trolls was at home, I ran
off in the direction of the smoke. But I had gone very
few paces when one of the trolls saw me, and, running
after me, struck me on the cheek, so that I have never lost
the bruise, and seizing me in her arms, took me back again
to the cave. After this, they looked after me diligently
enough.

"Once the younger troll said to the elder, 'How is it

that whenever I touch the bare cheek of Olafur, it seems to burn me like fire?'

"The other replied, 'Do not wonder at that; it is on account of the prayer which Oddur the wry-faced* has taught him.'

"In this way I passed three years; and when I knew that the season for charcoal-burning was come, and that there would be people on the other side of the wilderness assembled for the purpose, I pretended that I was sick, and could not eat any food. They tried every means in their power to cure me, but all in vain, I only became worse.

"Once they asked me whether I could not mention any delicacy for which I had a fancy.

"I said, 'No, except it were shark-flesh, which had been dried in the wind for nine years.'

"The elder one said, 'This will be very difficult to get you, for it is not to be found anywhere in the whole country, but at one farmer's house in the west, Ögur. At any rate, I will try to get it.'

"Then she strode off in search of it. Directly I saw that she was gone, and that the younger troll was busily engaged in catching trout, I took to my heels, and never ceased running towards the smoke of the charcoal-fires until I arrived here safely."

* So called by the troll, as he was a bishop and good Christian, two equally abominable qualities in the eyes of a troll.

When they had heard his story, the burners mounted
their horses and took Olafur as speedily as possible to
Skálholt. On the way, when they had just crossed the
Brúará, whom should they meet but the ugly old troll
herself, who came tearing down the rocks towards them,
and crying, " Aha! there you are, you wretch!"

Olafur, at the sound of her voice, went mad, and tried
to break away from the men, so that it was all they could
do to hold him back.

Then the troll seized hold of a horse which stood near
her on the rocks, and tearing it asunder, threw the pieces
over her shoulder in her fury, and ran back to her cave.

When the news arrived at Skálholt, they took Olafur to
the bishop, who kept him by him for a few days, and
then sent him into the east part of the country, out of
the reach of the trolls, having cured him of his madness.

The Troll in the Skrúdur.

Long ago, the priest's daughter at Hólmar, near the
Reidarfjördur, was lost from her father's house, and though
search was made for her in all directions, both by sea and
land, was not found again.

At the mouth of the Reidarfjördur there is a high rocky
island called Skrúdur, upon which the priest used to graze
his sheep, from the end of the autumn till the spring.

" When they had fastened their boats, they sat down near the beach, drenched as they were, and to while away the time, sang songs about the Virgin Mary."

[To face page 138.

But after he had lost his daughter, it happened that every winter, for several years, his best wethers always disappeared.

Once, in the winter, some fishermen were caught in a storm at sea, and were compelled to take shelter under this rocky island. When they had fastened their boats, they sat down near the beach, drenched as they were, and to while away the time, sang songs about the Virgin Mary,—when suddenly the rock opened, and a gigantic hand came out, with a ring on each finger, and the arm clad in a scarlet velvet sleeve, which thrust down towards them a large bowl full of stirabout, with as many spoons in it as there were fishermen.

At the same time they heard a voice saying, "My wife is pleased now, but not I."

When the men had eaten the stir-about, the bowl disappeared into the rock in the same way as it had appeared. The next day the storm had abated, and they rowed safely to the main land.

At the same season in the year following, the fishermen were again driven to seek shelter on this island by violent winds; and while they sat near the beach, they amused themselves by singing songs about Andri the Hero; when the same hand appeared from the rock, holding out to them a great dish full of fat smoked mutton, and they heard these words, "Now am I pleased, but not my wife."

So the fishermen ate the meat, and the dish was taken back into the rock. Soon afterwards the wind fell, and they were enabled to row safely to shore.

Some years passed away, until Bishop Gudmundur visited that part of his diocese, in order to bind the malignant monsters in rocks and waters and mountains, by his prayers. When he came to Hólmar, he was asked by the priest to consecrate the island Skrúdur ; but the same night, the bishop had a dream, in which a tall and splendidly dressed man came to him and said, " Do not obey the priest's injunction, nor consecrate Skrúdur, for it will be very difficult for me to move away with all my chattels before your arrival. Besides this, I may as well tell you, that if you come out to visit that island, it will be your last journey in this life." So the bishop refused, on the morrow, to consecrate the island at all, and the troll was left in peace.

The Shepherd of Silfrúnarstadir.

A man named Gudmundur lived once upon a time at a farm called Silfrúnarstadir, in the bay of Skagafjördur. He was very rich in flocks, and looked upon by his neighbours as a man of high esteem and respectability. He was married, but had no children.

It happened one Christmas-eve, at Silfrúnarstadir, that

the herdsman did not return home at night, and, as he was not found at the sheep-pens, the farmer caused a diligent search to be made for him all over the country, but quite in vain.

Next spring Gudmundur hired another shepherd, named Grímur, who was tall and strong, and boasted of being able to resist anybody. But the farmer, in spite of the man's boldness and strength, warned him to be careful how he ran risks, and on Christmas-eve bade him drive the sheep early into the pens, and come home to the farm while it was still daylight. But in the evening Grímur did not come, and though search was made far and near for him, was never found. People made all sorts of guesses about the cause of his disappearance, but the farmer was full of grief, and after this could not get any one to act as shepherd for him.

At this time there lived a very poor widow at Sjávarborg, who had several children, of whom the eldest, aged fourteen years, was named Sigurdur.

To this woman the farmer at last applied, and offered her a large sum of money if she would allow her son to act as shepherd for him. Sigurdur was very anxious that his mother should have all this money, and declared himself most willing to undertake the office; so he went with the farmer, and during the summer was most successful in his new situation, and never lost a sheep.

At the end of a certain time the farmer gave Sigurdur

a wether, a ewe, and a lamb as a present, with which the youth was much pleased.

Gudmundur became attached to him, and on Christmas-eve begged him to come home from his sheep before sunset.

All day long the boy watched the sheep, and when evening approached, he heard the sound of heavy foot-steps on the mountains. Turning round he saw coming towards him a gigantic and terrible troll.

She addressed him, saying, ": Good evening, my Sigur-dur. I am come to put you into my bag."

Sigurdur answered, "Are you cracked? Do you not see how thin I am? Surely I am not worth your notice. But I have a sheep and a fat lamb here which I will give you for your pot this evening."

So he gave her the sheep and the lamb, which she threw on to her shoulder, and carried off up the mountain again. Then Sigurdur went home, and right glad was the farmer to see him safe, and asked him whether he had seen anything.

" Nothing whatever, out of the common," replied the boy.

After New Year's day the farmer visited the flock, and, on looking over them, missed the sheep and lamb which he had given the youth, and asked him what had become of them. The boy answered that a fox had killed the lamb, and that the wether had fallen into a bog; adding, " I fancy I shall not be very lucky with *my* sheep."

" *So he gave her the sheep and the lamb, which she threw on to her shoulder, and carried off up the mountain.*"

[*To face page* 142.

When he heard this, the farmer gave him one ewe and two wethers, and asked him to remain another year in his service. Sigurdur consented to do so.

Next Christmas-eve, Gudmundur begged Sigurdur to be cautious, and not run any risks, for he loved him as his own son.

But the boy answered, " You need not fear, there are no risks to run."

When he had got the sheep into the pens about night-fall, the same troll came to him, and said :

" As sure as ever I am a troll, you shall not, this even-ing, escape being boiled in my pot."

" I am quite at your service," answered Sigurdur, in-trepidly ; " but you see that I am still very thin; nothing to be compared even to one wether. I will give you, how-ever, for your Christmas dinner, two old and two young sheep. Will you condescend to be satisfied with this offer of mine ? "

" Let me see," said the troll ; so the lad showed her the sheep, and she, hooking them together by their horns, threw them on to her shoulder, and ran off with them up the mountain. Then Sigurdur returned to the farm, and, when questioned, declared, as before, that he had seen nothing whatever unusual upon the mountain.

" But," he said, " I have been dreadfully unlucky with *my* sheep, as I said I should be." Next summer the farmer gave him four more wethers.

When Christmas-eve had come again, just as Sigurdur was putting the sheep into their pens, the troll came to him, and threatened to take him away with her. Then he offered her the four wethers, which she took, and hooking them together by their horns, threw them over her shoulder. Not content with this, however, she seized the lad. too, tucked him under her arm, and ran off with her burthen to her cave in the mountains.

Here she flung the sheep down, and Sigurdur after them, and ordered him to kill them and shave their skins. When he had done so, he asked her what task she had now for him to perform.

She said, " Sharpen this axe well, for I intend to cut off your head with it."

When he had sharpened it well, he restored it to the troll, who bade him take off his neckerchief; which he did, without changing a feature of his face.

Then the troll, instead of cutting off his head, flung the axe down on the ground, and said, " Brave lad! I never intended to kill you, and you shall live to a good old age. It was I that caused you to be made herdsman to Gudmundur, for I wished to meet with you. And now I will show you in what way you shall arrive at good-fortune. Next spring you must move from Silfrúnarstadir, and go to the house of a silversmith, to learn his trade. When you have learned it thoroughly, you shall take some specimens of silver-work to the farm where the dean's

three daughters live; and I can tell you that the youngest
of them is the most promising maiden in the whole country.
Her elder sisters love dress and ornaments, and will admire
what you bring them, but Margaret will not care about
such things. When you leave the house, you shall ask
her to accompany you as far as the door, and then as far
as the end of the grass-field, which she will consent to do.
Then you shall give her these three precious things—this
handkerchief, this belt, and this ring; and after that she will
love you. But when you have seen me in a dream you must
come here, and you will find me dead. Bury me, and take
for yourself everything of value that you find in my cave."

Then Sigurdur bade her farewell and left her, and returned to the farm, where Gudmundur welcomed him with
joy, having grieved at his long absence, and asked him
whether he had seen nothing.

" No," replied the boy; and declared that he could answer for the safety of all future herdsmen. But no more
questions would he answer, though the family asked him
many. The following spring he went to a silversmith's
house, and in two years made himself master of the trade.
He often visited Gudmundur, his old master, and was
always welcome. Once he went to the trading town of
Hofsós, and buying a variety of glittering silver ornaments, took them to Miklibœr, and offered them for sale to
the dean's daughters, as the troll had told him. When
the elder sisters heard that he had ornaments for sale, they

K

begged him to let them see them first, in order that they might choose the best of them. Accordingly he showed them his wares, and they bought many trinkets, but Margaret would not even so much as look at the silver ornaments.

When he took leave, he asked the youngest sister to accompany him as far as the door, and when they got there, to come with him as far as the end of the field. She was much astonished at this request, and asked him what he wanted with her, as she had never seen him before. But Sigurdur entreated her the more the more she held back, and at last she consented to go with him. At the end of the field Sigurdur gave her the belt and handkerchief, and put the ring on to her finger.

This done, Margaret said, " I wish I had never taken these gifts, but I cannot now give them you back."

Sigurdur then took leave and went home. But Margaret, as soon as she had received the presents, fell in love with their giver; and finding after a while that she could not live without him, told her father all about it. Her father bade her desist from such a mad idea, and declared that she should never marry the youth as long as he lived to prevent it. On this Margaret pined away, and became so thin from grief, that the father found he would be obliged to consent to her request; and going to the farm at which Sigurdur lived, engaged him as his silversmith.

Not long after, Sigurdur and Margaret were betrothed.

One day the youth dreamed that he saw the old troll, and felt sure from this that she was dead; so he asked the dean to accompany him as far as Silfrúnarstadir, and sleep there one night. When they arrived there, they told Gudmundur that Sigurdur was betrothed to Margaret. When the farmer heard this, he said that it had long been his intention to leave Sigurdur all his property, and offered him the management of the farm the ensuing spring. The youth thanked him heartily, and the dean was glad to see his daughter so soon, and so well, provided for.

Next day Sigurdur asked the farmer and the dean to go with him as far as the middle of the mountain, where they found a cave into which he bade them enter without fear. Inside they saw the troll lying dead on the floor with her face awfully distorted. Then Sigurdur told them all about his interviews with the troll, and asked them to help him to bury her. When they had done so, they returned to the cave and found there as many precious things as ten horses could carry, which Sigurdur took back to the farm.

Not long after, he married the dean's daughter, and prospered to the end of his life, which, as the old troll had prophesied, was a long one.

The Night-trolls.

Two trolls, who, quite contrary to the custom of trolls in general, had taken a great fancy to a church in their neighbourhood, determined to do it a service by taking an island out of the sea and adding it on to the church property. So they waded out one night till they reached one of a group of islands which suited their notions, and having rooted it up they proceeded to take it to shore, the man pulling before, and the wife pushing behind.

But before they could accomplish their task, dawn broke in the east, and they were both suddenly turned into stones.

And there they stand in Breidifjördur, to this day, the husband troll a tall and thin rock, the wife troll a short and broad one, and are called still " old man," and " old woman."

The Story of Bergthór of Bláfell.

In heathen times a troll named Bergthór married a wife, and lived in a cave called Hundahellir, on Bláfell. He was well skilled in the black art, but a very mild-tempered and harmless troll, except when provoked. Near the mountains stood a farm called Haukadalur, where an old man then lived.

One day the troll came to him and said, " I wish, when I die, to be buried where I can hear the sound of bells and running water; promise, therefore, to place me in the churchyard at Haukadalur. As a sign of my death, my large staff shall stand at your cottage-door; and, as a reward for burying me, you may take what you find in the kettle by the side of my body."

The farmer made him the promise, and Bergthór took leave of him.

Some time afterwards when the servants went out of the farmhouse at Haukadalur early in the morning, they found standing by the door a great wooden staff, and told the farmer of it. As soon as he saw it he recognised it as that of Bergthór, and having caused a coffin to be made, rode in company with some of his men to Blåfell. When they entered the cave, they found Bergthór dead, and placed him in the coffin, wondering among themselves to find so large a corpse so light as his seemed to be. By the side of the bed the farmer discovered a large kettle, and opened it, expecting it to be full of gold. But when he saw that it contained nothing but dead leaves, he fancied that the troll had played him false, and was much wroth. One of the men, however, filled both his gloves with these leaves, and then they carried the coffin with Bergthór in it down to the level ground.

At the foot of the hill they stopped to rest, and the man who had taken the leaves opened his gloves and found that they were full of money.

The farmer seeing this, was struck with astonishment, and turned back with some of his servants to get the rest of it; but, search as they would, they could find no traces of either cave or kettle, and were obliged to leave the mountain disappointed, as everybody else, who made the same search, was too.

They buried the body of the troll, and the mound which marked where they placed him is called " Bergthór's barrow " to this day.

GRYLA.

We cannot conclude our stories of trolls without giving a description of Grýla, a bugbear used to frighten children quiet, which is almost horrible enough to frighten them to death.

Grýla had three hundred heads, six eyes in each head, besides two livid and ghostly blue eyes at the back of each neck. She had goat's horns, and her ears were so long as to hang down to her shoulders at one end, and at the other to join the ends of her three hundred noses. On each forehead was a tuft of hair, and on each chin a tangled and filthy beard. Her teeth were like burnt lava. To each thigh she had bound a sack, in which she used to carry naughty children, and she had, moreover, hoofs like a horse. Besides all this, she had fifteen tails, and on each tail a hundred bags of skin, every one of which bags would hold twenty children.

Grýla had a husband named Leppalúdi, a scarecrow, and they had twenty children. In addition to these, they had thirteen more (whom Grýla is reported to have borne before she was married to Leppalúdi the scarecrow) called Christmas-men, as they were supposed to come to human abodes about Christmas time, and take away the naughty children.

More is told about all these trolls which is not worth repeating.

STORIES OF GHOSTS AND GOBLINS.

Murder will Out.

Once upon a time, in a certain churchyard, some people who were digging a grave, found a skull with a knitting-pin stuck through it from temple to temple. The priest took the skull and preserved it until the next Sunday, when he had to perform service.

When the day came, the priest waited until all the people were inside the church, and then fastened up the skull to the top of the porch. After the service the priest and his servant left the church first, and stood outside the door, watching carefully everybody that came out. When all the congregation had passed out without anything strange occurring, they looked in to see if there was any one still remaining inside. The only person they saw was a very old woman sitting behind the door, who was so unwilling to leave the church, that they were compelled to force her out. As she passed under the porch, three drops of blood fell from the skull on to her white head-dress, and she exclaimed, "Alas, murder will out at last!" Then she confessed, that having been compelled to marry her first husband against her will, she had killed him with a knitting-pin and married another.

She was tried for the murder, though it had happened so many years back, and condemned to death.

KETILL, THE PRIEST OF HÚSAVÍK.

There once lived a priest at Húsavík, whose name was Ketill. Finding the churchyard rather crowded, he dug up a good many of the coffins; saying, "that they were no use where they were, but only took up room," [and used them for firewood.

Some time after, in a kitchen, three old women were sitting round the fire where some of the coffin-planks were burning. A spark flew out and set fire to the dress of one of them, and, as they were sitting close together, the flame quickly caught the dresses of the other two, and burnt so fiercely, that all three were dead before any one could come to their assistance.

Next night the priest saw a man come to his bedside who said, " Do not endeavour to make room in the church-yard by taking out our coffins and burning them ; you see that I have already killed three old women, and if you go on in this way I will kill many more, and fill up your graves for you quicker than you will like."

The priest took the warning, burnt no more coffins, and saw no more ghosts, nor were any more old women killed.

White Cap.

A certain boy and girl, whose names this tale telleth not, once lived near a church. The boy being mis-chievously inclined, was in the habit of trying to frighten the girl in a variety of ways, till she became at last so accustomed to his tricks, that she ceased to care for anything whatever, putting down everything strange that she saw and heard to the boy's mischief.

One washing-day, the girl was sent by her mother to fetch home the linen, which had been spread to dry in the churchyard. When she had nearly filled her basket, she happened to look up, and saw sitting on a tomb near her a figure dressed in white from head to foot, but was not the least alarmed, believing it to be the boy playing her, as usual, a trick. So she ran up to it, and pulling its cap off said, " You shall not frighten me, *this* time." Then when she had finished collecting the linen she went home; but, to her astonishment—for he could not have reached home before her without her seeing him—the boy was the first person who greeted her on her arrival at the cottage.

Among the linen, too, when it was sorted, was found a mouldy white cap, which appeared to be nobody's property, and which was half full of earth.

The next morning the ghost (for it was a ghost that the girl had seen) was found sitting with no cap upon its head, upon the same tombstone as the evening before; and as nobody had the courage to address it, or knew in the least how to get rid of it, they sent into the neighbouring village for advice.

An old man declared that the only way to avoid some general calamity, was for the little girl to replace on the ghost's head the cap she had seized from it, in the presence of many people, all of whom were to be perfectly silent. So a crowd collected in the churchyard, and the little girl, going forward, half afraid, with the cap, placed it upon the ghost's head, saying, "Are you satisfied now?"

But the ghost, raising its hand, gave her a fearful blow, and said, "Yes; but are *you* now satisfied?"

The little girl fell down dead, and at the same instant the ghost sank into the grave upon which it had been sitting, and was no more seen.

A Ghost's Vengeance.

Some years ago, two friends were conversing together on various subjects, and, among others, on corpses.

" If ever I happen to find a dead man," said the one, " I shall do my best for it, and bury it."

" For my part," replied the other, " I shall take no such trouble, but pass it by like any other carrion."

Some time passed away, and one day Ketill (that was the name of the latter), while out walking, found the corpse of an old woman lying in the road, but passed by without paying the slightest attention to it.

Next night, after he was in bed, this old woman appeared to him and said, " No thanks to you for your neglect of me; for you did me neither good nor evil."

And she looked so horrible, that he jumped out of bed, grasped a large knife that lay near him, and chased the spectre from the house, cursing and swearing, and crying, " Shall I stab you, you old witch?"

After this he went to bed again, and fell asleep; then he saw the old woman a second time, holding her lungs, all clotted with blood, in her hand, and making as if she was going to strike him with them. So he jumped out of bed with the knife, but before he could reach her, she had disappeared.

When he had got into bed again, and was asleep, she

came a third time, and made as if she would strangle him
So a third time he jumped out of bed with the knife, but
failed in reaching her before she vanished.

And this hag's ghost followed the unhappy Ketill all
his life, and drove him with her wrath and spite into an
untimely grave. Whether Ketill's friend ever found a
corpse and had a chance of carrying out his charitable
intentions with regard to it, this story narrates not, neither
does it so much as hint at what reward he would have
got for his pains.

DRY BONES.

There were once two friends, the elder of whom was a
drunkard. It happened that the younger was betrothed
to a girl, and had invited the elder to his marriage-feast.
But before the time came the drunkard died. The wedding
ceremony was performed, and the feast held at the church
in which he was buried.

That night the bridegroom dreamed that his friend came
to him, and addressed him in piteous tones, saying, " Pour
out one keg of brandy into my grave, for my dry old bones
are athirst."

Next morning the bridegroom emptied a cask of brandy
on to his friend's grave, and never saw his ghost again.

THE BOY WHO DID NOT KNOW WHAT FEAR WAS.

There was once a boy so courageous and spirited that
his relations despaired of ever frightening him into obe-
dience to their will, and took him to the parish priest to be
brought up. But the priest could not subdue him in the
least, though the boy never showed either obstinacy or ill-
temper towards him.

Once in the winter three dead bodies were brought to
be buried, but as it was late in the afternoon they were
put into the church till next day, when the priest would
be able to bury them. In those days it was the custom to
bury people without coffins, and only wrapped up in grave-
clothes. The priest ordered these three bodies to be laid
a little distance apart, across the middle of the church.

After nightfall the priest said to the boy, "Run into the
church and fetch me the book which I left on the altar."

With his usual willingness he ran into the church, which
was quite dark, and half way to the altar stumbled against
something which lay on the floor, and fell down on his
face. Not in the least alarmed, he got up again, and, after
groping about, found that he had stumbled over one of the
corpses, which he took in his arms and pushed into the
side-benches out of his way. He tumbled over the other
two, and disposed of them in like manner. Then, taking
the book from the altar, he left the church, shut the door

behind him, and gave the volume to the priest, who asked him if he had encountered anything extraordinary in the church.

"Not that I can remember," said the boy.

The priest asked again, "Did you not find three corpses lying across your passage?"

"Oh yes," replied he, "but what about them?"

"Did they not lie in your way?"

"Yes, but they did not hinder me."

The priest asked, "How did you get to the altar?"

The boy replied, "I stuck the good folk into the side benches, where they lie quietly enough."

The priest shook his head, but said nothing more that night.

Next morning he said to the boy, "You must leave me; I cannot keep near me any longer one who is shameless enough to break the repose of the dead."

The boy, nothing loth, bade farewell to the priest and his family, and wandered about some little time without a home.

Once he came to a cottage, where he slept the night, and there the people told him that the Bishop of Skálholt was just dead. So next day he went off to Skálholt, and arriving there in the evening, begged a night's lodging.

The people said to him, "You may have it and welcome, but you must take care of yourself."

"Why take care of myself so much?" asked the lad.

"*Then there fell down on to the floor of the kitchen half a giant—head, arms, hands, and body, as far as the waist.*"

[*To face page* 162.

They told him that after the death of the bishop, no one could stay in the house after nightfall, as some ghost or goblin walked about there, and that on this account every one had to leave the place after twilight.

The boy answered, " Well and good; that will just suit me."

At twilight the people all left the place, taking leave of the boy, whom they did not expect to see again alive.

When they had all gone, the boy lighted a candle and examined every room in the house till he came to the kitchen, where he found large quantities of smoked mutton hung up to the rafters. So, as he had not tasted meat for some time, and had a capital appetite, he cut some of the dried mutton off with his knife, and placing a pot on the fire, which was still burning, cooked it.

When he had finished cutting up the meat, and had put the lid on the pot, he heard a voice from the top of the chimney, which said, " May I come down ?"

The lad answered, " Yes, why not ?"

Then there fell down on to the floor of the kitchen half a giant,—head, arms, hands, and body, as far as the waist, and lay there motionless.

After this he heard another voice from the chimney, saying, " May I come down ?"

" If you like," said the boy ; " why not ?"

Accordingly down came another part of the giant, from the waist to the thighs, and lay on the floor motionless.

Then he heard a third voice from the same direction, which said, "May I come down?"

"Of course," he replied; "you must have something to stand upon."

So a huge pair of legs and feet came down and lay by the rest of the body, motionless.

After a bit the boy, finding this want of movement rather tedious, said, "Since you have contrived to get yourself all in, you had better get up and go away."

Upon this the pieces crept together, and the giant rose on his feet from the floor, and, without uttering a word, stalked out of the kitchen. The lad followed him, till they came to a large hall, in which stood a wooden chest. This chest the goblin opened, and the lad saw that it was full of money. Then the goblin took the money out in handfuls, and poured it like water over his head, till the floor was covered with heaps of it; and, having spent half the night thus, spent the other half in restoring the gold to the chest in the like manner. The boy stood by and watched him filling the chest again, and gathering all the stray coins together by sweeping his great arms violently over the floor, as if he dreaded to be interrupted before he could get them all in, which the lad fancied must be because the day was approaching.

When the goblin had shut up the coffer, he rushed past the lad as if to get out of the hall; but the latter said to him, "Do not be in too great a hurry."

"I must make haste," replied the other, "for the day is dawning."

But the boy took him by the sleeve and begged him to remain yet a little longer for friendship's sake.

At this the goblin waxed angry, and, clutching hold of the youth, said, "Now you shall delay me no longer."

But the latter clung tight to him, and slipped out of the way of every blow he dealt, and some time passed away in this kind of struggle. It happened, however, at last, that the giant turned his back to the open door, and the boy, seeing his chance, tripped him up and butted at him with his head, so that the other fell heavily backwards, half in and half out of the hall, and broke his spine upon the threshold. At the same moment the first ray of dawn struck his eyes through the open house door, and he instantly sank into the ground in two pieces, one each side of the door of the hall. Then the courageous boy, though half dead from fatigue, made two crosses of wood and drove them into the ground where the two parts of the goblin had disappeared. This done, he fell asleep till, when the sun was well up, the people came back to Skálholt. They were amazed and rejoiced to find him still alive, asking him whether he had seen anything in the night.

"Nothing out of the common," he said.

So he stayed there all that day, both because he was tired, and because the people were loth to let him go.

In the evening, when the people began as usual to leave

the place, he begged them to stay, assuring them that they would be troubled by neither ghost nor goblin. But in spite of his assurances they insisted upon going, though they left him this time without any fear for his safety. When they were gone, he went to bed and slept soundly till morning.

On the return of the people he told them all about his struggle with the goblin, showed them the crosses he had set up, and the chestful of money in the hall, and assured them that they would never again be troubled at night, so need not leave the place. They thanked him most heartily for his spirit and courage, and asked him to name any reward he would like to receive, whether money or other precious things, inviting him, in addition, to remain with them as long as ever he chose. He was grateful for their offers, but said, " I do not care for money, nor can I make up my mind to stay longer with you."

Next day he addressed himself to his journey, and no persuasion could induce him to remain at Skálholt. For he said, " I have no more business here, as you can now, without fear, live in the bishop's house." And taking leave of them all, he directed his steps northwards, into the wilderness.

For a long time nothing new befell him, until one day he came to a large cave, into which he entered. In a smaller cave within the other he found twelve beds, all in disorder and unmade. As it was yet early, he thought he could do

no better than employ himself in making them, and having
made them, threw himself on to the one nearest the
entrance, covered himself up, and went to sleep.

After a little while he awoke and heard the voices of
men talking in the cave, and wondering who had made the
beds for them, saying that, whoever he was, they were
much obliged to him for his pains. He saw, on looking
out, that they were twelve armed men of noble aspect.
When they had had supper, they came into the inner cave
and eleven of them went to bed. But the twelfth man
whose bed was next to the entrance, found the boy in it,
and calling to the others they rose and thanked the lad for
having made their beds for them, and begged him to
remain with them as their servant, for they said that they
never found time to do any work for themselves, as they
were compelled to go out every day at sunrise to fight their
enemies, and never returned till night. The lad asked
them why they were forced to fight day after day? They
answered that they had over and over again fought, and
overcome their enemies, but that though they killed them
over-night they always came to life again before morning,
and would come to the cave and slay them all in their
beds if they were not up and ready on the field at sunrise.

In the morning the cave-men went out fully armed,
leaving the lad behind to look after the household
work.

About noon he went in the same direction as the men had taken, in order to find out where the battle-field was, and as soon as he had espied it in the distance, ran back to the cave.

In the evening the warriors returned weary and dispirited, but were glad to find that the boy had arranged everything for them, so that they had nothing more to do than eat their supper and go to bed.

When they were all asleep, the boy wondered to himself how it could possibly come to pass that their enemies rose every night from the dead. So moved with curiosity was he, that as soon as he was sure that his companions were fast asleep he took what of their weapons and armour he found to fit him best, and stealing out of the cave, made off in the direction of the battle-field. There was nothing at first to be seen there but corpses and trunkless heads, so he waited a little time to see what would happen. About dawn he perceived a mound near him open of itself, and an old woman in a blue cloak come out with a glass phial in her hand. He noticed her go up to a dead warrior, and having picked up his head, smear his neck with some ointment out of the phial and place the head and trunk together. Instantly the warrior stood erect, a living man. The hag repeated this to two or three, until the boy seeing now the secret of the thing, rushed up to her and stabbed her to death as well as the men she had raised, who were yet stupid and heavy as if after sleep. Then taking the

phial, he tried whether he could revive the corpses with
the ointment, and found on experiment that he could do
so successfully. So he amused himself for a while in
reviving the men and killing them again, till, at sunrise,
his companions arrived on the field.

They were mightily astonished to see him there, and
told him that they had missed him as well as some of their
weapons and armour; but they were rejoiced to find their
enemies lying dead on the field instead of being alive
and awaiting them in battle array, and asked the lad how
he had got the idea of thus going at night to the battle-
field, and what he had done.

He told them all that had passed, showed them the
phial of ointment, and, in order to prove its power, smeared
the neck of one of the corpses, who at once rose to his
feet, but was instantly killed again by the cave-men.
They thanked the boy heartily for the service he had
rendered them, and begged him to remain among them,
offering him at the same time money for his work. He
declared that he was quite willing, paid or unpaid, to stay
with them, as long as they liked to keep him. The cave-
men were well pleased with his answer, and having embraced the lad, set to work to strip their enemies of their
weapons: made a heap of them with the old woman on
the top, and burned them; and then, going into the mound,
appropriated to themselves all the treasures they found
there. After this they proposed the game of killing each

other, to try how it was to die, as they could restore one another to life again. So they killed each other, but by smearing themselves with the ointment, they at once returned to life.

Now this was great sport for a while.

But once, when they had cut off the head of the lad, they put it on again wrongside before. And as the lad saw himself behind, he became as if mad with fright, and begged the men to release him by all means from such a painful sight.

But when the cave-folk had run to him and, cutting off his head, placed it on all right again, he came back to his full senses, and was as fearless as ever before.

The boy lived with them ever afterwards, and no more stories are told about him.

The Two Sigurdurs.

A farmer once had a son named Sigurdur, who was so ill-tempered that no one could live in peace with him.

One day it happened that a man whose name was also Sigurdur, came to the farmer's house and asked shelter of him for the winter, which the farmer consented to give him. The stranger did nothing but play the flute, and the farmer's son became so fond of him that he cared for nobody else.

In the spring the stranger went away, and Sigurdur became so sick of home-life that he also left the farm and went in search of his beloved namesake. From house to house, from parish to parish, and from district to district, he went, continually asking for Sigurdur. At last at a certain priest's house where he made the same inquiry, they told him that a man of that name had just died there, and lay in the church. On being admitted into the church the boy sat down by the open coffin, intending to watch over it all night.

At midnight the corpse of Sigurdur (for it really was his friend) rose from the coffin and left the church, but his namesake sat still and awaited his return. At dawn the corpse came back, but Sigurdur would not let him, in spite of his entreaties, return to his coffin before telling him how he had spent the night outside the church.

So the dead man said, "I have been looking over my money. Now I must get into the coffin."

"No," replied the other; "you must first tell me where your money is.'

"In one of the corners of the family-room," said the other.

"How much is there of it?"

"One barrelful."

"Did you do nothing," again inquired the youth, "besides counting your money?"

The corpse denied it, but when the living Sigurdur

pressed him to tell him how he had been employed, on pain of refusing to admit him into his coffin again, the other answered, "Well, then! I have killed the priest's lady, who has just had a child."

"Why did you commit so mean a crime?" asked Sigurdur.

"Because," replied the corpse, "during her lifetime I tried to seduce her, but she always resisted my persuasions."

"How did you kill her?"

The dead Sigurdur answered, "I drove all the life in her body into her little finger."

"Can she not be revived?" asked the youth.

"Yes! If you can untie the thread that is round her finger without shedding any blood, she will come to life. And now I really must get into my coffin."

The other only allowed him to do so on his promising that he would not ever try to move again.

In the morning, as soon as the sun was fully risen, Sigurdur left the church and entered the family-room, where he found everybody plunged in grief, and, on his asking them what was the matter, they told him that the priest's wife had died in the night, and nobody could tell her complaint. So he asked permission to see her, which was granted him, and having gone up to the dead woman and undone the cord which he found round her little finger, he urged back the life from it into her body, and she sat up alive and well. Then he told the priest about his interview with the corpse of Sigurdur, and, to prove his words still further, showed him the money hidden in the corner of the family-room. The priest thanked him cordially for the good service he had done him, and after this Sigurdur became as much beloved as he had before been hated.

THE DEACON OF MYRKÁ.

A long time ago, a deacon lived at Myrká, in Egafjördur. He was in love with a girl named Gudrún, who dwelt in a farm on the opposite side of the valley, separated from his house by a river.

The deacon had a horse with a grey mane, which he was always in the habit of riding, and which he called Faxi.

A short time before Christmas, the deacon rode to the farm at which his betrothed lived, and invited her to join in the Christmas festivities at Myrká, promising to fetch her on Christmas-eve. Some time before he had started out on this ride, there had been heavy snow and frost; but this very day there came so rapid a thaw, that the river over which the deacon had safely ridden, trusting to the firmness of the ice, became impassable during the short time he spent with his betrothed; the floods rose, and huge masses of drift-ice were whirled down the stream.

When the deacon had left the farm, he rode on to the river, and being deep in thought did not perceive at first the change that had taken place. As soon, however, as he saw in what state the stream was, he rode up the banks until he came to a bridge of ice, on to which he spurred his horse. But when he arrived at the middle of the bridge, it broke beneath him, and he was drowned in the flood.

Next morning, a neighbouring farmer saw the deacon's horse grazing in a field, but could discover nothing of its owner, whom he had seen the day before cross the river, but not return. He at once suspected what had occurred, and going down to the river, found the corpse of the deacon, which had drifted to the bank, with all the flesh torn off the back of his head, and the bare white skull visible. So he brought the body back to Myrká, where it was buried a week before Christmas.

Up to Christmas-eve the river continued so swollen, that no communication could take place between the dwellers on the opposite banks, but that morning it subsided, and Gudrún, utterly ignorant of the deacon's death, looked forward with joy to the festivities to which she had been invited by him.

In the afternoon Gudrún began to dress in her best clothes, but before she had quite finished, she heard a knock at the door of the farm. One of the maid-servants opened the door, but seeing nobody there, thought it was

" *The horse leaped over the black and rapid stream.   At the same moment the head of the deacon nodded forward.*"

[*To face page* 174.

because the night was not sufficiently light, for the moon was hidden for the time by clouds. So saying, " Wait there till I bring a light," went back into the house; but she had no sooner shut the outer door behind her, than the knock was repeated, and Gudrún cried out from her room, " It is some one waiting for me."

As she had by this time finished dressing, she slipped only one sleeve of her winter cloak on, and threw the rest over her shoulders hurriedly. When she opened the door, she saw the well-known Faxi standing outside, and by him a man whom she knew to be the deacon. Without a word he placed Gudrún on the horse, and mounted in front of her himself, and off they rode.

When they came to the river it was frozen over, all except the current in the middle, which the frost had not yet hardened. The horse walked on to the ice, and leaped over the black and rapid stream which flowed in the middle. At the same moment the head of the deacon nodded forward, so that his hat fell over his eyes, and Gudrún saw the large patch of bare skull gleam white in the midst of his hair. Directly afterwards, a cloud moved from before the moon, and the deacon said—

> " The moon glides,
> Death rides,
> Seest thou not the white place
> In the back of my head,
> Garún, Garún?"

Not a word more was spoken till they came to Myrká, where they dismounted.

Then the man said :

> "Wait here for me, Garún, Garún,
> While I am taking Faxi, Faxi,
> Outside the hedges, the hedges ! "

When he had gone, Gudrún saw near her in the church-yard, where she was standing, an open grave, and half sick with horror, ran to the church porch, and seizing the rope, tolled the bells with all her strength. But as she began to ring them, she felt some one grasp her and pull so fiercely at her cloak that it was torn off her, leaving only the one sleeve into which she had thrust her arm before starting from home. Then turning round, she saw the deacon jump headlong into the yawning grave, with the tattered cloak in his hand, and the heaps of earth on both sides fall in over him, and close the grave up to the brink.

Gudrún knew now that it was the deacon's ghost with whom she had had to do, and continued ringing the bells till she roused all the farm-servants at Myrká.

That same night, after Gudrún had got shelter at Myrká and was in bed, the deacon came again from his grave and endeavoured to drag her away, so that no one could sleep for the noise of their struggle.

This was repeated every night for a fortnight, and Gudrún could never be left alone for a single instant, lest

the goblin deacon should get the better of her.   From time
to time, also, a neighbouring priest came and sat on the
edge of the bed, reading the Psalms of David to protect
her against this ghostly persecution.

But nothing availed, till they sent for a man from the
north country, skilled in witchcraft, who dug up a large
stone from the field, and placed it in the middle of the
guest-room at Myrká.   When the deacon rose that night
from his grave and came into the house to torment Gudrún,
this man seized him, and by uttering potent spells over
him, forced him beneath the stone, and exorcised the
passionate demon that possessed him, so that there he lies
in peace to this day.

THE SON OF THE GOBLIN.

The farm Bakki (now called Prestbakki, in Hrútafjördur)
once stood further north than it does now, and the reasons
of its being moved from its ancient to its present position
are as follows.

It happened that a certain farmer's son courted the
daughter of the priest who lived at Bakki, but met with a
refusal of his offers, which grieved him so sorely, that he
fell sick and died, and was buried at the church near the
priest's house.   This had happened in summer.   The
winter following, people noticed a certain strangeness in

M

the demeanour of the priest's daughter, for which they could not account.

One evening, it happened that her foster-mother, an old woman and a wise withal, went out to the churchyard with her knitting, as it was warm enough, and the moon had but few clouds to wade through.

Some time before this, her foster-child had told her that since his death her old lover had often been to see her, and that she found herself now with child, whose father had assured her that the infant would prove an ill-fated one; and the unfortunate girl had asked the old woman to try to prevent, from that time forth, her ghostly lover's visits; and it was for this purpose that the good dame had gone out into the churchyard. She went to the grave of the young man, which was yawning wide open, and threw her ball of thread down into it, and having done so, sat down on its edge to knit. There she sat until the ghost came, who at once begged her to take up the ball of thread from the grave, so that he might enter his coffin and take his rest.

But the old woman said, " I have no mind to do so, unless you tell me what you do out of your grave thus at night."

He answered, " I visit the priest's daughter, for he has no means of preventing my doing so. Ere long she will be delivered of a boy."

Then the old woman said, " Tell me this boy's fate."

" His fate," replied the other, " is, that he will be a priest at Bakki, and the church with all its congregation will sink down to hell the first time he pronounces the blessing from the altar, and then my vengeance will be complete, for the injury the priest did me in not allowing me to marry his daughter during my lifetime."

" Your prophecy is, indeed, a great one, if it meets with a fulfilment," answered the old woman; " but are there no means by which so horrible a curse can be prevented ? "

The ghost replied, " The only means are for some one to stab the priest the moment he begins to pronounce the blessing; but I do not fancy that anybody will undertake that task."

When she had gathered this information, the old woman said to him, " Go now into your grave, and be sure never again to come out of it."

After this the old woman drew up her ball of thread, and the corpse leaped into the grave, over which the earth closed itself. Then she recited over the grave some magic spells, which bound the corpse in its last rest for ever; and returning home, told nobody what had passed between her and the goblin-lover.

Some time afterwards, the girl was delivered of a fine and healthy boy, who was brought up at Bakki by his mother and his grandfather (though the latter did not know who its father was). In his early youth people saw that he excelled all his companions both in mind and body; and

M 2

when his education was complete, and he had arrived at he proper age, he became his grandfather's curate.

Now, the old woman saw that something must be done to prevent the approaching ill-fate, so she went to her son, who was a man of great courage, and one who did not shrink from trifles, and told him the whole story of her interview with the goblin, and begged him to stab the young priest directly he began to pronounce his blessing from the altar, promising herself to take all the consequences of the deed. He was at first very unwilling to do this, but when she pressed him with earnest entreaties, he at last made the promise she required, and confirmed it with an oath.

At length the day came on which the young curate was to perform service for the first time, and the large congregation assembled in the church were struck with his eloquence and sweet voice. But when the youth stood at the altar and raised his hands for the benediction, the old woman signed to her son, who rushed forward and stabbed him, so that he fell dead on the spot. Horror-struck at this fearful act, many rushed forward and seized the murderer, but those who went to the altar to raise the priest found nothing of him but the top bone of his neck, which lay where he had been standing. Every one now saw that what had happened was no every-day murder, but that some goblin had had to do with it; and the old woman, standing in the midst of them, told them the whole story.

When they had heard it they recovered from their panic, and thanked her for her foresight, and her son for his quickness and courage. They then perceived that the east end of the church had sunk down a little into the ground, because the priest had had time to pronounce the first few syllables of the blessing.

After this, the farm of Bakki was so haunted by goblins that it was removed from its old to its present situation.

THE STORY OF GRÍMUR, WHO KILLED SKELJÚNGUR.

A certain man was named Kári, the son of Össur. He was the nephew of Hjálmúlfr, who had made himself possessor of Blönduhlíd, extending from the river Djúpadalsá to the river Nordurá, and who dwelt at Hjálmúlfsstadir, and is buried in the barrow called Ulfshaugur, south of the farm.

Kári came from Norway, in company with Hjálmúlfr, made himself possessor of the land between Nordurá and Merkigil, and dwelt at the farm called Flatatúga; whereupon he was named Túngukári.

He had a son, Thorgrímur, a strong and wise man, who married Ashildur, daughter of Thorbrandur, of Thorbrandsstadir, in Nordurárdalur, and with her he received the property belonging to the farm Silfrastadir, where he began his life as a farmer, and became very wealthy in flocks and herds.

Thorbrandur lived at Thorbrandsstadir, to a high age, and possessed, besides this farm, one called Haukagil. At the former of these he built the famous hall, so much spoken of in the Sagas, through which the highway ran, where there were tables of provisions always ready for every passer-by. Thorbrandur was buried on the other side of the river Nordurá, where a large mound was raised above him, in a place he had himself chosen, whence he could see over both Thorbrandsstadir and Haukagil.

Thorgrímur of Silfrastadir had a son by his wife, named Grímur, who was one of the handsomest and best-grown men in Skagafjördur. He had also a daughter, named Ingibjörg, who was both winsome and wise, and was looked upon as one of the chief ladies in all that neighbourhood.

Thorgrímur had large flocks, as his pasture-grounds were good, and was therefore in need of an active herdsman, if he wished all to go well with his sheep. Once it happened that a vessel from Norway came into the harbour of Kolbeinsá late in the summer. Thorgrímur, with many other farmers, rode down to the ship, the merchants of which had on board, besides other wares, a certain bondman named Skeljúngur. He was tall, strong, and of an indomitable temper.

Thorgrímur, being apprised by the merchants that this man was for sale, went to him and asked him for what work he was fit.

Skeljúngur answered, "Thralls are not fit for much. But in good weather I have not refused ere now to watch sheep, and if you will, I can do so still."

Thorgrímur said, " I will risk buying you if you will guard my sheep, which are numerous, and their pastures dangerous."

" Do as you like," answered Skeljúngur.

So the farmer purchased this bondman, and took him home to Silfrastadir, where he commenced his duties as herdsman towards the beginning of the winter, and Thorgrímur soon perceived that the man had the strength and courage of two, in everything he undertook.

Skeljúngur was very obedient to his master, but could not agree with the other men of the farm, and least of all with Grímur.

Amongst the servants at the farm was a bond-maid named Bóla, who was fiendishly evil-minded and malicious, insomuch that nobody could come to any understanding with her. Many fancied that her nature partook of that of the trolls; and her quarrels with Skeljúngur were so fierce and frequent, that the farmer had repeatedly to interfere between them.

At last, Bóla ran away from Silfrastadir in a fit of rage, and every one was convinced that she had taken up her abode in a deep rocky gulf, near the farm. In this gulf there were three high waterfalls, as a little river ran through it. The approach to the two lower ones was difficult; to the uppermost one, under which Bóla was supposed to have taken up her abode in a cave, nearly impossible. From this place she infested the neighbourhood, part of which, with the gulf itself, was subsequently called by her name.

Once, early in the winter, Thorgrímur lost five of his best wethers from Skeljúngur's keeping, and it was suspected that Bóla had taken them. Skeljúngur became very cross at this, and wanted to find out whether she had taken them or not. But the farmer entreated him to run no such risk, assuring him that it would be far better to remain quiet. The man obeyed him, and, for the present, desisted from any search into the matter.

Next autumn eight wethers were lost from Skeljúngur's charge, who still did not endeavour to find them, as the farmer had begged him not to do so.

The third autumn ten more were lost, and then Skeljúngur became so enraged that he would not listen in the least to what the farmer said. So he ran off in a state of blind and mad rage, like that in which the warriors of old could fight their best, and hastened to the gulf, and over the waterfall into the cave; which leap has been since called " Skeljúngur's leap."

Now, after this, nothing distinct is known concerning his struggle with Bóla; but the story runs, that, after a fierce and long fight with her, he contrived to suffocate her in the deep pool beneath the fall. This done, Skel-

júngur returned to the farm, and said that he fancied the
stealing of his sheep would not be continued now; but
Thorgrímur, far from pleased, held his peace.

People soon found that Skeljúngur's temper had become
more diabolical than ever, since his struggle with Bóla, so
that it became almost impossible to treat with him; but he
still continued faithful and attached to his master, and so
time passed quietly on.

Now we must return to Grímur, the son of Thorgrímur,
who had lived with his father to manhood, and was now
the most active of all his fellows.

One day Grímur came to his father, and said, " Advance
me some money from my inheritance. I wish to travel
hence and become acquainted with the customs of other
countries; for to sit here at home like a girl will prove but
a scanty advantage to me."

The farmer replied, " You shall not need to ask twice.
I will give you money enough; but I have a foreboding
that at some future time we shall need you here; and then
you had better be at home than away; and I fear that you
will have some great dangers to overcome."

Grímur answered, " I will run the risk;" and after this
went on board a vessel belonging to some Norway merchants, with plenty of money for his travels. He took an
affectionate leave of his father, and sailed away. But the
ship had started very late, having been prevented from
sailing by the Greenland ice, and when once at sea, was so

hard tossed by storms, as to lose her way and be driven hither and thither all the rest of the summer. At the approach of the winter, they were, in a heavy snow-storm, carried near the shores of an unknown country, where there was no harbour, and where the coast was surrounded by cliffs. Here they were wrecked, and every life was lost, and all the merchandise swallowed by the waves; Grímur alone being able to swim to shore, where he wandered about forlorn and tired, not knowing whither to go, till he heard the sound of some one cutting wood near him. He went in that direction, and found a young and strongly-built man, hewing wood with a large axe.

Grímur saluted this youth, who courteously received him, and asked him about his journey, and how he had come there.

Grímur answered, " I am an Icelander, by name Grímur. My ship, with all its merchandise and all my companions, has been wrecked, and all lost but myself. Tell me now, to what land I have been driven; who is its ruler? and whom do I now address? "

The other replied. " I am your namesake, for my name is also Grímur. You have come to the wildernesses of Greenland, a long way from the thickly-inhabited districts; but my father's hut is not far hence. His name also is Grímur, and my mother's Thórhildur, and I have a sister, two years older than myself, named Ingibjörg. No one else lives in the house, nor have we many neighbours.

Now, as matters stand, I think you can do no better than accompany me home to my father, appeal to his good feeling, and see what comes of it. And I suppose he will do better who aids you than he who is against you."

To this the Icelandic Grímur agreed, and the young men went towards the hut together.

The cottage was neat and strongly built, and the Greenland Grímur brought his namesake into the room where his father was sitting; an old man of noble aspect, hale for his age, and active in all his movements. His wife, an aged woman, was very neat in her dress, and imposing in her demeanour.

The old man saluted his son kindly, and said, " Who is the young fellow with you ? "

His son replied, " He is an Icelander who has been wrecked on the shore, and has lost all his possessions. I beg you, my father, to help him, for he is an honourable and well-born youth."

His father said, " I was not curious concerning him, but as he has been driven to shore, to the compassion of his fellow-creatures, take him with you, my son, we bid him welcome for the winter."

The young men thanked the farmer for his kindness, and from that time became, as it were, brothers. Ingibjörg was a noble and lovely maiden, and she and the Icelander became much attached to one another, at which no one wondered, as all were fond of him.

So the winter passed, until shortly before Christmas-time, when it happened one day, that the brothers, while gathering drift-wood on the shore, saw a monster in woman's form, with large and repulsive countenance, approaching them.

She addressed them with these words:—" I must tell you, young men, that my mother Skráma, who lives in the mountains, invites you to her Christmas festivities, and is very anxious that you should accept her invitation."

The youths answered her only with curses, and spurned her invitation; whereupon she at once disappeared.

When they came home late in the evening, the old man asked them whether they had any news for him, but they said they had nothing new to relate to him. He continued, however. " I am sure that you have seen something unusual, and that you will not refuse to tell me the truth about it."

So they told him that they had seen the monster, and laughed to scorn her invitation; " for," they said, " what cared we for her ?"

The old man answered, " It will not do for you to reject her invitation. And now, I will give you some useful information. In the mountains some way from here, is a valley with a cave in it, in which lives a trollwoman, Járngerdur by name, who is an awful and malignant creature. Her two daughters live with her, Skinnbrók and Skinnhetta, who are very dangerous to have to do with.

Now, because I and Járngerdur have for long been opposed
to one another, and I have always had the advantage, she
will seek to take vengeance upon you, by her troll's arts.
But it will not do for you two to go by yourselves to her,
therefore I and my dog Grámúll will join your company.
This Járngerdur is the worst troll of all the infernal tribe,
and upon whomsoever her dying eyes shall fall, he will rot
alive beneath their glare, in that very hour.   Therefore we
must make all possible preparations, and take every pre-
caution, if we wish to escape from her alive."

The young men begged the old farmer to make for them
every needful preparation, declaring that they trusted im-
plicitly in his great experience.

On the morning of Christmas-eve they left the hut; had
to reach the valley through heavy snow drifts, and would
have lost their way to it, had not the dog Grámúll found
the path for them.   In the evening they saw before them
a large cave in some rocks, and following the narrow passage, came into it.   There was a blazing fire in the cave,
by which two young, monstrous, and hideous trollwomen
were sitting.

The one, Skinnbrók, said to the other, Skinnhetta, " See !
we shall not lie alone to-night, and to-morrow we will cut
those young men up for our Christmas feast.   But if this
old Grímur can carry out his intentions, we shall all perish.
I would that the old man could have some punishment for
his curiosity in coming here against our will."

Then Grímur the Icelander went close to the fire and said: "Is the Christmas meal ready? and the table dressed?"

The sisters started at this, and sprang to their feet; and Skinnbrók ran towards Grímur the Icelander, to struggle with him, saying, "I suppose you will not consider yourself the worse treated if you embrace such a fine lady as myself, before the Christmas feast?"

Then they fought together with brute fury, and dashed one another from corner to corner of the cave. After a while the Icelander found that, troll as she was, she began to flag and lose her breath; then he tried to trip her up, and at last flung her down so that her neck was broken, and he left her dead, he himself being tired and bruised after the struggle.

Now Skinnhetta, in her turn, attacked Grímur the Greenlander, and they had a long and fierce fight, each trying to throw the other into the fire; but at last Grímur succeeded in lifting her up from the ground and hurling her, head foremost, into the boiling kettle, where he kept her till she died. After that he rested himself.

Meanwhile, the old troll-mother had attacked Grímur the father, and their struggle was a deadly one. When the brothers saw that their father began to lose strength, they set the dog Grámúll upon the troll. The hound flew savagely at her, and tore her side so that her entrails were seen, and the dog rent them out. At this the troll fell down, and in dying fixed a horrible and ghastly glare upon Grámúll, till the dog rotted beneath her eyes, and crumbled to dust at her feet; and thus died Járngerdur and the dog that had slain her.

Then the men lighted a great fire outside the cave, and burned the bodies of the three trolls. They found over the. bed of the old troll a spear, which was a great rarity; glittering as glass, and adorned with gold. After this they searched all through the cave, and found many good things and valuable; all of which they bound into bundles and took away with them, the old Grímur carrying the spear, and returned home.

Here Grímur the Icelander dwelt for a long time, beloved by them all, but by none more than by the daughter, Ingibjörg.

The story now returns to Iceland. It happened that the winter after Grímur's departure, a meeting was appointed at Hofmannaflöt. To this many of the strongest men in the country, and even the giants and the mountaineers, came to make trials of their strength in wrestling. There came also Lágálfur, the son of Lítildrós. When he came from this meeting in the south, down the mountains to the Skagafjördur, he had to cross the river Nordurá, opposite to Silfrastadir. It was late in the day, and the snow drifted heavily, and just now Lágálfur saw a man of huge stature striding towards him along the bank of the river. The giant saluted Lágálfur, and asked him what news he had to tell. Lágálfur told him all the most important news, and asked with whom he was speaking.

The other answered: "I am Skeljúngur, and I come from my flocks. I dare say you are a great and strong man, but I am cold with standing over my sheep all day, and it would be good sport for us to wrestle a little, to warm ourselves."

Lágálfur replied: "I have for some time had good sport in wrestling with gallant men, but although you look like a rascal and a troll, I will not refuse to wrestle with you. Let each man look to himself."

Skeljúngur consented to this, and having thrown off their outer clothes, they began to wrestle. Lágálfur soon felt that Skeljúngur had the strength of two strong men, and that he must not spare his own strength against him. Now they wrestled with such fury that frozen stones started from the ground beneath their feet. When Lágálfur was tired of this undecided struggle, he tried to trip up his adversary, and a fit of blind madness and heroic fury seized them. At last Lágálfur lifted Skeljúngur by his hip and threw him so high, that when he fell both his thighs were broken upon the frozen ground, and both his shoulders dislocated. Then his enemy set upon him with such rage that he left him at the point of death.

After this, Lágálfur went to the farm Silfrastadir, where

all the people were already assembled in the family-room, and sang outside the window a verse, telling how he had fought with and subdued Skeljúngur.

> "Quickly over the earth I ran,
>   And dealt with that rascally shepherd-man ;
>   The strength-failing thrall himself brought it to be
>   That he should be dealt with so hardly by me.
>   The hair-brained fellow was beaten, and found
>   A good drubbing on the stony ground.
>   Skeljúngur scarcely will find him again
>   To watch his sheep and to guard the pen."

From this farm he went to another house, named Frostastödum, and stopped at that end of the house at which the farmer slept, where was a window through which he could see into the house. He saw the farmer sitting there, a grey-headed man, and heard him scolding his wife for having taken a handful of meal from the leather sack hanging in the roof over the farmer's head, and at last he struck her with his hand upon the cheek, so that she wept. Then Lágálfur thrust through the window the spear which he held in his hand, so as to cut the cords of the leather meal-bag, which fell down suddenly on the farmer's head, and sent him fainting to the ground. As soon as he saw that the farmer had recovered his senses, he retired from the window and sang,—

> "The meal-sack fell from the roof above
>   Upon the old man's pate,
>   And the beaten wife sat bewailing her fate
>   Till Lágálfur's spear avenged the sweet love."

N

Then Lágálfur went home, and henceforth is no more seen in our story, which returns now to Silfrastadir.

The farmer began to suspect something about Skeljúngur, when he heard Lágálfur sing at the window, and he supposed that the latter had left the herdsman unable to help himself. He therefore ordered his servants to search for Skeljúngur, but they could not find him, as the night was very dark. Early in the morning, the farmer started off with his men to search again for him. They discovered the place where Lágálfur and Skeljúngur had fought, by the trodden ground, and the stones which had been kicked up by their feet, but of the man himself they could find nothing.

After a little time people began to be aware that Skeljúngur did not lie quiet in death, and that he was a goblin, and now lived in the mountain close to Silfrastadir. And it became dangerous to pass through the valley, for he used to kill the horses of travellers, and their dogs, and mislead themselves. But Thorgrímur received the worst harm of all from him; for his herdsman was killed the following Christmas, and the same fatal thing took place till the third Christmas.

Now the story returns to Greenland again. Grímur the Icelander had lived there in all happiness with the good farmer and his family all this time. He had learnt many things, and excelled everybody in bravery and skill.

Once in the last spring the old farmer came to him and said to him, "This night I have seen many visions, and I suppose that your father is in hard need of you, for his herdsman has become a dangerous goblin, destroying his property and killing his servants, and I tell you that you are the only man capable of killing this monster. Now you shall make ready to return to Iceland, and I will give you a little ship for the voyage, in which Grímur, my son, and Ingibjörg, my daughter, shall accompany you. I see that your lines of fate lie together, and on your arrival in Iceland, you will marry your sister Ingibjörg to my son Grímur. He will bring her hither, but will return again to Iceland, where they will rear their family. Your fortune, however, will lead you away from your native land; but in whatever company you move, you will always be the foremost and best. And now I will equip you for your journey as well as I can."

Grímur the Icelander thanked the old man for his kind gifts, and promised to follow his advice.

When the ice had disappeared, the young men prepared their vessel for their voyage, and the farmer gave them everything they required, of the best quality. To the Icelander he gave many rarities, and, among others, the troll's spear which they had found in the cave, and, as he delivered it into his hand, said, "I think this will wear through many a rough combat."

After this the old Grímur bade farewell to his children

and to his future son-in-law, and wished them God-speed. So they weighed anchor and sailed away into the Greenland sea, and a long and rough passage they had, between the stormy weather and the ice, but at last they came safely into harbour in the mouth of the river Blanda, two days before Christmas.

The Icelander said, "I will ride as speedily as possible northwards to Silfrastadir, and I shall be none too early; but do you wait by the ship till my return."

So he procured two of the best riding-horses in the neighbourhood, and rode, dressed in glittering armour and carrying the troll's spear, along Blanda up through Vatnsskard. The snow had drifted, and the roads were heavy, but he rode so fast that, as the tale goes, one of his horses died in the middle of the journey, and the other by the wall of the grass-field of Silfrúnarstadir.

When he arrived there it was Christmas-eve, and the day far spent, and he went in to his father, who received him with great joy. Then he went to the family-room and threw off his riding-dress. He saw that all the people of the household looked sorrowful, and as he knew what was the cause of their sadness, he questioned them about Skeljúngur's habits. They told him that all night this goblin used to sit outside of the sleeping-room roof, kicking his heels into it, and that he was so dangerous, that no one dared go out after nightfall.

Grímur saw lying on the floor the fresh skin of the ox

which had been killed for the Christmas feast, so he took
it and cut out of it three strong ropes, and after that went
out of the house, and directed his steps southward, carrying the spear in one hand, the ropes in the other, till he
came to a mound called, after him, Grímshóll, where he
found a stone standing on the south side, broad at the
bottom and narrow at the top. Grímur went to it, and
pierced three holes through it with his spear. Into these
holes he put the three ropes, and made, by means of
loops, three nooses, which could be drawn tight against
the stone. This accomplished, he returned home, where a
merry Christmas feast awaited him, for every one was glad
of his return, and none more so than his father. As the
night advanced, Grímur begged all the people to go to bed.

The servant men of the farm slept in a dormitory near
the entrance, where there were many beds. Grímur lay
down on the bed nearest the door, wrapped up in the fresh
ox-skin from which he had cut the cords, and through the
head of which he could see the door. One lamp was burning in the room, and Grímur told all the others to be
neither afraid nor troubled if anyone should come uncere-
moniously into the house. Every one, with silent dread,
expected Skeljúngur, and thus, in perfect quiet, some part
of the night was spent.

After midnight some one was heard to mount on to the
house and ride astride of the dormitory roof, kicking his
heels with such fury that every rafter cracked again.

Then this house-rider jumped down, and, coming to the door, kicked it open.

Skeljúngur (for it was he) rolled his horrible eyes round the room, till none of the men could move for fear. When he saw that there was a new sleeper in the room, he went up to the bed nearest the door and caught hold of the ox-skin, but Grímur held it so tight that the other could not move it. Finding this, the other pulled with all his strength; but Grímur put his foot against the wainscot, and pushed against him till he broke the wainscot down. Then in their struggle they arrived at the door; and Grímur, seeing that he could not resist Skeljúngur except by stratagem, lay on the skin and let the other drag him out, planting his feet, however, against everything that came in his way, and thus they came to the outer door. Skeljúngur dragged the skin from the door across the field, in a southerly direction, but Grímur made the dragging as difficult for him as he could by planting his feet against every hillock and every stone that they passed. Active as the goblin was, he now began to be tired, and at last they came to Grímshóll.

By this time the night was far advanced towards dawn, and Grímur fought then and there more fiercely than ever, contriving finally to bind him to the stone by means of the nooses which he had prepared. Having securely fastened Skeljúngur to the rock, he went home in order to procure fire and fuel for burning him.

But when he came back he found that both Skeljúngur and the stone had disappeared. He judged that the direction the goblin would have most probably taken with his load was a southerly one, down the slope of the mountain, so he followed that way. After a while he saw before him Skeljúngur dragging the great stone behind him with great difficulty. Then Grímur ran up to him and cut off his head, and, fetching the fire and fuel, burnt him there. After that he took his ashes to a well close by and threw them in, and, according to the current story, two fishes, covered with blue hair, sprung from them, and lived there until the Nordurá changed its course and swept over the well, when the fishes disappeared.

The stone, bound to which Skeljúngur lost his second life, is yet to be seen standing by the highway, sunk deep into the ground, and there is still one hole visible, which was pierced by the iron spear.

The poet Hjálmar Jónsson, who has written this story, asserts that he has seen, in his youth, two holes in the stone, the lower one of which was close to the surface of the earth. But this was forty years ago, and nobody can tell how large the stone may be.

On the spot where the goblin was burnt, was afterwards built a farm called Skeljúngsstadir, which is mentioned in Sturlínga, for Eyólfur the Vehement rested there with his men when he attacked the Earl Gissur at Flugumýri.

Skeljúngshellir, or the cave of Skeljúngur, is also to be found in the adjacent mountain.

Now we will return to Grímur, who went home after this struggle very weary. Everybody in the farm thanked him with fair words for the riddance he had made, and everybody agreed that no one was his equal in all Skaga-fjördur. Now he told his father about his journey to Greenland, and mentioned all the conditions he had made with his Greenland friends, asking him frankly to consent to them, for that he had to thank those men for his preservation; nor, declared he, would his sister be better off with any husband than with Grímur the Green-lander.

Thorgrímur said that all their agreements should stand unbroken. "And my daughter," he continued, "shall go with your friend to Greenland, for I know that they will return and settle in Iceland to rear their family around them."

Grímur thanked his father for his kind answer, and his sister's departure from home was prepared for with all possible liberality, and both her father and brother accompanied her to the vessel lying in the mouth of the Blanda. Thorgrímur gave her a large number of gold and silver ornaments, and to Grímur the Greenlander a new body of sailors, sending also with him gifts for the old man in Greenland. Then they parted in affection, and when

Thorgrímur kissed his daughter at farewell, he wept tears of fatherly love.

With a fair wind, Grímur the Greenlander and his bride sailed away.

Thorgrímur and his son rode northwards to Silfrastadir, taking with them Ingibjörg of Greenland, who was looked upon as very beautiful, and who made a right good wife; for, a short time after this, Grímur married her, and their marriage was a happy one. It was soon found that Grímur, after his struggle with the goblin, had become very irritable, and it was impossible for his neighbours to agree with him; so they induced him to go south, to Borgar-fjördur, but having dwelt a short time there, he sailed from Iceland with his wife Ingibjörg, and settled in Sweden, where he raised up a family, and none of his descendants are known to have come to Iceland.

And where he dwelt he became celebrated for his bravery.

People say that Grímur the Greenlander returned to Iceland with his wife Ingibjörg, and settled at Skaga, between Skagafjördur and Húnaflóa.

His son was Thorgrímur, the Weatherwise, who lived at Keta.

His son was Grímur, who lived at Hafnir.

His son again was Grímur, who lived there after his father's death, at the time when Thorgerdur Kolka came from Hornstrandir and built the farm called Kolkunes, trusting herself to Grímur's honour.

The priest Eyólfur of Vellir mentions her in his "Antiquarian Transactions" as a benevolent woman, and one of great account, and says that at her death a miraculous earthquake took place, doing much damage, both at Skaga and at other places, and swallowing up the farm Gullbrekka, with all its inhabitants and cattle.

And there is now a great slough where the farm formerly stood.

And thus ends the story of Grímur, who killed Skeljúngur.

MISCELLANEOUS.

The Story of Jón Asmundsson.

In the district of Boyarfjördur, once lived a poor married couple. The man's name was Asmundur. They had many children, whose names have not been handed down to us, except that of the eldest, and he was called Jón. At this time, so severe a season was prevailing, that Asmundur was obliged to leave his home and his children, who were scattered about the country and brought up, one here and one there, at the houses of various farmers.

Now there lived at Reykjavík a priest, named Christján, and he it was that took Jón into his house, and brought him up as his own son. Jón grew into a fine and handsome lad, and was stronger than any of his fellows. But he was always very quiet, and seldom opened his mouth, unless first spoken to. He was, moreover, hardworking and willing, and became before long a great favourite, not only with the priest himself, but with every member of the household.

One summer, according to yearly custom, a trading vessel arrived at Reykjavík. Its owner was a foreign merchant, who carried on a large business at this season; but of his name no mention is made. Among other people with whom he had dealings was Christján, the priest. One day while Christján was on board the ship, it fell out that they came to talk about strong men. The merchant, being himself well-built and powerful, went up to where four barrels of rye lay bound together, and, seizing them by the rope which was round them, lifted them all together as high as his knee. When he had put them down again, he said, "There! let anyone prove himself my match in lifting, and I will give him three half-pounds of gold by weight."

When the priest returned home, he told his foster-son what he had seen, and how the merchant had promised three half-pounds of gold by weight to any man that should match him in lifting, and encouraged the boy to make the trial. To this Jón agreed without wasting many words. So they went together to the ship, and Christján told the captain that the lad would like to try his strength. The merchant pointed out the rye barrels to Jón, who, going up to them, lifted them on to his shoulder as if they were but a handful of feathers, and when he had walked with them to and fro upon the deck, put them down again in their place.

When he saw this, the merchant changed colour, but weighed out the three half-pounds of gold, and paid them over to Jón, begging him, as he took leave, to come and pay him one more visit on board the ship before he sailed away. This Jón promised to do.

One day, shortly before the time the merchant had fixed for sailing, the priest came to Jón, and reminded him of his promise to visit the ship. Accordingly Jón went, and Christján with him, and the merchant received them with all due honour, begging Jón to come with him into the cabin for a few words he wished to say in his ear.

But when he saw that the priest was going to make one of their party, he turned round to him, and said, "Friend, you can stay up here a while; we have no need of you."

Christján, however, was not to be put off, but assuring the merchant that he would not disturb them, or be in their way, followed them down into the cabin.

Then the merchant said to Jón, "You have not yet done with me; for next year I shall bring with me a boy for you to wrestle with, and if you get the better of him in that game, I will weigh you out five pounds of gold."

Jón agreed to this, and when he and Christján had taken leave, the merchant sailed away.

For some time everything went on quietly, and the winter set in. One day the priest asked Jón whether he remembered the agreement he had made with the foreign merchant before his departure.

Jón answered, that it was so slight a matter that he had never yet given it a thought.

But the priest said, " Indeed it is no such child's play as you think; for the boy that this merchant will bring for you to wrestle with, is none other than a fiendish and monstrous black man, and get the better of you he surely will, unless you employ craft against him. I will find out speedily some means for gaining you the victory, for ere three weeks of the summer be over the merchant-ship will come into harbour."

Jón nodded, but said nothing, and seemed in no way troubled by the news; nor did he give himself the least pains about it till the time came.

Before three weeks of the summer were over, as Christ-ján had foretold, a vessel was seen making for the harbour of Reykjavík from the open ocean. It was no sooner in sight than the priest went to Jón, and, warning him of what he now might expect, dressed him in a peasant's frock of black wool, and clasped a belt round his waist; when he had thus equipped him, he gave him a little, bright, sharp-edged dagger, which he bade him keep ready

to his hand, hidden in the sleeve of the woollen frock. He
further told Jón, not to attempt to resist the negro's attacks, as the latter would fling him easily over his shoulder.

"I," said he, "will take good care that you fall on your
feet. But, after a while, challenge the negro to take off
his shaggy mantle, and do you make ready in your hand
the dagger, that when he rushes upon you a second time
you may thrust it into his chest."

The anchor was scarcely dropped before a boat sped
from the vessel, and set on shore a black man of giant's
build, dressed in a shaggy mantle, who, directly he saw
the priest and the lad standing close to the sea, rushed at
Jón, and, seizing him in his arms, flung him like a pebble
over his head, high into the air. But the boy fell on his
feet, and forthwith challenged the black to fight without
his woolly mantle, that they might the more easily try
their skill in wrestling. To this the negro consented; but
while he was doffing his cloak, Jón made ready in his
right hand the sharp-edged dagger which the priest had
given him, and when the other ran blindly upon him,
thrust it into his breast once and again. But yet they
wrestled together for a while, and assuredly even now Jón
would have got the worst of it, were it not that his black
woollen frock served him as armour against the heavy
blows of the negro.

At last the fight came to an end, and Jón slew his
enemy.

O

Then he and Christján went on board the vessel, where they found the merchant, and saluted him.

"Well," said the latter, "and how went the fight?"

The priest answered, "If you will look towards the shore, you will see·the negro lying dead close to the waves. That is how the fight went."

Then the merchant was exceeding wroth, and said, "Aha! you have not acted like brave and true-hearted men. This lad has but fought by craft and with steel."

"But," replied the priest, "however that may be, he has deserved fairly the prize; for, whereas you promised to bring a lad to wrestle with him, you have brought an evil-souled, giant-built black."

To this the merchant had no answer ready, so, as needs must be, paid into Jón's hand the five pounds of weighed-out gold, which he had promised to the winner in the wrestling. Then, smoothing his angry brows, he begged Jón to come and see him once more before the ship sailed, which would be in the latter end of the summer.

Everything went on as usual till a short time before the merchant had determined to sail from Reykjavík, and then the priest reminded Jón of his promise to visit the merchant before his departure, offering at the same time to accompany him, and be present during the interview. They went, therefore, to the vessel and greeted the merchant, who received them with great politeness, but, as before, begged Jón to go a little aside with him, as he had something particular to tell him. Christján, however, followed close upon their heels, and the merchant, seeing him, said, "You need not trouble yourself to come so close; what we speak about has nought to do with you."

But the priest was not to be put off so, and saying, "I will neither leave the side of my foster-son, nor will I interrupt your converse," kept still close to them.

Then the merchant said to Jón, "Next summer I will bring with me a little whelp against which you shall try your strength, and if you get the best of the fight, I will weigh out into your hand seven-and-a-half pounds of good gold."

Upon this they parted; Jón and Christján returning on shore, and the merchant sailing away.

Now the summer passed away, and a great part of the winter passed away without Jón making any preparations for, or saying a word about, the next visit of the merchant.

One day the priest asked him whether or no he remembered the merchant's words and promise.

"Not I," replied Jón.

"But," said the priest, "this visit of his will bring almost as much difficulty as his last one. The whelp he promised to match against you, ere half a month of the summer be past, is nothing less than a large and cruel deer-hound, and to get the best of the fight we must devise some wile, for your strength will be as nothing."

But Jón only answered, " Devise, then, for me," and there he let the matter rest, occupying himself no further about it.

Ere half a month of the summer was over, a vessel appeared in sight, sailing from the open sea towards Reykjavík.

Then the priest went to Jón and said, " The merchant will now soon be in harbour, and you must be ready for him." And he made him put on again the black woollen frock which he had now woven through and through with links of iron. He gave him, at the same time, a spear, with moveable barbs, which would spread out and tear the flesh into which they had been thrust, and, placing on the point of this a piece of meat, bade Jón watch his chance and thrust it with all his strength down the dog's throat.

When he had thus equipped him he led him down to the shore.

Scarcely was the anchor dropped, when a boat sped from the vessel, and placed upon the beach a large and evil-eyed deer-hound, who, directly he saw Jón advancing towards him, rushed at him with mad fury, and would have torn him to pieces on the spot had not the frock, with its links of mail, saved Jón from his teeth. Over and over again the brute rushed upon him, each time with greater rage and strength. But Jón, who escaped un-scathed from each attack, watched his chance, and keeping the piece of meat always before the dog till the beast opened its mouth to snap at it, thrust it with all his force down its throat, till, in a short while, it lay dead at his feet.

Then they went out to the ship and saluted the merchant, who received and returned their greeting surlily enough. But feign and conceal as he would, he could not hide from them the wrathful red blood that filled his cheek and brow and swelled his lip.

" We have come to claim the gold," said the priest; " my foster-son has fairly earned it."

" Fairly, forsooth!" replied the merchant. " He has fought like a brave man in truth, by wile and craft and steel. He has no claim to the gold, he has not kept to our agreement."

" Neither have you," the priest returned, " for you promised to bring a whelp, and have brought a wild beast to match it against this lad." So the merchant, who could not deny this, put the smoothest face he could upon the matter and weighed into Jón's hand the gold. Just before Jón and the priest left the ship, the merchant begged the former to come once more to see him before he weighed anchor and sailed away at the summer's end. Jón promised to come.

Now the time came round at which the merchant had fixed to sail, and Christján reminded Jón of his promise to go once more and visit him, saying, at the same time, that he himself would take good care to be present at their meeting. Accordingly they went on board the ship, whose anchor was even now being weighed. Just as before, the merchant begged Jón to come down with him into the cabin, as he had something particular to say to him, and when he saw Christján following them, turned round to him with a fierce look and cried, " Stand back, and meddle not where nothing concerns you."

" I do not wish to meddle," said the priest, " but I will not leave my foster-son." And as he seemed firm about this the merchant said no more; so they went all three down to the cabin.

Then the merchant took down from one of the shelves a book, out of which he pulled a leaf and waved it quickly before Jón's eyes, as if to prevent the priest from seeing its contents. But Christján caught a glance of some of the words written upon it, without the merchant's knowledge. Then he returned the leaf to the book and the book to its place, saying to Jón, " If you do not bring me next summer, when I come back here, the book from which this leaf was taken, I will brand you as a fool and a faint heart; but if you bring the book I will weigh you out fifteen full pounds of good gold."

With these words they parted, Jón and Christján going home, and the merchant putting at once to sea.

When one week of the summer was still left, the priest asked Jón whether he had yet given a thought to the task with which the merchant had charged him for the next year.

Jón answered that it had never entered his head.

Then the other asked him whether he had known the leaf that the merchant had shown him, but Jón said, "No."

"No wonder," answered Christján, "for it was none other than a leaf from the devil's manual, which the merchant has bidden you bring him, and this is surely no slight or easy matter. But I have a brother who is a priest in the worlds below, and who is the only man that can help you to procure this book. Make yourself ready, therefore, at once for the journey, for you must spend with him in the lower regions the whole winter, from the first day to the last."

So Jón addressed himself to his journey, and when he was all ready for starting, the priest gave him a letter to his brother down below, and a ball of thread which would run before him and guide him. When he wished him Godspeed, he warned him most strictly never once to look back on the way, and never to utter a single word the whole winter through. The youth promised, saying, he thought this surely easy enough.

Bidding his friend and foster-father, Christján, farewell, he flung down on the ground the ball of thread, keeping one end in his hand, and it ran quickly along before him, he following and never looking back. After a while they came to a mountain which lay north of Reykjavík, and in

which appeared a passage leading deep into the earth.
Into this the ball ran. Soon it became so dark, and the
passage so rough and difficult, that more than once Jón
stopped, doubting whether to go any further or to turn
back. But every time he paused the ball pulled so hard
that he was encouraged to go on, and still followed it in
spite of difficulties. Thus, for a long way, they went on,
till all at once the place became light, and Jón saw lying
before him a vast and charming green plain over which the
ball still rolled till it came to a farm as big as a town, and
stopped at the door of one of the houses, where Jón picked
it up from the ground. At this door Jón knocked, and a
girl came out, neatly and plainly dressed, and of modest
mien, and, as Jón thought, the most winsome he had ever
seen. Jón nodded to her, and gave her the letter, which
she took without speaking, as well as the ball of thread,
and went with them into the house, leaving Jón standing
at the door. In a few minutes she came back, and with
her another girl younger than herself, who looked hard at
Jón, and turned back into the house. But the other took
him by the hand and led him through some passages into
a room, where stood one small table, one chair, a bench,
and a bed.

In this room Jón lived for a long time, till he thought
the winter must be far advanced. He saw no one but the
young girl, who came every day into the room, brought
him his meals, and made his bed, but never spoke to him,

" Soon it became so dark, and the passage so rough, that Jón stopped, doubt-ing whether to go any further."

[*To face page* 216.

nor did he, the whole time, hear the sound of a human voice.

One day, however, there entered the room a tall and handsome man, dressed in a long black cassock. This was the brother of Christján, the priest in the infernal world. He bade Jón good-day in a sweet and courteous voice, but Jón merely nodded in reply.

Then the other asked him if he knew how long he had, by this time, remained in the worlds below.

But Jón was still silent, and only shook his head.

The priest then said to him, " You have done well to keep so long and so firmly silent. But you may speak now, as the winter is over, and this is the first day of summer. Your task is accomplished, for here is the book you came to seek. Take care of it, and give it safely into my brother's hands. You must start hence to-day, as the merchant will arrive before a week of the summer be fully past. The owner of this book will miss it just about the same time, and claim it first from the merchant's hands. Therefore bid my brother buy every scrap of the merchandise on board the ship, and beware to land it before he delivers the volume into the captain's hands. Be bearer, too, of my love to my brother. My daughter shall go with you to point out the way." And with these words he took leave of him.

Then the girl who had served Jón all the winter, came to him and led him from the house, and they walked on sadly, holding one another by the hand. What they talked about now that Jón's tongue was loosed, nobody knows. However, at last the girl stopped and said she could go no further, as it was now easy enough for him to find his own way home. And these were her last words, " Now we must part, though it go nigh to break our hearts for sorrow. We cannot live together, for neither can you dwell here below, nor I in the world above. But, in the course of some months, I shall bear you a child. If it be a boy, I will send it you when it is six years old; but if a girl, when it is twelve. I pray you, receive it well." She then gave him the ball of thread. And when she had embraced him, with many tears, left him.

He, sad at heart, flung down the ball, which rolled before him, leading him this time, not through dark and difficult caverns, but along such a smooth and smiling country, that Jón knew not when he had left the one world and entered the other. Towards the close of the first week in summer he arrived at Reykjavík and was received joyfully by Christján, to whom he gave the book, and his brother's love and message.

The very next day the merchant arrived in harbour, and he had no sooner dropped anchor than the priest hurried on board and saluted him, but their greetings were just about as warm and cordial as the north-east wind. These over, the priest told him that, as a harsh and severe season had just prevailed and provisions were scant all through the near country, he wished to buy the whole stock that lay on board, and land it at once. They soon came to an agreement, and in a few days all the merchandise was landed.

No sooner was the last bale on shore than Christján and Jón went on board the vessel. When they had saluted, the merchant immediately asked Jón how he had succeeded in fulfilling the task wherewith he had been charged.

" Pretty well," said Jón.

Then Christján gave the book to the merchant, in the name of Jón, and mightily astonished the man was when he saw that it was the right one, but paid out the gold at the priest's request without saying any more about it. This Jón took, and after they had bidden adieu to the merchant, he and Christján jumped into their own boat and rowed quickly to shore.

But they had no sooner stepped out on to the beach, than the sea became, all at once, rough and stormy, and when they looked towards the merchant's vessel, lo ! it was no more to be seen. The devil had claimed his manual.

After this they returned to the priest's house, where no small wealth was now stored up, and Jón stayed there for another half-year. Always quiet and reserved, he was ten-fold more so since his return from the lower worlds. At the end of that time the priest, who had noted the youth's melan-choly, taxed him with having fallen in love with one of the daughters of his brother, the priest in the subterranean world. But to this Jón made no reply. Then Christján went on to offer him one of his own daughters (he had three, whose names we know not), whichever he loved the best, as a wife, thinking that this would perhaps free him from the thrall of his sadness. Jón chose the youngest of the three, and the priest married them, and giving his daughter no mean marriage present, settled them in a neighbouring farm, which could boast of the best land for many a long mile round.

Here they lived for many years in unbroken love and great prosperity, and had not a few children, but never the whole time did Jón bate one jot of his sadness.

At the end of twelve years, it happened one day that, as all the household were assembled in the family-room, a knock was heard at the door. Jón sent one of his sons, a lad about six years old, to the door to see who was there. The child returned, saying that there stood outside a little girl of wonderful beauty, who had asked him sweetly to say in the house that she wished to speak to her father.

At these words, it was as if a ray of sunshine had passed across Jón's face. He rose from his seat and ran eagerly to the outer door. The little girl, directly she saw him, ran up to him, and throwing her arms round his neck, kissed him fondly, calling him her own dear father. Jón returned her embrace with the greatest joy and love. She told him that her mother, the daughter of the priest in the worlds below, had sent her to him, bearing her sweetest love. Jón took the child by the hand and led her in to his wife, to whom he told the whole story of her parentage, begging her at the same time, as she loved him, so to treat the little girl as one of her own. The woman, being of true heart, welcomed the child with open arms and became a fond mother to her, from that day forth. They called her Sigrídur, and she grew up among them, a sister to the other children, and was lovelier by far and by far more accomplished than any girl of her own age, round about for many a stretch of long miles.

At the end of three years, Sigrídur, whose beauty was in everybody's mouth, asked her father's leave to pay her mother a visit in the worlds below. Jón granted it willingly, telling her that, if she would, she might stay a whole year with her mother, and making her the bearer of his sweetest love.

The year over, Sigrídur came back and was welcomed with delight by her father and all the family. She told Jón that she brought him her mother's dying farewell, together with the message that he himself had but one month more to live. Far from being grieved by this news, Jón seemed glad, and for the whole month no one noticed any change in his conduct, except that his heart was lighter than heretofore.

At last Jón made a settlement of all he possessed, giving by far the greater part of his property to Sigrídur, and his personal wealth to his wife and other children, who were well off with it. And every one thus saw that he was most fond of his daughter from the lower regions; and what, all things considered, was the wonder? When Jón died, many felt deeply his loss and wept bitterly for him; for he had been a good man and a warm friend.

Some years afterwards Sigrídur married a young and hopeful peasant, and their farm throve till none in the district could compare with it. They lived happily and everybody looked up to them with respect and fondness. Of their many children the descendants are scattered widely through the south country.

The Money-Chest.

It happened, once upon a time, that a large party of men were travelling together, and pitched their tent, early one Sunday morning, on the fresh sward of a fair green meadow. The weather was bright and warm, and the men being tired with their night's journey, and having tethered their horses, fell asleep, side by side, all round the inside of the tent. One of them, however, who happened to be lying nearest the door, could not, in spite of his fatigue, succeed in getting to sleep, so lay idly watching the other sleepers. As he looked round he discovered a small cloud of pale-blue vapour moving over the head of the man who was sleeping in the innermost part of the tent. Astonished at this he sat up, and at the same

moment the cloud flitted out of the tent. Being curious
to know what it could be and what would become of it,
he jumped up softly, and, without awaking the others,
stole out into the sunshine. On looking round he saw
the vapour floating slowly over the meadow, so set himself to follow it. After a while it stopped over where lay
the blanched skull of a horse upon the grass, in and about
which hummed and buzzed a cloud of noisy blue flies.
Into this the vapour entered among the flies. After
staying a while, it came out, and took its course over
the meadow till it came to a little thread of a rivulet,
which hurried through the grass. Here it seemed to be
at a loss how to get over the water, and moved restlessly
and impatiently up and down the side of it, till the man
laid his whip, which he happened to have with him, over
it, the handle alone being sufficient to bridge it across.
Over this the vapour passed and moved on till it came to
a small hillock, into which it disappeared. The man stood
by and waited for it to come out again, which it soon did,
and returned by the same way as that by which it had
come. The man laid his whip as before across the stream
and the vapour crossed upon the handle. Then it moved
on towards the tent, which it entered, and the man who
had followed it saw it hover for a minute over the head of
the sleeper, where he had first seen it, and disappear.
After this he lay down again, and went to sleep himself.

When the day was far spent and the sun was going

down, the men rose, struck the tent, and made preparations for beginning their journey again. While they were packing, and loading the horses, they talked on various things, and, among others, on money.

"Bless me!" said the man who had slept in the innermost part of the tent, "I wish I had what I saw in my dream to-day."

"What was your dream, and what did you see?" asked the man who had followed the vapour.

The other replied, "I dreamt that I walked out from the tent, and across the meadow till I came to a large and beautiful building, into which I went. There I found many people at revel in a vast and noble hall, singing, dancing, and making merry. I stayed some time among them, and when I left them and stepped out from the hall, I saw stretched before me a vast plain of fair green sward. Over this I walked for some time, till I came to an immensely broad and turbulent river, over which I wished to cross, but could find no means of doing so. As I was walking up and down the bank thinking how I could possibly get over it, I saw a mighty giant greater than any I had ever heard of, come towards me, holding in his hand the trunk of a large tree, which he laid across the river. Thus I was able to get easily to the other side. The river once passed, I walked straight on for a long time till I came to a high mound which lay open. I went into it, thinking to find wonderful treasures, but found only a single chest, which, however, was so full of money that I could neither lift it, nor, though I spent hours over it, count the quarter of its contents. So I gave it up and bent my steps hither again. The giant flung his tree across the river as before, and I came to the tent and went to sleep from sheer weariness."

At hearing this, the other who had followed the vapour was mightily pleased, and, laughing to himself, said, " Come, my good fellow, let us fetch the money. If one could not count it, no doubt two can."

" Fetch the money ! " replied the man. " Are you mad ? Do you forget that I only *dreamed* about it ? Where would you fetch it from ? "

But as the other seemed really earnest and determined, he consented to go with him.

So they took the same course as the vapour had taken, and when they came to the skull, " There is your hall of revel," said the man who had followed the mist some hours before.

" And there," he said, when they stepped over the rivulet, " is your broad and turbulent river, and here the trunk the giant threw over it as a bridge." With these words he showed him his whip.

The other was filled with amazement, and when they came to the mound, and having dug a little way into it, really and truly discovered a heavy chest full of golden pieces, his astonishment was not a whit the less. On their way back to the tent with the treasure, his companion told him all about the matter.

Whether they complained of the weight of the money-chest or gave up counting its contents in despair, this history relateth not.

THE BLACK SCHOOL.

Once upon a time, there existed somewhere in the world, nobody knows where, a school which was called the Black School. There the pupils learned witchcraft and all sorts of ancient arts. Wherever this school was, it was somewhere below ground, and was held in a strong room which, as it had no window, was eternally dark and changeless. There was no teacher either, but everything was learnt from books with fiery letters, which could be read quite easily in the dark. Never were the pupils allowed to go out into the open air or see the daylight during the whole time they stayed there, which was from five to seven years. By then they had gained a thorough and perfect knowledge of the sciences to be learnt. A shaggy grey hand came through the wall every day with the pupils' meals, and when they had finished eating and drinking took back the horns and platters. But one of the rules of the school was, that the owner should keep for himself that one of the students who should leave the

school the last every year. And, considering that it was
pretty well known among the pupils that the devil himself was the master, you may fancy what a scramble there
was at each year's end, everybody doing his best to avoid
being last to leave the school.

It happened once that three Icelanders went to this
school, by name Sœmundur the learned, Kálfur Arnason,
and Hálfdán Eldjárnsson; and as they all arrived at the
same time, they were all supposed to leave at the same
time. Sœmundur declared himself willing to be the last
of them, at which the others were much lightened in mind.
So he threw over himself a large mantle, leaving the
sleeves loose and the fastenings free. A staircase led
from the school to the upper world, and when Sœmundur
was about to mount this the devil grasped at him and
said, "You are mine!" But Sœmundur slipped out of
the mantle and made off with all speed, leaving the devil
the empty cloak. However, just as he left the school the
heavy iron door was slammed suddenly to, and wounded
Sœmundur on the heels. Then he said, "That was pretty
close upon my heels," which words have since passed into
a proverb. Thus Sœmundur contrived to escape from
the Black School, with his companions, scot-free.

Some people relate, that, when Sœmundur came into
the doorway, the sun shone upon him and threw his shadow
on to the opposite wall; and as the devil stretched out his
hand to grapple with him, Sœmundur said, "I am not the

last; do you not see who follows me?" So the devil seized the shadow, mistaking it for a man, and Sœmundur escaped with a blow on his heels from the iron door.

But from that hour he was always shadowless, for whatever the devil took, he never gave back again.

SŒMUNDUR LEAVES THE BLACK SCHOOL.

When Sœmundur was abroad, and while he stayed in the Black School, he forgot all about himself and his family, on account of the many wonderful things he saw and learned. He forgot, at the same time, his own name, and so all his companions in the school called him "Buft."

One night, as Sœmundur was asleep, he dreamed that Bogi Einasson came to him and said, "Surely you act ill, Sœmundur, in entering this school, in forgetting your God, in giving yourself up to witchcraft, and in losing your Christian name. If you care aught for your future welfare, it is time for you to return."

"That I cannot by any means manage to do," said Sœmundur.

"More fool you," said Bogi, "for entering a school that you cannot leave at your pleasure. However, if you are willing to return home, I know how you can contrive it."

Sæmundur answered, " You know everything, Bogi; we are all children to you in wisdom. Yes, I am willing enough to return."

Then Bogi said, " Take my advice, and when you leave the school, throw your cloak loosely over your shoulders. As you go out somebody will grasp at you, but slip out of the cloak and make the best of your way off. You have most to fear the schoolmaster, for not long after you are gone he will miss you. But when you are fairly on your way, take off the shoe from your right foot, and fill it with blood, and carry it on your head all the rest of the first day. In the evening the schoolmaster will observe the stars, in whose movements and aspects he is right well skilled, and seeing round yours a bloody halo, will think that you are killed. Next day as you travel, you must fill your shoe with salt and water and carry it on your head. During the day he will not trouble himself about you ; but at night he will again examine the stars, and, seeing round yours a watery halo, will imagine that you are drowned in the sea. On the third day you must open a vein in your side and let the blood from it trickle into your shoe. Then you must mix some earth with it, and carry the shoe on your head, as you travel, all the rest of the day. In the evening when the master examines the stars, he will see round, yours an earthy and blood-stained halo, and will suppose that you are dead and buried. But afterwards he will find out that you are alive and well, and will wonder at your cunning, and pride himself on having been the means of your learning so much wisdom. And the end of it will be, that he will cease persecuting you, and rather wish you well than otherwise."

With these words, Bogi Einasson left him.

And after all, it was in that very way that Sœmundur left the Black School, and returned safely to his own country.

Sœmundur gets the Living of Oddi.

As Sœmundur, Kálfur, and Hálfdán were returning from the Black School, they heard that the living of Oddi was vacant. So they all hurried to the king, and each asked it for himself. The king, well knowing with whom he had to deal, promised it to him who should be the first to reach the place. Upon this Sœmundur immediately called the devil to him and said, "Swim with me on your back, to Iceland; and if you bring me to shore without wetting the skirt of my coat, you shall have me for your own." The devil agreed to this, so he changed himself into a seal and swam off with Sœmundur on his back. On the way Sœmundur amused himself by reading the book of the Psalms of David. Before very long they came close to the coast of Iceland. When he saw this he closed the book and smote the seal with it upon the head,

so that it sank, and Sœmundur swam to land. And as,
when Sœmundur got to shore, the skirts of his coat were
wet, the devil lost the bargain, but the former got the
living.

The Fly.

The devil did not forget either this or any other of
Sœmundur's tricks upon him, and constantly looked out
for a chance of doing him a bad turn. Many and many
a time he tried to revenge himself upon him, but always
in vain. One day he turned himself into a very small
fly, and hid himself under the skin of the milk in the
porringer, hoping this way to get into the stomach of
Sœmundur the learned, and kill him. But no sooner
had Sœmundur lifted his porringer to drink out of it
than he saw the fly, and wrapping it up in the skin
of the milk, he put it into a bladder, and placed the
bladder on the altar in the church. So there the fly
was obliged to stay till Sœmundur had finished performing the next service, which took a long time. And
it is confidently told that the devil never enjoyed himself
less in all his life. When service was over, Sœmundur
undid the bladder and set the devil free.

KALF ARNASON.

When Kalf Arnason was in the Black School, he made a present of himself, it is said, to the devil. But when he got back to Iceland, he began to think that his promise was, after all, neither agreeable nor convenient, and puzzled himself to no purpose to find some way of escape from its fulfilment. At last he bethought himself of Sœmundur the learned, and determined to ask his counsel on so knotty a point.

When Kalf had stated his difficulty, Sœmundur advised him as follows: "Let one of your bull-calves live, and call it 'Arni;' after a while this one shall beget another, which you must call 'Kalf,' and then you will have 'Kalf Arnason.'"

The other took his advice, and in course of time the devil came to claim the fulfilment of the bargain, saying, "I want Kalf Arnason."

"Oh, with all my heart," said the man; "what objection can there possibly be to that?"

And forthwith went and fetched the second calf, which he presented to the devil, saying, "There, you have Kalf Arnason."

As the devil could not deny this, he must needs put up with it, though he grumbled at being played so shabby a trick. So off he went without Kalf Arnason, who died a natural death, at a high age.

Other things are related of Priest Sœmundur the learned, and how he died, triumphing, as usual, over the devil; but those we repeat not here.

BISHOP SVEINN THE SAPIENT.

This is a story of second-sight. Sveinn the Sapient was one of the bishops of Skálholt, and was considered to be a man of more than ordinary learning, and moreover gifted with prophetic powers. Some people used to declare that he understood the language of the ravens, but others that the ravens with whom he held intercourse were neither more nor less than spirits under that disguise. Many years before he came into his bishopric, and while he was still a pastor, it happened once that he was sent from Skálholt to perform the service at another and distant church, and took with him a lad named Erlendur Erlendsson. On the way they were overtaken by so heavy a storm of snow, that they were unable to ride against it, and therefore dismounted and stood by their horses.

After a while the lad began to despair, and said piteously that he thought they should never leave the place alive.

But the bishop chid him for his cowardice, and bade

him behave like a man. "For," said he, "our lives will be mightily changed when I am Bishop of Skálholt, and you have married the daughter of Thorvardur the wealthy, at Mödruvellir."

Erlendur answered, "That you may become Bishop of Skálholt is, I know, no such unlikely thing; but that I, poor as I am, shall ever have a chance of marrying so rich a lady, is quite out of the question."

"Never doubt the possibility of God's gifts," returned the bishop, "for what I have told you will surely come to pass. And this shall be the sign that my words are true; when you ride to fetch your bride, there shall suddenly fall such a shower of rain, that its like for heaviness shall not be within the memory of any man."

Towards morning the storm ceased, and Sveinn and the lad remounted their horses and rode on to the end of their journey.

Now, after years had gone by, it came to pass that Sveinn was made Bishop of Skálholt, and that Erlendur Erlendsson became an accomplished man, and married the daughter of Thorvardur the wealthy, at Mödruvellir. And, as he rode to fetch his bride on a bright warm day, and was close to the grass-field of the farm at which she lived, suddenly there fell such a shower of rain, that even the driest places were immediately under water. Then he remembered the words of Sveinn the Sapient.

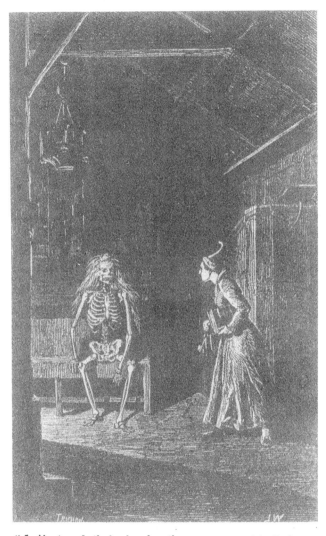

" *Looking towards the benches where the women were wont to sit, she saw there a human skeleton with long yellow hair!*"

[*To face page* 235.

The Skeleton in Hólar Church.

Once, on a winter evening, it happened that Jón Arason, Bishop of Hólar, wanted a book which he had left lying on the altar in the church, so called his household folk together, and asked which of them would do him the favour of fetching the book for him. They all shuddered at the idea, and all drew back, except one maid-servant, who declared herself quite willing to go, and not in the least afraid.

Now the bishop having enemies—as who has not?—had made a tunnel from his own house, which was called the Palace, underground to the church, with a view to being able, if need should ever be, to take sanctuary at a moment's notice, and unobserved.

Through this tunnel the maid went, having procured the keys of the church; but when she had taken the book from the altar, she determined not to go back through the tunnel, which she had found dismal and ghostly, but rather round the other way. So she walked down the church with the keys to the outer door; and looking towards the benches where the women were wont to sit, she saw there a human skeleton with long yellow hair! Amazed at this, but in no way frightened, she went up to the figure and said, "Who are you?"

Upon which the skeleton said, "I am a woman, and

have long been dead. But my mother cursed me so that I can never corrupt, and return to the dust whence I sprung. Now, therefore, my good girl, I entreat you to release me from this ban, if it lies in your power."

" But," answered the girl, " it does *not* lie in my power, as far as I now know. Tell me how I can help you."

Then the skeleton replied, " You must ask my mother to forgive me my faults, and to annul her curse; for she may very likely do for the living what she refuses to do for the dead. It is a rare thing indeed for the living to ask favours of the dead."

" Where is your mother, then?" asked the maiden.

" Oh," said the other, " she is here, there, and everywhere. Now, for example, she is yonder in the choir."

Then the maiden went through the door into the choir, and saw sitting there on one of the benches a wondrous ugly old woman in a red hat, to whom she addressed herself, asking her to be good enough to forgive her daughter, and remove from her the curse. After pausing a while, plainly unwilling, the old hag answered—" Well! it is not often that you living people ask favours of me, so for once I will say to you yea!"

Having thanked her for her goodness, the maiden went back towards the outer door, but when she came to the place where she had seen the skeleton, found there only a heap of dust. So she went on towards the door, and as she opened it she heard a voice from the inner part of the church, which cried after her, " Look at my red eyes, how red they are ! " And without looking round, she answered, " Look at my black back, how black it is !"

As soon as she had shut the door behind her, she found that the churchyard seemed to swarm with people who were shouting and screaming direfully, and who made as if they would stop her. But she, summoning up courage, rushed through the middle of them, without looking either to the right or to the left, and reached the home-building in safety.

As she delivered the book to the bishop, she said :

> " So loud were the voices of the Goblin band
>   That five echoes for each were found
>   In the mountain-rocks, though far they stand
>   From Hólar burying-ground."

The Wizards in the Westmann Islands.

During the time when that dread pest, yclept the Black Death, raged through Iceland, eighteen sorcerers banded together, and went out to the Westmann Islands, in order to escape, as long as possible, the scourge. When, after a while, by means of their magic arts, they discovered that the plague was abating its fury, they were curious to know how many people were left alive in the country.

So they agreed to send one of their company to land, that he might find how matters stood, and make his report to the others. They chose for this errand a man who was neither first nor last in the knowledge of their arts; and when they put him ashore they told him that if he did not return to them by Christmas-day next, they would despatch a Sending to him who should kill him.

Far and wide wandered the man, north, south, and east, without finding a single living soul. All the dwellings stood wide open, and from floor to roof, even on threshold and on hill, lay the dead. At last he came to a house which was shut up, and through his wonder at this half hoped to find there still some signs of human life. He knocked loudly at the door, which was instantly opened, and there came out a young and beautiful damsel, who, half-wild with joy to see again a living man, answered his salutation by falling on his neck, and embracing him; telling him at the same time with many tears that she had thought herself the only living creature in the whole land.

She begged him to stay with her some time, which he consented to do, and they went into the house and held a vast deal of talk together. She asked him whence he came, and what was the object of his journey; and he told her all about the company of wizards, their desire to know how many people were left alive in the land, and their strict command to him to be back in the Westmann Islands before next Christmas-day. But she begged for his company as long as he could possibly afford it her; and he, pitying her loneliness, agreed to stay with her some time. The girl told him, that within many and many a mile not one soul was left alive; for she had made a week's journey from home in all directions, hoping to find some one still living, but quite in vain.

So the man abode there, and Christmas-day drew nearer and nearer, until, at last, he felt bound to tell the girl that he must leave her now, or suffer the punishment of death for his disobedience to the commands of the other sorcerers. But the girl would not hear of his going so soon, and coaxed him to stay yet a little longer, saying, that surely his companions were not such unmerciful and heartless folks as to kill him for so slight a fault as staying with a poor lonely woman. By these words she quite overcame his determination to leave her till Christmas-eve came round. Then, said he, he truly must leave her as he valued his life. At first she tried to persuade him to stay with her by caresses and prayers; but finding him deaf to them, she changed her tone, and said, " Well, my good man, since you *will* go, go ! and reach the Westmann Islands by Christmas-day if you can. I wish you luck in your journey, and somewhat more than common speed ! " Then the man suddenly bethought himself that more than common speed must indeed be his, if he would make the journey in time; and so, knowing that it was totally useless for him to start now for the Westmann Islands, resolved to stay and await his death where he was. He passed the night in a sad state of mind; but the maiden, on the contrary, was as lively as lively could be, and asked him if he could now see what was going on among his companions. He said they had just rowed the Sending ashore from the islands. So she sat on the foot of the bed, which was near the door, and he lay behind her. After a while, he told her that he felt a strange heaviness come over him, which he knew to be owing to the magic arts of the wizards. Having told her this, he fell into a deep sleep.

By and by, the girl, who still sat at the bed's foot, woke him, and asked him if he knew now where the Sending was, or his way.

He said, " Within the bounds of the farm," and fell back again into a sleep so deep, that, shake him as she would, she could not rouse him from it.

When she had sat there a little while longer, she saw a brownish vapour enter the house through the open door. It glided softly towards her, and standing still before her, took the figure of a man. " Well," said the girl, " what do you want here? "

The Sending said to her, " I am sent hither by the wizards of the Westmann Islands to slay this man, who has broken his word to them—as one who knows not what truth is. Move, therefore, from the bed, for while you sit there I cannot reach him."

" All in good time," replied she.   " But, first of all, you must do me some service."

The Sending asked what service she would of him. " Make yourself, for instance," she answered, " as large as you can."

This, he said, he would assuredly do, willingly enough. Accordingly he made himself so large that he quite filled the house.

" That will do," said the girl.   " Now, for instance, make yourself as small as you can."

So the Sending shrunk down and down and down, till from a monstrous giant he became the smallest fly you ever saw.

" Aha," said she, and stuck him forthwith into an empty marrow-bone, which she had in her pocket, and corked him in.

Then putting the bone back in her pocket, she woke the man.   He started up, wondering that he was yet alive, and she asked him where was now the Sending.

" I know not," said he; and she answered, " I thought your companions were no such great wizards as you made them out to be.   Trouble yourself no more about them; they will not slay you just yet; but let us spend Christmas-day in mirth and joy."   So they spent Christmas-day in such revel as befitted the time and a late escape from death, and laughed and sang, till the rafters had not heard the like of it for many a long year.

Q

Now, as New Year's-day drew nigh, the man fell again into his old sadness, and became so gloomy that the girl noticed his strange manner, and asked him what ailed him.

He answered, "The wizards on the Westmann Islands are now preparing another Sending, and when that shall come here, it will be no easy task for me to escape from it."

"Oh," said the girl, "just wait till I have tried its strength, and then it will be time enough to be afraid of it. Meanwhile don't trouble your head about either your friends on the island or their threats."

And since the maiden was so light-hearted, he thought that surely he would be but a coward to be dull and sad, and accordingly put the brightest face he could upon the matter.

On New Year's-eve he spoke to the girl, and said, "Now the Sending has been put ashore; and, gifted as it is with all the wrath of the wizards, it comes apace."

She begged him to come with her, and led him across the country till they came to a place where the grass was high and the shrubs were thick. In the midst of this, the girl stooped down, and removing a low mound of earth and grass which stood at her feet, came to a large slab of stone, which she lifted, and, by so doing, disclosed a passage, leading far below ground. They entered the passage, and after walking for a long time in darkness, greater than that of the blackest night, they came to a cavern, which

" *Near this light, in a mean and wretched bed, lay an old man of the most horrible aspect.*"

[*To face page* 242.

was dimly lighted with some fat, burning in a human skull. Near this light, in a mean and wretched bed, lay an old man of the most horrible aspect. His eyes were as red as blood, and his mouth reached from ear to ear; and as for his nose, no words can tell its length and colour. So frightful was he, that the wizard quaked at the very idea of going near him.

"Oho!" said this old fellow, "strange news you have to tell me, no doubt, foster-daughter. It is long enough since I saw you last. What can I do for you?"

The girl told him all about the wizard, and his friends in the Westmann Islands, and how they had despatched a Sending to slay him, and in what way she had treated the same. Upon which the old man waxed quite lively, and asked to see the marrow-bone. So she immediately took it out of her pocket and gave it him.

As soon as he saw it, he waxed even livelier than before, and became at last so very brisk, that he was really quite another man. Taking the bone in his hand, with every appearance of pleasure, he turned it about and patted it, and rubbed it all over.

While he was mumbling over the bone, the girl noticed the islander growing sleepier and sleepier, and, at length, said to the old man, "If you will aid me at all, aid me now, for I know full well that the Sending is near at hand."

Without more ado, therefore, the old fellow took the

cork out of the bone, and out crept the fly, whom he patted and stroked, and to whom he said, "Go now. Receive all the Sendings from the wizards on the Westmann Islands, and swallow them."

Immediately, with a loud roar like thunder, the fly flew from the cavern; and when it came to the upper world, behold! it became so large, that one jaw reached up to the heavens, and the other touched the earth; and when not only one Sending, but two or three came, it swallowed them all down; and so the islander was saved from the malice of his companions.

After thanking the old man for his timely help, the girl and the Westmann islander returned to the farm, where, as the story goes, they became man and wife; lived to a good old age, and increased and multiplied. Thus was the land repeopled. As for the other wizards, mighty little more was ever heard about them; just enough, indeed, to amount to nothing.

Priest Hálfdán and Ólöf of Lónkot.

A certain old woman, named Ólöf, lived at a farm called Lónkot, in the parish of Fell, of which Hálfdán was the priest. She was very wise, and very well skilled in magic, but by no means amiable, and rather given to quarrelling. She and Hálfdán never got on well together, and many were the high words that passed between them, whenever they met.

One day in the autumn, the priest, and some of his servants, were out fishing, and had had the luck to catch a large halibut. As, however, the weather was sharp and frosty, the rowers paid little enough heed to the fish, but blew ruefully on their chilled fingers, and grumbled at the cold. Seeing this, Hálfdán said to them, "What would you give me, my lads, if I caught a good large hot sausage for you now?" They shook their heads, and said that he could not do so, skilful as he was, and looked more wretched than before. But the priest threw out a line over the edge of the boat, and in an instant dragged up on the end of it a large sausage, so hot that it bubbled and sputtered again. The rowers could hardly believe their eyes, but spent a mighty short time in wondering, finding that the best way to test the reality of the sausage was to eat it; which they forthwith did. But when they had finished their meal, lo! the halibut was no more to be seen.

"Aha!" said the priest, "something the old woman must have for her hot sausage."

The truth was that Hálfdán had enchanted the sausage from Dame Ólöf; but she (like many other good folk we could mention) was not disposed to give a thing away when she could sell it at a price, so she paid herself by enchanting the halibut from Hálfdán.

Priest Hálfdán and the Devil.

One winter, when it was rather late in the season, it chanced that Priest Hálfdán was in great need of dried fish for household use, his home stock having quite run out. He sent in all directions to his neighbours' houses, offering to buy from them what fish they could spare, but they were in just the same plight as himself, for the season had been bad everywhere, and the people suffered much from it.

As was the custom in those times, the priest kept a large number of fishing-boats at Grímsey, where there was also lying a vast quantity of fish, stacked for the winter. But so stormy was the weather at this time, and so dangerous the sea, that all hope in this quarter was quite cut off.

But Hálfdán, who saw no pleasure in starving when there was fish to be had somewhere, called in the devil, and said to him, "If you will go to Grímsey, and bring me thence dried fish enough for the rest of the winter, without wetting them, you shall have my soul. If, however, I find one drop of water upon the fish, you shall lose your bargain."

The devil was not a little pleased at this, and snatched at the offer hastily enough, making, however, the condition that the priest should provide him with the craft.

"Oh yes," said Hálfdán, "what easier?" and forthwith gave him an old kitchen coal-scuttle. But bad as this ship was, the devil was bound to make the best of it, so addressed himself to his journey late in the afternoon.

Next morning the priest's wife went out to see how went the weather, and the priest called out after her, saying, "How looks the sky?"

"Fair enough," said she; "but there is a dark cloud in the north which covers rapidly the heavens."

"Aha," replied her husband, who was still in bed, "it is time to get up then; the devil has done his work right speedily."

Upon which he got up, and dressing himself in haste, left the house. The devil was now quite close to the shore, but when he saw Hálfdán he lost his courage, and started in his seat, so that the surf broke over the coal-scuttle, and wet the tails of all the fish. As soon as he had landed, he delivered the great bundle of fish to the priest, who was not long in finding the water upon their tails, and who at once declared himself to have got the best of the bargain.

To this the devil had nothing to say, and was thinking of looking very crestfallen, when — so says the story — the priest cut off the wet tails of the fish, and flinging them into Old Nick's face, cried, "There! There is freight-payment for you."

Ever since that, the thinnest part of a fish's tail has been called "the devil's flap."

Priest Eiríkur's Handbook.

Now you shall hear several strange stories about Priest Eiríkur of Vossósar, who seems to have been as wonderful a person as Sœmundur the learned himself.

The fame of his learning, and his wisdom, more particularly in the Black Art, was so widely spread abroad, that many young men used to come to him, and ask him to teach them, even from quite distant parts of the country. But he used to put those who came to him to some sort of trial, and if he found them worthy of his pains, well and good, he taught them as much as they could learn; but if they failed to please him, he sent them off about their business.

Among others once came to him a lad, who craved his instructions in magic.

"Stay with me over next Sunday," said Eiríkur to him, "and come with me that day to Krysivík; and after that I will tell you my mind."

Accordingly on Sunday morning they rode from home together, but when they came to a tract of country, called Sandur, Eiríkur said, "Oh! I have forgotten my handbook. It is under my pillow. Go therefore and fetch it for me, but beware not to open it."

The lad returned for the book, and rode back with it, longing, but not daring, to look into it. When he arrived however at Sandur, his curiosity got the better of his wisdom, so he opened the book and looked into it. But suddenly he found himself surrounded by a countless host of devils, who cried, "What shall we do? What shall we do?"

"Do?" answered he quickly, "why, plait cables out of the sand."

Upon which they all sat down, and fell to their task.

But the lad rode on till he caught up Priest Eiríkur, who was, by now, far in advance, and gave the book to him.

"You have opened it," said the priest.

"No," said the lad, "not I."

When they were on their way home again, and came to Sandur, there were all the devils hard at work, though, to be sure, they had not yet made a single rope between them. As soon as the priest saw them, he said, " I knew well enough, my good lad, that you had opened the book, in spite of your denial; but you have acted with such presence of mind, that I see plainly it will be well worth my while to teach you."

So from that time forth the lad became Eiríkur's pupil.

The story does not say a word more about the devils who tried to plait cables out of the sand at Sandur, but there can be no doubt whatever that, after a while, they must have given up the task as a fruitless one. For they are assuredly not at work there now.

EIRÍKUR AND THE BEGGAR-WOMAN.

One day two men came to Eiríkur at Vossósar, and begged him to teach them the magic art. He looked very much amazed at the idea, and said that as he knew nothing of magic, he could teach them nothing; "but," continued he, "you have come far, and are weary; spend therefore the night at my house, and be welcome." They agreed willingly to this, and after a good supper rested that night at the priest's house.

Next morning betimes, Eiríkur asked them to ride with him round the farm, and see his fields and stock. They had ridden but a very little distance from the house, when an old woman met them who had a child at her breast, and walking up to Eiríkur, begged him in piteous tones and with many tears to help her in her need. But Eiríkur became wroth, and roughly telling her that he should do nothing of the sort, made as if to ride quickly past her. She however caught hold of his bridle, and entreated him again, in the name of Heaven, to help her, as she was a widow, and had neither home, nor food, nor money. At this Eiríkur waxed still more wroth, and cried, "I am weary to death of this eternal whining; a good thing it would be, I think, if some one were to kill all you beggars, troublesome wretches that you are!" Still the old woman wept and clung to his bridle.

Then Eiríkur, turning to the two men, said, "You must kill this old hag for me, if you wish me to teach you any of my magic."

One of them answered him, "Never thought I, Eiríkur, that you were so godless a man. No such crime as this will I commit, whatever price I get for it."

"I see no particular harm in it," said the other stranger, "and if Priest Eiríkur will it, I will slay this old witch with pleasure. Surely it is a good thing to rid the land of the like; and they ought to be themselves thankful to be so soon quit of their wretched lives." With which words he would have ridden at the beggar, but lo! she was no longer with them.

"Aha!" said Eiríkur, "*you* may go your way, my friend; never will I teach such a heartless, impious fellow."

But the stranger, who had first spoken, he took to himself as his pupil.

The raising up of this old woman by jugglery was one of the many ways in which Eiríkur was wont to prove those who came to him to learn magic.

EIRÍKUR'S SATURDAY AFTERNOON.

Eiríkur was wont every Saturday afternoon to disappear from his farm, without anybody's knowing whither he went.

Once a youth, who was learning under him, moved by curiosity, begged leave to go with him, on one of those occasions, but met, for a long time, with an utter refusal.

" You will gain no good by it," said Eiríkur; " you will do better to remain at home."

However, as the youth only became more urgent in his entreaties, the priest at last yielded to them.

Some weeks passed, and one Saturday the priest bade the youth follow him. They walked together till they came to a hill which stood in the farm inclosure, or tún. Eiríkur knocked with his staff upon the mound, which at once opened of itself, and out came an aged lady, who greeted Eiríkur in a friendly manner, begging him to enter. There came out, too, a maiden, who took the young man by the hand, and bade him also come in. So they went in, and came to the family-room, all round of which a number of people were sitting. Eiríkur and the youth took their seats by the door, the latter being next to it. Nobody spoke a single word, a thing which the young man found strange enough; but great indeed was his wonder when the two ladies left the room, and after a while returned with a huge trough and a knife, and, going up to the first man on the other side of the door, took him, threw him down, cut his throat with the knife, and let his blood run into the trough. Then they took the next one, and treated him in the same way, and thus the third, and the fourth, and the fifth, and so on, always in order. But the strangest part of the whole business was that nobody made the slightest resistance, or betrayed the least fear, nor did anybody speak. Then the youth looked at Eiríkur to see what he thought about it, but Eiríkur was quite unmoved. Still the ladies went on slaughtering each man in his turn, amid a silence only broken by the bubbling of the blood, till they came to Eiríkur, whom they took, flung down, and slew in the same manner.

By this time the youth had seen a great deal more than enough, and starting up with a loud cry took to his heels, and never ceased running till he came to the farm. When he arrived there, pale and breathless, and with his knees knocking together with fear, whom should he see leaning against the door-post but Priest Eiríkur himself.

"What are you running so fast for, my man?" said he. "Are you in a hurry?"

At this the other looked sheepish enough and did not know what to say, for he at once saw that he had been duped by one of the priest's juggling tricks.

"Ah," continued Eiríkur, "I always thought, my good

fellow, that you had not the courage to see anything out of the common, and now I am sure about it."

The Horse-stealers.

Priest Eiríkur always warned all the herdsmen and other lads in the neighbourhood of Vossósar against taking his riding-horses without his leave, as horse-stealing was very common in those parts, assuring them that if they disobeyed him it would be at their peril. This put an end to the thefts for a long while, for the herdsmen held Eiríkur in great awe, and knew full well that he meant what he said.

Two boys, however, thinking they could have a capital ride without its ever coming to the priest's ears, mounted two of Eiríkur's horses, which were grazing far from the farm. But they were no sooner seated than off ran the horses at a mad pace towards Vossósar, without their being in any way able either to guide or check them. As soon as they saw that the horses were not to be managed, the lads tried to throw themselves off on to the ground, but lo! that was not to be done, for their trousers had grown to the horses' backs.

"This won't do," said one of the lads; "we must get off somehow, or the horses will take us to Priest Eiríkur himself, and I don't at all care to fall into *his* hands."

" They were no sooner seated than of ran the horses at a mad pace towards Vogsósar." [*To face page* 254.

With these words he took a knife from his pocket, and cutting that part of his clothes which had grown to the horse's back, thus freed himself and leaped on to the ground.

But the other, either because he was not sharp enough or because he did not wish to spoil his trousers, stuck where he was, shouting for help. So the horses galloped home to Vossósar, the one with the screaming lad on its back, the other with the patch of trousers.

The priest was outside the door when the horses came running home, and stopping them he took the patch of cloth from the back of the one, and said to the boy who sat looking very helpless and miserable on the back of the other, "Well! you find stealing the horses of Priest Eiríkur of Vossósar great fun, no doubt. Get off, now, and take my advice, never touch my horses again, or it will be the worse for you. As for the other lad, he had more spirit than you, and deserves to be taught a little, for he promises to turn out a hopeful fellow."

Soon after, it happened that the boy came to the priest, who showed him the piece of cloth, and asked him whether he knew it.

Without betraying the least fear, the lad told him all about the matter.

Eiríkur, as much pleased with his openness as with his presence of mind, smiled, and bade him come henceforth and live with him, an offer which he gratefully accepted.

So the youth dwelt long with Priest Eiríkur, and was very faithful to him, and learned of him—so people say—more than most folk know of the ancient art of magic.

Eiríkur and the Farmer.

In Eiríkur's parish of Vossósar, there lived a certain farmer who never went to church, and, having a grudge against the priest, used, on purpose to annoy him, to go out fishing on the Sunday, whenever the weather was favourable.

One Sunday, Eiríkur was going to church to perform service, and passed on his way the house of the farmer, who, guessing when the priest would go by, just managed to be putting on his skin leggings at the moment. Seeing this, Eiríkur addressed him with courteous words, and asked him if he would not, for once, go to church that day.

The farmer rudely said "No," and continued putting on his skin trousers, without paying any further heed to the priest, who left him and went on to the church.

When service was over, Eiríkur returned home the same way as he had come, and passing the farmer's house, saw him through the open door, sitting with one leg of his skin trousers on, and the other off.

"Ah, my friend," said the priest to him, "I dare say you

have had a good draught to-day, since you are back so soon ?"

But the farmer, looking very crestfallen, was obliged to own that he had not moved from the spot since the priest had seen him last, and begged him to free him, as he could neither lift hand nor foot.

Eiríkur answered, " If you find the devil strong enough to hold you now, what think you will he be able to do with you by and by ?" and with these words freed him from the seat, to which, by his magic arts, he had bidden the devil bind him.

Ever after this the man went to church on Sundays, and became one of the best men in the parish.

EIRÍKUR AND THE BISHOP.

The Bishop of Skálholt heard from time to time such stories of the witchcraft and strange doings of Eiríkur, that at last he thought it high time to strip that priest of his gown. So one winter, he sent eighteen of the pupils from the school, bidding them, in his name, publicly to strip Eiríkur of his robes and deprive him of his office. They started on their journey one fine day, not a little proud of their errand,—for it showed how much trust the bishop put in them ; and as they rode along, talked very big about

R

the same, and would do mighty things when it came to the point.

One morning, Priest Eiríkur got up very early and went out of the house. After a while he came back, groaning heavily as if in pain or sorrow, and bade his people not on any account to let the beasts go out to pasture that day, as, said he, he thought he saw some signs of foul weather. Shortly after, there came on so fearful a storm, and so deep a fall of snow, that the people who wished to cross from one part of the farm-buildings to another, could scarcely stand out of doors for the wind and heavy drift. A little after noon, somebody knocked at the door, and the priest, on opening it, found that it was one of the youths sent by the bishop; so he asked him in. After a while, came another, then another, and then a fourth, till by evening every one of the eighteen had come. They had lost their way in the snow-drift, and been separated from one another, and thus it was that instead of coming to Vossósar in a body they came singly. Eiríkur treated them with the greatest hospitality, gave them changes of clothes, stabled their horses, and had withal so winning a manner, that his guests became too fond of him to be able to carry out the bishop's orders, to strip him of his gown. Accordingly, next morning they started from Vossósar with the kind farewells of Eiríkur, and in course of time came to Skálholt.

When the bishop heard how their journey had ended,

and that they had done nothing whatever, he was filled
with displeasure, and vowed that he would go to Vossósar
himself, and see how Eiríkur would get off then.

Now the winter passed away, and when the summer was
at its full, the bishop left Skálholt with a numerous band,
and when he arrived at Vossósar pitched his tents outside
the wall of the tún. This being on a week-day, the bishop
determined to wait till the Sunday, and then to strip the
priest of his gown. He warned his men earnestly to
receive nothing from the hands of Eiríkur, and having
given them this order, took his way to the house and
called the priest before him.

Eiríkur received the bishop cordially, and was so very
merry and so perfectly at his ease, that his reverence did
not know how to begin. So he asked to see the church.
Eiríkur therefore took him to it, and the bishop could not
help being pleased with the good order everything there
was in.

But while the latter was in the church, one of his
servants passed by in order to get fire from the farm, and
Eiríkur, who was in the porch, called the man to him, and
having greeted him in the sweetest and most friendly way,
pulled a bottle of wine from his pocket and begged him to
taste it.

" No," said the man, " I dare not, it would be against
the bishop's strictest orders."

But the more he refused the more Eiríkur pressed him,

till at last the man, overcome by his entreaties, put his mouth to the bottle and took a draught. And it was not such a very short draught either, for he thought that in all his days he had never tasted such good wine. When he had drunk he begged Eiríkur to give him the bottle, that he might refresh the bishop with it anon. Secretly laughing at the success of his trick, Eiríkur willingly gave him the rest of the wine, and off went the man with the bottle in his pocket.

Then the bishop came out of the church and returned to his tent, while Eiríkur went home and waited to see how things would turn out.

At dinner, the servant-man poured the wine into the bishop's glass, who had no sooner tasted it than he quite changed his mind about Eiríkur, and after dinner went to the priest's house, and stayed a week there in the greatest mirth and good-fellowship. At the end of that time he returned to Skálholt with all his company.

This was the way in which Eiríkur duped the bishop and kept his gown on his back.

EIRÍKUR AND THE CONVICT.

North-west of Vossósar, in the great lava plain, there is a cavern called Gapi, which is often used as a shelter and resting-place by travellers passing that way.

In this cavern Eiríkur hid a convict (this history saith not why) for a whole summer, and so enchanted the place, that neither could anybody find the cave itself, nor the cairn of stones which had been raised on a neighbouring hill to mark it.

The convict was from one of the eastern districts, namely, Sída, and having murdered another, had been condemned to lose his head.

The whole summer the man remained there, while papers were sent all over the country describing him and offering a reward to any who should catch him. Priest Eiríkur having got one of these bills, sent the convict himself with it to Sída, having first so transformed him by magic art that nobody could know him, and bade him say that the murderer had been caught in the district of Selvogur, and was now sitting, loaded with fetters, in the church at Strand.

Upon hearing this, the people of Sída at once set off southwards, and, coming to the church at Strand, found there sitting, loaded with chains, the man whom they sought. So they seized him and took him to the east, and made preparations for cutting off his head, according to the sentence which had been passed upon him. But when it came to the point, the axe would not cut, and bent at every stroke upon the man's neck. Accordingly the good folk of Sída were obliged to give up the attempt, and agreed to take him on board a ship bound for Denmark, in which country they hoped the axes would be a little sharper. But no sooner had they taken him on board the ship, than his human form vanished, and they found that they had put themselves to all this pain and trouble for a block of stone with two arms! The sailors, as soon as they saw this, made great game of the people of Sída, and rated them right soundly for their blindness, so that the good folk made all haste to shore covered with shame; not, however, before they had seen their convict hurled overboard.

Now they began to see that they had been made fools of by Eiríkur, and, bursting with rage, they determined to revenge themselves upon him for all the trouble they had been put to, and for the silly figures they had cut in the eyes of the Danish sailors.

To carry out their vengeance they bribed a man from the West firths who dabbled in magic to send a great cat to slay Eiríkur.

When Puss arrived at Vossósar, Eiríkur was outside his door in company with the young man who had formerly opened his handbook and bidden the devils weave ropes from sand.

The cat ran up with great strides and flaming eyes, and sprang at the priest's neck, intending to fix herself there and kill him; but Eiríkur was too quick for her, and, as the youth aided him with a right good will, Puss got the worst of the battle, and before very long lay dead upon the ground.

"The cat ran up with great strides and flaming eyes, and sprang at the priest's neck."

[To face page 262.

Now the story goes on to say that Eiríkur forthwith despatched a Sending to the man in the West firths, and put an end to him almost as quickly as to his goblin cat.

Also published by Llanerch:

The Saga of King Sverri of Norway
J. Sephton.

Bandamanna Saga
John Porter, illus. A. Selwood.

Cormac the Skald
W.G. Collingwood & J. Stefanson.

Handbook of the Old Runic Monuments
of Scandinavia and England
George Stephens.

Frithiof's Saga
George Stephens.

Thorstein of the Mere: A Saga of the
Northmen in Lakeland
W.G. Collingwood.

For a complete list of 100+ titles, small-press
editions & facsimile reprints, write to:
LLANERCH PUBLISHERS,
Felinfach, Lampeter, Dyfed,
SA48 8PJ.